A MONUMENTAL JOURNEY

A MONUMENTAL JOURNEY

"Our Journey Begins"

Richard L Cederberg

authorHOUSE®

AuthorHouse™ LLC
1663 Liberty Drive
Bloomington, IN 47403
www.authorhouse.com
Phone: 1-800-839-8640

This book is a work of fiction. Places, events, and situations in this story are purely fictional. Any resemblance to actual persons, living or dead is coincidental.

Published by AuthorHouse 10/19/2013

ISBN: 978-1-4184-1207-4 (sc)
ISBN: 978-1-4184-1206-7 (hc)
ISBN: 978-1-4184-1205-0 (e)

Library of Congress Control Number: 2004090873

DEDICATIONS / CREDITS

My wife, Michele Elizabeth Cederberg.

Lloyd William, Russell Grant, Debra Elaine, and my departed mother Elaine Louise. In so doing I offer something from **'Hymn of the Moravian Nuns of Bethlehem at the Consecration of Pulaski's Banner'** by Henry W. Longfellow

"Take thy banner!
But when night closes round the ghastly fight,
If the vanquished warrior bows, spare him!
By our holy vow, by our prayers and many tears,
By the mercy that endears
Spare him!-He our love hath spared!
Spare him!-As thou wouldst be spared!"

My Grandsons . . . AEDIN, HUNTER, and NOAH

The Santa Barbara Gang: Karen England, Nick Tepper, Barbara Fields, and Ed Oberweiser. I have many good memories about you guys that have endured through the years.

PHOTOGRAPHY AND AUTHOR PICTURE BY: MICHELE ELIZABETH CEDERBERG

One

My narrative begins . . .

Following eight years, and more intense studying than I had ever believed possible, I was routinely awarded a PhD in English Literature, Scandinavian Mythology, and the Ancient Northern languages. At first I was quite satisfied with my accomplishment because of a general awareness that I'd done something honorable in the pursuit of a higher education. Sadly there was nothing lasting in this reverie, and soon I began viewing the world system, and my place in it, from a more guileless perspective. With some degree of horror I realized that I was being groomed as just another player in a soulless machine, whose primary purpose was to churn out automatons for the global work market, and a lifetime of servitude and tax-paying.

Something changed in me shortly after this realization.

I began questioning seriously where personal fulfillment and happiness dwelt in this. And, despite what most considered an unparalleled victory for me in college, I'd become disillusioned with where my education was taking me. It was during these 'blurred' times that something exceedingly deeper (than my intellect) began swaying me to bolster myself for a monumental change. I didn't know what to think. The notions were undeniable, of course, and flooded upon my tenuous frame of mind with the regularity of the tides. Daily, it seemed, I was consumed with what this may foreshadow. In only a matter of weeks I began having vivid dreams about leaving my birth home, my father's powerful business influences, my family's great financial security, and branching out on my own to become a self-sustaining individual. How wonderful this prospect was, and how greatly I reveled in it. I began fancying traveling to the Southwestern United States and embarking upon (what the Australian Aborigines referred to as) a *'walkabout'* in search of answers to the unending questions continually haunted me about my true purpose for being alive. My dreams increased in frequency, and intensity, during this time, and so did my frustration.

Hello . . . My name is **Gabriel Proudmore.** Today is my twenty-sixth birthday, and also the first day of the first month of the sixth year since the political upheavals escalated worldwide. Sadly, the prognosis for all United Nations members is grim. Lawlessness has undermined most cities with rampant drug use, burgeoning witchcraft, brutality, murders, theft, and a scourge of corrupting alternative lifestyles. Life, for most, has been down-graded, on all levels. Most societies, worldwide, are caught up (now) in the swirling edges of a mysterious spiritual maelstrom. Very few understand the implications or the signs. Be that as it may, regions of the planet are being ravaged regularly by storms (of fierce proportion) worsened by escalating solar flares, the weakening of the ocean's salinity from polar melt, and mankind's consummate failures, spiritually, and also, as caretakers of God's Earth. **My narrative begins** several months after my graduation from Aberdeen University . . .

Two

An amazing turn of events

The ***Belanthian***, one of my father's mammoth oil tankers, was coming to port. **Proudmore Oil Inc** used eight colossal oil tankers worldwide: the ***Tanager***, the ***Absinthe***, the ***Evelyn*,** (named after my mother) the ***Sac Doyle*,** (named after one of my father's favorite authors, Sir Arthur Conan Doyle) the ***Na Hearadh***, (named after one of my father's favorite islands in the Hebrides) and the ***JMuir***, (named after one of my Grandfathers personal lifelong friends, John Muir, the naturalist and conservationist). The oldest tanker in the fleet was the ***Trelantier***. It was the very first vessel father had built in the early years and she was only two years away from being decommissioned. My father Edwin and I were both born and raised in Aberdeen Scotland. Every generation as far back as our family tree recorded, was born in Scotland, the Outer Hebrides, or scattered throughout the Orkney Islands. What had always intrigued me about my family's history were the Norse warriors and explorers in our ancestry that had prospered up in the Orkney Islands for generations. Knowing these facts had stirred something in me, (since my early teens) that I'd never been able to put to rest. Someday I hoped to have more understanding.

After telling my father about my decision to go to Southern California, he threw a fit and began yammering on about booking my passage aboard the *Belanthian.* My father had always been tenacious in his resolve, and he'd always been steadfast in his opinions about my safety, my life, and how I should be perceived abroad. 'The respected traditions of my family must be upheld in your sojourn to Southern California.' He would lecture. Knowing that most of the time I balked when he was in these moods, today he was trying to pressure me with the promise of paying for my first class passage. He declared emphatically that I would travel comfortably, eat superb food at the captain's table, and have a great amount of leisure time during the duration of the journey. Seeing that I was not in the least persuaded, Father began to entice me with something that almost changed my mind. He offered me a generous monthly allowance that would cover all the expenses for the extent of the whole journey. He had devised a well-structured financial plan and, as he explained it, the worldwide reputation of the Proudmore's would be reflected in how I was seen, how I lived, how I carried myself, and how utterly essential it was to have enough money. How could I refute this logic?

'My son will not be perceived as a traveling vagabond or a gypsy,' he bellowed that afternoon with an affected bravado.

I'd learned from past experience that sometimes I'd have to feign acceptance of father's demands, when he got into his moods, because I couldn't win with him. If I didn't fuss or resist him, and if I pretended to agree, invariably, the more affable part of his personality would return. I must confess, though, that my father had become predictable over the years and I used this, quite often, to my benefit. When he'd returned to a more palatable frame of mind, we'd begin communicating again about how the world was changing, and how my life had become a wonderful mixture of his influences and personal example. Although my dad was driven and erudite, he also was feisty and opinionated, and my mother and I had been subject to his glowering behavior since I was a child. Today, during another episode of his castigating, something inside of me snapped; I flew into a rage and told him what I thought. Sadly, because there was no way that I could resolve my deplorable behavior; I bolted out of the house miffed and hurt. I was not a child anymore, and I certainly didn't need someone micromanaging my life.

My mind wandered as I walked. I remembered the outstanding three summers I'd spent on the *Isle of Harris* in the *Hebrides,* especially the last one when father had finally let me venture there by myself. I leased a small cottage on the western coast and had taken along only a backpack, essential clothes, hiking shoes, a digital camera, my laptop computer, and a powerful desire to explore. Finally I'd been given the opportunity to spread my wings and fly in skies devoid of my father's opinions and influence. The views were as breathtaking as any I'd ever seen, meadows and lochs, sandy beaches, mountains, moorlands and crofts. I spent several nights camped next to castles on enormous cliffs, and several nights on the white and turquoise *'Luskentyre* Sands'. Some were even spent on the brooding

'Lewisian Gneiss', a bizarre place that resembled a lunar landscape. I remembered . . .

A blaring air horn deposited me back into the reality of my surroundings. At first I was shocked. Somehow I'd reached the docks, but had done so without ever taking note of my route. There was a white three-masted schooner with red trim in front of me; the most magnificently proportioned vessel I'd ever laid eyes on. According to the footage markers, she measured out at one hundred and twenty feet in length. The name on the bow was ***Heimdall***. I saw four men and two women scurrying about on deck; they were energetic and animated. I heard one man laughingly say: "If it wasn't for Jonah's e-mail, I don't think I'd ever chosen Aberdeen to dock in."

"I really love that man," a lighthearted woman's voice laughed from the other side of the schooner.

"Aye Olaf, but it was timely, we needed to stop and repair the diesel. We've procrastinated far too long, and we really do need some supplies." I heard another man respond.

"I agree Rorek," the first man answered, "I just can't figure why he wants us to stay here eight days, the repair won't take that long, and the two of us can restock in an afternoon."

"Don't know," the man Rorek grunted, clearly unconcerned. "Ask Helga, she took down the message!"

"Helga . . ." a strongly muscled teenager with spiked hair yelled. "HELGA, get yur lazy butt up here!" His voice was animated.

"Wait a minute Garrett;" a barely audible voice responded from below decks, "I'll be there in a second." Seconds later an athletic brunette woman bolted out the only doorway on the pier side of the schooner; she was clutching a piece of paper.

"What did he say Helga?" The inquiry came from a muscular man descending from the center mast with a bag of tools.

The crew stopped what they were doing and gathered around Helga. The sun had set quickly that afternoon, or so it seemed. I really didn't know how long I'd been standing there watching and listening to them. For some reason I was totally engrossed in their activities and felt as eager, as the rest of the crew was, to hear what Helga was about to read. As they gathered together street lights began to flicker on along the dock. Moments later the running lights on the schooner came on in radiant symmetrical lines.

"Is everyone here?" I heard Helga ask.

"Let's see," one man said, "yep we're all here little sister."

"OK then, Jonah sends love, and he hopes everyone is healthy and happy. He was also given another vision last night about something we're supposed to accomplish here in Aberdeen. Here, let me just read what he wrote." Helga shrugged.

> *Greetings to all, I hope everyone is healthy and happy.*
>
> *I know my request to dock in Aberdeen Scotland for eight days must have seemed weird, but GOD has shown me the timing for your stay there is crucial. You're going to meet a scrupulous young man, probably in his middle twenties, and highly intelligent. He has a very important mission to accomplish, and it's going to be with us. He comes from an affluent family in Aberdeen, but has over the years developed a different outlook spiritually than his family would have hoped. He will be listless, kind of in-between seasons; I hope you know what I mean here guys. Anyway, I've seen that Christ has a powerful call on his life to help us accomplish something concerning the changing weather conditions the last six years, and the runic writings and graves we found recently. I really don't*

> *know any more than this, Wait a minute people, strange, I feel strongly drawn to prayer right now; I'll finish this letter when I'm done, talk to you soon.*

Trying to understand what I was hearing was confusing. I was struggling seriously with the preposterous possibility that the e-mail had been written about me. But how could this be? Who was Jonah? Who were these people? Why had I come to these docks at exactly the time that this letter would be read? Helga continued:

> *I know that this is going to be hard to understand guys, but I just finished about an hour's worth of intense prayer, and the Holy Spirit has shown me something puzzling. WOW! The young man you're going to meet is listening to you, right now, while you're reading this e-mail from me. Good grief! Let me know as soon as you've confirmed this. Praise GOD! I love and miss you all. Smooth sailing. I'll confirm routes with you around the end of February,*
>
> *In Christ's awesome love, Jonah*

Was Jonah somehow talking about me? When a picture of my father's grim face appeared suddenly in front of me I felt as if I may puke. He would certainly not approve of this, and I already heard him yelling, 'what do you mean God told him that you were supposed to go with them,' while he held mother by her hands and tried to console her weeping. 'You will not leave with a crew of people you've never met before on such a small vessel. Son, please, you don't know anything about sailing. Please be reasonable!' At that moment I decided to head back home, but for some reason my feet wouldn't work. Suddenly one of the deck hands walked briskly towards the bow and began uncovering a spotlight. Chuckling quietly he started whistling an old Scottish melody. Within seconds the rest of the crew had joined in. The powerful beam began scanning up and down the dock; for the longest time it seemed to float around me. Suddenly the intense beam had found me. I was busted big-time!

"There he is," the man on the spotlight shouted. "Praise GOD," all of them chorused together. "Greetings friend and brother, come aboard the *Heimdall*."

Three

Aboard the *Heimdall*

Helga and the blonde woman were both standing at the rails waving and smiling. Helga quickly folded the piece of paper, she'd read from, and stuffed it into her back pocket. The strong looking man, John, started cranking the gangplank out towards the dock; apparently they weren't fooling, they really did want me to come aboard. Now my heart was thumping like a drum, and I had begun rationalizing my own uneasiness. The plank was creaking and groaning as John turned the large wheel; the sound reminded me of the discomfort in my stomach. After about two minutes the plank came to rest noisily on the concrete dock thirty feet from where I was. Helga ran down.

"Come on Betsy let's go meet him."

"I'm right behind you," Betsy grinned.

I'd never been a gregarious person. As far back as I could remember I preferred my studies, hobbies, reading, exploring, and writing. I loved working on the hybrid computer my father had built for me, and I loved watching old adventure movies and taking pictures. In my late teens I'd fancied myself becoming a musician and following in the footsteps of my all-time heroes, Jimi Hendrix and Jeff Beck. Sadly I couldn't muster the discipline necessary and besides; I sounded awful and had no rhythm. I'd given up on musical stardom in my second year of college and sometimes the disappointment still ate at me. I'd never liked team sports; just couldn't understand the mentality of athletes, or the constant aches and pains. I had, however, grown fond of pool and billiards, this probably because there was always a playing table and game room in my parent's mansion. As it was, my father could never defeat anyone except me, so I played and played and played. As I got older my proficiency at the game improved. Then, much to my father's chagrin, I ended up playing better than he did and the game just wasn't as much fun anymore for him. I had only one girlfriend in my whole life, Ingrid, but she'd moved to Maine (in the United States) during my last year of college. Regrettably her departure had left a deep pining in my heart. This, in turn, aggravated a quandary of self-doubt about finding anyone else, and, also, encouraged an asocial attitude that I could not shake. The Proudmore's were one of the most prominent families in Scotland; this because of my father's accomplishments. Because of this my mother's social functions were legendary and everyone wanted to attend. As it turned out, I was never invited to any of them because (much to my parent's dismay) my people skills were seriously lacking. Often mother referred to me as a social klutz. But I didn't care; I hated the phoniness that accompanied the upper class and their pompous functions. I couldn't help being who I was. I'd been sheltered and spoiled, by a powerful and affluent family, and I despised everything about it except the freedom that being rich afforded you. Unfortunately even that was an encumbrance at times.

Helga and Betsy had swiftly reached where I was standing; thankfully their presence tore me away from my thoughts. My first inclination was to hug them; both were stunningly picturesque women. Curiously I felt close to them without knowing them, but I resisted my impulses and remained quiet.

"Hi, I'm Helga, and this is my best friend Betsy."

"Hi," Betsy smiled, "what's your name?" Just as I began to respond, five more people circled around me.

"How long have you been standing here listening?"

"Wuzzup dude?"

"Have you been in Aberdeen long?"

"What do you do for a living?"

"What do you think about the drought?"

I began feeling like a punching bag while the seven men and women lovingly thumped my back and shoulders and shook my hand. Gracefully responding with affable smiles, I kept shaking my head politely, then without warning, everyone suddenly got quiet. "What's your name?" Helga asked once again, looking at me straight in the eyes. "Uh . . ." I rubbed my nose nervously. "My name is Gabriel Baaldur Proudmore, and it is my sincere pleasure to meet all of you. I feel uniquely honored, quite frankly, and profoundly baffled to make all of your acquaintances. I find it rather curious to be standing here this evening and, at this juncture, contemplating these compelling but perplexing thoughts about what I've seen and heard this evening."

"Huh?" everyone murmured, looking at each other and shaking their heads.

"What—the—heck did that mean dude," someone on the outside of the circle asked.

Self-conscious, now, I smiled awkwardly. For the next thirty minutes we milled about on the dock talking and laughing. I was getting more and more inquisitive to know who these people were and who this person Jonah was. Also, and most importantly, why I was purportedly going to embark with them in seven days. Having boarded the schooner around seven-thirty, according to my watch, I was seated in what appeared as a recreation room next to a kitchen. Helga, seeming to be the most forthright, stood up first.

"Speaking for myself and the others here; welcome aboard the *Heimdall* Gabriel." There was clapping, whistling, and several vulgar sounds from the back of the room in the shadows. "I know that what's happened for all of us today is truly a miracle, and we all praise God for it. It must also be established before we go any farther . . ." Helga's voice suddenly turned resolute, "that we are all born-again believers in the Risen Christ. What we do and pursue in our lives, individually, and on this voyage, we do for His glory. This is our way, and this is the God we've chosen to love and serve." Respectfully I nodded towards Helga in agreement. "I'd like first to let the crew introduce themselves to you, and let them tell you what their responsibilities are. Let's start here at my left and go around clockwise. Alright Betsy, you start."

"Hi Gabriel, my name is **Betsy**, I'm twenty-eight years old. I'm originally from Cedar City Utah and I'm the cook aboard. I'm also an aspiring deckhand, and I help Lizzy with the sail repairs."

"Hello, I'm **John**; I'm thirty-six years old. I'm from Boise Idaho. I'm the carpenter, electrician, plumber, and lead diver aboard. I'm also a deckhand and an ex navy seal; it's nice to make your acquaintance."

"I'm **Rorek**; I'm forty-seven years old. I was born in Stavanger Norway. I do all the engineering, repairs, and welding aboard. I keep the diesel and all the mechanical systems running smoothly, I'm also a diver, and an adventurer, I also help out with new installations."

"Greetings, I'm the captain and navigator aboard this wonderful vessel. My name is **Olaf**. I was born in Stavanger Norway as well, and I'm forty-four years old. Welcome aboard the *Heimdall* son.

"My name's **Elizabeth**. I'm the oldest; fifty-four years. My family is from Scotland but no one seems to know where I was born. Gosh I don't even know where I was born, that's so strange. Somehow someone somewhere lost my birth certificate you know. Well, anyway, I'm the doctor and nutritionist aboard, and I repair the sails. Actually, you know, Gabriel, I also trained to be a thoracic surgeon; I just couldn't stay in one place though, I am easily bored. I love meeting people and going to different places, so I work regularly on the *Heimdall.* It's so nice to meet you."

Suddenly a loud belch startled me. From back in the shadows a strongly muscled teenager with wildly spiked hair, shorts, and red tennis shoes shuffled into the light. He was grinding his head up and down to some rhythmic beat only he heard. Sitting down hard, and slumping back, he looked up slyly and grunted: "My name's **Garrett** dude; I'm everybody's slave on this dingy."

"GARRETT . . ." the crew chorused.

"You old dudes are helpless without me," he blurted. Sitting up for a moment, he shook his head and then quickly slumped back down into his chair. Immediately I remembered my own teenage years. Unable to suppress a grin I began chuckling quietly. I liked him, a lot.

"Sorry Gabriel," Helga quipped. Immediately she went over to Garrett, put her arms around him, and then gave him a hug and a kiss on the cheek. "Garrett's eighteen years old." She began with her hand on his shoulder. "He comes from a broken family. He was born in San Diego. He's a fine boy, but he hasn't made peace with his parents' divorce yet. He's been with us for two years. He's a deckhand, an exceptionally gifted boxer, a weight lifter, and he's very strong, too. He's also a diver and he takes care of many of our computer problems. He's talented, way beyond his years, and we all love him dearly."

"Amen," everyone murmured. Garrett was slouched down, eyes staring at the ceiling, and smirking with his cheek in his palm.

"Gabriel, my name is **Helga**, I'm thirty-three years old and I was born in Santa Barbara, California. I'm responsible for the computers and communication aboard. I'm also an assistant deckhand. It's really quite a miracle to meet you."

For the next four hours the crew and I talked and laughed marvelously together. They established with me that they were studying the drought and changing weather conditions, its dreadful effects on civilized life, and what was happening to humans around the world in light of Biblical prophecy. They explained, in detail, the powerful friendship they'd each maintained with Jonah. All agreed he was a uniquely gifted man of God whom they all trusted explicitly in spiritual matters. They also told me about their avid interest in an old Northern legend concerning a Viking family that had allegedly made the voyage all the way to Southern California. The legend contended that one hundred plus pilgrims had sailed all the way down from the Orkney Islands across the Atlantic. Their route had remained a mystery for many centuries and not one scholar had ever effectively ascertained how they really got to the West coast of the United States. The legend maintained that they'd migrated up into the Laguna Mountains, out into the Anza Borrego desert, and possibly as far north as southwestern Alaska. They practiced a new religion called Christianity, and from these teachings many of the old missions in California had been established. I wondered: if this was true could it somehow be related to the Proudmore's past history and our closely guarded family secrets in the Orkney Islands?

In my whole life I'd never felt as close to anyone, in so short a time, as I did with these people. It felt as if I'd known them my whole life instead of just half a day. It was also evident that I'd been accepted from the very first moment by these people. At the behest of Captain Olaf we all joined hands and prayed for God's guidance and wisdom in the upcoming phase of our journey; this behavior was very foreign to me. When I finally left for home I was firmly convinced that I'd found a new family with them. My experiences with religious legalism weren't anything like what these people were showing me. There was nothing dark or hidden here. They had a sincere and loving responsibility to one another, and went out of their ways to help each other in any way they could. They loved one another dearly and were not ashamed to openly admit it. The crew had prayed for me specifically, about my needs and my family's needs, and we had all thanked God for delivering me to them and them to me, on time, in health, *and* unharmed. We prayed for continuing finances and unity in all our endeavors together. Now my path seemed clearer than I'd ever known it to be, and I felt a deep peace inside that I just couldn't figure. According to what the crew had shown me I was right where GOD had intended me to be, at the appointed time, and with the very people I was supposed to be with. It was puzzling to me how I knew this, not only with my mind, but also with my heart. The crew invited me back at eight for breakfast and prayer. Helga had mentioned that all the repairs and restocking of the kitchen supplies, and everything else we needed to accomplish, would commence after breakfast. Tomorrow I was going to meet Jonah, via the internet, and talk with him for the first time; I was looking forward to meeting this inscrutable Godly man. The only thing left for me to do was to tell Mother and Father that I'd be embarking with strangers for an indeterminate period of time. In my heart I knew that this was already in God's hands.

Four

Jonah

How could Jonah have known about me? I'd never met the man. And why was he so positive that I was supposed to be aboard the *Heimdall* when it left port March 1st? Jonah lived in Pine Valley in Southern California. He wrote books. He was a Viking researcher and he took expeditions of scientists, geologists, church groups, and artists, into the remote areas, to reveal the secrets he had discovered in his many explorations. I had nothing in common with him, and he had nothing in common with me, but the miracle that happened to me *Feb 22nd at 5:30pm* will always fill me with childlike wonder. Like grandfather and John Muir, whose respective births and deaths in the same years had truly mystified me, Jonah's first correspondence will always captivate and enchant my memories as long as I live. We exchanged e-mails several times before I set sail with the crew. And during this time I began to understand a little more about this inscrutable man. An undeniable camaraderie was developing with Jonah. It was like he'd been a lifelong friend, or an older and wiser brother that knew things about me that I didn't even know about myself. He was a man whose life and pursuits truly reflected a faith and dependence on the Creator. And it hadn't been learned in books, universities, or tedious philosophical debates. He was a spiritual warrior who studied and prayed diligently. He was a man who took the Gospel of Jesus Christ and the Holy Bible literally. He was a man who ardently believed that a personal relationship with the Risen Christ was the most imperative pursuit in life. There was something about Jonah's spirituality that exposed the deep barrenness in me. And there was no earthly way I could have ascertained this with any of my own human reasoning. I readily acknowledged a peaceful witness deep inside me that, over the months and years, became my best and most trusted friend. It was a still small voice that I came to love and depend on. I knew, beyond a shadow of a doubt, that a very special path had opened up for me to follow that had not been contrived by human intellect. Jonah's spirituality seemed impractical to the ritual of daily surviving, and it railed against much that I'd been taught all my life. My education contended that if science can't prove it, and if there wasn't something tangible that you could see, feel, smell or touch, then it just did not exist. For generations my family had been staunchly Roman Catholic. But to my understanding Catholicism was only a legalistic cathartic ritual that dealt with the surface of man's problems and yearnings. Jonah's encouragements to pursue Christ defied all human reasoning and logic. It contradicted everything I had learned in the universities and inside the seminaries in my youth.

'Fear and ignorance is a formidable motivator,' I remembered Jonah saying in one letter. 'By the time the wangling aspects of fear have subsided, it's not uncommon to find yourself enslaved by your own delusional intrigues, and aghast at the gullibility and foolishness you've incorporated into your life.' We could only shake our heads at what nincompoops we'd been. Even the most intelligent people had been affected and manipulated. It was in those early conversations that I became privy to a deeply complex spiritual man with a powerful vision, that apparently I'd been destined to become part of.

Without any fuss my mother and father had yielded to my desires to join with the crew and had wished me the best in my endeavors. To say I was shocked would be an understatement. I was truly convinced God must have prepared their hearts beforehand to accept what they had no way of understanding. Eagerly I accepted fathers offer of a generous monthly allowance. The crew and I prayed together and they felt, too, that it was God's will to accept his gracious proposal. It seemed that God had heard our prayers and answered. I wanted to know much more about God and His son Jesus, but from a Christian perspective, not a Roman Catholic one. Father had also encouraged me to take along the powerful new laptop computer and digital camera that he'd designed specifically for the business. The last night before departure mother invited everyone over for dinner. It was wonderful to be in a room full of people that I admired, respected, and was beginning to love. It was truly a blessing, too, watching my parents bond with my new friends. There were no cigars, no liquor, no vile humor, no high society phoniness, just respect and intelligent conversation for the extent of the whole evening. I believe I saw father wipe away a tear, at one point, and it touched me very deeply. I felt closer to my parents this evening than ever before, and somehow I knew they would figure into the upcoming adventure in ways I could only dream about.

Five

The journey begins

There were five berths aboard the *Heimdall.* Helga and Betsy shared one, Rorek and Olaf shared one, Lizzy had her own, and John and Garrett shared one. Apparently, lately, Garrett and John were having trouble coexisting in the same space.

"John snores too stinkin' loud," I heard Garrett whine on the deck that morning. "I want my own room; homey I need my own space to create in."

"Hey chill out little brother, you snore too, and you need to wash your socks more often, they stink." John replied grimacing.

"Oh yah dude, you sound like an old buffalo at night. And your feet are so stinkin' rotten it makes me wanna puke!" Garrett complained.

"Come on guys, we've got work to do, Settle down!" Captain Olaf ordered with a stern look. Garrett kicked the floor and walked away. John grunted, shook his head in disbelief, and hit the rails with both fists. Me, I just chuckled softly. I liked Garrett and John, and I enjoyed their grumpy honesty. I looked forward to establishing a durable and long-lasting friendship with both of them. Captain Olaf issued me a small berth next to him. It was farther forward than any of the other rooms. Apparently for two years they'd used this particular room as a kind of a catchall and it was a frightful mess. The crew reassured me that there was a bunk somewhere under all that junk and, as soon as we were underway, their very first priority would be to help me clean up my new room and get me moved in. Thirty minutes after retiring Helga and Betsy burst from their room and began running up and down the hallway excitedly announcing that Jonah had sent another e-mail. Sleepily we all moved out of our berths.

"Is everybody here? Helga inquired. Everyone yawned, while Garrett muttered crossly for having been awakened. "Jonah sent a very significant message this time. I'm assuming this will probably change our original plans and, most likely, reshape the first part of our journey. If Captain agrees, we'll be stopping off in the Azorean Archipelagoes to pick up Roxanne."

"Whoa . . ." everyone murmured quietly and looked at each other with wide eyed expressions.

"I wonder how long she's been out there," Betsy queried.

"It'll present an interesting route change for us," Olaf pondered.

"This is very exciting," Lizzy added, "I've never been there before; I understand that they're gorgeous."

"Won't this take us out through the disturbance?" Garrett asked.

"I'm not sure,' the Captain shook his head. "But I'll consult the charts and check the computer later; I'll have more information for us tomorrow during breakfast, ok?"

"Aye-Aye sir," Garrett said snapping to attention. Olaf smiled and winked at Garrett as he saluted with both hands. "At ease, sailor," he laughed. Who was Roxanne I wondered. And why she was presently in the Azorean Archipelagoes? I wondered also what she did, and how she fit in with this crew. "Here's what Jonah wrote," Helga began.

Greetings brothers and sisters:

I hope and pray that you are all in good spirits and excellent health. Roxanne left our cabin in Pine Valley around the time the Heimdall docked in Aberdeen. Gods timing is evident here. Our first intentions were for her to travel down to Revillagigedo to follow up on the stories about the writings she'd learned were found in the newly discovered caves there. Apparently they're Runic, and the interpreter has begun to confirm our suspicions that the Vikings really had landed there on their way to America. According to some of the old writings, the tribe was there for about eight months due to illness and hunger. Anyway, at the last minute, she received an e-mail from a colleague vacationing in La Coruna, informing her that another set of caves had been unearthed during those earthquakes in the Atlantic, January this year. Evidently these caves are in the Azorean Archipelagos. The event purportedly collapsed the whole side of one of the larger hills on the westernmost island of Flores and has completely exposed three caves that had been previously hidden. When

Roxanne heard about this she was stunned; she decided that traveling there was more important than going to Revillagigedo at this point in time. I believe the timing here is excellent and, with a minor deviation, it's not too far off your route. I want you to stop off in the Azores and help her out. She might be finished by the time you get there. If she is, please just pick her up. She'll sail the rest of the way with you. I think she wants to stop off at Revillagigedo on the way back. She'll confirm this at that time. The University of Porto has already dispatched two researchers writing their theses; Resell and Lira; you probably don't know them though. They flew into Sao Miguel, and landed at Ponta Delgada airport, on the 25th of Feb, and then charted a small plane so that they could get into Flores. Apparently there were more airline disputes, and this was the only transportation they could find. They e-mailed Roxanne and informed her that the shorelines are very treacherous and the beaches are black volcanic sand. They also said that there are seven lakes and six volcanic craters in approx sixty-five square miles. Apparently one has lava oozing out of it since the earthquake WOW! I'm not a Geologist, but that can't be good. Roxanne is there now. She flew over to Lisbon Portugal and was able to find a small postal flight directly into Flores. She e-mailed me on the 27th, and informed me she was in good spirits, and very busy. The caves, according to her, are stunning. I told her my intentions for you guys to stop and pick her up. She was really excited. She sends her love. Her address is Roxanne@worldnet.net I'll write you again in a few days. I love you all dearly,

May the Holy Spirit guide and bless you tomorrow on your departure and journey. Smooth sailing! Say hi to my new friend Gabriel; tell him to keep writing. Also, tell him that I praise God that he's with us. Olaf, please consult the main website about the disturbance, something new and strange has developed.

In Christ's love, Jonah

It was an enlightening and significant letter. I was beginning to understand that these people were also pursuing stories and legends about Viking explorers, but why? I began to ponder the incredible events that had overtaken my life in just the last seven days. I hadn't talked about my family's history yet to anyone; there was still way too much work to accomplish before departure. I was nervous about my effectiveness, especially being a ship hand. And there was some apprehension about how I was going to fit in and what my duties would be. Whatever they ended up being I was going to pursue them with honor and forthrightness. Being the son of Elwin Sebastian Proudmore it could be no other way. Perhaps there'd be an opportunity, at some point, for an in depth discussion about Roxanne's involvement and her fascinating work. If Roxanne had left *our* log home in Pine Valley and flown to Portugal, did that mean Roxanne was Jonah's wife, or was she his sister, or perhaps a relative? There were still many unanswered questions, and I suppose I needed more patience. I remembered somewhere it saying: *'For everything under heaven there is a season'.* If this was true then my season of understanding must be at hand. I glanced down the narrow hallway at the rest of the crew's faces. They all seemed surprised, but because everyone was bone tired we agreed to discuss it over breakfast the next morning. It seemed tomorrow was going to be a day of transition and challenges.

Around three am I was abruptly awakened by the exaggerated sloshing of the *schooner* in the water. Outside the "*Belanthian*" was being maneuvered towards the dock by four powerful tug boats. I remembered my father had mentioned the tanker would be a few days late getting into port. He'd also mentioned about engineering problems they'd encountered with the electrical crossovers in fluid switching, and also something about intermittent electrical shorts in the hydraulic gate valves. He hadn't seemed concerned, so I'd just listened. The *Heimdall* was dwarfed by this behemoth. The displacement of water must have been six feet as the tanker went by. I'd forgotten how utterly gigantean these vessels were, and what engineering genius they represented. As I settled back down on the pallet I was gripped by a bewildering fear. How vulnerable I was allowing myself to become. Though I'd never been out to sea, and didn't know anything about sailing, here I was preparing to embark with seven others across the Atlantic Ocean. I guess I was going to grow up real quick.

When I awoke the following morning it was foggy, and the sea gulls were noisily agitated about something. I appeared to be the last one up. My wristwatch read 6:15, but I'd recalled the Captain saying we were going to leave at six. I wondered if there was something wrong. Maybe plans had changed and they'd decided not to take me along. After unlatching my porthole window I heard Olaf and Rorek talking earnestly. The captain was issuing orders to John, Garrett and Helga, in a sailing language I had no knowledge of. After a series of irregular coughs the diesel started with a low pitched rumble. I heard Rorek mention to Olaf that there was still a sizable leak in one of the bilge pump seals, but it was something that he could take care of once they were out to sea.

"Olaf, we've acquired all the parts we'll need for just about any problem we might encounter for the next six months, so please don't worry."

"That's a relief brother, I'm really glad that you and John found what we needed in Aberdeen. That close-out sale helped; finances are low. John's sure turned out to be a real asset, praise God. He's exceptionally skilled, don't you think?"

"Most assuredly agree brother," Rorek nodded. "Don't you have something to do?"

"Yes! I forgot! I've got to chart the new route," Olaf slapped his forehead. "I haven't gotten any work done yet. Jonah asked me to access the main website, concerning the disturbance, and I haven't had time to do that either. I can't help but feel something has changed brother, possibly for the worst, and he wants us prepared."

Rorek nodded with compassion and said: "Don't worry little brother; we'll get through whatever it is, and we'll do it together."

"I guess we're stopping at Edinburgh to pick up that new navigational software," Olaf continued. "I understand that it's been entirely updated and it allows us to continually uplink the GPS twenty-four hours a day. That'll be a real benefit you know. Also, Garrett talked to them two days ago and he's convinced we should update our system with it."

"Let's do it then brother," Rorek agreed. "Garrett's become a real asset since he joined. I trust him now. Remember those first few weeks? Good grief, I thought we'd made a mistake hiring the kid. He really is gifted, a little peculiar, but certainly gifted."

"I agree . . . I love that boy also." Olaf said shaking his head.

"I thought we were going north past Thurso."

"We're not anymore," Olaf frowned. "After I consult the charts I'll have a clearer picture. I'll be up in the wheelhouse if you need me."

"Are you as hungry as I am?" Rorek asked with a chuckle. Olaf nodded affirmatively and walked away.

I'd finally made it up on deck. After shouting a tenuous good morning, everybody stopped short for an instant, waved, and then offering me their hearty good mornings. Not knowing what to do I just stood and watched. "Bout time you got up," Garrett yelled down from the forward mast. I waved back with a half-hearted smile. Everyone, except Betsy, was on deck preparing for departure. The wonderful aromas, wafting up from below, told me she was busy in the kitchen. An hour later a bell started clanging. At once the whole crew let out a thunderous hallelujah, dropped what they were doing, and ran below decks. Eagerly we all flooded into the galley and sat down in hungry anticipation. While Betsy brought in plates of eggs, bacon, fruit, pancakes and hot cinnamon rolls, Helga and Garrett hustled in with the coffee, orange juice and utensils. For some reason Garrett was making faces at me as he worked. "That's a real nice hairdo slam-dunk. If you want, I'll loan you my hair brush so you can fix that nasty bird's nest. Oh wait; maybe that's Scottish style aye?" I knew I'd forgotten to do something this morning, so I sheepishly smiled back and said: "Thanks for the reminder Garrett; I'll use my own hair brush, thank you."

When everything was served Olaf stood up and tapped his coffee cup to get everyone's attention. "Today's the day folks," he announced. "We're embarking on a new adventure, and, with God's help, we'll accomplish what He's given us to do for the glory of His kingdom, amen?" The whole table erupted in cheers and whistles of agreement. "Garrett, would you lead us in prayer son?" Without the slightest hesitation Garrett bounced up and asked everyone to join hands.

"Holy Father . . . in Jesus' name, we all give you thanks for what we are about to receive, please bless this nourishment to our bodies. Father, we also pray for good health and continued wisdom in the coming days and weeks ahead. Thank you for these people and the wonderful skills that you've blessed them with. Thank you for my roommate John, and please forgive me for my complaints and rudeness towards him. Give our Captain the wisdom he needs to guide us safely towards our next destination, and please let this new software we're going to buy be effective in our journey. Lord, thank you ahead of time for our safety, success and victory, In Jesus Name . . . oh, by the way Lord, thank you for our new friend Gabriel. I pray that you will fit him into this crew the way that you desire, and give him the skills that are necessary to accomplish what you put him here to do. I ask all this in Jesus name . . ."

Everyone chorused a hearty amen, and then the breakfast feast commenced. John nodded towards Garrett. Both smiled at each other and I saw John's mouth quietly form the words, 'Thanks dude. I love you too.' Garrett smiled and gestured with both thumbs up. For twenty minutes everyone ate quietly. Near the end of the meal Olaf stood up again and proceeded to clarify his intentions concerning our journey.

"As you all know now, we're on our way to the Azorean Archipelagoes, specifically the Island of Flores, to pickup Roxanne, who by the way is Jonah's loving wife of sixteen years, if you were curious Gabriel." I acknowledged the Captain with a smile and a nod. "I've consulted the charts about our new route and have positively decided to head south. We'll be stopping off in Edinburgh to pick up the new navigational software I ordered. I've been assured that this is the best program on the market for navigating around and through the disturbance. It appears that many of the traditional ocean currents are changing. I read on the internet, just before breakfast, that in certain areas the water is dying and has actually changed color. According to the reports it's turned brown and has a rancid smell. In the western United States the northern and southern borders of the disturbance are constantly fluctuating now. Apparently sometimes the disturbance makes a landfall and then heads farther out to sea. Sometimes it disappears altogether and nobody knows why. There are reports of additional shifts in the color spectrum, especially in those areas where the disturbance has touched. According to the experts the phenomenon isn't localized only to the troposphere, it purportedly goes up through the stratosphere and the mesosphere." The Captain paused for a moment to sip some coffee and clear his throat. "Lord willing, our new route will keep us isolated from this thing. The software will allow us to depend more on GPS information, and less on our compasses and what we physically see. Hopefully this should prove very favorable for us. Does anyone have any questions?"

Everyone shook their heads no, more than likely because none of us knew what to think about it yet.

"All right then," Captain Olaf continued, "let's finish all the preliminaries we need to accomplish before getting underway. We'll be leaving this morning at 8:30 hours. Thanks for listening. Also, thank you Betsy for a wonderful breakfast. Ok people let's get it done!" Everyone pushed back their chairs and snapped to attention. Then all chorused in unison, "Aye Aye sir," while the Captain smiled from ear to ear. "By the way Gabriel," Captain Olaf added, "I want you to help Betsy clean up the galley. Rest assured I haven't forgotten you. Once we're underway your berth will be cleaned and organized."

Captain Olaf's demeanor had begun to change. I knew he was going to be a leader that I could respect and look up to; perhaps he would even become a teacher to me and a good friend. For the next hour or so there was a lot of commotion and shouting. Rorek had gone below decks. Soon a dull rumbling was vibrating up through the wooden decks as he increased the diesel's rpms. Garrett and John were casting off lines and carefully rolling them up. Helga was in the crow's nest testing new electronic equipment recently tied into the ships computers. She was motioning dramatically as she talked with Captain Olaf on the two way radios. The Captain was nodding his approval and smiling. Lizzy was lashing down loose equipment and tying off what she called the halyards; she was singing a melody I remembered my mother singing to me in my youth. The whole crew was either whistling or humming along with her. Even though I felt a curious sense of peace as we all worked together, I couldn't shake the insecurity that had gripped my stomach about leaving Aberdeen. Betsy and I had finished the dishes and everything was stowed safely away. We'd been up on deck for about fifteen minutes when suddenly she moved away and began helping John and Garrett. Nervously I stood around waiting for someone to shout at me, teetering on this strange precipice where my inner frustrations and ignorance collided. I got my wish sooner than expected.

"GABRIEL," the Captain barked.

"Yes sir," I responded uneasily.

"Put up our colors son, and also put up the Scottish courtesy ensign on the starboard halyard amidships, we're leaving!"

What? What were the colors? An ensign? Amidships? What was the halyard? On my left side, Garrett ran up suddenly and stopped. "Dill-dork . . ." he pointed, "put up those two flags over there, on those two lines right there. Don't worry ace, it took me a year to understand sailing lingo, and I'm a much faster learner than you are, Gabriel von dimwit." He laughed uproariously, punched my shoulder, and then dashed off to his other responsibilities. The *schooner* started moving away from the dock. Impulsively I grabbed hold of the railings and sucked in a quick breath. We were at last underway. Around us the sea gulls were getting agitated and their cries had increased in intensity. Somberly I looked back towards home and waved goodbye. What in the world had I gotten myself into?

Six

South towards Edinburgh

March 1st

The Captain steadily increased our speed to the harbors limits. When I glanced up at him in the wheelhouse, his face was reflecting a confident determination that filled me with peace and a warmhearted respect I needed to feel for the leader of this vessel. At home I'd been very confident in my own world. My life was well defined, methodical, and I controlled how each day progressed. Here it was different. I was in circumstances remarkably unfamiliar to me, and I was dependant on everyone else around me. To some degree I felt helpless, but none of my new friends seemed concerned at all about my lack of knowledge, or my insecurities. They must have seen something in me that I couldn't see in myself and had fortunately (for my sake) accepted me for who I was. The next thirty minutes Captain Olaf kept an eye on everything happening on deck. He talked with Rorek often about the bilge pump. But every time they finished, the Captain seemed in good spirits, so I assumed all was well.

"JOHN, GARRETT!" The Captain bellowed suddenly from the wheelhouse stairs.

"Aye," they both responded immediately.

"Take the plugs out of the scuppers stem to stern!"

"Aye aye Captain," they both replied.

"Check the capstan too; make sure that it's been locked down."

"Already done sir," John waved. Captain smiled, nodded his thanks, and climbed back up behind the wheel.

We passed by the *Belanthian on our way out of the harbor.* The gigantean tanker was already tied to the off-loading piers, and station crews were removing the crude oil. For some reason I started shaking. And then I started feeling apprehensive about something that had nothing at all to do with my own insecurities. Something was wrong, but I had no idea what it was. Quietly I began praying, 'God, please help me understand this odd feeling that I'm having about father's vessel.' The schooner was cutting through the water smoothly now. I'd overheard, a few days prior, the crew saying how grateful they were for the schooners 'planing hull' that was engineered to glide effortlessly through the water at low and high speeds. Where I was standing on deck the ocean air was extremely invigorating in my face. Around me the seagulls had grown in numbers. Betsy brought up some old bread from the galley. Smiling modestly she handed me one of the large remnants and we both started breaking them into pieces and throwing them into the air. For some reason I felt shy when Betsy was near, and I had been since the first moment we'd met on the docks. My thoughts churned uncertain in me as I tried to rationalize the warm flow of feelings pumping through me. There was something about her that deeply affected me, especially when she was near, and my inability to open up and communicate was vexing. The gulls were wildly feisty now and all were squawking noisily in their competitions for the small chunks of bread.

"Oh, good grief," Betsy cried out. A blob of seagull poop had been deposited on her forehead and was slowly dripping down over the bridge of her nose. As she tried to wipe it off I broke out into laughter. Alarmed with my reaction she ran below decks distraught. The Captain was livid. "STOP IT RIGHT NOW!" He shouted from the wheelhouse door. "Do *not* feed the gulls Gabriel; they're making a mess on my vessel." Mortified I quickly shook my head in agreement. "Don't fret honey," Lizzy whispered, suddenly appearing at my side. "The Captain hates gulls. He thinks they're filthy, and I have to agree with him. Come on, we'll get out the hose and spray this mess off." I nodded in agreement, and offered my thanks.

As I'd been promised, Olaf assigned Helga, Betsy, Garrett and John to help me clean out my new berth and we worked together for six hours to accomplish the task. The biggest problem was finding places to store what had accumulated for the last two years. While we were cleaning I discovered that the electrical outlets didn't function. John assessed and diagnosed the problem and then quickly repaired it. According to him, they'd been capped off to avoid any potential for fire. After offering my thanks, I unloaded my baggage and computer and put everything in its place. When they'd left I opened up the small porthole, and breathed in deeply the invigorating sea air. At last I had my own space and I was at peace.

We'd all been issued two way radios. They were very powerful, and the clarity of the voices was superb, even in noisy situations.

I concluded this was an excellent way to stay in touch with each other at all times, no matter where we were, on or off the vessel. Captain Olaf asked Helga to take me up to the crow's nest and explain the weather station that John and Garrett had installed the week prior. Intrigued, I followed Helga up the lofty center mast to a small platform with chest high railings. When we'd reached the top I was afflicted with light headedness and a queasy sensation momentarily in my stomach. The sea was choppy this morning, and the water was blackish in appearance. I wondered if this was some foreshadowing of our journey. The dense fog was beginning to lift, the skies were still overcast, and the air was crisp. Our perspective here had changed dramatically. The view on deck paled in comparison to the view in the crow's nest; it was truly breathtaking. From this perspective *Heimdall* was an elegantly graceful vessel with craftsmanship beyond compare. The weather station was an updated smaller version of what my father had been using aboard all of his tankers for years. It had an anemometer, (to register force or speed of wind and direction), barometric pressure, temperature, a rain gauge, atmospheric radiation, chemical depiction, and color spectrum analysis. There was also a new feature included, that allowed us to track weather anywhere, via GPS with absolute precision. Of course this feature still had to be installed, but our stopover in Edinburgh would provide us with the software we needed to utilize not only this feature, but also Virtual Earth Watch capabilities as well. I told Helga how familiar I'd become with this technology the last few years, and, also, about my father's utilization of the same tech aboard all of his tankers. Based on my confident outspokenness of its operability and features, Helga tentatively deferred responsibility of the unit's daily operational chores to me, pending approval from Captain Olaf. Excitedly I began to explicate what I knew to her.

"What I admire about the VEW tech is its ability to zoom out on land and water surface areas, and compass a large or small, precisely detailed image. We can also zoom down on very small geographies with absolute accuracy. The images are amazingly clear and color perfect. Helga, I can zoom down onto the deck of the *Heimdall* and see the faces of our crew, as long as there are no cloud covers to obstruct the satellites view." Helga was getting excited the more I shared with her. "Do you see this small platform here?" I asked pointing to a part of the unit that had nothing attached to it.

"What's that for?" She asked.

"That's where the satellite dish attaches, and without that; all the features I've explained to you would never be able to function."

"Wow! No wonder Captain Olaf wants this new software. You know, given the changing global conditions, and this new route we're going to take, this new technology will definitely keep us aware of what's going on around us, that's a fact!"

"Absolutely right," I agreed with her. "We can ascertain what's on any vessel, the kind of people aboard her, even what they're wearing, as long as they're up on deck. We'll be able to see them on the computer screen long before we can see them with our own eyes. We'll be able to zoom down on Flores, exactly were Roxanne is working, and see what she's doing. We'll be able to communicate with each other in real time with no time delay distortion in the image, or the voices. As soon as the new programs installed, we can get started; it'll be a lot of fun."

Quite unexpectedly Helga began dancing and spinning. Bewildered I quickly pressed myself against the railings to give her more space. Both her hands were thrust up towards Heaven and she began thanking God for the privilege of being alive and for the people she was involved with. "This is very exciting." She raved after her puzzling behavior came to an abrupt halt. "It's obvious Gabriel that the understanding you have of this technology will help our endeavors a lot. I'm really eager to get the new software installed; we'll have to get your computer networked with the other computers aboard, and also with the station up here. Are you willing to get started right away?"

"I'd love it," was my response.

"Ok . . . I'll talk to the Captain." Helga confirmed.

Unexpectedly I began feeling a sense of worth; maybe my computer skills would prove more useful here than I'd anticipated. While descending the mast I noticed the sun was starting to disperse certain parts of the cloud cover overhead; the effect was enchanting. Where sunlight had pierced through, the water had become crystalline and translucent. The blackish color had changed to a grayish green and it was interlaced with striated ribbons of greenish brown. I noticed that our wake was leaving two slowly dispersing lines of white foam, trailing back lazily off the vessels stern. We'd both paused momentarily on our descent to take in the mesmerizing change when all at once Helga let out a whoop that almost made me lose my footing. Cupping her hands together, she yelled down to the crew: "LOOK OVER THERE!" she pointed. A pod of dolphins had surfaced and were racing along with the schooner about twenty yards off the port side. All of them were jumping and diving playfully with each other at precisely the same speed we were moving.

"They're pacing us!" Helga cried out. "Gabriel, no matter where we've been in the past, aboard this vessel, the dolphins have always seemed to enjoy traveling with us. Sometimes they're around for many days, even weeks. BETSY!" Betsy had just come up from below decks, and was brushing out her freshly washed blonde locks. When she heard Helga's cry, she looked up. "LOOK!" Helga pointed excitedly. Betsy ran to the bow and leaned over the railing as far as she could. A moment later she turned back around and waved with a huge smile that pierced my heart and deposited a kind of tenderness in me that I hadn't experienced for over two years. Suddenly I was flooded with memories of when I'd first met my sweet Ingrid in Aberdeen. Here again, halfway down the mast, curiosity moistened my heart with the sweet residue of Betsy's fleeting smile and, for a moment, I felt as if I could fly. The rest of the crew were congregated now at the bow and had begun whistling and waving at the dolphins. Apparently they appreciated the crew's attention, because they started jumping higher and became more comical and spirited. When we'd reached the deck Helga and I joined the rest of the crew to enjoy the comic relief the dolphins were offering. After watching awhile we began, one by one, to disband and head back to our berths or unfinished work. Helga had been the first to vanish; I assumed she'd gone to talk with Captain Olaf about our discussion concerning the weather station. Later, when I saw her, she was smiling and exuberant. "Olaf was very excited when I told him about your knowledge and skills with this new equipment. Congratulations Gabriel; you're now officially a working member of the crew." After her short dialogue, she reached out and shook my hand. "What it means, simply, is that you and I will be working closely with Captain Olaf every day with navigation, charts, and record keeping, or anything else that needs to get done."

"Oh wow, gosh, honestly?" I asked in amazement.

"Yes . . . the Captain was genuinely upbeat Gabriel," Helga continued, "he sincerely wants you involved on this voyage. He was also intrigued when I told him about the other functions we could add to the overall system. He wants you to research those prices on the computer and get back with him. If it's within our budget we'll purchase those upgrades in Edinburgh. See, you're already proving useful, so you shouldn't ever worry about fitting in here."

"Well . . . . Ok! Thanks for that Helga. I've never been to Edinburgh, though, and I have no idea how to get around."

"Captain said Garrett and you could take the raft into town together," Helga continued, "Garrett's been there three or four times in the last few years, and he knows his way around fairly well. According to the Captain we're going to anchor outside the surf line, instead of docking, and stay for a day or so. It'll give you and Garrett a chance to get into town, see a few sights, and make the purchases. Captain wants us to work out the bugs while we're anchored, just in case we need to replace something defective. We don't want to have to turn around and come back you know."

"Oh sure, I agree! You said something about a raft?"

"It's behind the wheel house covered with a tan tarp. It's an eighteen foot hard rubber raft with a fifty-five horse power motor; come on." Helga motioned as she turned on heel and made her way towards the stern. I was totally shocked when she showed me; I'd walked past it at least twenty times since I'd been aboard; it stuck out like a sore thumb, but I'd never seen it.

We were making good time. After finishing with us Rorek went back to the wheel house to talk with his brother. I could tell those two Norwegian brothers really loved and respected each other, and, considering their jovial demeanor; it appeared everything was going smoothly our first day out. The Captain saw me watching them; he nodded and gave me a thumb up. Around one pm we passed Arbroath, and were anticipating anchoring outside of Edinburgh around seven that evening. Over lunch, we all agreed that Garrett and I should take the raft into town first thing in the morning. Hopefully tonight I could get some sleep. I was sluggish from the previous night's restlessness and needed to sort out the feelings I'd gotten when we'd passed the Belanthian. Something peculiar had happened to me then, but I was far too tired to try and figure out what it was. Maybe I'd have time tomorrow. We were sailing south now. And when we'd passed roughly where the city of St Andrews was, we'd be changing our course and heading inland towards Edinburgh. I was more excited now than ever. The Captain seemed pleased. And Rorek was elated because repairs on the bilge pump had been successful. "It was just a top seal," he shared with us, "and now it's as good as new again." After finishing he walked away laughing and dancing an old sailor's jig.

I'd been in my berth close to two hours, writing an e-mail to my parents, when I was startled by a sharp rapping at the door. "Hey Gabriel," I heard a muffled voice say.

"Yah," I answered.

"Hey dude, its Garrett, can I come in?"

"Sure, hold on." I pushed back my chair, went over and opened the door. Garrett sauntered in.

"Gimme five homey," he grinned. I held out my palm and he slapped it hard. Smiling slyly he went over and plopped down on my disheveled bunk. "This place looks better than it ever has since I've been aboard this dingy, well, everything except this nasty ass bunk." Garrett stretched out his legs and, with his head bent up against the wall; he started playing his invisible drum kit.

"Really, I'm truly delighted about all of this; I'd never seen such a mess as the one that was in this room. And by the way, the beds messed up because I took a nap earlier." I grimaced defensively.

"Whatever dork," he shot back, and got up to leave.

"Are you a musician Garrett?"

Garrett smirked, but quickly relaxed and replied: "I have my own drum kit man; it's at my dad's house in San Diego. He lets me store it there while I'm away. I've always had dreams, you know, playin' music professionally and makin' it. My dad was professional for years; He told me it was a dead end being an artist in this crumby world, nobody really cares, but if you're good, then everybody wants a piece a' you. I nodded calmly as he spoke, it seemed he was going to open up a little, and I didn't want to interfere with the delicate process. "Did you know that my dad and Jonah know each other?" He asked. I shook my head no. "Yeah, they work in the studio sometimes; those dudes are bomb, you should hear their recordings. They told me when my chops get better that I can do some session work with them. I really love my dad dude. He taught me a lot about people and life, and what to do, and what not to do, in different situations. He gave me a good foundation about personal relationship with Jesus Christ too." Garrett slowly began shaking his head and his eyes began glowing intensely. "I think, after my mom walked out, I would 'a probably killed myself if I hadn't been grounded in Christ . . . anyway dude." Sitting up suddenly, he changed the subject. "I'm looking forward to Edinburgh tomorrow. I'm glad you have those skills you told Helga about. Captain Olaf's bomb, but don't tell him I said so." He gestured at me with a clenched fist and smiled. "I've been in Edinburgh before. I know a place we can rent scooters. Cap said we could stay the whole day if we wanted. He's givin' us money for pizza, or whatever." Garrett smiled feebly as he stood to leave.

"I'm really looking forward to it, Garrett," I said, quickly standing and offering him my hand. "I'm really glad you and I are going."

"Me too dude." Garrett murmured.

"Are you ok?" I queried.

"Yah I'm fine," he replied with sudden resolve. "Catch ya at breakfast doc, thanks for gabbin' with me." After that, he shuffled out and closed the door behind him. In that moment I realized that I liked Garrett a lot and I really looked forward to a burgeoning friendship and our adventure in Edinburgh the following day.

Seven

A sinister encounter

During the night we anchored *about* a mile offshore the city of Edinburgh Scotland. I'd decided to retire early, figuring that catching up on my sleep was the best thing I could do to maintain my vitality and health. Thankfully I'd slept like a baby and had awakened focused with an eagerness to take on the world with these people. It was six am, the sun had crested the horizon, and the air was briskly pungent with the smell of salt. When I sauntered into the galley Betsy was alone and busily involved with her preparations for another morning meal.

"Good morning sunshine," she proclaimed brightly.

"Morning Betsy . . . what time did you get up?"

"I usually get up around 5:30 to get breakfast started."

"Wow, that's pretty early."

"It depends a lot on what's going on; there's a lot factors that could change my schedule."

"Can I have some coffee please?"

"Sure, it's in the urn over there" she pointed, "and it's fresh."

"Gabriel, I need some help this morning, I'd appreciate the extra hands?"

I began to stutter and stammer. "Uh . . . . I guess so. Is Garrett busy, doesn't he usually help out with the food? You know I'm not very good at cooking Betsy, but anyway, well, ok . . . I guess."

Betsy straightened up, turned, and glared at me in the eyes. "Garrett is busy. He's preparing the raft for you guys to go into Edinburgh after breakfast. John got up early to help him gas it up and prepare for the trip, too. Two people need to winch it into the water, so that's why he's not helping out this morning ok?" Betsy was beginning to get flustered, and I certainly didn't want to get into an argument with her.

"Well, ok then, sorry to upset you, how can I help?" I'd utterly relinquished my defenses, smitten once again by that 'unfathomable something about her' buzzing around my head like bees. I guess I liked this woman and should probably accept it. With a newfound resolve I straightened up, squared my shoulders and, with a sigh and shrug, consigned myself to helping her in any way that I could. As I was rolling up my sleeves to begin I recalled that somewhere it said it was 'better to give than to receive', so I became Betsy's assistant chef with a smile on my face.

The rest of the crew wandered in just before seven. When they were seated Captain Olaf stood up, tapped his coffee cup, and led the morning prayers. After we'd eaten, and while they were picking up the dishes, Betsy paused near me and whispered in my ear: "Thanks so much for helping this morning, you did a groovy job. So, maybe you can help out more often if I need it?" She smiled and moved away before I could respond. Looking down I impulsively wiped some crumbs off my pants; I was embarrassed, but quickly succumbed to the delightfully sweet warmth that crept up in the form of a smile.

"All right," Captain Olaf began abruptly, "QUIET NOW!" He tapped loudly on the table top with his knuckles. "All right then, Garrett and Gabriel will be heading into Edinburgh today to pick up our new software for the weather station. Helga and I are both excited about the excellent potential these programs will offer in our upcoming endeavors. When the software's installed and functioning properly, we'll bring everyone up to par on the new capabilities this new tech will offer us, and also how we'll use this to protect ourselves out on the ocean. The world is changing rapidly people." The Captain paused, brooded for a moment, and then he continued. "According to what I've read on the internet, the last few days, the disturbance has destroyed everything it's touched, but now it's not maintaining the original boundaries (it's had) for the last five or six years. It's begun moving around at will, and no one knows why. Heck, nobody really knows anything about this phenomenon. I have a hunch this will be the most perilous voyage we've ever been on before. Truthfully I'm struggling with some apprehension about what we're getting ourselves into, and I want us all to be prepared spiritually every day, and I also want our tech tools up to date. I'm convinced God has put Gabriel on this vessel for a specific reason. I believe, somehow, that he's made our crew complete. There are eight of us now people. That's the number of new beginnings. I find this remarkably thought provoking. I know we don't understand everything God is doing with us, but we'll muster the faith necessary to make this journey happen together. I also trust that He will reveal to all of us, in His perfect timing, what needs to be done and when. Also guys, good news. Our financial grant was renewed yesterday, so . . ." The Captain's voice got louder to compensate for the escalating commotion, "we've got the money for another six months of work." The whole crew jumped up with whistles and catcalls as the Captain spun in circles. Betsy and Helga started dancing together; John and Rorek started punching each other in a mock fight; Garrett began played his invisible drums; Lizzy began conducting a silent orchestra as her long white hair flowed rhythmically with Garrett's wild poetic movements. It was obvious the crew was ecstatic about this news. I realized that the renewed grant, and my father's promised assistance, had placed our voyage in a very favorable financial position and would allow us to continue in the pursuit of our goals.

"Just for the record," Olaf interjected, "Gabriel is now officially helping Helga and me with navigation and satellite imaging. I haven't told him yet, or anyone else for that matter, but I think he would also be well suited to help us out with our logs and digital photographic records too." The Captain looked at me quizzically with his eyebrows up. I shook my head affirmatively and glanced around the table for looks of approval. Everyone started clapping and whistling and I heard Garrett's animated voice cutting through the hullabaloo. "Bout time you did something to earn your keep dude. You can't be sleepin' the whole trip." The next moment I got hit in the head with a rolled up napkin. The laughter increased now; something extraordinary was going on and I felt very proud to be part of it.

"Also . . . ," the Captain continued when the laughter and chatter had subsided, "as of now, we'll be staying anchored here until our new software is installed and functioning. Is everyone in agreement?" Everyone shook their heads affirmatively after which the Captain turned and pointed at the world map on the rear wall. "Our route to the Azorean Archipelagoes will take us south along the eastern shores of England, through the North Sea, out through the English channel, and then south/south/west through the Bay of Biscay towards northern Spain. I want to try and avoid the shipping routes as much as possible. I read on the internet this morning that a large tanker, filled to capacity, hit a sunken vessel in the center of the channel. Apparently it took ten super tugs to pull it off the wreck. The outer hull, up around the bow, was damaged severely, but it didn't breach the inner hull, so no crude was lost. Praise God for that miracle," Captain Olaf looked up towards heaven and began shaking his head in thanks. "I'm planning to stop at the barges near Roscoff for fuel and fresh supplies. Unless I hear from Jonah we'll continue on to Porto Spain. We're going to pick up new equipment the University will be delivering to us at the docks. Hopefully we'll be able to fit it all onboard; I'm sure you're aware that we don't have a whole lot of room left since Gabriel joined." Everyone murmured and shook their heads in agreement. "After that our plan is to proceed to Lisbon for diesel fuel, fresh water and supplies again, and lay over for a day or two to rest. The disturbance is about seventy miles off the Portuguese coast now, and, according to my sources at the Coast and Geodetic center there, it's never made a land fall yet. They told me that hundreds of people in Lisbon have moved off the coast and out of the city. There's a significant relocation going east towards the Spanish border. Fear is spreading quickly, and I understand that there's a lot of lawlessness. We'll have to be on our guard and prepared for the worst when we dock there. We'll be heading directly through the disturbance for the very first time on our way out to Flores. I want all of you to pray about possibly using some of the new laser technology we've read about over the last few months. It might be wise to have some high tech gadgets to defend ourselves. We really don't have to discuss this in detail now, just keep it tucked in your minds as a possibility, we'll all decide before we reach Porto. If anyone has any ideas let's talk about it. Perhaps the University could loan it to us for research purposes; I'll check with Roxanne this week, ok? That's all I know now. Does anyone have any questions?"

"I think we need to get the boys on their way, Olaf," Rorek said standing up pointing at the clock, "it's after eight, and they both have a long day ahead of them. The rafts ready, gas tanks full, life jackets are aboard, and I gave them that first aid box we purchased in Trondheim last year. Also I gave them two long range radios. All they need now is some money." Olaf nodded in agreement, and with a motion of his head instructed Rorek to get it out of the safe.

Helga stood up. "Before you go Rorek let's all join hands and pray for Garrett and Gabriel's success and safety today in Edinburgh. And let's thank God for the financial grant that came through for us." Everyone agreed. By eight thirty we were aboard the raft. Garrett had started the motor and was letting it warm up while we got ourselves situated. While maneuvering into my life vest I glanced up at the Captain; he was staring at the northern horizon; his face was etched with concern. There was a very large bank of incarnadine altocumulus clouds looming across the whole northern skyline. Rorek joined him, and they both seemed to be intently discussing something of a serious nature. A few moments after Garrett had gunned the motor and taken off the radios crackled into life.

"Garrett, Gabriel, come in please, this is Captain Olaf." Garrett quickly slowed the raft down and showed me how to use the radio.

"This is Gabriel sir, go ahead."

"Boys, the northern horizon looks threatening. We have a red mackerel sky moving towards us this morning, can you see it?"

"That's affirmative sir," I answered, turning back around and waving at the schooner.

"Rorek and I have decided to anchor in the harbor. The barometer is falling quickly and I'm concerned a really big storm is brewing. If the storm hits before you and Garrett get back, find a place to stay in town for the night. Do not ride the raft back in the storm, that's an order!" The Captains voice was authoritative.

"No problem Captain, we copy you, and understand," I replied.

"That's good son, see you both either tonight, or when the storm passes. Please stay in touch!"

"Copy that Captain; see you soon, take care." I stood up and waved as Garrett increased our speed. "It doesn't sound too promising dude." Garrett shouted over the whine of the motor. I shook my head and turned back to keep an eye on the approaching shoreline.

"Hey Gabriel!"

"Yeah!"

"Wanna take the wheel super dude?"

"Yeah . . . sure I do."

Garrett brought the raft to a sudden stop. Following some cursory instructions, we changed places. With some trepidation I gripped the wheel and slowly pushed the throttle lever forward. After about ten minutes we'd reached the harbor entrance and passed through the 'Dragons Jaws'. Edinburgh's skyline loomed like a pencil sketch on the horizon in front of us. When we were about halfway into the harbor Garrett took the wheel back. He'd been scrutinizing the shoreline for a particular landmark he'd remembered from the last time he was here. After twenty minutes of squinting we found the rock formation, and then maneuvered in to tie off on a small piling next to the pier. Based on the presentiment Captain Olaf had about a storm coming down from the north we decided to pay for two days in advance. Apparently the owners of the docks and bait stations were anticipating the storm as well and they offered to stow our raft in one of the floating garages for no extra charge. Gratefully we accepted the offer, waved goodbye, and started towards the city.

Edinburgh is magnificent. Over the last couple days Garrett had shared some facts and figures with me. But the pictures he'd shown me, and the descriptions I'd read, did no justice at all to what I was seeing with my own eyes. The city is built on a hodgepodge of many hills and valleys. During the eighteenth and nineteenth centuries this charismatic geography was expertly enhanced by a succession of gifted and distinguished Georgian and Victorian architects. The results were truly breathtaking. We passed a large ornate bronze plaque, informing us that the city had been named after *Edwin,* a king of ancient Northumbria. Edinburgh had been a 'Royal Burgh' since the twelfth century, and had been universally accepted as the capital of Scotland since the fifteenth century. As a flock of seagulls moved in noisily around us we passed another sign that read: **Welcome to Portobello**. Apparently we'd come ashore outside Edinburgh's *'quaint suburb by the sea'*. It was a beautiful place with sandy beaches that spread out as far as the eye could see. After a while we came to a very large estuary intersecting the bay. In-coming salty tides, here, met the fresh water of the out-flowing river. This confluence created a considerably muddy area of agitated water. Here the seagulls were quite disconcerted and were foraging noisily for food. As we walked we came upon another sign advertising **Edinburgh's Glorious Golf Courses**. I remembered father raving about these before he'd succumbed to the knee injury that had regrettably ended his golf game. I recalled him saying there were twenty-eight courses within the city's boundaries and they were all as pristine as the Queens castle. *'Fit for a king, tho' the waefu' may wager the holes, it'll make a pauper out 'a ye quickly.' he would laughingly brogue.*

Finally we found the rental service. And after signing the agreement we were given two scooters. Edinburgh was immense, about one hundred square miles, and we needed to cover a vast area and didn't have a lot of time. Garrett purchased a street map and, when we'd stowed our small bags in the hard luggage boxes, we pushed the starter buttons on the handlebars and the motors whined and pinged into life. After they'd warmed up for several minutes, we were off. Our first stop would be *Northern Marine Weather Technology* on Cockburn St to purchase our new software. The ride took twenty minutes. When we arrived we saw that the store front had been boarded up. There was a sign, hanging cockeyed on an old rusted chain, informing passerby's that the business had moved. Unfortunately the new address had been sprayed over by vandals. After shutting down the scooters we pushed them off the old deteriorating cobblestone road. After several minutes of puzzling, and taking in our gloomy surroundings, Garrett perked up. "Dude, they have internet cafes in this city; Reality X, and WEB13. I remember we can access *Northern Marines* website from one of those and find out where they've moved too. Let's see," he contemplated, rubbing his forehead and kicking the crumbling sidewalk, "where were they?"

"Do you think they might be listed on this map you purchased Garrett?" I asked, reaching into the luggage box.

"What am I, a mind reader?" He snapped. At once aware of his brusqueness, Garrett looked up sheepishly and said: "Sorry that was rude. This place is creepy. Let's look at the map, you're probably right Gab."

There were several dislodged cobblestones from the old street lying in the gutter so we used them to hold done the edges of the map.

The wind had picked up and was bringing with it scattered clouds and loose trash swirling in and around the abandoned doorways. A random gust suddenly blew the shops broken sign back and forth; it began making an eerie squeaking sound. A door slammed down the street, almost simultaneously accompanied with the sound of broken glass. Garrett and I straightened up. Realizing that this part of town was, by and large, abandoned, we began feeling on edge. Hunched over in a dirty brown hooded cloak a sinister figure had stumbled out from one of the many deserted shops; he was talking indistinctly. Stopping suddenly he threw down an old brown bag that shattered when it hit the cobblestones. Looking up at the sky he began shaking his fist. We stared at each other uneasily and shook our heads. Having stopped what we were doing now, our full attention was glued on the sinister figure shuffling up Cockburn Street. Cursing and mumbling he crossed over the street six shops up. Suddenly he turned towards us and began scowling repulsively. With one hand gesturing at us rudely he cursed us and then turned and vanished into an adjacent alley. Something was gravely wrong with this old neighborhood, and that disturbing man had rattled our emotions.

“There’s something funky here.” Garrett whispered glumly. “I don’t remember Edinburgh ever having any neighborhoods like this before. This place gives me the creeps dude!”

“Let’s see what we can find out from this map.” I suggested, in an effort to change our focus and to shake off the disconcerted feelings the wind, strange sounds, and that sinister character had given us. “Here’s a list of different places. Edinburgh Castle, a thousand years of history on a bloody volcano, what’s up with that?” I looked over at Garrett and he just shrugged his shoulders. “Who knows!” he grunted. “What else is there?”

"The Royal mile, the Palace of Holyrood, Holyrood Park, Greyfriars Kirk, Edinburgh Zoo, Royal Yacht Britannia, Camera Obscura, that's not what we need. Oh, here's a list of Lochs. Earn, Tay, Venacher, Loch Lomond, nope; this isn't what we need either." I was beginning to get annoyed; maybe the map didn't have the information we needed. "Wait, here it is Garrett, Internet Cafes . . ." Garrett moved closer and started reading.

"Alrighty then super dude, Cyberia, Electric Frog, here we go, WEB13, that's where I was before. Let's see, here it is on Bread St, right off of Lothian Road. You ready? Let's leave now." I nodded in absolute agreement.

An hour later we'd found WEB13. And after we paid the fee, Garrett accessed the *Northern Marine Weather Technologies* website. We discovered they'd moved to a newer building. According to the web page; they were now over on Hanover St. A phone call was placed and we introduced ourselves. We were informed our software was already packaged and ready for pickup. The satellite dish had also arrived, and payment had been made on-line by credit card the previous day. The secretary spoke highly of Captain Olaf and Helga and she apologized for any inconvenience the trip over to Cockburn St had caused us. She told us the neighborhood had deteriorated, six months previous, when a group of disturbing people had moved in. They'd apparently migrated down from somewhere up north, possibly Norway, or some islands farther north, but she wasn't sure.

"They smell terrible, like they never bathe, and their behavior is unpredictable and bizarre." She told us. "They're hateful and all the businesses in the area suffered financial consequences. Ninety percent of the cash flow disappeared in all the shops; everyone stopped doing business in the neighborhood. Some business owners were hurt trying to fight back when their properties where assaulted.

They have astonishing strength and make sounds like animals when they're resisted or confronted. They certainly don't like anyone in the areas that they've staked out for themselves. They wear dark cloaks that cover their entire bodies, apparently to hide the facial deformities and the grotesque color of their skin. We were very happy when this new property opened up for us; we were getting terribly despondent about being confronted by them. Well gentlemen, I'll see you both when you get here, your new software's right up front on my desk. I look forward to seeing you. Good day!" With that she concluded and hung up. What a story that'd been.

For hours we rode around in silence, taking in the sights, and deeply absorbed in our own thoughts. After we'd picked up the software and satellite dish, I suggested we stop somewhere and eat. Garrett eagerly agreed. "I'm so hungry; I could eat the Loch Ness monster dude. I know a great place about half a mile from here, right over there in Portobello where we landed. Follow me!" Revving his scooter hard he screeched his back tire and zoomed off.

Ravenously we both devoured a late lunch. Afterwards we talked about the puzzling character we'd encountered on Cockburn St. We both surmised that he was surely one of those afflicted crazies the secretary had described. Quietly we prayed at the table and thanked God for protecting us in that horrid neighborhood. Outside our window the skies mackerel appearance had changed to black. Something was approaching. There were low rumblings and brief flashes of lightening, now, accompanied with erratic smatterings of rain on the street and windows. As we watched the radios began crackling.

"Gabriel, Garrett, this is Captain Olaf, come in please."

"Go ahead Captain," Garrett responded.

"Garrett, we're anchored now over near the estuary by Portobello. How are things with you? Have you picked up the new software yet?"

"Things are well boss; we picked up the software about six hours ago. The lady was very nice and spoke highly about you and Helga. Their business moved, so it took us longer than expected to find it, and by the way Captain, we're in Portobello right now. Captain, do Gabriel and I have a weird story to tell you when we get back."

"I look forward to hearing it. Listen to me now. This storm is moving in fast. According to the Global Weather Service, there's a massive hurricane blowing off eastern Greenland. First word came from a Russian freighter that reported the winds had risen steadily for about two hours, and was up around eighty-five mph. The ships barometer had plunged to 28.25 inches in less than an hour and they were desperately looking for safe haven. They were confirmed about five hundred miles from Iceland. I don't believe the full force of the storm will reach this far south though. Forecasters at the 'Norwegian Weather Bureau' predict it's going to turn due east towards their western coast. They've activated the whole Northern network with a hurricane advisory. The storm has huge potential, with the possibly of twenty foot storm surges. There's also a possibility that Iceland is going to take a terrible beating. Coastal cities are evacuating. Meteorologists have determined the storm is moving at thirty miles an hour, it sounds grim. Satellite photos confirm the storm veering east from the original southern direction. We're going to stay glued to the internet and Navtex reports for the next few hours here. I'm looking forward to being able to use our new software boys."

"Captain Olaf, what do you want us to do, stay in town, or come back to the schooner?" Garrett asked uneasily.

"What's your status son? Do you have lodging yet? Have you eaten anything since you left this morning?"

"We're in a restaurant right now and we just finished eating. Rented two scooters, but we don't have any lodging yet. There's a hotel right across the street so it wouldn't be too difficult for us to get a room."

"Good! Stay the night but try and get back by seven tomorrow morning. If my hunches are right, this storm will be fierce for awhile but pass rather quickly. Lord willing we'll be able to shove off early tomorrow morning. Let's see, its six o'clock now, well, for sure boys get back here before eight . . . ok?"

"Roger that Captain; we'll be there on time, promise, unless I can't wake Gabriel." Garrett smirked and punched me on the shoulder.

"We'll see you tomorrow then, bright and early. If anything changes on our end we'll contact you; keep the radios on. Lord willing, tomorrow we'll all be heading out towards the English Channel. I hope you both had a fun time."

The rain got torrential as we got up to leave; the storm was upon us now in full fury. Lights began flickering as the cities power grids began to fail. After we'd stowed our scooters and paid the garage hand, we ran for the front door of the hotel clutching the new weather software and satellite dish safely under our jackets. Just as I reached down to turn the handle; Garrett nudged me in the ribs and whispered: "Look over at the end of the street by that alley dude." At once my flesh began to crawl. Standing in the downpour, staring straight at us, was the same sinister man we'd seen on Cockburn St earlier in the day.

Eight

An urgent e-mail & sails ahead

"Captain, this is Gabriel, what's wrong sir?" Around five-thirty we'd been awakened by the sudden crackling of our two way radios; Captain Olaf was agitated and despondent. "Gabriel we've gotten an urgent e-mail from Roxanne. There's been another earthquake. The Labrador Sea, approximately six hundred miles northwest of the archipelagos and 7.2 on the Richter scale. According to the Lisbon on-line weather services they're expecting a tsunami to hit the islands at any time. The volcano's become more active. She's confirming emissions have tripled and the atmosphere is filling with sulfurous fumes and ash. Thank God the winds generated by the hurricane are working to their advantage. They're pushing the fumes due west, off the island. The lava's flowing towards the eastern shores, away from them, and into the sea. Resell and Lira are with her. They're working shifts around the clock to catalog and package as many of the artifacts as they can. They've taken over two hundred digital photographs of the runic writings, and she says the information is astonishing. I've received some of the photos on my computer; and I definitely agree with her, they are truly a remarkable find. She'd hoped to be finished with her work and off the island three or four weeks from now, but this earthquake has understandably alarmed them. They've been forced to push that date forward; she sounds desperate, and wants us to hurry. Apparently the airlines are on strike again and all flights, in and out, have been terminated for the time being. As of yesterday they're stranded on the island. Boys, you need to get motivated; unfortunately now we'll have to install everything while we're moving. I really didn't want to do it this way. I hope and pray that everything's in order, and we don't end up needing something else. I want to leave Edinburgh as soon as possible. Did you copy?"

"We copy you loud and clear Captain, we're on our way," Garrett responded, while hastily pulling on his trousers, "I'll have the rental service pick up the scooters here at the hotel; they're already paid for through today. We'll just run down to the docks. We're only about three blocks from the raft; I don't think it'll take much time."

"Copy that Garrett," the Captain answered, "Good idea about the scooters son; it will save us some time. Betsy has breakfast ready, so you can eat when you get aboard; we're waiting on you, please hurry. Also Gabriel, there's some news I've received that's going to affect you specifically. I'll tell you when you get aboard, it's not good son."

"Roger that Captain, we're on our way."

The Captains last few words baffled me; what could the news be, and why wouldn't he tell me. As we were preparing to check out, Garrett called the rental company and told them about our predicament. They assured us that there was no problem; they'd done it many times before. They wished us both luck, and smooth sailing, and said they'd see us next time around. Considering the disquieting encounter we'd had with that sinister looking man, the previous night had progressed uneventful. Garrett and I had prayed together before turning in, and both of us upon awakening had found our sleep thoroughly refreshing. We'd informed the desk clerk about our suspicions concerning the character. We were assured it would be reported to the police immediately. The desk clerk had also mentioned that those *crazies* were moving around more at night, especially during the last thirty days. There'd been a number of reports from prominent leaders around the city, and all of them were voicing complaints about their unhealthy appearances at the most inopportune times. They'd also become a controversial topic on the television over the last few weeks. As soon as the police had responded to his call he'd smiled and said goodnight. We both waved appreciatively and hurried up to our room to retire.

Speedily we checked out of the hotel and waved goodbye. I glanced down at my wristwatch; the time was *5:55*. Stopping briefly, we both carefully repositioned our bags and purchases. The software, and satellite dish, had begun bouncing around and we both feared that they would get damaged. As soon as we felt they would transport safer, we started jogging again in the direction of the pier. It took about fifteen minutes to reach the floating garages where the raft was stored. The beaches were strewn with wreckage from the gale. Many dozens of the smaller craft had been thrown up on the beach; most were lying on their sides severely damaged and broken in pieces. I noticed large shapes up by the surge wall; several whales had floundered and perished during the storm. It looked apocalyptic.

The sea gulls were numerous near the bodies and all were fiercely agitated. Some were flying in a strange ritual around them, some were perched on top of the corpses dancing, and some were pecking and screaming loudly. The scene on the beach was one of chaos and wide spread damage. The dock owners met us and hastily informed us that their property had thankfully survived the storm intact. They also mentioned that some good people would be contacting their insurance companies and starting over. We saw exactly what they were talking about; many businesses had been completely destroyed and were lying in piles of rubble. After we thanked the two workers for their help we both boarded the raft. As he pulled away from the pier we shouted our thanks once again, and waved hasty goodbyes.

"Where did the Captain say the schooner was?" I asked.

"Around the estuary somewhere, dude." Garrett scanned the bay with a pair of small binoculars he'd found stowed in the rafts storage locker. "I can barely see anything."

The weather was still a bit unstable; there were many dark clouds and occasional rumblings of thunder. A heavy mist, overhanging the water, made it difficult to see any more than fifty or sixty yards around us. "I have an idea Garrett." Swiftly stopping the raft I picked up the radio. Garrett lowered the binoculars and stared at me curiously. According to my wristwatch it was *6:35.*

"Captain Olaf, this is Gabriel, do you copy sir?" Garrett suddenly gave me a thumb up; apparently he understood my idea intuitively.

"Go ahead; this is Rorek, Captains indisposed."

"We can't see the schooner through this wretched mist; can you switch on the spotlight for us?"

"John, turn on the spotlight," Rorek barked. "Aim it towards the estuary; the boys are having trouble. Gabriel, let me know as soon as you see us."

"There they are!" Garrett yelled, pointing west.

"We see you Rorek, we're on our way!"

Five minutes later we were alongside the schooner. The time was *7:10.* We'd made it back home in an hour and forty minutes. With our help, John hoisted the raft out of the water and secured it. Garrett and I put the new software and satellite dish up in the wheelhouse and came back down to help secure the bowsprit preventer lines. When we were finished Rorek announced we were ready to go. Moments later we were moving out of the harbor. Garrett and I were ravenous, so we proceeded down to the galley at once. Betsy had been kind enough to keep breakfast warm for us. When we entered I noticed she was deeply agitated about something.

"What's wrong Betsy?" Garrett inquired. She shrugged her shoulders and told us that we needed to discuss it with the Captain.

"How was your trip?" She asked. We both smiled and shook our heads ok.

John appeared in the doorway and welcomed us back. He told us we'd be helping him install the new equipment. "Captain wants it installed ASAP. We'll get started in about thirty minutes. He can't raise sails until we've finished the project so we need to make some good time here, guys. Good to see you back. Enjoy your meal." Garrett and I both nodded as he exited the galley, smiling while we continued stuffing our faces with Betsy's eggs and French toast. Lizzy wandered in next. After filling her coffee cup she stopped by our table and warmly hugged both of us. "I'm so thankful you're both back safe." She smiled broadly. "Things are changing so quickly out there boys. We've got a long and challenging journey ahead of us and we need each other now more than ever. I love you both. See you soon." After we'd finished eating we thanked Betsy and joined the others on deck.

"Garrett, go below and install the new programs on the main computer," Rorek began as we all huddled together for a meeting. "Helga's having problems with configurations; the new software is proving a bit difficult to load. Figure out the problem for her ok? She's getting a bit fussy."

"No problem boss," Garrett answered. "By the way, do you know what's wrong with the Captain?"

"Olaf's preoccupied with plotting our course son; we've got to make excellent time from here on out." I could see Rorek was getting irritated; he kept pursing his lips and looking away.

"What about the news he's supposed to talk to me about," I asked awkwardly.

"We'll talk about that later." Rorek glared sternly. "Look, Gabriel, I don't want to hear any more, understand, end of story!"

"Alright! We'll talk about it later then." There was clear tension aboard that wasn't there when Garrett and I had departed the previous morning. But trying to comprehend the change was rather difficult being that I'd been angered by Rorek's tone.

"What do you want me to do?" I asked cautiously.

"I want you and John to go above," he said pointing up, "I want you to install this satellite dish here, wire it into the stations port with these weather proof connectors, seal all the connections with that stuff in the blue can over there, run this special shielded cable down through the white conduit to me, and then I'll tie it into the central hub myself. Let's get it done!" John and I promptly began preparing to go aloft. Strapping on the tools we needed, we began our ascent up the center mast.

"Wait a minute!" Rorek barked tersely. John and I turned to see him motioning for us to come back down; he looked remorseful.

"Let's pray before we start, I'm sorry about the outburst." Sighing in relief, we both shook our heads and agreed.

The installation took almost six hours and everything installed flawlessly. Betsy brought up sandwiches and tea so we could eat as we worked. When she handed me my food she looked at me demurely and said: "I'm glad you're back safely, Gabriel, I missed you." All I could do was smile because my tongue was tied in knots. She was so lovely, and this expression of caring caught me completely off guard. Turning away with another smile, she hurried below decks.

Several times, during the morning, I'd glanced up at the Captain. Each time, though, he seemed busy with piloting the craft south. At one point he'd smiled and waved back, but otherwise I felt invisible to him. Had I done something wrong? Garrett found the computer problem quickly and had corrected it. "I really think he should be promoted to deck swab first class Captain." Helga joked, laughing wildly over the radio. Then the radios suddenly went silent. I could only imagine what was happening between them. I glanced up at the Captain; it was the first time I'd seen him laughing today, and it helped me overcome my insecurity.

"Captain Olaf!" It was Helga. "We have an image now on our screens, and relevant information is coming down from the satellites. GARRETT, stop it! Let go of me you little turd! CAPTAIN, make Garrett stop!" She wailed frantically. Apparently Garrett had, once again, gotten the best of Helga, but all the Captain was doing was smiling. Five minutes later she radioed again. "Do you have an image yet Captain?" There was about two minutes of silence and then Olaf confirmed that his computer had image also. "Thank you all for a job well done today," Captain Olaf told everyone a few minutes later, "God is blessing us. By the way Gabriel, go down and make sure your laptop is networked properly. If you need help, son, please ask. Also, check and make sure that Helga and Garrett haven't killed each other." Captain chuckled and keyed off the radio. Smiling, I ran down to my berth and performed the necessary tests. Five minutes later I radioed that everything was in working order, and that Garrett and Helga were both still alive.

We were approximately forty kilometers off the English coast, now, and we would be maintaining this heading all the way down past Sunderland and Scarborough. After Scarborough, we'd be passing through the prime meridian and then by the East riding of Yorkshire and the Wash, after that past the cities of Great Yarmouth in Norfolk, and Lowestoft in Suffolk. "When we get beyond these areas, we'll be taking on a new tack son," Rorek continued, "eighty kilometers out into the North Sea, southwest smack down the middle of the Strait of Dover, and past the white cliffs. Then we'll head down through the English Channel towards France. Olaf mentioned taking us out through the Bay of Biscay, there's something he wants to find there." Rorek grunted and began shaking his head. When I looked at him questioningly he just shrugged his shoulders. "Son, there are some things he doesn't even talk to me about lately. We'll be hoisting sails soon; we can make much better time that way, you realize we have a lot of miles to cover to reach Flores don't you?" I nodded yes. "By the way Gabriel, from Olaf and me, you fellas did a fine job in Edinburgh. Keep up the good work; I'm very proud of you." After nodding his head politely he sauntered off. This had been a compliment that I wouldn't take lightly.

Thirty minutes later the Captain gave the order to hoist sails. Within thirty seconds everyone was up on deck and busily focused on their individual tasks. Olaf radioed and motioned for me to stand back and watch. "Make yourself available son." He instructed. "If someone needs you Gabriel, they'll ask. Also my young friend, *get ready to fly*!" Within minutes the electric motors had hoisted all the sails into place. Most of the procedure was mechanized now, so getting them into position took much less time than the older conventional ways. The crew moved about silently, with calculated steps, during the whole process. The efficiency utilized in accomplishing this reminded me of an exquisite ballet my parents had once taken me to. There was idiosyncratic beauty when people worked together this way. Rigidly focused determination and not one movement wasted or misplaced. It was as if they danced together like a well-oiled machine. These people were experienced professionals and I was most impressed. The schooner had begun leaning slightly to the left. Accompanied with a soft hissing sound the vessel began slicing through the water. With loud snapping sounds, all the sails had accepted the ample wind and filled tightly, suddenly the vessel began moving very swiftly.

"Captain, fifty yards off the port bow."

I made my way up to where John was tying preventers on the bowsprit and looked at him inquisitively; he pointed out to sea and began laughing. Our dolphins were back jumping and racing along with us. Soon everyone was laughing and praising God. The speed of the schooner had steadily increased. According to Captain Olaf, we had reached thirty-five knots. We really were flying. I began to understand why the men kept their hair short and also why the women tied theirs back when we were under sails. The smell of the salt air had quickly intensified; seemingly proportional to the speed we were moving at. It was truly exhilarating. The wake from the bow had increased dramatically, and the dolphins were maneuvering effortlessly in the peeling wave. The crew appeared to me like characters in a movie, or, perhaps from an old novel like Herman

Melville's 'Moby Dick', or Jules Verne's, 'Twenty thousand leagues under the sea'. I was captivated with the feelings flooding through me now and I felt I had no cares. We were flying entirely under sails and my temperament was fast becoming euphoric.

Nine

Hurricane Rachel / the Belanthian tragedy

Captain Olaf joined us for dinner at eight. Relieved, finally, after a wearisome day, he'd graciously, and thankfully, deferred the responsibility of piloting the vessel to his older brother Rorek through the long night time hours. Captain had plotted our course meticulously and explained that in order to accomplish our recently altered mission; we'd be traveling around the clock, using sails during the day and the diesel at night. Roxanne was in harm's way, and we were her only hope of rescue at this point. Once again she'd e-mailed the Captain about their seemingly hopeless circumstances and Olaf had responded to her; he'd also e-mailed Jonah with his ideas about Roxanne's deteriorating situation on Flores. He was still awaiting Jonah's reply. The Captain's spirit was grave. He'd deferred the evening prayer to Lizzy who, after sensing the Captains stricken demeanor, had offered to lead. Her prayer was compelling; a loving request for assistance that encompassed every facet of the crews, and our friends, dilemma. She was undeniably a woman who walked with, and trusted in, the Risen Christ. After she finished the crew ate dinner in silence.

Two hours before dinner I'd gone on-line to find out more information about Hurricane Rachel. I'd discovered that it had originated off South Western Iceland somewhere in the middle of the infamous drought zone, between 58 and 65 degrees North Latitude. Apparently Iceland had been hammered by powerful winds, and excessive amounts of rain had fallen in Reykjavik. Mercifully, the worst part of the storm had never made landfall there. The storm supposedly became massive after leaving the droughts peculiar northern coordinates and encountered the Arctic Sea on the North Eastern side of Iceland. The hot and frigid fronts colliding caused the hurricane to split into two different storms; the lesser storm heading south towards Ireland and the United Kingdom, and the greater storm heading north. This collision had caused both to spin in opposite directions. After going around the southern parts of Iceland, the mega-storm had taken a due east course towards Norway's Faroe Islands. Slowly changing to an east/north/east heading, it made its way towards the coasts of Nord-Trondelag, and Nordland, on Norway's western shores. After the southern edge of the storm raged across Denmark's Faroe Islands, it shifted north/north/east towards the Arctic Circle, and then across the prime meridian into the Norwegian Sea. After raging north, eighteen hundred kilometers, the storm veered northeast over the southern tips of the islands of Svalbard Norway and into the Barents Sea. The storm was generating eighty mile an hour winds and high seas on the western shores of Norway. Curiously, though, Nord-Trondelag and Nordland were spared any major damage. The last reports put the hurricane downgraded to a severe storm; this was the part that we'd just endured.

When we began our meal I couldn't get what I'd learned about Hurricane Rachel out of my mind. The strange split that caused one storm to develop into two different personalities bedeviled me. Was it possible that this was a kind of picture of something we were going to encounter in the coming weeks? I was very thankful this crew ate healthy. I knew my increased physical activity, and these outstanding daily meals, would be beneficial to my tenuous health. Throughout the meal my mind was immersed in speculation about the storm and also what'd happened since we'd left Aberdeen. There was assuredly some higher power at work in our lives and, without knowing how; I knew our steps were being guided daily. When Betsy and Garrett had put the galley back in order, Captain Olaf pushed back his chair. For a moment he stood quietly staring ahead and chewing his lip.

"I suppose the best way to do this is to just tell it straight." He admitted, shrugging his shoulders, "Gabriel, there's been a tragedy aboard the Belanthian."

Intuitively I focused my eyes on the Captain's emotive face and breathlessly waited for the distressing lexis to begin. Sweat started to bead up on my forehead and I began recalling those peculiar feeling's I'd gotten while we passed the tanker that first morning.

"There's been a terrible explosion aboard the tanker;" he continued. "Investigators think it was caused by hydraulic switching valves that malfunctioned. Apparently insulation on the high voltage control wires melted and created dead shorts all over the ship." For some reason, while the Captain was speaking I happened to glance over at Lizzy. She was hand in hand with Helga and Betsy, and they were all praying quietly. "There was a conflagration aboard her shortly after the explosion took place, the whole bow of the tanker, and halfway down her port side was ripped wide open. There were bodies all over the water and piers. The fire was so intense that decks one through eight, on the forward third of the tanker, have either melted or collapsed. The fire suppression systems malfunctioned shortly after the control meltdown. Before city or harbor fire crews could be dispatched a third of the ship had been destroyed. Choking black smoke spread miles throughout the city. The phone service was overwhelmed with hundreds of calls, from as far away as five miles. Many people were going into respiratory shock from the toxic clouds. The whole tanker has nosed down eighty feet towards the bottom of the bay. Most of the crude in the forward holds had already been pumped out so there was a minimal amount a spillage. According to the last reports they believe the whole tanker could have been emptied of crude the night before but the fuel tanks had been filled for the next voyage. The death count is high; as of now over sixty dock workers and seamen lost their lives trying to escape. There are twelve reported deaths inland, but that could go up." The Captain took a few breaths, looked out the porthole for a moment, and then continued. "Gabriel, your mother and father were out in the Hebrides vacationing when they were first alerted to the tragedy. The company sent out a helicopter to fetch them and bring them back. They're fine son, just fine." Sighing, the Captain closed his eyes, momentarily transfixed. I also sighed in relief and hastily wiped away the tears that had begun blurring my eyes. The news about mother and fathers safety had given me strength. I wondered if the e-mails I'd neglected to read were about the Belanthian. "Before dinner tonight I called the Harbor Master," the Captain continued, "he informed me that the conflagration was under control and ninety percent extinguished. The damage, however, was beyond belief. All the offloading piers were destroyed, and there was dead fish everywhere. News crews had been flown in from all over Europe. The initial reports are saying it was the worst harbor disaster in Aberdeen's history. The Harbor Master said the death count hadn't been tallied; unfortunately it appeared things were worse than they'd thought at first. The main concern is that there are still many more people under water, trapped inside the vessel. They have over a dozen divers working around the clock, but there's still no word yet. The hull is a twisted mess underwater, and the damage to your dad's tanker is in the millions. The harbor could be hindered for a year or more." The Captain suddenly walked over and sat down next to me. "Gabriel, didn't your father want you to travel to Southern California aboard the Belanthian?"

"Why yes he did! And I knew right from the start Captain that I wasn't supposed to travel aboard that tanker. Something just never felt right about it. Do you think that I could of . . . ?"

Betsy interrupted. "Yes Gabriel, you could have been aboard and been killed."

"That's right Gab, what a miracle you weren't," John added. "Captain wasn't the tanker scheduled to leave port the following morning for the Mediterranean?"

"I believe so John. I remember reading that she would be in port three or four days. They'd brought in extra crews to unload the crude as fast as possible because of the quick turnaround. Let's see, its March 4th, you're right John, they were leaving the next morning."

Lizzy began ranting emotionally. "That settles it, and what a terrible predicament for those poor people. How in the world can something like this happen? I can't believe it. Gabriel, honey, you would have been aboard the Belanthian and very possibly killed. Oh thank God you weren't. But all those poor people, I just can't believe this. It's horrible!" Betsy grabbed Lizzy's hand and Helga grabbed the other; large tears were flowing down all their cheeks. I was shocked at the reaction from them. I felt remarkably loved in that moment, more so than ever before in my life. Everybody started talking amongst themselves.

'I'd been spared miraculously;' I overheard John say to Olaf.

"God has a plan for you, dude, and it's with the *Heimdall.*" Garrett's voice cut through the din from across the room. "It's as plain as the nose on your face. That's so cool." Turning towards the Captain he added, "I see this as a sign, boss, for Gabriel and us."

The whole crew responded with a hearty amen and started rejoicing. Something profound was happening to me right at that moment. It was something that I'd never experienced before in my whole life. It was like oil was being poured down on the top of my head. Impulsively I reached up to see what had spilled on me, but there was nothing, my hair was completely dry. What a peculiar sensation. "We need to pray right now. Let's all join hands." Captain Olaf cried out. The crew was standing in a heartbeat and began thanking God for what was transpiring for us. After we'd finished, Betsy brought up coffee and a meal for Rorek to sustain him through the night. He was extremely grateful. Considering that he hadn't pulled a night shift for over two years he was a bit apprehensive about being able to stay awake. After retiring, I checked the e-mails I'd neglected. Father *had* written to inform me about the tragedy, and also to confirm that he and mother were safe. *'Please don't worry!'* Father assured me several times during his correspondence. *'The insurance companies will cover everything that the company has lost son. The worst heartbreak was loss of life. I lost some old and dear friends. It will be impossible to replace good people like that.'* He also informed me that he'd opened an on-line account and ten thousand dollars had been deposited on the second of March. *'Use the encrypted password I told you about Gabriel. If there's ever a need for more, contact me, and I'll get more money into the account. Your mother and I love you very much, and I don't want you or your new shipmates to stress about finances. I'm proud of you, son, Godspeed!'*

I decided at that moment to continue the journal I'd begun on March 2nd, and to do so faithfully every day. A record needed to be kept about everything that was happening to me, to the others, where the journey took us, and what we were all experiencing and learning together. After writing a quick reply to father and mother I collapsed in my bunk and quickly embraced a blessed sleep.

Ten

Sailing non-stop

March 5th

The Captain's plan was to sail non-stop until we'd successfully reached our destination. Despite this we were all in high spirits as we prepared to cross the Atlantic Ocean towards the greater and Lesser Antilles, into the Caribbean Sea, and through the Panama Canal, with Southern California as our eventual destination. I wondered about the fates of Roxanne's assistants, Resell and Lira. What would they do? They had no way to get to their homes in *Vila Real, Portugal.* The airlines had discontinued service into and out of the archipelagoes because of the problems. And if they'd be joining us aboard the *Heimdall,* how could we accommodate them? There was no room for three more people and all the artifacts. The radio suddenly squawked into life. "Gabriel this is Garrett, do you copy." As I reached for the radio I glanced out through the porthole. The weather was overcast and foggy. Why did this vessel suddenly feel so small and oppressive?

"Go ahead Garrett," I replied sullenly.

"Are you coming to breakfast? We're waitin' on you."

"Give me a minute, I'm on my way. What's on the menu?"

"Blueberry pancakes, country fried ham, orange juice, coffee, and hot cinnamon rolls with butter. Sorry dude, John and I ate all the rolls; you're just too late homeboy."

Garrett's smirky tone had alerted me instantly to the fact that he was goofing with me. "I'm on my way chump, and I'll be kickin' your sorry butt for eatin' my sweets!" Both were laughing hysterically as I keyed off the radio. Mysteriously I was in good spirits again. I needed to get out of myself today and enjoy my friends. Breakfast, as always, was a delight, and, of course, Garrett had been kidding, so I greedily ate my fill of hot cinnamon rolls, smothered in butter, and leaned back satisfied.

Part of the day would be devoted to learning about sails, sailing logic, and familiarizing myself with the tricky names of some of the parts on the schooner. I learned that the tallest mast was called the main mast. The mast before the main mast was a foremast. And the mast or masts after the main were called the mizzenmast. I learned that the square sail is the oldest type of rectangular sail. And this is held up by a horizontal spar called the yard. The yard is attached to the mast in a way that allows it to be turned both in the vertical and the horizontal plane. The *Heimdall* was a full square-rigged computerized ship. It had three masts and carried electrically operated square sails on all of them. When Captain Olaf had to return to the wheelhouse Betsy and Lizzy continued his lesson.

They schooled me in the art of sewing and mending sails, and more sailing terminology. "A square sail has four edges and four corners and the vertical edges at the sides of the sail are called leeches." Lizzy explained. "The upper edge, which is attached to the yard, is called the head, and the lower edge is called the foot. The two lower corners are called clews, and I'm sure right about now, young man, that you don't have a clue." Both laughed as I grimaced. My mind was spinning from all of these unfamiliar terms, but I didn't care, I'd enjoyed the hour with them exceedingly. I felt comfortable being around Betsy. She made me smile a lot with her soft humor and quiet intelligence. Later in the day, while pondering some unrequited memories, I finally said my farewells to sweet Ingrid, the love of my youth. While I was leaning on the forward railing, feeling sorry for myself and wiping away some tears, a dolphin jumped suddenly out of the water and looked at me directly in the eyes for a moment. I was shocked. The experience was like a thunderbolt that changed my heart completely. I knew now it was time to get closer to Betsy.

The weather was moody. We'd all awakened to the sloshing of water around the vessel and a persistent stem to stern rocking in seas that had begun developing sizeable waves. The wind was approximately seventy degrees off the starboard bow, and it was blowing westerly near twenty knots. Our speed had slowed from twelve to five knots, and the brothers needed to discuss options. We were in the English Channel now and the Captain ordered the crew to hoist sails. Shortly after that the diesel went silent. The last few days of travel had spoiled us. The seas had been smooth and we'd covered a great distance in a decent amount of time. After passing by the Isle of Thanet, in Kent England, we began navigating the Strait of Dover. A dense fog was keeping us from seeing any farther than one hundred yards. Because of this the legendary *White Cliffs* remained invisible. Olaf informed us that instead of getting out into the middle of the channel we were going to stay closer to the Southern shores of England to avoid the more impetuous seas in the middle of the channel. It made sense to me. Since the wind was blowing the swell towards France, we would sail in calmer seas closer to the English coastline. Eastbourne was coming up on our starboard, and we'd be sailing close enough to see the legendary Isle of Wight. Our course would then take us southwest across the channel and past the Northern shores of Guernsey UK in the Channel Islands. We'd be stopping near Roscoff France to fill our diesel tanks, replenish fresh water, and buy supplies. The original plan had us stopping in La Coruna Spain or Porto Portugal. But the decision to stop sooner was logical; we could always use fresh supplies. Our new heading would take us past the western shores of the ILe D' Quessant, offshore Brittany France, and south into the Bay of Biscay. There was a lot of mystery surrounding this legendary bay and Olaf hadn't spoken a word to anyone about what we'd be doing. We passed very near the Isle of Wight around six pm. And because the fog had lifted we were given a beautiful view of her rock-strewn shoreline. This was the very Isle that Jimi Hendrix had played his last concert on. Dinner was served at seven, just about the time Rorek had reassumed the vessels wheel and his nighttime duties. Everyone was famished and in really good spirits. After John had offered up evening prayer we all eagerly devoured Betsy's culinary inventions.

Later, after we'd finished, Olaf stood up and tapped the table. "Jonah's written us again. He's given us more information concerning our voyage, and a confirmation for me personally about a scuba diving job in the Bay of Biscay. I know that I've been quiet with everyone, but I assure you that Jonah asked me to keep this confidential until he could confirm the coordinates, and determine whether we would even be able to accomplish such a thing in our circumstances. Why don't you go ahead and read it now Helga." Helga stood up and began.

Greetings brothers and sisters of the starship Heimdall . . .

Hopefully all is well with you. Olaf informed me your voyage so far has not been entirely uneventful. Congratulations Garrett and Gabriel on a job well done in Edinburgh. And kudos for your successful integration of the new software and satellite dish. We're certainly going to need all the help we can get in the weeks and months ahead. There are reported altercations with the 'crazies' from all over the globe. The newspapers have given them an official name; they're referring to them now as the ***Mortiken****. The researchers, Roxanne works with, believe they might be a sect of ancient Vikings that gave themselves over to various ancient witchcrafts. There are positive sightings now in many countries, on some islands off the European coastlines, and also in the UK. There are confirmed infestations in the western areas of France, specifically in the provinces of Finistere and Morbihan, so stay prayerful and be on your guard. There are also confirmed sightings in Scotland, Finland, Ireland, Greenland, the Orkney Islands, Canada, and possibly Alaska. There are also (albeit at this point in time unconfirmed) reports of some infestations around Los Angeles and south of Santa Barbara in the Channel Islands. Things are changing quickly. Gabriel, keep up the good work, you are a blessing son, I'm very thankful you're with us. I've been in contact daily with my wife. Her last letter confirmed conditions calming down a bit* *from a few days prior. The tsunami that the BBC and weather updates on-line from Porto predicted missed the Archipelagos entirely. Praise God for this. Satellite photos put the tsunami on a heading towards Ireland. I understand that at one point, after dragging over some reefs north of the Archipelagoes, the wave reached a height of one hundred feet. I think you all understand that if this wall had hit Flores no one would have survived. Thank God for this. The high winds from Hurricane Rachel have successfully blown most of the volcanic ash west, away from the islands. The lava stream has slowed down and good weather is returning. I believe that God is opening up a window of opportunity for us to get something special accomplished.*

Now, to put light on the mystery that Olaf has been keeping from all of you. There is a dive we've decided to accomplish, and I've sent the precise coordinates to Olaf encrypted in a separate e-mail. There's a high precedence here folks. For hundreds of years there've been many shadowy tales about a sword forged from a metal unknown at that time in metallurgy. Apparently this one sword represented the whole of Christianity overcoming the pagan philosophies and bloodthirsty practices of that era right within the Viking nation itself. The symbol on the handle was a sword being plunged into the head of a dragon, and the inscription on it read: ***Christ before all Else****. Allegedly, the sword came with the Rognvald's on their voyage to Southwest America. Yesterday Roxanne confirmed that the runic writings on the cave walls have described two ships, out of the fifteen* *that began the journey from the Orkneys, sinking in a violent storm around an area the scribes described as the* ***'Shallows of Three Rocks'****. Roxanne and her assistants spent three days analyzing the pictographs and runes. They're confident it's accurate. There's a small township, Concello de Carino, on the Iberian Peninsula in Galicia Spain. We're thinking that if we form an equilateral triangle from specific coordinates in Carino and on the top of the Estaca de Bares, directly north, the top point of the triangle should take us exactly where we think our destination is. I've discovered what appears to be a small circular reef around that area. According to legend, the reef has three two hundred foot vertical rock formations in the center of it forming an obtuse triangle; they apparently stick straight up like towers. The water is only about fifty feet deep and, considering how deep it is in the Bay of Biscay, this will help us out tremendously in our dive. The rocks are in close proximity to one another, no more than two hundred feet apart. This must be the 'Shallows of Three Rocks'. Your mission, if you decide to accept, is to find that sword people. Hahahahaha! The writings have confirmed the name of it to be,* ***'Tempest'****. I'll have more information on this later. I love you all dearly. I pray God's richest blessings on all of you. Please be safe and trust your leader. I'll be in touch as soon as Captain confirms your approach to Carino. Love Jonah*

Eleven

A savage battle with the mortiken

March 6th 5:45 am

A heavy mist clung obstinately to our jackets, hair, and skin and was coalescing, occasionally, into salty little droplets that made their way down towards the tips of our noses. Huddled together outside the wheelhouse door, sipping hot coffee under one of the deck lights, we were all mulling Jonah's informative and disturbing e-mail. I cringed at the idea of ancient bitterness lurking in the shadows ready to entangle us in an insidious ancient blood feud. I recalled Jonah's choice of the word 'infestations' as his description for the Mortiken military incursions and their territorial occupations. I kept seeing an image of militant cockroaches under my bunk preparing to strike me in my sleep. The thought made me shudder and I was flooded with compassion for those beleaguered people forced to confront this reemerging evil. How many had already died in their malevolent agenda I wondered. What had I gotten myself into?

Eager for handouts, a flock of noisy seagulls were circling near the stern of the vessel. Exasperated, Captain Olaf left our huddle with an indignant grunt, found a broom, and began swinging it in an attempt to shoo away the birds. After ten minutes Captain Olaf finally gave up. Betsy told us breakfast today was going to be simple; hot cereal, fresh fruit and orange juice and we could serve ourselves whenever we found the opportunity. "Our fruit, vegetables and meat are almost gone," she continued. "And since we won't be docking again until Porto, I want to purchase as many supplies as we can on the barges. We're low on all stocks and I don't think we can wait until we get to La Coruna. Since we don't know how long we'll be working on this new job I'm considering it prudent to be well stocked and ready for anything." Everyone agreed. We were preparing, now, to dock for the first time since departure. Given this we all took it upon ourselves to inventory the stores, and then lists were compiled and given to Betsy.

There was a moderate breeze blowing. The morning skies were rapidly clearing as the sun prepared to break from the east and embrace the rugged geography. The weather yesterday had changed to our advantage after we'd passed the Isle of Wight. The calmer seas, and bountiful winds, had filled the sails for most of the afternoon and this had helped increase our speed to fifteen knots. We'd covered a good distance during the night, and had already passed Guernsey UK in the Channel Islands and the Golfe de St.-Malo. We were nearing Roscoff in Finistere France where we'd be docking on the offshore barges. Captain was allotting four hours to refuel, replenish our fresh water, and accumulate whatever supplies Betsy deemed necessary from our combined lists. I informed Captain Olaf that the on-line account had ten thousand dollars available to us. “Thank you Gabriel,” Captain said, smiling and nodding, “God is good, and He *is* supplying our needs. I’m very thankful that your father has chosen to support our endeavors. I’m very much impressed with his generosity.” I thanked the Captain for his gracious comments.

Around three the Captain ordered sails down. All jumped to the task. Thirty minutes later the diesel was reverberating through the wooden decks. As we neared the small islands southwest of Roscoff France the seagulls at last flew off. Olaf cheered resoundingly. A magnificent silence remained in their absence. The dolphins were still with us. All were clacking, playing, and jumping near the bow. Betsy brought up some of the older bait and threw in overboard. Greedily they devoured the tasty morsels with great clownishness and enjoyment. Rorek had awakened from his sleep and was up in the wheelhouse poring over navigational charts with his brother. Helga had been up in the crow’s nest for close to five hours. She’d been observing the shorelines, and the other vessels, through powerful binoculars. Suddenly a distraught voice crackled over the radios. “Captain Olaf, port towards the shore, what is that?” Olaf motioned for Rorek to take the wheel and he picked up the telescope on top of the charts. “There seems to be fires and some explosions over there,” he replied back. “I can’t tell if it’s Roscoff, Helga, we’re too far away.”

“Copy that. I wonder what’s happening there, something feels dreadfully wrong!”

“Can’t say lass, we’ll keep an eye on it. Would you mind staying up there a while longer and keep us informed?”

“No problem sir, I’ll watch for any changes, Helga out.”

In the distance dark clouds were billowing up over the city. Occasionally they were being accented by bright mushrooming flashes of orange and red. It appeared dozens of structures were burning. Thankfully the wind was blowing the bulk of the smoke back towards the Golfe de St.-Malo and not towards our present position.

"Barges dead ahead Olaf," Rorek yelled from the bow. Carefully Olaf guided *us* towards the small wooden dock through the circular eddies and erratic currents formed by hidden rocks in the shallower water. John and Garrett were fore and aft yelling to each other while they unrolled the lines that would secure the vessel to the barges small pilings. Lizzy was on the bowsprit tying something around one of the jibs and waving at a woman standing outside the market. Betsy was bringing up plastic containers and stacking them next to the railings. Suddenly Helga cried out from the crow's nest." Captain, there's a small smack off our stern out about a mile or so. It's kept the same distance from us for most of the day, never closer, never farther, I can't say for sure, but I think it's been following us." The Captain, being completely preoccupied with docking the vessel, motioned for me to answer Helga. I noticed a look of dismay on his face, and then, I began to feel a certain amount of uneasiness stirring in my own spirit.

"Captain can't answer right now. Could you please wait until we're docked?" I asked hurriedly.

"No problem," Helga answered, "I'm coming down anyway."

I'd seen this expression before on the Captain's face and, more often than not, it was the foreshadowing of something unpleasant. The Captain was speaking impatiently with the barge foreman and pointing towards the fuel inserts. Three dock workers had begun unrolling fuel hoses along the length of the pier; all were jabbering disconcertedly and pointing out at the approaching smack. Why was there such uneasiness in everyone about this? Perhaps it was just coming in for bait, or food, or perhaps they wanted to sell some fish they'd caught. I remembered that a smack was a small fishing boat rigged with a sail, (like a sloop for daily excursions) and equipped with a well used for keeping the fish alive and fresh. I noticed that the dolphins were no longer with us; they'd vanished when the Captain began maneuvering towards the barges. Why? The smoke in the distance was obscuring a clear view of the coastline now. But I could still see some inconsistent movement over to the far right. Squinting, with both hands over my eyes, I saw now that a raging fire had spilled out through a tiny estuary on the far left of the city; perhaps from a ruptured fuel tank spilling out into the ocean; it reminding me of the mythical Phelgethon. Could this be a foreshadowing of some type of evil making its way towards us? I trembled as stark images from Jonah's recent e-mail began gnawing at me. Helga was down from the crow's nest now and she was clearly annoyed with my attempts at trying to explain what I'd seen on the far right of the city. In frustration she took the binoculars to see for herself. With a gasp she spun around and proclaimed: "There are six more of those smacks heading towards us."

Garrett and John had lowered the gangplank. Rorek was supervising the refueling but had become disgruntled trying to make sense of the frustrating dialect they were jabbering. Betsy and Lizzy were up in the market. The Captain, Helga and I were huddled together to keep an eye on the smacks. We saw twenty-eight ominous figures in all six. They were dressed in long cloaks with hoods that obscured their faces. The Captain ordered Garrett and John to go below for the shotguns and baseball bats. Then he called Betsy on the radio and told her to see if they had any twelve gauge shotgun shells and, if they did, to buy as many as they had. It was obvious now that the owners of the barges were preparing for an altercation. Their dialect was a strange mixture of French and English, so it was difficult for me to interpret anything except a few phrases. What I interpreted was that Roscoff had been attacked by a vicious band of mortiken from up north. There were many dead on both sides and parts of the city were burning from the booby traps they'd set. Two hundred Marines were being transported on helicopters from Morlaix, but they were still several hours away. The barge workers were barring the doors and windows around the outer perimeter of the buildings; most of them had belted pistols and knives.

"Captain Olaf . . ."

"Betsy what is it," Olaf answered.

"They had two hundred shotgun shells, so I bought them all."

"Excellent, good job, John's on his way to help; are you guys almost done?"

"I heard that Captain," John interrupted, "and I'm on my way."

"Maybe ten more minutes Captain." Betsy answered.

"Copy that, but please hurry, we have to get out of here!"

"Alright Captain, we understand." John ran like a sprinter across the gangplank and up towards the market. Moments later he'd brought back four large boxes of shells.

"Garrett, go below and get those bandoliers in the forward storage bin next to my room," Capt Olaf barked, "hurry son!"

"On my way boss," Garrett responded, scrambling off.

Helga and I had been watching the six smacks through the binoculars; they were now about half a mile away. It reminded me of the boatman in *Clash of the Titans* taking passengers over to the Isle of the dead to encounter the Medusa. The smacks were partially obscured now by a mist forming two feet above the surface. Several were cursing and denigrating us, and then, something unnerving happened. All of them, except the rowers, stood up. And then, in an unsettling unison, all swayed hypnotically together while the oars continued swishing in the water. The scene was eerie. Slowly they moved closer.

The refueling was completed. The ladies and men were back aboard. All the supplies had been stowed and all of us were armed. Captain Olaf had holstered a 357 magnum and he was clutching an oak bat. Rorek had a long knife clenched in his teeth and, a small snub-nosed pistol in a hip holster. John had two twelve inch titanium knives and a sawed off shotgun. His countenance had changed dramatically; it was as if an old part of him had come back to life. He had donned a sleeveless tan military shirt, baggy long jeans, and boots popularized in the Desert Storm conflict many years back. His face and arms were covered with black tribal markings which gave him a frightening aggressive appearance. I remembered him telling me, when he'd introduced himself the first night, that he was an ex-navy seal. This fact brought me some reassurance.

Nervous tension was thick in the evening air. And it seemed that our wristwatches now ticked with an exaggerated persistence which only accentuated the vocalizations of the mortiken approaching us. Suddenly the chanting ended. Clutching my oak bat tightly I braced myself. At Captain Olaf's behest we joined hands and prayed for wisdom, strength, safety, a warrior's spirit, and, also, for God's will to be done. A wonderful sense of peace and focus filled us when we'd finished. The mist had risen now about three feet from the surface. After we'd cast off our fore and aft lines the gangplank was cranked in. The setting sun had begun casting shadows on the wooden deck. After glancing up and down the length of the schooner Olaf put down the bat and started the diesel. As he was maneuvering away one of the market employees began waving franticly and pointing towards the stern. At once he disengaged the transmission and slammed the diesel into idle. Hunched over like a large cat he deftly jumped from the wheelhouse door and onto the deck. With clenched teeth he pulled out his 357.

EVERYONE, PREPARE YOURSELVES!" Rorek ordered tensely. Helga was secured firmly on the small halfway platform up the center mast. Methodically she was loading and sighting in the high powered rifle. Lizzy and Betsy were perched on top of the wheelhouse; both were crouched down behind the parapet walls. Both had shotguns with fully loaded bandoliers and were glancing nervously up and down the length of the deck. Garrett, John and I were spread out along the starboard railing with our backs to the cabins. Garrett was near the bow, I was in the middle, and John was near the stern. Garrett was quietly verbalizing his drum sounds and swinging his bat in large overhead circles to stretch out his muscles.

The mortiken appeared suddenly on the stern deck. My stomach was gripped by a sudden jolt that made me nauseous and light-headed; thankfully it passed as suddenly as it had taken me and left me feeling stronger than I'd ever felt in my life. Silently I thanked God. For several moments the savages stared at us like zombies and postured evilly. It was like an evil pack of wolves eyeing their prey. Their intentions were evident; they were here to kill us. A strange growling rumbled from their throats as one lifted a club over his head. John raised one of his knives and answered the challenge with a warriors scream.

"You are so freakin' ugly!" Garrett snarled. One of them roared at Garrett and then all began stomping the deck. "You dirt-bags picked the wrong vessel to board," Garrett yelled back. "We're gonna kick all yur ugly asses!"

Two rushed forwards. With two shotgun blasts John sent one forcibly back over the stern railing. The other maneuvered behind him angrily and attempted to grab his throat. John snatched him up and then viciously body slammed him on the deck; one of his knives slashed across the throat precisely. He was dead in seconds. I was shocked at how rapidly he had reacted. Cautiously I maneuvered towards Garrett on the bow. To my left Rorek had been confronted by two that had appeared suddenly from behind the wheelhouse on the port side. One hit him with a heavy club on the chest. Rorek collapsed to one knee gasping. A rifle shot rang out and his assailant collapsed instantly. To his right another was preparing to bring a smaller club down on his head. Olaf screamed and Rorek spun around to the left and bounced back like a wild animal. In one perfectly executed move his knife slashed across the throat. It was gruesome. Blood gushed out everywhere as he fell dead. Garrett shouted that three more were coming up by the forward anchor chain. Instantly I spun around and noticed that Betsy and Lizzy were now on the opposite side of the wheelhouse roof. They were responding to the cries for help on the barges. Instantly they both opened fire. Like a frenzied cat Garrett had scurried up the rope ladder on the foremast until he was about ten feet above the deck. Hovering momentarily he suddenly jumped and brought his bat crashing down on a deformed gray head. The man crumpled. A second rifle shot rang out as I was offering Garrett a hand up. Another of them fell back over the railing into the water. Helga's eye was deadly accurate and we both cheered. The third vanished suddenly around the front of the forward cabins. He wanted no part of Helga. We both heard Captain scream for help. Both of us spun on heel and ran towards the wheelhouse where he was involved in a grim battle. An enormous brute was attacking him and screaming violently. Captain's face was grim and set as Garrett and I maneuvered towards him. Another cry for help had Garrett suddenly swerve away. "Dude, I gotta help John, be strong big brother!" The Captain had fallen to one knee and was bleeding. Stealthily I made my way up behind the brute. Captain was praying, "God please give me strength." The brute turned towards me with a savage expression. "Your false God will never help you *or* this puny man!" He was speaking in an old Orknean Scottish dialect I clearly understood. Something came into me. Overwhelmed with rage I swung my bat as hard as I could. The man fell to one knee screaming in pain. His arm was limp and completely useless. Quietly I thanked God and then glanced over at the Captain to make sure he was alright. Beaming proudly he told me he was. "Help the others, son!" he pointed towards Garrett and John. "They're in trouble."

Garrett and John were both deeply involved in a brutal skirmish against twice their numbers. Like two muscled gladiators both were moving together with shocking ferocity against their attackers. One suddenly appeared ghostlike from the shadows and slammed John in the back with a club. John stumbled forward and cried out. Roaring in anger Garrett dropped his bat and launched himself forcibly at him. "You coward piece of shit, I'm gonna kill you for that!" he screamed savagely. Fiercely two granite fists pounded his jaw and forehead repeatedly. I was shocked. My little brother was like a wild gorilla. Slowly the brute stumbled back until at last, with a loud scream, Garrett delivered a final blow that toppled him back over the railings and into the dark water below.

"GABRIEL," the Captain shouted.

I saw at once that the mortiken I'd hit with the bat was attempting to maneuver towards him. As he did the hood of his djellabah slipped off his head. Brightly illuminated in the deck light, his hideously deformed gray face shocked me. Failing in his attempt to stand, he fell to both knees and looked up at me straight in the eyes and began growling like an animal. I felt spellbound, and couldn't move my legs, as the huge deformed body inched towards me. Captain fired once and the man fell forward onto his face. Before I could gather my wits, Betsy, Lizzy and Helga began screaming; they were pointing towards the stern. "There's seven more coming over!"

Racing by me Garrett turned and shouted: "you havin' fun yet dude?" I hardly recognized him. He was bleeding badly across the forehead and out of one of his nostrils. A sudden high powered blast from Helga's rifle changed my focus. Another of them slammed back against the rear rails behind me and crumpled in a heap. And then, after several more shotgun blasts, two more were lying on the rear deck in pools of blood. For a moment I felt sickened and confused. John and Garrett had formed a defensive stance back to back. Because of this they were given enough time to gather their wits before re-engaging the new onslaught. Savagely John clothes-lined the first of them; I was shocked at his power. The blow was so forceful that the boots were left behind as the man hurtled back over the railings into the water. Laughing Garrett pulled another attacker from John's back and began beating him mercilessly with his fists. Rorek leaned over the railing and put one precise shot into his head as Garrett pummeled down his antagonist quickly. With a wild yell Garrett kicked him in the face and then picked him up and heaved him into the ocean. A deadly shot from Helga's rifle ended any possibility of him ever coming back aboard. John was grabbed roughly from behind by the last two. They hated John and Garrett. I could see in John's face that he'd been hurt. Three shotgun blasts from the wheelhouse put one attacker down instantly. Sadly some of the buckshot hit John. Crying out he dropped his knife and clutched his left triceps; blood was flowing out through his fingers. Rorek shouted to duck. As John did Rorek's blade swiftly slashed across another attackers shoulder and chest. For a moment the air was full of blood. Screaming the mortiken jumped into the dark waters to escape the second swipe. With a vengeance Garrett picked up John's shotgun and pumped three shots at the mortiken now flailing in the water. When he'd finished he raised his fist in victory. John had fallen to one knee. He was grimacing in pain as he feverishly tried to tie something around his upper arm to stop the blood flow. Captain Olaf shouted a warning. Another group was approaching Garrett out of his line of sight. Garrett understood. Thrusting up forcefully, he brought the butt of his shotgun to bear on the man's jaw. He crumpled on both knees. Olaf's 357 roared twice. Garrett and Olaf both nodded at each other in thanks.

There was yelling from the pier. The workers were pointing towards the schooner. Multiple shotgun blasts roared repeatedly from the roof of the wheelhouse towards the barges. In my field of vision I saw that John was safe and that Captain Olaf was lying in a heap next to the wheelhouse stairs. He was face down, breathing hard, and blood was pooling on the surface. My hackles were up as I crouched down to tend to him. Suddenly I noticed a shadow moving towards me from the rear part of the wheelhouse. Standing with a fierce yell I swung my bat blindly. I heard a crunch of bones as it connected. The man screamed and fell on his rear. The impact knocked me off balance, as well, and I stumbled back against the rubber raft. Captain's weapon roared twice. The attacker crumpled. Before I had time to think I heard Garrett and John screaming for assistance. It was Helga now who was in danger. After regaining my stance I glanced up at the center mast and saw that a dark shape was indeed climbing towards her. My heart crawled up into my throat and caused me to feel like vomiting. I could see Rorek was completely spent.

He was on all fours groaning. As I approached he barked 'no' and pointed at the center mast where the last mortiken was climbing up towards Helga. She was clawing franticly at her tether as the monster approached. In a sudden gust of wind the hood fell back off his head. He was absolutely hideous. Who were these creatures? Garrett was standing at the bottom of the mast and Captain Olaf had taken careful aim. Both were waiting for an opportunity to intervene. Forcefully the man grabbed Helga's ankle. In desperation she cried out. Incensed John scrambled up and grabbed his cloak. Valiantly he thrashed to escape John's grip but he wasn't strong enough. John pulled him down next to him and, in one deadly motion, slashed across his throat. "You filthy scum," he roared as he threw him out into the night air. As soon as the man hit the water the ships running lights flickered on. I could see that what remained of our confrontation around us was gruesome. Nine bloodied corpses lay scattered by the stern, the wheelhouse, the center mast, and at least eight others were in the sea. Within moments John was back on deck, leaning against the mast, clutching his bloody triceps. Helga was crying on his shoulder. Rorek had been rendered unconscious and was bleeding from his mouth. I watched the Captain stumble back up the stairs into the wheelhouse. Wiping at the gash across his cheek; he engaged the transmission and the schooner began to move. Garrett limped over and sat down next to me. From the waist up he was covered in blood. I was shocked at his appearance and began to cry in fear and exhaustion. Breathing hard, he sighed almost inaudibly, "Man, I've never been in a fight like that before. I can't believe we survived."

"Get rid of the trash, and hose off the deck as soon as possible!" The Captain ordered hoarsely. "We're leaving!"

"Aye Aye sir." we replied with wearied sighs.

I began shaking, as the adrenaline started dissipating, and began feeling light-headed. A moment later I vomited violently over the side. I could hear weeping. A moment later I saw Lizzy on deck with a triage kit. At once she brought Garrett under a bright deck light and washed him thoroughly. He was in bad shape. The cuts on his forehead were all the way to the skull and he was slipping in and out of consciousness. After injecting Novocain on his forehead, in several places, she started stitching the wounds closed. Betsy tended to the others. John was next for stitching and Lizzy began as soon as she'd finished with Garrett. Helga stayed next to him as Lizzy worked. Rorek was unconscious, still, and Olaf was piloting the schooner. As soon as Lizzy gave us permission we began pushing the corpses overboard and hosing off the deck. As we worked I noticed something stuck under the rubber raft next to the wheelhouse. As soon as I'd picked it up I knew what it was. It had been around the neck of the one the Captain had killed.

"Take a look at this!" I held it out to Lizzy. Turning away from John for a moment, her eyes opened wide. It was a square blue and yellow medallion with black points on all four corners. It was about three inches long on every side, and on it was carved an image of a deformed man in a Viking helmet. What could this possibly mean?

Twelve

Mayday from the Barque Belem

March 7th

The *Heimdall* was gliding silently through tufts of steam fog formed from the water being warmer than the air. It was a mesmerizing sight. The spirit aboard was somber. Lizzy had just finished sterilizing, stitching, and bandaged everyone's wounds. And even though she was exhausted; she was in the wheelhouse caring for, and ministering to, Captain Olaf and Rorek. She'd served them a special tea blend to help sooth them through the emotionally difficult aftermath of the battle. Betsy was crying softly. Still deeply distressed she was lying in the fetal position near the capstan. Garrett was sound asleep under a blanket in the exact place Lizzy had stitched his wounds. He'd lost a lot of blood, and would (more than likely) sleep twenty-four hours because of the physical trauma. He'd proven to be a magnificently skilled young warrior, far surpassing his young age. His four years of boxing lessons, and weight training, had proven invaluable in our violent struggle. Garrett and John's physical prowess, as well as John's six years as a navy seal, Rorek's deadly expertise with the long knife, Captain Olaf's ability with the 357, and the ladies skills with weaponry, had taken the enemy off guard and had defeated them soundly. I'd ascertained that more than thirty mortiken had attacked the docks and twenty of them had been killed aboard the schooner. And though God's hand had clearly been upon us, we'd paid a price.

Garrett: thirty-eight stitches on the forehead and several more on the right ear lobe. Captain Olaf: sixteen on the right cheek. John: twenty-two stitches on the left triceps, and a puncture wound on the left pectorals minor. Rorek: severely bruised on the chest and left arm, and, at this point, in terrible pain and finding it difficult drawing breathe.

All the women had made it through unscathed. I knew that if it hadn't been for them, our numbers might have been diminished this morning. Most of the crew had found secluded spots to meditate and rest. I'd fallen into a deep sleep finally around two-thirty, and considering that I'd slept on a hard deck, covered only with a life boat blanket, I was remarkably refreshed and alert upon awakening at six-thirty. After scrutinizing the main deck it appeared that I was the first one up. Captain Olaf was still in the wheelhouse piloting the schooner; he appeared haggard. "Gabriel, would you please get me some coffee?" He asked when he saw I was awake. "Sure Captain," I shook my head in agreement. After stretching out the pain in my hip I slowly made my way down to the galley. After filling two stainless steel thermoses I hobbled back to the wheelhouse. The Captain asked me to take the wheel for a moment as he opened the first thermos and gulped down two cups. "Helga's sleeping on top," he said pointing. "Awaken her please. Tell her there's information from Jonah and the commander from Morlaix on the computer."

"Aye Captain," I answered giving the wheel back. As I turned a distress call blared over the radio.

"Mayday, mayday, this is the Belem, over . . . mayday, mayday, this is the Barque Belem, over . . ."

"Take the wheel Gabriel!" the Captain ordered.

"Sure Captain," I responded. Pulling my body back up the three steps into the wheelhouse, I clutched the huge wheel, and leaned my body weight back against his stool.

"Keep us on this heading son!" Captain Olaf said, pointing at the brass compass.

"Go ahead Belem," the Captain responded.

"Mayday . . . Mayday . . . this is the Barque Belem, over . . ."

"This is Captain Olaf aboard the *Heimdall,* go ahead Belem."

"Captain Olaf, so good to hear your voice sir . . . this is Captain Jacque Frerris'. We've got an emergency. Do you have a ship's surgeon aboard sir?"

"Yes sir we do, a very good one."

"We have two crewmen with compound fractures, Captain Olaf. Our surgeon was unable to make the voyage and now, sir, we have an emergency that no one onboard is qualified to handle."

"Where are you located sir?" Captain Olaf responded, hurriedly pulling out a chart.

"Sixty kilometers North West of Pointe du Raz. We were enroute to the city of Quiberon, off the coast of Morbihan when we were hit by a rogue wave. It was enormous. We are presently at a standstill; do you have an operational GPS?"

"Certainly we do . . . yes sir. Can you send me the Belem's coordinates?" Captain Olaf asked. The conversation between the two went on for fifteen minutes. The Captain of the Belem went on to say that the military raid on Roscoff had proven successful. Over two hundred Mortiken had been defeated. 'The barges were unharmed,' I heard him add, 'and business will resume by the end of the week.'

Captain Olaf related our previous evening's encounter and the Captain saluted our ship and crew for a job well done. He also informed Captain Olaf that our exploits were already being touted on French radio. They were calling us warriors of a righteous cause against this new global threat. The Captain motioned for me to get on the radio and wake up the crew and alert them that we had another emergency. With one hand holding the enormous wheel, and one hand keying the transmit button, I alerted the whole crew that they needed to rendezvous ASAP at the wheel house. Everyone, except Garrett, sleepily responded. After consulting the charts, and ascertaining the coordinates Captain Frerris' had sent us, Olaf determined we were only forty-three kilometers from the Belem. There was still no wind; certainly not enough to hoist our sails. When the crew reached the wheelhouse we all put our arms around each other and sighed; what in the world were we going to do now? Olaf related the facts about Captain Frerris' dilemma. Because of the lack of wind it would be impossible for us to reach the Belem in a favorable amount of time. As a result we'd be using the raft. "Lizzy, get what you need for two surgeries." The Captain instructed her and then he turned towards me. "Son, you're going to captain the raft; you're the only one who can accomplish this presently. Betsy, they'll need food, and also stow two gallons of fresh water. John, please get two of the long range radios fully charged and a shotgun with a loaded bandolier. At full throttle you should arrive at the Belem in about an hour and fifteen minutes Gabriel; we'll be about three hours behind you. We have no choice, it has to be accomplished. Please remember that these men are in terrible pain, and God has put them in our path. I promise all of you; as soon as this is completed we'll all get some rest. Now . . . let's pray!"

Lizzy and I boarded the raft. "Hey doc!" When I looked up I saw Garrett looking down from the bottom rail. His head was bandaged and he was very pale. Smiling weakly he waved. Waving back, I stood up and saluted him. Betsy arrived and knelt down next to him and began changing the dressing on his forehead. Helga arrived next with food and water. When Betsy finished she kissed his cheek. A toothy grin spread out over Garrett's battered face. Smirking, he gave me a big thumb up. I knew then that Garrett was going to be alright, and I sighed gratefully. "See you soon little brother," I waved.

Captain Olaf handed me a quickly sketched chart. We had provisions for one day: two gallons of fresh water, two long range radios, a shotgun with twenty-five shells, the surgical instruments and drugs necessary, and raingear, just in case. My stomach began churning as we moved away from the schooner. Suddenly, in my peripheral, I saw dark shapes moving near the side of the raft. All on deck began laughing and pointing. Over on the starboard two dolphins had surfaced and were on their sides waving at us with their flippers. I was overwhelmed with a surge of joy, because I realized that God had sent our friends to help guide me towards the Belem. With renewed spirits we roared off in the direction of the other vessel. The dolphins were very fast. Not only did they keep up with us, they swam in front of us, jumping and playfully rolling off to our right and left. Zigzagging back and forth under the raft, they began jumping up on our starboard and port sides, and splashing us as we raced along. I felt exhilarated with the brisk wind in my face.

At one point, it seemed as if we were off our compass heading and I shouted my concerns to Lizzy. She turned from where she was clinging tightly to the bow rope and yelled back reassuringly, "Trust the dolphins!" The outline of the Belem appeared on the horizon an hour and ten minutes later. I was overjoyed. A moment after we'd seen the Barque there was a sharp retort of small cannon fire; I knew they were acknowledging our approach. Most of the crew was congregated on the decks as we pulled alongside. It was obvious they were relieved to see us. Once aboard two men quickly whisked Lizzy below decks and Captain Frerris' motioned for me to join him in the wheelhouse. Following a terse greeting and handshake, I was politely reminded to radio Captain Olaf of my arrival. Captain was overjoyed to hear we'd arrived safely and was intrigued with my recount of how the dolphins had helped us navigate accurately. "We'll rendezvous with you in three hours Gabriel." The Captain informed me. "The crew sends their love. Also Garrett sends two thumbs up, and said he thinks you're *'the bomb'*. Son, tell me what that means later will you . . . Captain Olaf out."

It was time for the midday meal and I was invited to join the Captain in his personal stateroom adjacent the wheelhouse. Eagerly I accepted and sat down to a sumptuously prepared meal. During the conversation the Captain told me he was familiar with my father's company. Four years prior they'd met on the 'Isle of Harris' in the Hebrides where they'd both been vacationing. It was sometime later when Lizzy at last joined us from below. She informed the Captain that both men were out of harm's way and resting peacefully. The breaks had been very serious and both would be out of commission for a minimum of six months. As she was explaining the convalescing procedure we were startled by another canon retort and a crewman bellowed loudly. "The schooner *Heimdall* is approaching on the port stern, Captain." The Captain stood, snapped his heels, nodded respectfully at Lizzy, shook my hand vigorously, and then excused himself and exited the wheelhouse. Fatigue came upon us like a sudden rain. The last twenty-four hours had taken their toll. Lizzy hugged me warmly and we both walked out near the stern rails to watch.

Thirteen

Through the Bay of Biscay

Dinnertime was nearing and the sumptuous aromas of Betsy's cooking wafted tantalizingly throughout the vessel. Towards the west the sun appeared extraordinary in size as it slowly dipped down into the horizon; to me it was like an undulating fiery orange dimensional portal beckoning the courageous to step through. At this moment, however, that wasn't me. Several hours had passed since we'd bid adieu to the Belem. Just before we disembarked Captain Frerris' mentioned to our Captain that there was a stretch of shallow sandy reef parallel to Pointe du Raz where we could anchor safely and rest. Navtex reports were projecting excellent weather along the western coastline of France for the next several days. In this we rejoiced.

Once we were over the reef Captain anchored us, bow and stern, on a sandy mound in four fathoms. According to the charts we were now officially in the Bay of Biscay. The crew congregated at precisely 7:30 for dinner. Helga informed us that another e-mail from Jonah had arrived that she'd be sharing with us after the meal. Considering what we'd all been through in the last twenty four hours, the crew still had a positive outlook. We were all grateful to be alive, and together embraced this special celebratory time with eagerness. The meal tonight was platefuls of spicy beef tacos and Betsy's epicurean Mediterranean salads. While I was delighting in the meal, and the crew's lively camaraderie, a line out from a Bret Harte short story came to me that I'd read a few days earlier: 'A Night at Wingdam.' Altered slightly to oblige our present numbers, the line seemed appropriate to what I felt at the moment. *'Eight souls with but one single thought, eight hearts that beat as one.'* Captain told us, as we ate, that we'd be anchored at our present location three nights and two days and then sailing through the Bay of Biscay non-stop towards the small township of 'Concello de Carino' on the Northwest Iberian Peninsula in Galicia Spain. After we'd finished eating Captain Olaf stood up, as was his custom of late, and tapped his glass.

"We've all been through, well, speaking for me, and hopefully everyone else, a most challenging and life changing incident in the last twenty four hours. I want to extend my appreciation to all of you for the incredible teamwork that was exhibited against this despicable enemy. God's faithfulness and grace, and our warrior skills, saw all of us through this dreadful ordeal. Hopefully we won't be tested this way again. But if we are we all know now that we're capable, with God's help, of rising to the challenge and overcoming an evil that's spreading now all over our planet. Garrett, John, Rorek, Gabriel, you were all incredible, and I want to thank you all for your perseverance and skills. Ladies, all the men agree that if it wasn't for your marksmanship, we'd probably all be dead. Thank you one and all." Because of the stitches in his cheek the Captain found it difficult to smile. So after acknowledging the crew's appreciation he sat down amidst the applause and motioned at Helga to go ahead with Jonah's e-mail. "Thanks Captain," Helga said. "I'll read this quickly guys so we can all get some bunk time."

Brothers and Sisters . . .

Captain Olaf informed me, in great detail, of your exploits off Roscoff last night. I commend all of you for an incredible victory, and your hard fought battle. I raise my hands in thanks to God for preserving you and our vessel. As I'm writing this letter the news services are flooding with reports about an unknown schooner of valiant men and women that successfully thwarted the Mortiken on the refueling barges near Roscoff France. They don't have any names yet, and I believe that this will work to our advantage for safety's sake. We don't want to become a high profile target for the Mortiken. Tell Garrett I've informed his father about his inspiring performance against the Mortiken. He cried while I shared with him the warrior his son has become. He asked me Garrett that you please e-mail him; he'd love to hear from you. At least send him your address so he can write you. He respects and loves you a lot son. Gentlemen, ladies, praise God for you and our shared vision. May God continue to guide and bless our journey for His glory! You're all incredible.

Now, for some good news . . . Roxanne and I are planning to rendezvous with all of you in Concello de

Corina for our endeavor on the 'Shallows of three Rocks.' Resell and Lira will remain on the island to continue cataloging artifacts and packing them for transportation to the West coast aboard Heimdall. The weather on Flores has calmed and all of us see this as a good opportunity. We feel that this dive is important enough for us all to be together. We'll be bringing some very special equipment from the university we've been allowed to use for triangulation purposes. You'll be amazed at this tech; we'll be able to test the efficiency of our new software also. Did you know that no one has ever found the Shallows of Three Rocks; this is very puzzling to me. Our grant will cover all expenses getting there and back. Roxanne will fly into La Coruna 7am on March 13th and wait for me in the Plaza de Maria Pita by the statue. I'll be flying into La Coruna four hours later on the 13th, and then at four pm we'll both be catching a small research vessel going up north into the Bay of Biscay towards Gijon. They've agreed to drop us off at Concello de Carino on the morning of the 14th. We'll rendezvous with you then. I love you all dearly, and we both look forward to working with you until March 21st. Roxanne will then return to Flores to prepare for the Heimdall's arrival, Lord willing around April 1st. I'll be returning to Pine Valley on the 23rd, and taking a small church group up to Ghost Mountain in the Anza Borrego, with the intention of writing a book. See you all soon. I praise God for all of you, and love you all so much.

In Christ's love, Jonah

March 8th

I finally stumbled up on deck around nine am. I couldn't stop yawning and my eyes were having trouble opening. It seemed unseasonably warm to me and there was a funny smell on the wind. Looming in the distance was a mountainous coastline that looked like the backbone of a fallen dinosaur. Around the vessel seagulls were squawking noisily. They seemed especially interested in the bait Helga and John were using for fishing. When I'd finally awakened I saw the opportunity to notate what I saw and to draw pencil sketches of the diversity of life around us. We were the only vessel in sight. Somehow the isolation was offering me certain essentials that were beginning to prove therapeutic with the blur of feelings that churned in me. On the same spot where Olaf and I had defeated the Mortiken leader, I began to notate various feelings about life and my recent ponderings. I recalled a verse from a *C.S. Lewis* poem, 'Posturing', that somehow encapsulated the emotional conflict I'd had since joining. *"Because of endless pride reborn with endless error, each hour I look aside upon my secret mirror trying all postures there to make my image fair."* It seemed so true of me. And even though I'd been, (and in certain ways was still) a self-centered sort of dweeb, I really hadn't even been aware of it until I'd started working with these people. It was during these moments of revelation that I purposed to trust God, and my shipmates, in all things, and not worry so much about what I couldn't do, or how I was perceived. I realized what an enormous ego I'd developed from my schooling, and the pampering I'd always received for being born a Proudmore. It was painfully apparent to me now that God, in His mysterious mercy, had moved me away from those days of gloating and self-centeredness, and He'd done it for my own good. I was going to apply myself to humbly learn and help out in every way I could, and what I didn't know, I would most assuredly learn.

I began notating what I was seeing in my journal. Great Skuas, Arctic bonxies and Gannets abounded here. An hour earlier a flock of Grey Phalaropes had whizzed over the schooner. Also I'd seen three Shearwaters flying so close to the water's surface that they seemed to be running on top of it. Over a period of several hours all the birds lost interest in us and flew inland. Around me the crew was at peace. Captain was reclined on top of the wheelhouse sipping Lizzy's special tea, soaking up the warm sun, and listening to a sermon from David Wilkerson from New York. Bits and pieces of what he was preaching came to my ears occasionally, but one thing I specifically and clearly heard was: *'When God takes His people into hard places, He expects them to act on His promises to them from His word, and not from what they see and feel. God's word is life to all who trust and believe'.*

John and Helga were still fishing on the bow. I asked them where Garrett was. John told me he'd decided to write his Pop. Apparently Jonah's request had moved upon Garrett's spirit so effectively that he'd decided to reestablish a connection with him. It was inspiring news.

March 9th

Everyone was delightfully laid back now; our time of rest was working wonderfully. Most battle wounds and emotions were healing nicely. Rorek was finally able to come up on deck to enjoy the pristine weather. He was deeply engrossed in a book about scuba diving off the Northern Spanish Coast. His facial color still wasn't good. In fact it was getting worse and that bothered all of us. Lizzy had been doting on him since the battle and I could tell, in her occasional expressions, that she also had some misgivings about his state of health. I wondered what the next few days would bring for him. Garrett was reclined in the sun on top of the raft. Lizzy had removed his bandages so the stitches could breathe. He was listening to music in headphones and calmly sipping her potent herbal tea. His forehead and left cheek had become blackened severely. The vicious blows, and knife wound, he'd endured at the hands of the Mortiken were strikingly apparent in the bright sun. Considering the violent encounter he'd been through I was amazed at the good humor he still possessed. Garrett was an amazingly gifted teenager with a warrior's spirit. I'd never met anyone like him. Already he had garnered enormous respect from me for his multifarious abilities and passion for life. Captain Olaf was in the wheelhouse marking charts and wolfing down Huevos Rancheros. Lizzy was sitting on a chair next to Rorek so she could keep an eye on him. She was quietly knitting something and softly humming some old Scottish melodies. Helga was aloft adjusting the electronics on our weather station and, also, fine tuning the advanced functions in the new VEW software. Betsy was below decks preparing the sea bass they'd caught the day before. John was bringing up scuba gear from storage and running pressure tests on regulators and air tanks. His left pectoral minor was swollen and blackish where he'd been stabbed, but he'd retained only seventy percent mobility on the arm where Lizzy had stitched his left triceps; he was in good spirits and healing nicely. The day passed quietly and uneventfully. Thankfully the gorgeous weather was persisting. Dinner was served at 7:30, and we all dined voraciously on Betsy's gloriously prepared pan seared sea bass with parmesan noodles, steamed vegetables, and buttermilk biscuits.

March 10th

I awoke abruptly to the sound of gusting wind. It was six am. I began distinguishing the shouts of Captain Olaf, Helga and John on deck, they were preparing to hoist sails and leave. I also noticed out of the corner of my eye that I'd received another e-mail from father.

"Gabriel," the radio suddenly squawked, "roustabout son, we're leaving and I need you to do Garrett's duties. He's developed dizzy spells, and Lizzy suggested a couple more days rest. Do you copy?"

"Coming Captain," I replied with a sudden surge of adrenaline. Quickly pulling on my pants and shirt, I stepped into my tennis shoes and bolted out the door struggling with the left arm of my windbreaker. As I flew past Garrett's berth I shouted a determined good morning.

"Don't work too hard dude!" was the muffled reply. "Thanks a lot for your help, I owe you one."

Apparently the last few days of warm, settled, high pressure weather conditions were coming to an end. The air was cold this morning, and the skies had a scattering of whitish gray clouds. Ice crystals, falling from higher faster moving clouds into the calm air above, were forming Mare's tails that had the appearance of swiftly brushed paint strokes, feathering away at the ends. The sea was dappled with an abundance of small waves, and depending on the velocity of occasional surges of wind, were cresting and forming whitecaps. A few days earlier, in one of our many conversations, Captain Olaf had informed me that in 1805 the British Admiral, Sir Francis Beaufort, had devised a scale for determining wind speed and velocity from the countenance of the sea. As much as I remembered from our talks, we appeared to be at Beaufort #4 in a moderate breeze. In the distance, towards Iceland and Greenland, the skies were bulging with darkening mammatus clouds. Fierce thunderstorms were forming northwest of our present position. Bright flashes of lightening had already begun stabbing at the water. Twenty minutes later the sails billowed open and we were once again slipping gracefully through the water. Quickly we reached a speed of thirty knots, and found the winds greatly in our favor. After listening to several Navtex reports, Rorek hoarsely informed the crew that the Atlantic Ocean was filling up with fronts and fast moving depressions. The northern storm, in the distance, appeared to be moving south out of the Norwegian Sea and moving just west of us. This was welcome news. Betsy brought fried egg sandwiches, coffee, and orange juice up on deck shortly after we'd gotten underway, and for the remainder of the day she checked on us all regularly.

The day passed quickly. All of us were busy keeping the vessel trimmed and moving efficiently. Having the biting wind in our faces, and the brisk ocean air filling our lungs, was truly an exhilarating experience. Helga was up and down the center mast several times, adjusting the stations VEW capabilities to the encrypted parameters Jonah had sent Captain Olaf. The images were pristine. Lizzy was below tending to Garrett and Rorek and we saw neither of them for most of the trip. Garrett had been instructed to stay in bed until his fever had broke, and Rorek's health was deteriorating quickly; he was sweating profusely, unable to work more than an hour at a time, and he'd become very despondent and withdrawn.

March 13th-Cabo Ortegal sighted.

John and Olaf had split their shifts piloting the vessel. Twelve hours on, and twelve hours off, enabled us to travel twenty-four hours a day without interruption. During this time I was also given opportunities to pilot the *Heimdall* while the others took well deserved breaks. It was an overwhelming experience really, feeling the wheel in my hand and being responsible for keeping us on our southern heading. What had seemed impossible for me two weeks previous was now actually happening. Non-stop sailing had been difficult for all of us, but we were all still energetic and focused on our goal. I had witnessed, (and had notated) an enormous amount of life along the way. Beaked whales, dolphins, sperm whales and pilot whales abounded in the Bay of Biscay. We'd also caught fleeting glimpses of other vessels traveling north or south. At one point, we'd passed so close to one square-rigged tall ship that we could clearly see her crew scurrying about on deck; for at least five minutes we all waved at one another. In the English Channel the water had been a murky grayish green, but as soon as we'd passed over the edge of the continental shelf it had changed to a deep blue-black. The water below us now was anywhere from one thousand to four thousand fifty meters in depth depending on how close we were to land. A group of boisterous dolphins had joined us the morning of the twelfth. All day they raced along with us, playing and jumping, until seven that evening when a large group of pilot whales showed up suddenly from the northwest. Immediately the dolphins veered east towards Bordeaux France. The pilot whales stayed with us throughout the night and for most of the next day. Each of them had a bulbous snout with a distinguishing dorsal fin and were anywhere from three to ten feet in length. For many hours they swam along with us on each side of the schooner. Occasionally one or more moved in close (starboard or port) and would roll up on their side and stare at us curiously with one big black eye. It was moments like these that gave life a special meaning to me.

Several hours later

"Land ho Captain, straight off the bow sir." Helga shouted.

"Copy that Helga; let's get the sails down crew. Oh, by the way, listen up now people. It is my most sincere pleasure to announce the return of our incomparably talented, and incredibly humble resident teenage phenomenon . . . Ladies and gentlemen, let's all give a warm round of applause in welcoming our very own Garrett back to work."

Garrett bounded up the stairs and strutted onto deck, grinning from ear to ear fervently playing his invisible drums. "I'm back dudes and dudess's." He yelled excitedly, spinning around in circles with his hands upraised. The crew let out a loud shout of appreciation. It was so good to see our little brother again. He'd been sorely missed. As we lowered and stowed the sails John brought the *vessel back* on the diesel to navigate towards the harbor entrance clearly visible now off our starboard bow.

Fourteen

Concello de Carino

Our first view of the small fishing town was exhilarating; sandy beaches, high cliffs, rugged shorelines, and all within our field of view. Helga had been scrutinizing the harbor through the high powered binoculars when she suddenly let out a whoop. "I see Jonah and Roxanne; they're standing at the end of the jetty." Roxanne was dancing and waving wildly. Jonah's large toothy grin, and thumbs high above his head, reminded me a lot of Garrett, whose persistently endearing affectations continually kept us all amused. When we passed through the narrow harbor entrance the *Heimdall* was no more than forty feet from where Jonah and Roxanne were standing on the jetty. The ladies began shouting back and forth.

"Good to see you! Praise God you're here and all safe. You feel better Garrett?" Jonah grinned and threw a small pebble at him.

"I'm getting better Jonah, thanks for asking. I wrote my pop."

"I'm proud of you son, it was the right thing to do, you're becoming a Godly man."

Slowing his pace slightly from the vessels momentum, Jonah turned his attention directly towards me. For the first time ever Jonah and I were looking at each other. Our communications had been intensely informative and I'd gained a lot of respect for this man. About three weeks ago our paths had mysteriously merged in Aberdeen over the internet, and since then my life had begun to change in ways that I'd never dreamed. Jonah looked down momentarily as he waved; his head slowly began bobbing as he looked back up, and what rose up in his features turned into another large toothy smile. I was whelmed with an irresistible emotion; at once my heart was touched with compassion and respect for this enigmatic man. I saw Jonah reach over and gently touch Roxanne's arm. He whispered something in her ear, and then he turned and proudly pointed at me. "Gabriel, it's so good to finally meet you," she shouted, and then turned back to her conversations.

John registered with the harbor master. After anchoring we lowered the raft over the side as Jonah and Roxanne made their way back to the wooden pier where several small suitcases and two oddly shaped polyurethane cases were waiting. Jonah was tall and had short brown hair. He appeared strong physically and had a compelling nature that was obvious from where I stood. There was also a peculiar kind of light around him that didn't seem to be natural. I could see at once that Roxanne was his perfect compliment. With an eloquent persona and radiant personality; she seemed to influence everyone around her with love and encouragement. She was a striking woman with long blonde hair braided in the back, and, without looking muscled; she appeared charmingly athletic and healthy. She wore round black glasses which accentuated her assiduous intelligent image. Immediately what struck me was how they both looked together. When they moved apart they seemed unfinished, but when they moved back together, or in close proximity, they seemed like a confluence of pure rivers. I knew that these two people loved each other very deeply, and had something very special together. Our introductions were brief, but insightful, and there was hugging, kissing, and accolades from both of them about our battle with the Mortiken.

Dinner that evening was splendid. Betsy had created something that amazed us all. *First course:* Iceberg Mediterranean wedge with hot house cucumber Lolla Rosa and Maytag Blue Cheese. *Second course:* Grilled sea bass over Porcini Mushroom Risotto with White Truffle oil, and fresh Vegetable Ratatouille (stew). *Third course:* Desert was a wonderfully satisfying Raspberry Crème Brule. No one had any idea that Betsy was so gifted in the culinary arts; she had truly enchanted us all. Sensing our eagerness to dine this way regularly, she reminded us that this was a special occasion and not to get spoiled. Laughing we all consigned ourselves to tomorrow's beans and weenies. After everyone had finished, and the dishes were washed and put away, Jonah got up and began talking with us about life's peculiar challenges, and also the equipment he and Roxanne had brought along.

"First I'd like to say how incredible it is to be here with all of you. It really has been an unbelievable three weeks for Roxanne and I, and it's truly astonishing how God has put this particular group of people together. The skills we possess together now form an all-inclusive team. He has given us such a remarkable vision to accomplish.

Gabriel, we are both exceptionally honored that we're finally able to make your acquaintance, this is so incredible. You truly are a God given miracle for Roxanne and me; we're really looking forward to working together with you and enjoying your skills. We're all hoping for a long and productive relationship son."

I got up and warmly shook his hand. My heart was deeply touched listening to Jonah's words and watching Roxanne's mannerisms and smiles; I felt extremely honored and privileged to know them. When I sat back down, I felt slightly embarrassed by the attention, but eagerly awaited the rest of Jonahs thoughts.

"Most of my life I've stood on a shoreline gazing out at this seemingly unattainable place I've wanted to arrive at, and regardless of whether I maintained a clear view of it, or there was obstacles shrouding it from my clear perspective, I never lost hope, or the yearning to embrace it. I've never seemed to have the right circumstances or the financial means though, only a persistently passionate desire along with the skills necessary to do my part, these things accompanied with a vision that I insistently and prayerfully pursued. Roxanne and I share the exact same dreams people. All of our lives we've been confronted with the very same obstacles in the pursuit of those dreams, the bewildering negativity, and harmful gossip of others, and the frustrating lack of finances to complete the vision. There seems to be two types of people in this world, those who have a lot for themselves, but don't have much to give to others, and those that have a lot to give others, but don't have much themselves. I realize that this is an oversimplification of a much more insidious problem with human nature, but I surely hope you get my drift. God's perfect timing is involved in all that He calls His people to do, I know that now beyond a shadow of a doubt. I once heard a man postulate on the radio that 'our efficiency without Christ's daily sufficiency will

end up in our being grossly deficient in all of our endeavors'. Amen! I believe that God has finally given us the right grouping of players and Christ centered association we need to cross over and claim the dream. That alliance and grouping is all of us here right now in this room tonight. We've all been chosen by Christ Jesus for something He needs accomplished in this time. I'm so thankful for the love and caring that we all share for one another, you know that's the key with God's people, we have to be bound together in love for Christ Jesus, and then bound together in zealous love for one another. There's no room for apathy in our endeavors! Three weeks ago Roxanne and I would've never considered this a viable option to pursue, but because of an unexpected argument with his father, Gabriel appeared on the Aberdeen docks that special evening and joined forces with us, mysteriously making our numbers complete. He caught the vision also. God is so good, He opens doors when we least expect it, and lovingly nudges us through, even if we're afraid and approach life too intellectually. I really feel good about our quest and the journey we've embarked on together. I have complete faith that we're the group of people God has chosen to find the 'Shallows of three Rocks', and the legendary 'Tempest'. Alright then, enough of that, now, let me quickly explain how this incredible technology we've brought along is going to help us discover what we're after. This is what's known as a Ceawatch Buoy." Jonah pointed at the large object on the floor next to him. *"It was constructed by a company called Banderboi Oceanographic. This is an impressively built, multi-functional floating platform. Communications are initiated by the Inmarsat satellite working in conjunction with the buoys chip and transmitter. The unit is incredibly powerful, and just recently it's been released to a small group of scientists and researchers like us to try. You know there's only one way that this got into our hands to use people, and that's because God willed it. It employs meteorological sensors; and an Inmarsat Satellite transmitter, air pressure sensors, data processor and storage, wave height and direction sensor, temperature conductivity, current meter, and a very powerful laser projector that uses small sensors to equilaterally triangulate anything, anywhere within one meter. The unit is powered by these black solar panels, so once we've placed this unit where we want it; we don't have to be concerned about anything. Tomorrow we'll be dropping it in the ocean directly north, several thousand yards offshore Carino. Then we'll be placing one of these small devices here on top of 'Vixia Herbeira' at a precise location, and one on top of 'Boya de Estaca de Bares' in the same fashion. We'll be monitoring this on our computers thanks to the new software you've just recently installed. Ok, that's all I have now, I'm really anxious to begin and I hope you are too."*

With that, Jonah nodded and sat down. Captain Olaf got up and led us in prayer and after hugging and saying our goodnights, we all retired.

March 15th The beginning of our third week out

There was a vibrant buzz on deck as everyone prepared to begin our search for the *Shallows of Three Rocks.* Lizzy had opted to stay aboard to help Helga with the computers; downloading the incoming information from the Inmarsat satellite would take two people. Lizzy also needed to inventory the stores of medical supplies that'd been depleted from the Belem incident, and the battle with the Mortiken. She strongly suggested that Rorek stay behind; he was still struggling with his breathing. There was also some fluid in one of his lungs that she was concerned about, and his color was worsening. Despondently he agreed and offered to monitor the two way radios, listen to the Navtex, and keep us informed about anything unforeseen that might interfere with our work. Betsy opted to go it alone today. She'd be going ashore to rent a small scooter to find the precise location on the escarpment and install the beacon. Helga had finally fine-tuned the new 'Virtual Earth Watch', and had begun monitoring us while we worked. She could watch everything we did, and the new programming would automatically adjust to our changing positions with the directional arrows on the keyboard. After a quick breakfast the raft was loaded and we all said farewells and shoved off.

The weather was excellent. Two foot swells caressed the rocky shoreline with the regularity of a fine Swiss watch. Captain Olaf, Jonah, Roxanne, John, Garrett and I, along with all the equipment and food and water for a day, churned out and over these perfectly shaped waves directly north with the coordinates established the night before. On the way out we passed a gnarled old man with shoulder length hair and a scraggly beard. He had a corncob pipe firmly clenched in his back teeth and he was working on a small punt. It was no more than eight feet in length and a tattered square sail, and erratic currents, were his only means of propulsion. The punt was colored red, yellow, and blue, and he was fishing the old fashioned way, without a pole. Tough leather gloves were his only protection as he bobbed the stout line up and down repeatedly in an effort to attract the fish. We all waved as the raft slowly trolled by. Without a word, or change of expression, he hoisted up a five foot spotted sand shark from the bottom of the old punt. With a partially toothless smile he grinned at us, and then resumed his tedious work. The scene had me remembering 'The Old Man and the Sea', by Ernest Hemingway, and I wondered if it was character's like this man that could have been the inspiration for his marvelous story.

Placing the Ceawatch buoy was easy. When the precise location had been ascertained we heaved it into the water and Jonah switched on the electronics. After the buoy had stabilized an energetic school of Muro's fish appeared around the submerged part of the structure and began sticking their noses up at us for food. "Oh man, it's a bloody shame we don't have a large net here with us." John groaned. All of us laughed and agreed. Minutes later Helga radioed with an affirmation that the buoy had made a reliable connection with the Inmarsat Satellite. "Roger that," Jonah radioed back, "God's hand is on our endeavors, Helga, and He will bless our efforts. We're proceeding north; we should reach the formations in an hour and a half, we'll keep you posted."

"Roger that Jonah," Helga responded. "Gabriel, pick up please." I grabbed my radio and keyed on. "What's up Helga?" I answered a little suspiciously after sensing the curious affectation in her voice. "Betsy asked me to tell you to be careful when you climb the formation today, and that she'll see you tonight. Ok, y'all take care, Helga out!" All in the raft turned with goofy half-cocked smiles. Jonah pulled his sunglasses down slightly under his right eye and peeked over while his eyebrow went up. He began shaking his head and grinning.

"Whoa homey," Garrett chimed with a playful smirk. "I didn't know something was happening with you two love birds. What's goin' on man?" I started to flush with embarrassment. "I think I like Betsy, ok? There I said it! I don't know Garrett, there's just something about her I can't put my finger on. I really do care about her. I know it's only been a few weeks, but what can I say."

"Dude, that's so cool," Garrett laughed lightheartedly.

"Alright guys," the Captain interrupted, "we can discuss this later. Let's get our minds back on work."

Two hours later we'd reached the **'Boya de Estaca de Bares'**; a formation of eight craggy vertical rocks in a circle just offshore.

There was also a tall flat topped rock, resembling a small volcano, directly in the center of the circle leaning slightly south towards the shore. After carefully watching the pulsing of the waves Captain chose a moment of lull and maneuvered the raft through a narrow opening between the two largest rocks. At first glance we saw two places to anchor. Directly east of the center rock the water was somewhat agitated and probably four feet deep. It we anchored here we would have to wade in about ten yards to reach a climbable area. There was also a shallower place, directly north of the cliffs, on the southern face of the center rock, where the water was considerably calmer. This area revealed a twenty foot wide bay carved into the bottom of the rock face on its southern side. Captain maneuvered the raft in closer. When we were near John tied the bow and stern lines securely at the base of the formation. It was strangely calm here. The wind gusting off the Bay was completely blocked. Jonah radioed *Heimdall* that we'd arrived and were preparing to climb the eight hundred foot rock. Jonah and Garrett joined John outside the raft and began wading around the base of the rock in both directions. They were searching for somewhere to pound in pitons so that we could begin our climb. Ten minutes later John let out a loud whoop. After wading back to the raft he informed us that there were steps and handholds carved right into the rock face that went all the way to the top. Someone in the past had, with great fortitude, chiseled them out. We all shook our heads in disbelief; it would certainly make the climb a lot easier. Roxanne was delighted with this news, and I too sighed in relief, having never rope climbed before in my whole life. We were carrying three backpacks with the triangulating beacon, four thin steel cables and tines to firmly attach it to the rock, binoculars, two radios, snacks, water, and Roxanne's digital camera. After praying Jonah ascended first, Roxanne followed, then me,

Garrett, Olaf, and finally John pulled up the rear; we kept a three to four foot distance between ourselves for safety's sake. A restless wind had begun whipping powerful gusts in as we climbed. It'd begun whistling eerily around the extreme east and west edges of the formation. We all deduced a storm was approaching from the north, but didn't know for sure because our view was blocked where we were climbing on the southern face. An hour later we'd safely crested the top of the formation. The climb was grueling and we were out of breath. One by one, as we pulled ourselves up and stood, an inexplicable awe fell upon us.

"There are Viking symbols up here," Roxanne finally began pointing, "runic writings and pictures everywhere, Jonah; it seems to begin here and go around the whole cap clockwise, it appears a story is being told. What in the world is this place? Look over here; see? There are two vessels under the surface with dozens of bodies lying prostrate. Here's a fancy looking box with two angelic guards standing next to it and one is holding a key. Another vessel seems to be tied down on the beach here with the bow pointing west, and, let's see; one, two, three, twelve more vessels appear to be sailing towards the west. There's one more here, a larger one further north in the Bay with different symbols. The occupants look deformed, and the vessel has four distinct bows pointing north east west and south. So what direction is it traveling in do you think?"

Roxanne took dozens of digital pictures as she walked the perimeter, and, after delineating half a dozen quadrants, she marked them all with chalk. She also notated, into her small leather ledger, dimensions and the possible meaning behind each one. Towards the northern edge Garrett had stumbled upon something interesting and cried out for everyone to 'beat feet'. He'd discovered a weathered oak lid that had been perfectly crafted to fit into a hole with a two inch overhang that acted like eves on a roof. Without a word, John pulled out his enormous knife, and, shortly thereafter he'd loosened the sticky seal around the edges and pried the wooden lid up; the hole inside was remarkably dry. We found an old rusted metal box with something white and smelly smeared around the outside edges; it had a faint etching of a sword and helmet over a shield carved on the cover. As John was dislodging the box the radios squawked. It was Betsy.

"I found the location and attached the sensor guys; we're ready on this end . . . copy?"

"Yes Betsy, we copy you . . . excellent job!" Jonah quickly answered. "Did you have any problems finding the location?"

"Not really, it just took a while; it's a long way. There's people living up here, they're cloistered and weird," Betsy whispered. Her voice had lowered significantly and she spoke in hushed tones after she'd begun answering Jonah's question. "They're not Spanish, Portuguese, or European, and they dress old fashioned like. They live in round wooden huts built under the rocky outcroppings of the cliffs; their dwellings are surrounded by tall tightly woven fences. The only reason I can see them now is because one of the gates is open. Two men approached me shortly after I'd arrived and asked me in English what I was doing. Why would they assume I spoke English? Anyway . . . I told them I was with a research team exploring the topography and sea life along the coast, and we were traveling on that big white schooner in the bay. I don't think they understood some of what I said because they started grumbling with each other in a strange language. I heard them say France twice though, and I heard them say the word Mortiken I think, but I'm not positive. I don't think they saw me attach the sensor. I covered it with brush anyway just in case."

"Good job Betsy, do you feel you're in danger?" Jonah asked.

"Not really. They're just peculiar looking people; they don't look like they belong in Spain though, but they do seem peaceful. Wait a second. Someone else is moving towards me; the other two are walking towards him now. Ok, now they've all stopped and they're talking together. He's speaking in English, too, and he's carrying a Bible. Do you think he's a missionary? He's got a radio like ours and he's listening to it. He's laughing for some reason and he just smiled at me. How weird. They seem very interested in protecting their privacy; they're all walking back towards the gate together. I don't understand this exactly. From the pictures I've seen; those two big men look like belong in some of the ancient tribes of Vikings we've studied. I know that sounds strange, because what would they be doing living up here in the high cliffs over Carino, right? On one of the larger huts I can just barely see a symbol; it looks like a sword and helmet carved on a big shield. I'm leaving now, its creepy here. They just shut the gate."

"Do you have a camera?" Jonah asked.

"Yes I have a little pocket digital."

"Take some photos of that symbol and the dwellings, and if it's possible, take some of the people's faces."

"I think I can do that, but I can't promise anything."

"Try your best; we'll see you when we get back, Jonah out."

John had pulled the metal box from the hole and had opened the rusted lid. There were twenty or so trinkets inside, an assortment of coins, several talismans and a brass key. There was also an animal skin, rolled up in good shape, with runic symbols on the outside. Roxanne and Jonah were stunned as they looked over each piece in the box.

"It's the Rognvald insignia," Jonah shook his head in disbelief, "they've actually been here Roxanne. They must be the ones that chiseled out the steps." One talisman mystified Roxanne. "I don't recognize this Jonah. I've never seen it before. No pictographs of this exist anywhere that I know of." Overhearing them, Garrett, Captain Olaf and I gathered around and peeked over her shoulder. Shuddering immediately we all jumped back.

"Holy crap," Garrett cried out. "Can you believe it Cap?"

"Oh gosh," Captain Olaf gasped. "Gabriel found this exact Talisman after the battle with the Mortiken Jonah; it was around their leader's neck. How in the world did it get here?" Jonah and Roxanne shook their heads in disbelief.

"The tide is starting to go out Captain!" John shouted from the other side of the formation. "We should probably get moving sir!"

Acknowledging him the Captain gave orders to leave. As we descended we speculated about the new find, the talisman, and what Betsy's encounter with the men up on the escarpment could mean. Maybe there was something useful on the rolled up animal skin that might answer some of our questions. "We have triangulation guys." Helga's voice crackled suddenly on the radio. "The sensors are working, and they're both talking with the Inmarsat and Ceawatch. They've given us a precise point out in the ocean. I believe we've located the *Shallows of Three Rocks*!"

Fifteen

A cloistered clan of Rognvald's

The extent of our discoveries hadn't really sunk in. Jonah and Roxanne were consumed with what they'd brought back and, directly upon our return, Helga and I helped them load all the information into the computer after which it was immediately sent off to the University of Porto and USC for assessment. Within an hour we received word that our two respective finds were a significant piece of the puzzle that fit together perfectly with what'd been established over our last year of research. The Rognvald's had lost two vessels and all aboard on the *Shallows of Three Rocks and part of the clan* had remained in Concello de Carino to establish another community; the reasons why were open to speculation. Dinner was served at eight, during which we discussed what we'd discovered and if it was, in any way, intrinsic to our journey. After dinner Roxanne shared a most illuminating story about our discoveries.

"As you all know our finds have confirmed that the Rognvald expedition crossed the Bay of Biscay and landed here in Galicia and, that after an indeterminate period of time, they continued their journey west. We've reconfirmed today that the Rognvald's lived on Flores in the Azorean Archipelagoes for a season. Let me explain the meaning of some of the petraglyphs we found on top: The two vessels we saw etched into the rock confirmed that there was indeed an accident involving two vessels that unfortunately hit and sank on a reef. The Rognvald scribes positively described this place as the *Shallows of Three Rocks.* According to the records painted on the leather scroll we've ascertained that thirty-five people lost their lives in the calamity. A large wooden container was being carried by one of the two ships and that was also lost. Considering the two symbolic angelic guards that were assigned to the box in the records we've assessed that this was indeed the symbolic Christian sword they were transporting called *Tempest.* The petraglyphs indicate a singular vessel being tied down on the beach with the bow pointing west. Now, with Betsy's discovery today, this beached vessel is indicative of a group of Rognvald's that stayed behind and established what Betsy discovered on top of the escarpment. We believe they've been cloistered there for some time preserving their way of life. Betsy will share more with us about her experiences today, Betsy . . ."

Betsy got up awkwardly. I knew at once she was shy in front of groups. She began with her head down and fumbling with her pockets. "Well, as you all know, I did meet two males. Um, well, they spoke English to me and although it was heavily influenced by some strange accent, uh, I could understand most of their questions. I uh, well, it was curious that they spoke English you know, and, um, knew that I spoke it also. They wanted to know what I was doing and who had given me permission to be there. You already know how I responded to them. They weren't rude, they were polite actually, but they scared me, they looked like Viking warriors. It always felt to me as if they were hiding something. I was able to get these four pictures here; one of the large symbols on the main dwelling, one of the missionary, and two of the clan's people. Jonah determined the symbol is a sword and helmet over a shield and the white man is holding a bible and spoke English with the other two men. Roxanne and I have determined that these two men here are dressed in Orknean styles. That's all I have. Ok Roxanne, it's your turn again."

"Thanks Betsy that was great. What an incredible day we've all had. Now, we can draw certain logical deductions here folks. One, these people are descendants of the Rognvald expedition, and two, they speak English because they've had a missionary in their midst teaching them for some time. How and why this came about is still a mystery. The symbol Betsy photographed was the same one we found on top of the Bares. The symbol we found on that box was also a sword and helmet over a shield. This *is* the symbol of the Rognvald clan and has been positively confirmed at both universities. The trinkets we found appear to represent the fashionable jewelry of the day. Personally I believe that there's a story connecting the symbols on the trinkets and the petraglyphs carved in the rock, but as of now we just don't have enough information to positively confirm this. The key we found could very well be the key that opens the large container the two angels are guarding in the petraglyphs, and also described and painted on the skin. The square blue talisman is undoubtedly the symbol of the Mortiken, but how it got up on the Bares is a mystery that I have no answers for. The fact that Gabriel found one after the battle allowed us to logically connect these two different circumstances. We might accept that the Rognvald's placed it in the box but there's no way to prove that. Obviously, we all know the Mortiken is a moniker the world media has designated to them. But we're still unsure about whom the Mortiken really are, or how the Rognvald's knew about them. Have the drought conditions and the changing environment in these afflicted areas been responsible for this sudden upsurge of violence in the last year or so? We just don't know and are presently relegated to hypothesizing the circumstance and reasons. Sometime in the next few weeks, Lord willing, we'll have a much more definitive picture. Also, we're unsure why Betsy heard the two men mention France and use the word Mortiken. It appears that they're also enlightened to what's happening in the world. But considering that they live so cloistered I don't understand how this could be. My preliminary analysis leads me to believe that there was a split in the early Viking tribes based on differing religious beliefs, but this also is still in the realm of speculation. I am confident that time and careful research will help us sort this out. Ok . . . the vessel, with the four distinct bows, must surely represent the elusiveness of the Mortiken. Considering the unpredictability of the direction they're traveling in, I believe this also represents that they could be anywhere at any time; an insidious foe trying to destroy everything the Rognvald's stood for. Considering what happened last week it would appear that this antagonist has made an enemy of all mankind now. Gabriel and I scanned the parts of the rolled skin that were unclear. We loaded them into the computer and sent it off to both Universities. Hopefully, when the information comes back, we'll all understand another part of this mysterious puzzle we're trying to solve."

Roxanne finished and sat down. Her talk had certainly been enlightening. We understood several more facts, now, about the diverse puzzle, and it was slowly beginning to take shape and look like something. As she was talking I was having a premonition about the Vikings in my past history, and why my family had kept it a secret for so many centuries. These thoughts were upsetting my stomach. I truly hoped that what I was beginning to suspect about my families past was incorrect. Captain got up and led in prayer. Afterwards he informed us that we would be taking the raft out in the morning to find the shallows. If we were blessed in our search we'd be radioing our coordinates to John and Rorek who'd then be moving the *Heimdall* out to commence with our preparations for our dive.

Sixteen

A dire emergency/ we make a monumental discovery

March 16th

It was twelve-thirty. A noisy commotion in the hallway had awakened me. When I stumbled out most of the crew was scurrying about under Lizzy's orders. Hurriedly she informed me that Rorek's condition had taken a turn for the worse. He was in a semi-coma, now, his lung had filled with fluid, and he'd developed a dangerously high fever. Lizzy instructed me to help Betsy and Helga bring some ice from the galley to pack around his torso. I knew he'd been struggling since the battle with the Mortiken, but I never once realized the seriousness of his condition. My heart began to hurt and a stream of tears began flowing down my cheeks. We'd been through so much and this seemed so unfair. Captain Olaf ran back from the wheelhouse to inform us that he'd contacted the *La Coruna Emergency Services.* A helicopter was on its way with an estimated time of arrival at thirty minutes. Jonah called everyone together and all joined hands.

Father in the name of Jesus Christ, we lift up your child, and our brother Rorek to You, and we ask for your merciful will to be done. Lord God, you know all things, and all things work together for good for those that are in your son Christ Jesus and called according to his purposes. You have put us together for your purpose's Lord, and we pray for our brother's complete healing. Lord God, in your mercy, please act quickly on this request. We all ask this in one accord. Lord your word says that if we ask anything according to your will for our lives you will hear from heaven and answer. So Lord God we ask for your mercy upon our brother Rorek, and for his complete healing, in Jesus' name.

Something shook me deep inside while Jonah was praying, something I'd never felt before. I was amazed at the depth of Jonah's faith in the unseen God, and I knew for sure that I had to know more about this kind of faith, and the daily expression of it. The helicopter arrived five minutes early and, being equipped with pontoons, landed successfully on the water thirty yards from the schooner. A number of people were gathered on the pier watching. Rorek was groaning and sweating as we lowered him down into the raft. Hastily we floated him over to the helicopter. Within a minute the **'Life Flight'** ascended in a flurry of wind and whipped-up water. The pilot waved reassuringly as he banked towards the west. Lizzy had decided to stay with Rorek and reassured us she would update us daily about his condition. After we'd stowed the raft, Captain Olaf called us together and informed us of more bad news. There'd been another earthquake in the Labrador Sea centered precisely on the Davis Strait, between Greenland and Canada's Baffin Island. It had been an overwhelming 8.7 on the Richter scale. Reports were coming in from as far as Nuuk and Holsteinborg in Greenland. From as far northwest as Clyde River, on the Baffin Island, there were reports of irreversible damage from (what the preliminary reports were saying was) the largest Tsunami in recorded history. Contact with all seagoing vessel's, in the Labrador Sea, had been lost, and there was apprehension that they'd all sunk or been disabled. The situation was grave; thankfully there wasn't a large human population along most of these coastal areas, but fears of an immense loss of life were still persisting. Wearily saying goodnight to one another we finally got back to bed at two. My sleep came with great difficulty and with many tears.

The crew congregated in the galley at eight. During a hasty breakfast of oatmeal and fruit we talked in detail about our plans for the day. Each of us was very concerned about Rorek. Captain Olaf had spoken to Lizzy earlier in the morning. She'd reported he was stable and resting peacefully. After x-rays were taken the doctor's found the problem within minutes. A large splinter, from a Mortiken club, had lodged itself deep inside his pectoral major and the skin had closed over it. It was what had caused the infection and fever and had to be removed surgically. The bacterium was of an unknown origin and required special antibiotics. Lizzy was reassured, and told us, that he would be up and about in ten days and ready for full duty in two weeks. Jonah ministered to us, after we'd eaten, about keeping our faith in God's plan, prayerfully trusting Him, and staying focused on what He'd given us to accomplish. I realized that walking in faith was sometimes way beyond a person's ability to comprehend.

Around nine Captain Olaf, Garrett, and I shoved off with all the necessary equipment aboard for our search. The raft moved out slowly through the narrow inlet. Despite the early morning trauma, and the devastating news Olaf had shared about the earthquake, the day felt glorious and we embraced it as a good diversion from all our other problems. On the way out we passed the same old gnarled fisherman we'd seen the day before. This time he waved heartily and smiled but he had no fish to show. When the land had become distant on the horizon another group of Muro's fish swarmed in around the raft and began nosing up for handouts. For a time this entertained us but then, as suddenly as they appeared, they vanished. Seconds later the reason for it became known; our friends the dolphins once again had joined us at a most auspicious moment in our journey. When they moved next to the raft, we reached over and began rubbing their noses and scratching their fins. They seemed to really enjoy this. But then, when we began vocalizing that we were glad to see them, they began jumping and splashing around the raft. It was as if they were celebrating our friendship and were happy being around us again. I kept my eyes glued to the laptop as Capt Olaf piloted the raft. As of now we were dead on course. Garrett had been the forward lookout for the last thirty minutes; he was up on the bow squinting through powerful binoculars for any sign of land or rocks. "I see somethin' Cap, off the port bow; it looks like a small cloud resting on the water." Olaf brought the raft to a stop. Stumbling forward, he took the binoculars to see what he was talking about. "There's a round cloud on the water Garrett," he concurred. "This is very curious; I wonder what it could be. Are we still on course Gabriel?"

"We appear to be, sir. The computer shows we're right on the mark. The cloud is about three miles more."

Captain Olaf nodded and then increased our speed to five knots. Thirty minutes later, after we'd lost sight of the coast; we decided it was time to eat. Helga had packed tuna sandwiches, chips, tea, and apples. She'd also sent along a wonderful trail mix of her own invention. Olaf stopped the raft once again and we devoured an early lunch with great enjoyment. It was peaceful here, and the brisk salt air was invigorating. In the distance an enormous freighter was dieseling southwest in the general direction of the Azores. Over east, in the general direction of Aquitaine France, a herd of whales was arching up and down and blowing enormous spouts of water. After they'd finished eating the dolphins swam ahead, in the general direction of the cloud, and began jumping and playing about two hundred yards off our starboard bow. When we'd finished eating Captain checked in with the *Heimdall* and then we continued on in the direction of the cloud. Ten minutes later we were floating just outside its perimeter. According to the computers (now blinking green) beacon we'd arrived precisely on the top point of the equilateral triangle.

"Raft, this is Helga . . . come back."

"Go ahead Helga. This is your humble loving little brother."

"Hi Garrett! Hey, according to my computer, you guys are directly on top of the shallows."

"Copy that big sister, our computer confirms it also. Helga, the Captain wants to talk to you . . . hold on a second."

"According to these charts, lass, we're over the continental shelf and the water here must be at least two miles deep. How could there be shallows in this area?"

"According to Inmarsat imagery, *and* the Ceawatch information, Captain, there's an extinct volcano near you. I'll check the VEW again to confirm this, give me a few minutes, Helga out."

The cloud was like a big stationary wheel of cheese. It was, in all probability, two hundred feet high, and appeared white and thick like cotton. What exactly was it? And how did it maintain these properties? Was this the *Shallows of Three Rocks*? Sunlight was piercing through the feathery outside edges right where the anomaly touched the water. It was being refracted (and reflected) by millions of small droplets of water that were creating an intense arcing band of colors in the air about eight feet up, and twenty feet out on the water's surface. This rainbow was richly visible from all angles and utterly mesmerizing. When Captain turned off the motor an eerie stillness descended on us like a blanket. Quietly the dolphins resurfaced next to the raft. We were rubbing them when the radio shattered the stillness.

"Raft, this is Helga, copy?"

"Go ahead Helga," Captain answered.

"Sir, we've run this test five times, you *have* found the Shallows. We can see you clearly on the VEW. You're stationary in the water on the southeastern edge, next to what appears to be a rainbow completely around the circumference of a cloud; the water is also a distinctive color in your immediate area, much different than farther out. We can't make out what's in the center. It resembles a donut kinda, like a circular wall surrounding something; Jonah thinks the wall is probably one hundred and fifty feet thick. He suggests taking the raft through to get inside the inner circle."

"Tell Jonah we'll take his advice and begin. We'll keep you posted lass, Olaf out."

The ocean was lightly choppy where we were, but where the rainbow was visible stillness hovered over the water. Considering the optical properties of water, to view a rainbow effectively the observer must be at a forty-two degree angle from the path of the sun's rays, but this particular phenomenon had seemingly overwritten the laws of physics. The water turned pale green as we approached the wall of the cloud; this confirming what Helga had viewed on the VEW. There didn't appear to be any sea life in our immediate area, except the dolphins. They were floating quietly next to us and seemed just as inquisitive about this location as we were. On the motors lowest trolling speed we entered into the cloud. As soon as we'd penetrated the outer edge Garrett disappeared. Once the raft was inside we couldn't see each other at all. Suddenly Garrett let out a loud shriek. "It's like a recording booth; the sound is so stinkin' dead; like crawling through cotton; you can't see nothin'."

"Kinda like swimming through milk, huh?" I added.

Garrett laughed. Inside it was syrupy with moisture, and in a matter of moments we were completely soaked. I took one of my fingers and wiped some of the moisture off of my left hand and put a drop on my tongue; it was perfectly pure tasting. After five minutes of creeping Garrett's enthusiastic exclamation broke the silence once again.

"Oh man, this place is awesome!"

When the raft had pierced the inner circle, the dolphins got much roused. Energetically that swam around, and under, us, but they were doing so without making any sounds. It felt as if we'd entered into another world. There was a distinct smell of sulfur and, considering what Helga had said about being over a very large extinct volcano here, I considered the possibility of vents purging gases from deep inside the earth as the probability for this odor. Inside there were (indeed) three enormous vertical rocks, and all with the appearance of multifaceted gems. To me they were similar looking to the inside of a geode and all were reflecting the sunlight in a multitude of prismatic colors. Being all similar in shape and size, they stuck straight up an incredible two hundred feet. The area here was possibly six hundred yards in diameter. And the formations were in (what appeared to be) a triangular formation; the separation between them (I roughly calculated) was somewhere between forty to sixty yards; differing slightly because of the obtuse shape. The water was about forty feet in depth, according to the captain, and the sea floor appeared sandy, with a smattering of different sized rocks. After viewing the area for several minutes we realized there were no observable aquatic plants, or marine life, here except our dolphin friends. Captain spied an area between two of the rocks where the water was perhaps six feet in depth. But directly out towards the inner wall of the cloud the water got much darker, almost certainly because the depth had increased dramatically.

"Heimdall, this is Olaf, over." The Captain's voice seemed to boom in the uncanny silence.

"Olaf, this is Jonah. We stopped trying to get a hold of you ten minutes ago because all we got was static."

"Roger that, the same was true on this end too. Jonah we've here, I'm looking at the three rocks as we speak. It's stunning brother."

"Olaf, that's phenomenal. Praise God. We can't see you on the VEW anymore. The cloud's seemed to disappear. There's something very mystifying here Olaf. As soon as the raft penetrated the outer edge of the cloud everything but the water vanished. Our weather station is giving us some indications of magnetic disturbances eighty thousand feet above us, perhaps this could be the reason we lost sight of you. We can just barely see some small whales or dolphins in your area. Are there any?"

"They've been with us most of the trip, Jonah, they're dolphins. Is the raft still visible?" Olaf asked.

"Sorry; we can't see you anymore, strange, because the equipment is still functioning perfectly. We do still have indication that you're directly above an enormous volcano mount though."

"We're certainly not over the continental shelf; the water here is pastel green and translucent. We can see the bottom clearly and there's a smell of sulfur in the air. Also, the dolphins are uneasy here; not sure why yet."

"Olaf, I'll be back shortly." There was a pause for several minutes and then Jonah radioed back; now the tone of his voice had changed. "Olaf, I strongly feel that you should head back at once. We'll move *Heimdall* out to the site tomorrow and start diving then. Do you copy?" Jonah's words bit the ears like cold wind. As he continued the only response from Captain was to nod willingly to his views. I'd never seen that before in him. While they were talking I started organizing the various aspects of this place and how I'd be notating it in my journal tomorrow. I remembered, too, that I had to charge my digital camera.

Seventeen

The mysterious stranger's story

March 17

Despite what we'd discovered yesterday all of us felt mostly dejected. Rorek and Lizzy were terribly missed. Gloominess weighed heavily on our hearts and minds, and the frustrating inability to offer anything to aid in his recovery was vexing. It appeared even Jonah's sagacious personality had become reticent as we prepared for the first day of diving; something was really bothering him. When Roxanne came up from below she was, at once, aware of the quandary her husband had found himself in and she pulled him aside. Together they went forward to the bowsprit. She put her arms around him and they began praying.

I realized that no matter how much we desire it to be different; life, at times, becomes an emotional struggle, fraught with redundant rancor and the unforeseen. At the most inopportune moments, we are beleaguered with the unknowable, and begin struggling fiercely against nasty little things besieging our minds which, during fleeting times of joyfulness, seem so inconsequential. I rationalized these dreary somber seasons were a requisite part of the human condition, and, it was in those moments of despair that we all strove harder to understand our small places in life's enormously complex puzzle.

Everyone except John seemed to be carrying a burden today; he was focused and energetic, and once again he was checking tanks, valves, regulators, and hoses for any problems. Being an Ex-Navy Seal, he was the obvious person aboard to head up the dive, and the only one who seemed educated enough to accomplish these duties. John mentioned to me that because of Rorek's condition, I would be diving in his place and needed to learn a few things. "Don't fret Gabriel, I can teach you all you need to know in an hour, it's a very shallow dive, it'll be easy." All I could do was nod and smile.

Garrett was the first one to notice a lanky man shuffling towards us on the jetty and he alerted Captain Olaf. "Hey boss, there's some weird lookin' dude headin' towards us. When I made eye contact he nodded and waved at me like he knew me. I've never seen him before boss."

Olaf climbed down from the wheelhouse and moved over towards the starboard rails. "Can I help you sir?"

"Yes sir! Hello! Captain is it? Olaf nodded. "Hello my name is Regan Pendleton. Good day sir, so very nice to meet you, very nice indeed." While the stranger was speaking, he removed his large straw hat; clutching it now with both hands he bowed slightly from the head several times, and then dropped the hat on the ground next to his feet. "I'm a missionary sir, and I've been working with the clan on top of the escarpment for seven years. I've been teaching them the English language, and refreshing them regularly in the Gospel of Jesus Christ." Everyone stopped what they were doing and moved over to where Olaf was leaning on the railing and talking. Jonah's temperament changed. I could see suspicion in his features when he heard Regan's voice. And then, when he saw the man, a strange expression came up in his features. He became fidgety, and increasingly nervous, as we all stood staring at him. I remembered the first time the crew all stopped and stared at me on the Aberdeen dock, and I was momentarily flooded with an unexpected compassion for this stranger's present dilemma. He was indeed a unique looking human, and possessed more than a few quirky mannerisms. For a while Garrett was on the verge of busting up; he kept poking me and snickering to get me to laugh first.

"Look at that dudes hair homey," he finally whispered, "looks like he cut if off of a horses butt."

Squirming restlessly the man's eyes kept darting up and down the jetty, almost as if he was expecting danger to suddenly appear from his periphery. Anxiously he bit at his lower lip and began clearing his throat as his eyebrows kept rising and falling regularly. He'd removed from his coat pocket, and was tightly gripping, what appeared to be a Bible; it was firmly pressed against his left hip. The thumb of his right hand was hooked into his right pocket and he was rubbing his forefinger and thumb together nervously through the material. He had a weathered face, deeply furrowed with lines, but he was not old chronologically. Thick blonde hair fell around his temples like feathers. And over the front of his ears the rest was sloppily pulled back into a pony tail that almost touched his waist. He had the humility of a clergyman, and the few words he'd spoken (thus far) had not sounded contrived, clever, or religious. It was obvious, however uncomfortable he appeared, that he had no agenda other than communicating with us. It was clear to me, too, that he possessed a restrained and intelligent spirit, and that he was articulate and insightful in the way he related; it also appeared that he was sensitive to the possibility of offending us.

"Sir, what exactly is it you want with us?" The Captain asked finally in an effort to end the awkward uneasiness. Immediately, as if a switch had been thrown, the man's demeanor changed. He stood up straight with a newfound confidence, squared his shoulders, and began. "Respectfully, I know about your mission sir, you've discovered the *Shallows of Three Rocks*. I have information that will prove invaluable to your endeavors. You and your vessel are known to us Captain. Sir; we all support you in your salubrious journey."

"I'm sorry . . . how did know that we discovered the shallows?" Helga asked with a look of consternation.

"Miss . . . I intercepted your radio transmissions yesterday, and although I felt like I was intruding, my curiosity got the best of me and I continued listening. I salute you on the discovery; no one has ever been able to find the shallows before."

"Mr. Pendleton, exactly why did you feel compelled to walk all this way today to share this information with us?" Roxanne asked.

"My lady . . . I encountered one of your crew two days ago by the village, a beautiful young woman who affixed a special transmitter for your triangulation purposes. Though I never spoke to her, I acknowledged her with a smile. I knew what she was there to accomplish. Your presence and mission here has provoked mistrust in the clan. When I left this morning the elders were in high counsel to decide what to do. I explained to them that your allegiances were with the Rognvald's, and convinced them that talking with you was in their best interest. I came to do just that." We were engrossed now with this man. But how in the world could he have known about our mission, and in so much detail?

"Come aboard then sir," Captain Olaf motioned towards the gangplank. "Let's discuss this further. Would you like some breakfast perhaps? You must be very tired and hungry from the walk."

"That would be wonderful sir; yes, I am famished. Thank you so much for your generous offer, I am indebted."

Captain asked John to bring up the portable table and eight chairs; we would be talking with the stranger on deck. He also radioed Betsy and asked if she would prepare something for him, and told her that this was the character she'd seen on the escarpment. Betsy seemed relieved; she'd expressed concerns earlier about the possibility of retaliation for invading their privacy, and she was thankful they'd sent an ambassador ahead instead. When Betsy brought up the strangers breakfast he promptly stood, lowered his head in respect, and didn't move. When his plates were laid out he sat down and ravenously devoured what was placed in front of him. After several belches, the stranger stood up with a new found composure.

"I haven't eaten this quality of food for seven years, it was delightful, thank you so very much for this blessing Captain. Now, let me begin. As I've already mentioned, my name is Regan Pendleton. I'm from the small town of 'Shelburne' on Lake Champlain in Vermont. I belong to a sizeable Christian congregation which employs over two hundred missionaries in various locations around the world. Our mission is to teach English and minister to the widely scattered clans of Rognvald descendants. There's over thirty that we know of between here and Southern California. Just last week I received encouraging news about the discovery of two more clans; one near Mt Logan in the Yukon Territory, and one in the outskirts of the city of Valdez in

Alaska. Our church has three locations. There's one in Shelburne, our main church is in Portland Maine on the Casco Bay, and there's also one in the Laguna Mountains of Southern California, two miles from the general store. For forty-five years we've been holding true to our churches founding father's vision to help prepare the Rognvald Viking remnants for the second coming of the Lord Jesus Christ. Now . . . brothers and sisters, the Rognvald's categorically made a journey that took over twenty years to accomplish, and many died. Here offshore Carino is the first disaster they encountered on their pilgrimage; they lost forty people and two vessels on, what they described in their records as, the 'Shallows of Three Rocks'. The great symbol of their Christian faith was lost also in that disaster. An incomparable sword, forged from a powerful new metal, called **'Tempest'**. The tribes originated up in the Orkney Islands. There they all prospered and grew strong for hundreds of years. All the centuries old tales we've heard are accurate, they were a very powerfully unique group of creative people that plundered anywhere and everywhere. There were sailors, hunters, farmers, craftsman, and savage warriors; a uniquely skilled people they were. A fearful reputation preceded them wherever they roamed, they were the mighty Norsemen. At some point, the exact date is elusive though; there was an enormous uprising between the two foremost tribes. One tribe embraced a religion called Christianity and a new book called the Holy Bible. The other faction embraced a host of diverse blood witchcrafts, which included human and animal sacrifice and the worship of fallen angels. The Rognvald family was the first to introduce Christianity to all the outlying tribes. And even though they met with fierce resistance in their efforts, they became the predominate tribe and eventually were embraced as the leaders of the Northern nation. The Baaldur family, who encouraged the continuation of witchcraft, and the early violent practices, were vilified, and finally excommunicated from fellowship with the others. The tribes quickly separated. And after a brief period of posturing and politics, they began warring in an effort to establish preeminence. The Baaldur tribe became known as the Baaldurians and, purportedly, because of their atrocious and dishonorable religious practices, over many generations, began developing bizarre facial deformities. I believe there is more to this than we know or understand. The ancient Baaldurians have become what we now know as the Mortiken. Another blood feud began between the two tribes approximately seven years ago. This seems to coincide with an overt increase of violence, murders, drug use and witchcraft prophesied in the Holy Scriptures just before the return of our Lord Jesus Christ. Even though we believe the seven year tribulation has not yet officially begun, I strongly sense that these signs are precursors to something cataclysmic coming in the near future."

Everyone sat stunned. The stranger had confirmed a theory that Roxanne had contended for years about a religious split in the Viking tribes that became violent. In just a few moments, Regan's words had reestablished the significance of our journey. I must also confess that into a vertiginous state I plummeted when I heard the stranger mention that the Baaldur's were the ones who continued to pursue witchcraft and evil. It had suddenly become clear, given that my middle name was Baaldur, why my family had kept this a secret for so many centuries. This was a curse of sorts, and my premonition the day before had been accurate. I sensed that I'd been prepared beforehand to hear this so I wouldn't drift into some kind of irreversible stupor.

"Mr. Pendleton . . ." Jonah began with an air of indifference. I could see that a kind of incredulous disbelief had gripped his thoughts and expressions. "You've been quite verbose about the amount of information you seem to be privy too. As a missionary to this clan for seven years, isolated in such a remote part of the world, how is it possible to be so self-assured about what you've related to us here? The young woman who prepared breakfast for you this morning distinctly heard the two men on the escarpment yesterday twice mention France and the word Mortiken. How could these cloistered people be in possession of knowledge about these facts? Actually sir, how is it possible that you have knowledge of these facts?"

The stranger visibly cringed at Jonah's indignant tone. Then he chuckled irritably, and began methodically rubbing his sweat beading forehead with the forefingers of both hands. For a while a contemptible look blazed in his eyes as he pondered an appropriate answer. As if suddenly awakening he stood erect, glanced sheepishly at everyone, and then bowed tersely. With a new found humility he turned towards Jonah and said: "Sir, forgive me my rudeness. I will answer your questions. Through the mail and UPS my church supplies me with the materials and money that I need to continue my work here. Three years ago I received a wireless computer that is solar powered from the people of my congregation. Considering that I would be living without electricity and plumbing, we all prayerfully decided to have this model developed by one of the engineers in our men's group, specifically for people like me in the field, so we can stay abreast of what's transpiring in these quickly changing days."

"Hmmm, I see . . ." Jonah responded. "Is this also how you know about our personal exploits?"

"Sir, we've known about your research for years. We truly do respect and admire you and your wife's work, and we discuss it often in meetings on-line. As you know, everything the University of Porto and Southern California publishes is in the public domain.

Your extensive works have been published on-line; even your music is known to us sir, I'm very fond of it. We've known about your intentions since March 2nd. Please remember that my job is to stay abreast of anything involved with the Rognvald's and the Mortiken. I apologize; I seem to have offended you in some way." The stranger looked remorseful and began chewing his lip again. Roxanne touched Jonah's shoulder to try and quell his mounting frustration.

"How could you *possibly* have known about our intentions on the second of March," Jonah blurted, "even I wasn't aware of them then?"

Captain Olaf stood and suggested that we all continue our conversations at a later date. It was already nine and our work was beckoning for us to commence. The stranger nodded and politely bid us all a good morning. Hurriedly he wrote something down on a piece of paper and handed it to the Captain. "It's my e-mail address, sir. Please contact me whenever there is a need. I am always at your service. Thank you once again for your hospitality. "After shaking the Captains hand he nodded politely at everyone, except Jonah and then disembarked. "There's so much more to talk about," he affirmed when he'd reached the jetty, "I pray Christ's richest blessings on your endeavors, a good day to you all." Regan reached down and retrieved the straw hat and put it back on. Circumspectly he glared up at Jonah from under the rim as he moved down the path. Jonah grimaced back, and then looked at Roxanne in disbelief. With clenched fists he hit the railings and stormed below decks.

Eighteen

Shallows of Three Rocks

The chemistry between Jonah and Regan was surprising and manifestly heated. Jonah had perceived something disturbing with what the man had shared. Several questions came to mind. First, was the stranger telling us the truth? And if so, why were Jonah, Roxanne, and the *Heimdall* being observed? How much did they know? And how far reaching was their knowledge? Exactly who were *they*, and why were *they* interested in our endeavors? It seemed as if some clandestine action had been launched against us, but I also saw the blessing in having been made known of these facts. We all decided it was better to let Jonah open up, when he was ready, instead of digging at him; it was imperative now that we focus our energies on the work before us this week. Hopefully, soon, we'd have answers to these troubling questions.

Captain Olaf weighed anchor at 9:15. After confirming his intentions with the harbor master, he maneuvered out through the narrow channel towards the open sea. Helga established our heading with the Captain, and shortly after, we were dieseling swiftly towards the shallows. John, Helga, and Roxanne were conversing about the sky over towards the west. In certain areas it was dark reddish and had developed undulating greenish borders. It looked bizarre. Jonah suggested it might be the magnetic bands which had, according to varied internet reports, become unstable in conjunction with the jet stream. There was also a very legitimate theory being promulgated in the same reports. This theory contended that an ever increasing number of coronal transients were the reasons for the drought. A ballooning of the suns outer corona, and solar prominences of flaming gases erupting from the suns surface, had begun reaching extraordinary heights of almost three million miles. When these transients reached the earth's magnetic field the bombardments were producing massive magnetic storms, intense heat, and changing weather patterns. Because of the frequency of these sun storms, especially in the last two years, frightening parameters were being established in various climates all over the earth, never before experienced in recorded history. Something incomprehensible was happening inside the sun. As it is, our atmosphere, the oceans, the land surfaces, and the snow and ice fields (which are the major components of the earth's climate system) all act in concert together to determine the earth's climate. But if anything at all changes the delicate chemistry between these complex components anything can happen to disrupt normal weather patterns anywhere. I knew now that the vexing drought patterns, over the last six years, had direct correlation to the anomalous increase of coronal transients the sun was producing. The Aurora Borealis, shimmering in swirling bands over the Alaskan forests, and now being seen in much lower latitudes, was caused by gases that glow when particles emitted by the sun struck the upper atmosphere. But this increase of bombardments was fifty times worse than anything ever recorded before; this is what the intelligentsia was hypothesizing had caused the abnormal shifts in earth's weather, magnetic fields, and the continuing changes in the color spectrum in the stricken areas. As a team, we'd agreed that these new widely discussed theories were the most plausible explanations we'd heard on the topic yet. We decided that we'd be keeping abreast, and always taking to heart, any new developments in the future.

The trip to the shallows occupied us with all the last minute preparations that trouble the beginning of any new dive. We would be using twelve aluminum 80 air tanks outfitted with standard K-valves and AGA Divator MKIII full face masks. These would allow us to communicate with one another wirelessly underwater for up to two miles. We'd be using a standard 50/50 travel mix to breathe underwater. John also had six forty cu ft pony bottles, and quick connects manifolds, we had the option to wear strapped next to our main tanks to extend our air supply. John said that he would assess the need for extra air on the first dive, depending on water temperature and depth, distance, and the physical complexity of our work. We had twenty bug bags available to carry everything we'd anticipated finding, and John had jury-rigged a winch for anything we were incapable of physically moving ourselves. John also had a waterproof digital camera he'd be attaching to his head harness with two small intensely powerful lights; it was his intention to let the crew watch what we were doing, especially when he was in the caves. In many circumstances this system would allow those onboard to see things that the divers often missed. We'd now completed an open visual inspection program of all the equipment and everything had checked out positive. John and Olaf were pleased and anxious to begin.

On the stern, Jonah and Roxanne were observing the shoreline through binoculars for any followers. Because (the unsettling encounter with) Regan had aggravated an apprehension that someone might try to sabotage our efforts, they'd decided to be as proactive about our safety as possible. Olaf ordered Helga to install new isolated frequency chips in all the radios and underwater wireless transmitters. Given the confession from Regan Pendleton, that they were openly eavesdropping on our private conversations, he wanted to maintain our privacy and with his excellent decision there was wholehearted agreement and optimism from everyone.

The cloud appeared as profoundly sedentary as it had the day before. Captain Olaf, again shaking his head in sheer astonishment, carefully steered us through the outer rainbow into the interior. The syrupy moisture once again soaked everything in a matter of seconds. About three minutes after the bow had penetrated the outside edge of the cloud we were safely inside. Everyone stared speechlessly when we were inside. Carefully the Captain maneuvered the stern north between the second and third rocks where the bottom was sandy and about ten feet deep. It was perfect here.

"Captain, I'd like to begin blowing bubbles with your permission." Olaf nodded back in agreement, and motioned for Garrett and me to drop the fore and aft anchors.

"John, have you decided who you're going to take?" Olaf asked after the anchors hit the water.

"First, I'd like to get in myself sir to evaluate the area, exactly what we're looking at, and then make a logical determination."

"Is everyone in agreement?" Captain asked, looking around at the group. Everyone nodded affirmative. "Let's get busy then, but first, let's pray for God's will to be done today. Jonah, would you lead?"

After prayer John climbed down onto the diving platform with only a face mask and dove into the water. He remained down for a minute and then resurfaced. Without a word he climbed back aboard and put on one tank and fins. Slipping the MKIII mask over his head he fell backwards into the water and disappeared from view.

John's first transmission came fifteen minutes later. "The hull is in excellent shape, Olaf. The bottom is mostly sandy, with a smattering of rocks. There are two twelve inch vents on the northwestern ledge releasing something into the water continually; it could be the sulfur component we were noticing in the air earlier. The northern edge is comprised of very rugged looking rocks and then the bottom drops off quickly, perhaps a hundred feet. Over the edge there the sand has a peculiar dark color, can't figure it out yet, it's different from the sand on the shallows. The face of the cliff is full of seaweed and little feather duster worms. It's strange really. These creatures are far more indigenous to the Mediterranean. The water is warmer here than I expected, but this will prove perfect for our endeavors. There's invertebrate life, too. I see coral and large sponges and the water's wonderfully clear. It seems there's visibility all the way down to the bottom, and, perhaps four hundred feet out. I'm going down farther Olaf; I'll report back in a few minutes. There's something stuck in the side of the cliff I want to investigate." We were all huddled around the receiver, captivated with John's report. Suddenly the quiet was rent by Roxanne's cry of astonishment. "Look at the sky . . . WOW!" The disturbance had found its way directly over the shallows and was beginning to immerse us in a dark reddish color that had changed the way everything appeared. The air became hot and heavy, and this was producing a low level irritability in each of us.

"*T*he color's changed down here, what's happening up there, clouds?" John asked.

"John, the atmospheric disturbance is directly above us, probably what you're noticing down there." Captain Olaf grumbled.

"Copy that Captain, John out." Thirty minutes went by before we heard another report from John. "We're over an enormous seamount people; it very well could be that old volcano you mentioned. The northern side drops down seventy-five feet to another sandy ledge and there are three caves in that cliff wall. We'll need to use all our diving lights to explore them. I've made my way around the western and eastern sides. The water is only about forty feet deep in those areas. I don't have enough air to hit the southern side. We'll have to do that in the next few dives. I'm heading back. Ask Garrett, Jonah and Gabriel to prepare; I'm going to need their help, John out."

Fifteen minutes later John was back aboard. Even though the anomaly was churning above us, and making everyone very irritable, John was talking excitedly about what we were going to accomplish in the next few hours. I could plainly see that he was in his principal environment as a diver, and now, as a new diving 'guppy', I felt safe under his tutelage.

"I'd like to explore the southern side tomorrow; I have a theory about something." John glanced over at the Captain for transference of leadership during the dive. Captain Olaf nodded vigorously and said: "John is in charge of all the dives while we're here. Give him your utmost attention and follow his instructions, I want no mishaps."

"Thanks Captain. I'd like to lay out simple quadrants," John continued. "Jonah; you've had experience in deeper waters, right?" Jonah nodded yes. "I've been down to one hundred feet John."

"Excellent! You'll be with me. We'll establish two shoot bags over the northern edge. Garrett and Gabriel will raise and lower them on two separate lines. We'll use these to bring up whatever we might find in the caves. Jonah and I will establish anchors on the cliff wall and install temporary lights. We'll need to explore these three caves; they're down about seventy-five feet. I swam through a thermocline sixty-five feet down on the northern wall. That means there's a boundary between two layers of water of different temperatures, it seems to be in conjunction with a halocline at the same depth. Meaning that in the same area we're working, we'll be encountering a boundary between two layers of water of different salinity, this shouldn't affect us though. There seems to be an outpouring of fresh water coming from somewhere around the vicinity of the three caves, which I don't quite understand yet. Hopefully we'll understand better when we're there. Alright folks, if there aren't any questions it's time to get to work. The environment up here is horrible, I hope it passes soon."

Thirty minutes later all four of us were suited up and in the water. Garrett, John, and Jonah were focused at once, but I was having a terrible time regulating my breathing. I began breathing too fast and started feeling sluggish and dizzy. Aware of my difficulties John swam over and instructed me to stay still, breathe slowly, and get accustomed to being underwater without moving. Then, when I felt less apprehensive, he told me to start swimming, and do slow somersaults, while I breathed regularly. John saluted and moved away. His advice really worked. Fifteen minutes later I was swimming around like a pro. All three gave a thumb up when they saw me swimming towards them. Complying with John's clear hand signals, I began helping them establish two lines for the bug bags. Roxanne radioed and told us the skies had cleared and the day was once again sunny and blue. The water transformed when the anomaly had moved away. Now it was a pale bluish green with great horizontal visibility. Bright sunlight, filtering down through small waves on the surface, was dancing in elongated striations on the sandy bottom. Jonah and John were forty feet below us; they were attaching lines and pulleys onto the rock wall. Their exhaust bubbles had begun to drift past us in varying sizes on the way up towards the surface. I could see the *schooner's* silhouette above floating lethargically. Garrett nudged me and pointed towards one of the rocks; a manta ray was flying lazily away from us towards the continental shelf in the Bay.

"Dude, we should put a saddle on that water bird and ride it."

"Go ahead man, you first." I gulped, cringing at the thought. Garrett was smiling now through his mask; he was bobbing up and down as if he was riding on the ray. I was learning to appreciate his strange sense of humor, and how it sometimes helped me deal with my perplexing fears. At first it sent a chill down my spine to realize how vulnerable we were underwater. We had no peripheral vision at all because of our masks. Still I felt comforted by the fact that God had allowed us to find this place, and I believed He was going to protect us here no matter what we encountered. Was this faith in action? John indicated to us that we'd accomplished enough for the first day, and we should probably all head back to the *surface.*

March 18

We were in the water at seven. At eight six lights had been successfully attached just outside the three cave openings; all were being fed by the *schooners s*econdary electrical generator. When the circuits were enabled the area was vibrantly illuminated. Like sudden sunlight breaking through dark clouds, rays of light stabbed out as undulating swords into the surrounding areas. After close scrutiny John and Jonah established the order in which they'd be exploring the caves as east to west. The formations around this area seemed quite ancient. They both concurred that the mount had been formed by a volcanic eruption but the volcano had been dormant for millennia. The first cave went thirty feet in and ended on a solid rock wall. There was nothing noteworthy here except two eels and a family of colorful sea anemones at the entrance. While Jonah and John were scrutinizing the cave walls, the agitation caused by their fins awakened a sleeping stingray about twenty-four inches in diameter. When it raced out of the cave it startled both of them and obscured the surrounding area in a murky haze of silt and sand for a few minutes. Our air was getting low so we resurfaced. While the tanks were being recharged we ate some lunch and discussed our continuing agenda. An hour and a half later we were all back in the water working. The second cave was only a small depression, perhaps twelve feet in diameter and about the same depth. Towards the rear there were two twelve inch vents in the roof that were pushing fresh water out with the velocity of fire hoses. John's hunch earlier had been correct; this was the explanation for the mysterious halocline in the area, and why around the entrance of the cave, and out at least a thousand yards north, the sand was filled with black basaltic particles and an inordinate amount of minuscule flotsam. The third cave turned out to be what John was hoping for. The entrance was smaller than the others. There was heavy suction at the entrance, similar to a vacuum cleaner, and when they got near the entrance it began to pull them in. Because of the possible danger John and Jonah buckled safety harnesses around their waists. These were connected to two spools of nylon rope, each eight hundred feet long, and anchored to the sea ledge with steel pegs. John entered this cave alone. After swimming in a hundred feet he reported he was seeing many irregular depressions filled with an incalculable amount of anything and everything held in place by the considerable pressure in the cave. Shells, seaweed, rocks, aluminum cans, netting, fishhooks, plastic bottles, and skeletons of fish were stuck to the walls as if they were glued. John said it looked like a pauper's art gallery. Our air tanks had begun to get low, again, so it was decided that tomorrow would be spent fully exploring this particular cave. John also decided that we'd be using two tanks so we could stay down longer than two hours.

March 19

Inside the cloud this morning a dense fog was making it hard to see any farther than six feet. Thankfully, after breakfast, the skies began clearing nicely and by eight we were in the water. John had fitted his MKIII headgear with the digital camera he'd designed when he was in the Navy Seals. The pictures coming back were crystal clear. We would all be wearing double #80 tanks, today, connected together by a small stainless steel manifold. This would allow us to stay down and work four hours uninterrupted. John's air mix was slightly different than ours today; he'd concluded that his descent into the cave might take him deeper than he'd previously anticipated, and he didn't want to have to turn back and waste time to procure a different gas mixture. Garrett and I were monitoring the two lines and keeping an eye below, above, and around the work area for any unexpected intrusions. Jonah was stationed right outside the cave entrance. He would be loading bug bags with whatever John found and then sending them up to us. After prayer John entered the cave at exactly 8:15. The following is what John communicated. His words were recorded on the vessels digital recorder as a working verbal log that we could refer to. The following entries are what we recorded and do reflect the occasional irregularities of John's MKIII breaking up.

8:15 am

"Just entered cave, appearance same as yesterday, pressure enormous going through opening—becomes less discernible when you're inside—definite feeling of more weight in here—different pressure than outside—cave is filled with junk everywhere—plenty of room to maneuver though. Beautiful shiny black walls, like skin of whales—I'm going back farther—John out."

8:30 am

"Reached rear wall of first cave, maybe five, six hundred feet in, two more tunnels branch off main tunnel—the smaller one right, maybe four feet in diameter—obstructed by sand—left tunnel same diameter—shut light off for a moment, utterly black, very spooky. Proceeding left tunnel, current through transition very powerful."

8:45 am

"Have reached area that's opened up a lot—can't see tunnel walls here anymore—depth gauge one hundred feet and moving deeper, do you still copy?"

"We copy John loud and clear. You breaking up occasionally, can't make out some of your words, your sentences are erratic." Jonah answered.

"We can hear you clear also John, but I agree with Jonah about the loss of some of your words." Helga added.

"Still receiving images *Heimdall*?" John asked.

"Affirmative, pictures are very clear." Helga confirmed.

"John, you're at the end of the safety tether, the spools are empty." Jonah said.

"Copy that Jonah—going to disengage, leave marker, large grouping of basalt columns here—good landmark to reference. Untied now, going forward, water very clear—calmer—strange pinnacle formations in this chamber everywhere—John out"

9:30 am

"In enormous chamber now—think its cone of volcano, swam around whole circumference—back now at basalt columns, pinnacles where tether tied off. Center of chamber very deep, spooky—farther than I can go with present air mix—equipment wrong—outside edges tons of junk—many narrow smooth pinnacles everywhere, strange! Light down here coming from above somewhere—need to investigate further. Three enormous columns here—must be directly under shallows—three rocks coming up from center of cone, struggling with conduction—water colder than tunnel—pulling heat from body quicker than should—going to continue though, have to find out why there's light here . . . John out."

10:30 am

"Dolphins here, can't believe it. Did they come past you Jonah?"

"No, nothing came past me. Garrett, Gabriel; did you see the dolphins come past your position?" Jonah asked.

"No, we haven't seen them since the first day we found this place boss." Garrett answered.

"Wonder how they got here . . . they want me to follow them . . . all nudging me in same direction, can you see this Helga . . . incredible. Have hour and a half more air . . . what do you guys think?" John asked.

"John, they got in some way other than the cave entrances, I think you should follow them for thirty minutes and then head back." Captain Olaf suggested.

"I agree also, go for it brother, and be careful." Jonah said.

"Copy that Olaf, Jonah . . . John out."

11:15 am

Dolphins led me to large sandy ledge up towards top of chamber can see more daylight here—can almost maneuver without lights now. Air getting low, water very calm—dolphin's excited small barnacled box and piece of metal pottery on ledge—I can see part of bow of boat buried in sand, Oh Lord—it must be part of the wreck!

On a hunch, John followed the dolphins after his last radio transmission. They brought him up and he surfaced in calm seas through another cave opening on the southern side of the shallows. It was a good thing; he had three minutes of air left when he resurfaced, he never could have made it back the way he came in. We all met aboard at 11:47 and decided to call it a day. Captain Olaf was anxious to get into the water, so he suited up and dove down to the caves entrance. After four trips back and forth, he successfully retrieved the lights and safety tethers and stowed them back aboard. He hadn't appreciated being on the radio today, and was anxious to be physically involved tomorrow. Then we'd be entering the site from the southern side, thanks to what the dolphins had shown us. As a reward Betsy fed them the thirty pounds of bait we'd purchased that night on the barges. The little buggers devoured every morsel and still wanted more.

Nineteen

A monumental discovery

March 20th

After prayer Captain Olaf resolved to flip-flop the schooners present position; now her stern would be facing south and her bow would face north towards the Bay of Biscay. As we saw it, this would offer a more advantageous working angle to winch up any artifacts or boxes we might retrieve from the site. We entered the water at exactly 7:30. Each of us had two tanks tied together with a modified steel manifold, hand held lights, bug bags, shovels, and a thin steel line from John's winch on the stern. Olaf would join us today and he was very excited and animated about his involvement. It'd been decided the night before that Garrett and I would be helping out with the physical aspects of retrieval today. Garrett had mentioned jokingly that their reasoning for this was because he and I were the youngest, the best looking, the most resilient, and they obviously needed our vibrant youthfulness to drag along their aging carcasses and carry on when they needed their naps. The night previous, Roxanne, Jonah and I had gone over all the information she and her assistants had accumulated from the Isla Flores site. From this effort we'd put together a physical description of the longboats the Rognvald's had used on their sojourn to Southern California. The vessels were about ninety-five feet in length, eighteen to twenty feet in the beam, with an enormous prow fifteen feet above the keel amidships. The vessels were clinker built with two inch thick oak planks, held together with something their metallurgists ostensibly had discovered that year, a mixture of steel alloyed with chromium and something else still unknown. We'd determined this was similar to our modern stainless steel and was virtually immune to rust and corrosion. The vessels were built with single lines of planking called strakes; these extending stem to stern along the hull of the vessel. The overall construction was strengthened by approximately thirty-five ribs. Steering was done with a large oaken rudder on a reinforced rear gunwale.

The dolphins were back again today and they were exhibiting a new trait; the nuzzling of arms, legs and shoulders. At first I was nervous; I'd never been in the water before with these creatures. Thankfully though, after a short time, I began to see this as an expression of their camaraderie with us and began to enjoy it. We reached the cavern John had discovered at 8:10 and entered through the southern entrance; it was a much easier ingress than the original entry. Roxanne radioed to tell us Helga was detecting three medium sized vessels on radar within twenty miles of our position. Two were sailing west and one seemed to be heading south directly towards our present location. While we were setting up I couldn't help but speculate, if we were fortunate enough to rediscover the 'Tempest' today, what would the ramifications of that be? To whom did the sword really belong? Would we have salvage rights and own it ourselves? If we found it, would we become a target for the Mortiken again? Would the clansmen consider it their property and try to take it away from us? Why hadn't anyone ever gotten as far as we had in the last three days? While Garrett and I set up the powerful lights, John, Jonah and Olaf began clearing away the sand that had accumulated around the wooden bow; this was the only part that was accessible and semi-visible. The construction had become fragile and our hitting it with the shovels caused the oak planks to separate; the wood remained intact though, and somehow maintained its original dimensions. This was an ancient Norse vessel, without doubt, and very similar to the description we'd put together the night before. The water was clear here, and there were no currents in this cavern. After thirty minutes of digging, Jonah finally decided to oblige the dolphins continual nudging and follow them fifty yards from our present position, Captain Olaf instructed me to take the largest light and go along with him. As Jonah approached the new area we both noticed another ledge, about twelve feet up, and what appeared to be another cave entrance almost entirely obscured by sand. The cavern was getting lighter, as the sun got higher, which allowed us to shut down half of the area lights we'd brought along. Jonah motioned for me to swim up and position the work light a few feet from the cave entrance. When it was in position we both began shoveling sand from the opening. We'd been shoveling for about fifteen minutes when the current picked up suddenly where we were working. Within a matter of seconds our area was thick with obscuring sandy clouds, but along the ledge where the others were working, I could see that the water was still remarkably calm. It seemed that the current was following a predetermined path and had skirted them; clearly it was flowing around them and then down into the crater and up the opposite side. After that it appeared to flow out the southern part of the cavern where we'd entered earlier.

"Helga, has anything changed above?" Captain Olaf asked.

"Yes sir! We're getting huge swells across the shallows; we're actually getting bombarded over the bow, it's covering the decks. It's a bit unnerving. Scuppers are all open, sir. We've shut the wheelhouse door, all the portholes, and all the doors going below so we won't flood, I'm concerned Olaf, will our anchors hold?"

Before the Captain could reply Jonah cried out. "The sand has shifted away from the entrance, the cave entrance is wide open and I can see boxes inside. Garrett, can you bring another light son?"

"No problem boss, I'm on my way."

"Helga . . . good call, lass, good call," the Captain answered. "You'll be alright! Tell the others the anchors will hold. You've done a fine job, all of you. Now, stay below until it passes."

"Roger that, Captain, thank you."

The strong currents had cleared where Jonah and I had been digging laboriously a few moments earlier. Inside I could see an assortment of boxes, semi-encrusted metal pottery, and a few oddly shaped copper lanterns. All were intact. On the first box we dragged out there was another faint etching of a sword and helmet over a large shield; this made it official, we'd found the site. The bow of the vessel was the only part of the ship that appeared intact, and Olaf and John's digging revealed only metal rivets and some two inch banding under the sand. Most of the structure had rotted away over the centuries and the second vessel was nowhere to be found. Given this John swam down into the crater as far as he could with his air mixture.

He reported back ten minutes later that he'd reached a depth of one hundred and fifty-five feet but had found no sign of wreckage; he was on his way back up. Removing what was still intact from the cave took about thirty minutes. We'd discovered eleven boxes of varying sizes, six lanterns, and eighteen pieces of metal pottery, including plates and cups. How this had all ended up in this one cave seemed somewhat miraculous to me. After putting what we wanted into the bug bags we swam them up. Then with ropes and nylon netting we helped escort the larger boxes to the surface. John's electric winch was proving invaluable to our retrieval efforts. With ease it brought the larger boxes to the surface. Roxanne was giddy with excitement as the dripping boxes were slowly hoisted aloft and lowered onto the wooden deck. With the help of the other girls, she removed everything from the nylon nets and laid them aside so they could be lowered again. Jonah swam back to the *Heimdall* and asked Betsy if she had any glass containers, like the kind used in preserving fruit. She confirmed she did. He asked if he could use two because he was going to take a sample of the water right where we were anchored, and, also, back inside the cave were we'd discovered the boxes and artifacts. His intention was to have the water tested for any unusual substances. Something had preserved these treasures and he was bound and determined to find out what that was.

A report had just come over the Navtex detailing another earthquake in the ocean. This one had registered 6.6 on the Richter scale, and was centered five hundred kilometers south of Ireland, and three hundred kilometers off the western coast of Brittany France. Warnings of possible thirty foot tidal waves had been dispatched to all vessels and freighters in the Bay of Biscay. The city of Brest in Brittany, the cities of Helston, Penzance and Plymouth in Cornwall England, and also the entire northern coast of Spain were on alert.

Was this what had caused the barrage of waves at the shallows? Had God protected us someway with this?

Lizzy contacted us about Rorek; he was ready to come home. Thankfully he was breathing freely again and the infection was gone. Lizzy and he listened amazed as Helga shared about our incredible discovery and subsequent progress the last four days. They were super anxious to be back aboard and resume their duties. Captain Olaf asked Helga to confirm our intentions with them of leaving the shallows today. Our journey to La Coruna was about to begin.

Jonah and Roxanne's flight was scheduled to leave La Coruna tomorrow at three pm. Their flight would stop over on Ponta Delgada for thirty minutes and then on to Newark New Jersey. Jonah would board a flight there to Baltimore Maryland, and from there on to San Diego. As we were preparing to leave we received an e-mail from Regan Pendleton. Jonah was livid. How he'd gotten Helga's e-mail address was a mystery. Regan expressed concern about our progress and wondered if we'd found the Tempest. He was also curious if we'd safely weathered the enormous waves that had inundated the area. At Jonah's behest, the Captain ordered Helga not to respond until God had given us wisdom about what we should do with this man's impositions. Because of time constraints, with everyone's itinerary, investigating what we'd found would have to wait until we were sailing between La Coruna and Porto Portugal. Everything, then, would be photographed, notated, and e-mailed to Roxanne and Jonah in encrypted attachments.

The dive was over. And what an adventure it'd been. What we'd been privileged to discover *had been a miracle by any standard.* Several of the larger cases had dimensions similar to what the petraglyphs and runes hinted at as being the case holding the Tempest. Now there was great excitement in all of us knowing that there was the possibility of a magnificent discovery. After thanking God for his great mercies, and also for keeping us safe during our work, we took some final pictures of the site and then Captain Olaf motored out. Once we'd retrieved the Ceawatch buoy we headed west, towards La Coruna, accompanied, once again, by our resolute friends the dolphins.

Twenty

8 stone tablets

Everything we'd salvaged had finally dried. After prayer we decided to open the largest and heaviest box in the collection. Roxanne set up a small table on deck. She had a ledger, her laptop, and a digital camera for the process. Carefully we photographed the distinguishing markings on the lid and the four sides. Measurements were taken, and sketches were drawn of all five views; this part of the work Roxanne always pursued alone. After pondering the dimensions from a more comprehensive perspective, I came to the conclusion that the case maintained the exact outside dimensions of the Rognvald vessels, at a 12:1 ratio. Considering the vessels were 95 feet in length, 1/12 of that length would be approx 7.91 feet, and, 1/12 of 20 feet at the width of the beam would be approx 1.66 feet. This particular box had almost precisely those dimensions, ninety-three inches by eighteen inches. It had been fitted together and sealed by highly skilled craftsmen. After thirty minutes of effort John finally broke the hardened seals and, under Roxanne's watchful eye, slowly pried the top off. The inside of the box was remarkably dry but reeked of something that reminded us of formaldehyde. Inside were eight smaller boxes. Each was uniformly and smoothly sealed, which gave the appearance of one uniform block of wood. On each of the lids was a sword and helmet over a shield. The boxes had been placed in a numbered sequence, left to right, as if to infer an order in which they should be opened or removed. These inner boxes were crafted meticulously and this had John mulling various approaches to opening them without ruining them. After a time of intellectualizing together, and laughing at Garrett's engaging humor, it was determined that the seals were hardened wax dabbled over with resin and sanded smooth; we assumed that this was what made the seam invisible to the wood surrounding it. During one of Garrett's humorous barrages we decided that one of his ideas was the best solution he'd suggested up to that point. The idea was to use a small Map Gas torch, with a wide tip, to try to shrink the seal. This proved productive and, a short time later, the first box was unsealed and opened. Garrett started to strut and flex his muscles. Then he began rapping along with his raucous verbalized beats that he was 'the man with the plan', and that 'the dingy would be lost without his steel trap of a brain'. For a while we laughed hilariously. These moments, when everything seemed to flow in harmony between us, were awesome.

There was a perfectly preserved stone tablet with small runic symbols etched over one side inside the first box. First, Roxanne stared without speaking, and then she hugged Jonah with a childlike fervency and began crying. After ninety painstaking minutes we had removed all eight tablets from eight small boxes. During the process Roxanne and Jonah were unwaveringly focused on making sense of the construction and interpreting the symbols into English. Later, at dinnertime, they both burst into the galley flushed with excitement. She informed us that these eight tablets revealed something entirely unknown from all their personal research and studies in the past. "Because these runes are pictures of sorts," Roxanne began, "and do not represent a linear thought process contingent on grammatical correctness, some of the writing seems to be the emotional frame of mind the writers were in while they were composing. What that means to us is it will probably sound a bit stilted in our interpretations into English. Needless to say, brothers and sisters, our Lord God has truly blessed us in this find, and, surprisingly enough, there are also several confirmations about what Regan Pendleton told us about earlier this week. Here's what they say:

<u>Tablets numbered 1-3</u>:

Legend has it; tale of Baaldur, hero man/god of light was killed by a mistletoe dart thrown by mischievous contriving Loki. In glowering shadows of eventide, evil was pronounced against clans of Rognvald, Valhalla shed tears of wrath. The greatest misfortune ever to befall men and gods required vengeance. Lovers of Baaldur united against the only enemy they knew, followers of the God of Truth and Light.

<u>Tablets numbered 4-6</u>:

We the many, followers of Jesus, son of Most High, hath united against evil clouds of Baaldur's hordes. Blood flowed deep on fields of sorrow and death reached up in hunger to devour us, generations fell lifeless in youth, heaps like mountains grew, while children screamed for retributions, and rivers of soothing. In bloody tribulations the vision came to great King Agar to build fifteen craft of new design and sail south to freedom, leaving along the journey, seeds on barren crags to multiply and tell stories of great men of battle. A sword was forged by the metallurgist Gamelin, metal undefiled in battle, plunged forth into the dragons head and inscribed: ***'Christ before all else'***

Tablets numbered 7-8

"This next one is a variation of Eddic Prose," Roxanne explained. "It appears that these two tablets were put in as an afterthought. Perhaps the need to do so came from a vision after construction was complete, or perhaps when they were preparing to embark on the voyage, or even after they'd done so."

Change has been thrust upon us

Fortune smiles indistinct in morning and eventide shades

Shadows embrace the unsuspecting travelers in vile lies

Treachery that lessens the path of Light and Truth

Hearts beat in sorrow watching our beloved shores diminish in the distant suns red setting in hope we unite under the symbol noble Gamelin in visions procured ***'Christ before all else'*** *inscribed upon helmets, swords, and shields, the symbol of King Agar, the beloved, taken yet a fortnight ago in deaths inexhaustible repose*

Together and wretched we sail the raging unknown to find destinies embrace and complete the vision in honor to our great king

In death he salutes us, and we will join him in New Jerusalem's golden sanctuary, to a place higher than Valhalla. In faith we will attain what was offered by the Christ's holy sacrifice our Eternal King and First love God, Holy and Omnipotent will grant us peace, wisdom, strength, and guide us through the raging battles that surely await us

In victory and Truth we claim what the Baaldurians have encroached upon, and the encumbrance of their deceptions we spit upon. Behind we leave fallen men, women, children, and heroes, alive only in memory we salute them in honor and forthrightness. Together we will raise the ***Tempest*** *in victory in that day of many collisions*

Twenty-one

Farewell to Jonah and Roxanne/ our encounter with a peevish spy

My respect for Jonah and Roxanne's awesome work had grown decidedly in the last week. Both were truly gifted individuals. Our time working together had gone by swiftly, but what we'd experienced and accomplished together was so much more than I could ever have imagined. When Roxanne had completed her analysis we all felt acutely aware of the responsibility we had with each other, and with God's help we would surely accomplish our journey and achieve its fruition. We were anticipating seeing Roxanne again around April 1st on the island of Flores. At that time she'd be boarding for the long journey across the Atlantic Ocean. There was a possibility that we wouldn't be seeing Jonah for a long while and that grieved us. Jonah was an integral part of what we were doing and his absence would surely be an encumbrance. Our dear friends influence, spiritually and intellectually, would have to again be consigned to the virtual realm. He reminded us that our finances must be used judiciously, and he encouraged us to read God's word daily and pray unceasingly about everything together.

"Our individual paths are in God's hands, and our journey is rife everywhere now with danger," Jonah explained. "We all must exhorted walk in faith and patience with the things we don't understand. Together or apart; we're still working towards the same goal. Our lives are not in *our* hands. The visions we've been given are Holy and only for us. Our timing is not God's timing, so we all need to be patient, and wait expectantly on the Holy One for the fulfillment of those plans. Let me quote something from Isaiah 40:31. *'But those who wait on the Lord shall renew their strength; they shall mount up with wings like eagles, they shall run and not be weary, they shall walk and not faint.'* Roxanne and I love you all dearly. This last week with you has been astonishing. Remember what we've accomplished as a team, something no one else in history has been able to do. Who can really say what God has planned in the near future for us? It's very possible we could be back working together within the month."

The whole crew responded with a hearty amen. I reminded everyone that the grant wasn't our only source of financial support anymore. My father's on-line account now had twenty thousand dollars in it and by the end of the month it would have thirty thousand. Father was more than willing to fund whatever was necessary to accomplish our goals; he was fully behind us now. As of today Captain Olaf's intentions were steadfast; we'd be sailing into the Caribbean Sea, through the greater and Lesser Antilles, and then on to Panama. The only other possibility was a much longer route. But this would only become a viable alternative based on the weather, drought conditions, geological anomalies, or anything else that may happen. The second option would take us south past the Falkland Islands, the Isla de Los Estados, around the legendary Cape Horn in the Southern Ocean, and then north up the western coast of South America. As of now Olaf and Jonah were still anticipating entering the Pacific Ocean through the Panama Canal, and then sailing northwards to the Islas Revillagigedo. All of us quietly knew, based on our past experiences of plans suddenly changing, that time would tell us whether or not we'd be sticking to this schedule.

The distance to La Coruna was about one hundred and fifty nautical kilometers. Presently we were sailing southwest along Galicia's rugged northwestern coastline past an assortment of verdant mountainous islands. It was gorgeous. The weather, according to the Captain, was so good that we wouldn't need to depend on our satellite navigation (GPS) or radar; we were making excellent time. In the wee morning hours, Captain Olaf pointed out the famous 'La Torre de Hercules' (the tower of Hercules) constructed in the second century AD by a Portuguese architect. It was well lit and stood majestically in the distance. This was the largest and oldest (still working) Roman lighthouse in the entire world. It was sixty-eight meters tall, and one hundred and twelve meters above sea level. Spanish legends told that Hercules had battled the evil giant Gerion here. He had killed the giant and built the tower on top of his bones and grizzly remains. Because of this legend La Coruna had incorporated the skull and crossbones image as part of the cities coat of arms.

Captain Olaf navigated into the La Coruna harbor at 8:15 am. The harbor, we'd been told, was full of wrecks and the chances of fouling an anchor, or crunching a hull, were well above average. Captain asked me to climb up to the crow's nest and sight the water below to avoid any possibility of calamity. It was an excellent idea and I was able to help him successfully steer around several disasters that could have fouled us terribly. When we dropped the anchor, twenty yards from shore, I noticed heavy linked chains were draped between four foot concrete posts along the whole length of the colorfully tiled boardwalk. The middle of the walkway was lined with round white glass globes on tall metal posts, and the waterfront buildings were painted brightly in reds, blues, greens and whites, similar to what we'd seen on the old fisherman's skiff off of Concello de Carino.

Jonah and Roxanne were ready to disembark at nine am. Reluctantly we all hugged and said our farewells. John loaded everything aboard the raft and then took them ashore. A taxi was waiting just off the water front. After they'd unloaded the Ceawatch Buoy and their suitcases, and had stuffed them into the taxi and on the roof, they turned, smiled, and blew kisses to us all. As they pulled away Roxanne's saddened face appeared in the rear window; fervently she waved goodbye as they motored up one of the streets out of sight.

Lizzy called Olaf at ten; they'd be rendezvousing with us that afternoon around four on the docks. Rorek was fed up with inactivity; he was so bored and cantankerous that he'd become difficult to deal with. Despite all his pissing and moaning the hospital was not releasing him until three today. Captain shared also that Lizzy had met an older gentleman at the hospital a few days earlier; apparently he'd shared a strangely compelling story with her. Before his retirement he'd owned a company that patrolled the Rias Baja's, specifically the 'Ria Pontevedra', and one farther south near the city of Bayona called the 'Ria de Vigo'. For forty years his company's responsibilities were to locate squatters and poachers and report them to the local authorities. According to him, there'd been an ancient legend passed down many generations about a tribe of Norsemen concealed miles upstream in the Pontevedra Province. These areas, we'd discovered, were mountainous landscapes, with thousands of complex inlets where rainfall traveled many miles down rivers, streams, and rivulets, and eventually emptied into the sea. Considering this, one could explore them for a lifetime and never fully compass their complexities. Like many other legends this story of the Norsemen was shared often around campfires, and on fishing expeditions, or when men got drunk and bragged about everything they knew and had done. There were numerous writings and sketches of what others had seen in several private collections (in Vigo) and all seemed to affirm the stories the previous generation had written about. Shadowy tales abounded about long boat sightings in the early mornings. But when the clansmen knew they were being watched they had simply disappeared into the mists. Although some adventurous types had pursued them, nothing was ever physically discovered that corroborated the many recorded sightings and old writings. Lizzy mentioned also that the old man had drawn a map years ago, and that he was willing to sell it for one thousand Euros. He had assured her the map would take us into remote places, rarely explored, and suggested there was a real possibility we could accomplish what no one else had ever been able to. Captain Olaf was certainly intrigued.

"Considering the success we'd just had on the Shallows, it might be beneficial to our overall efforts to attempt this," He mused.

After we'd prayed I reminded him that the maps cost was of no consequence. The on-line account was for situations exactly like this one. I also suggested that the information Lizzy had received from the old gentleman was not fortuitous, his story and map had offered us another opportunity for research in a geographical area that we'd never even considered looking before. And besides, it was on the way to our next destination, Porto.

"Captain, I think the idea is worth pursuing. We just might find another lost colony; that'd be way cool." Garrett said, perking up.

"I'm inclined to do it son. But I'd like everyone to go along this time, you know, if we do make an expedition out of it. I suggest that we put our heads together with Rorek and Lizzy and then make our final decision. What do you guys think?" The Captain looked around at everyone. Helga suggested we pray again before we decided anything. After we had we tentatively agreed to pursue the plan as long as Rorek and Lizzy both agreed. Betsy wanted to go into town for the evening. She suggested that instead of meeting Rorek and Lizzy on the docks that we rendezvous with them in the 'Plaza de Maria Pita' and have dinner in the outdoor café there. Captain Olaf nodded eagerly.

"An excellent suggestion Betsy; I love it. Let me radio Lizzy. I believe they can walk to the plaza from the hospital, it would do us good to see some sights and relax, perhaps even listen to a live band." Eagerly Garrett shook his head, and started playing his invisible drums and dancing. "Maybe they'll let me jam Cap. Yah dudes, dig it!" Garrett sang, spinning in circles. In the spirit of the moment the crew picked up an invisible instrument and started jumping and jamming along with our little brother. Suddenly the day had an exceptional enthusiasm to it.

Lizzy and Rorek were delighted and laughingly told us that they'd heard the main taxi service in La Coruna had (an hour earlier) gone on strike unexpectedly. Because of this there was no public transportation anywhere in the city. Both agreed that our suggestion was timely and that walking sounded very appealing. Plans were made to rendezvous with them at seven by the statue of Maria Pita. Captain called the harbor police to inform them about our intentions for the evening. He also explained to them that we were a funded research vessel and asked if they could keep an eye on things while we were in town. After mulling the prospect the sergeant agreed that he would help us for the sum of one hundred and fifty Euros. For this meager sum, (as he put it) they would patrol our anchorage every hour until six the following morning. Though captain balked at this he begrudgingly agreed to the terms. We found the sergeant waiting by the post office on the waterfront. With a certain amount of eagerness he relieved us of the money, stuffed it into his pocket, and shook the captain's hand.

"Have a wonderful time tonight in my beautiful city." The sergeant's smile was tepid.

"Thank you, we will," the Captain nodded with a grunt.

La Coruna's streets are narrow and evocative of many of the European villages I'd seen in my early travels. Only here old women weren't carrying bundles of sticks on their heads down cobblestone streets, and there were no chimney sweeps hobbling about like blackened snowmen looking for work. As we walked we took pictures of a few interesting churches, museums, and exhibitions of sculpture and art, seemingly on almost every street corner. We were amazed at the glut of eateries and bars; they were scattered about like pennies in a wishing fountain. Only a block from the waterfront chandleries began popping up everywhere. Some of them catered to the fisherman's needs, some to the leisure yachtsmen's needs, but most seemed geared to the fashion conscious sailor whose only real concern was being color coordinated so he could look the part in the local pubs and restaurants. The city also loved its local *Galego Beer*. There were signs everywhere describing the pleasures that consuming it would bring. And oh my, the scantily clad buxom women that would swarm around you while you imbibed large amounts of it.

"I really hate the lies that advertising pawns off on us. You know what I mean big bro John?" Garrett asked. John grunted and shook his head disdainfully.

"Since I was a teenager I've seen through the deceptions little brother. The biggest problem I've found, though, is the incredible amount of dummies that buy the lies, hook, line, and sinker." Garrett shook his head in agreement, and so did I.

Joie de vivre (a keen enjoyment of living) was bubbling in the air as the city slowly stretched out of its daytime lethargy and began putting on its festive nighttime costumes. The streets had begun pulsing now and, as the *buskers* and *promenaders* prepared to ply their colorful trades that evening, the excitement around us began seeping into our souls. About an hour into our walk we passed a large indoor market that Betsy immediately fell in love with. After fumbling in her purse for a piece of paper she wrote down the address to put into our computer records. There were many colorfully appareled people laughing and bargaining around the outdoor bins; all of them were looking for the best deals. Inside an ample variety of fruits and vegetables lay in colorful rows, tempting us to pick them up, caress them, smell them, buy them, and eat them. As it had been in the past, (on occasion) Garrett's inquisitive eyes noticed something curious in our immediate vicinity and told the Captain what he'd seen. Olaf glanced over discreetly at the man for a moment. Then he asked Garrett to watch for a while to see if he was indeed following us, and, if he was, to inform John later. Garrett nodded.

We'd been walking La Coruna's side streets for a while when Garrett finally nudged John and me. He motioned over towards a tall, square shouldered, fortyish man, in a beige panama suit, wearing a hat of similar color and brown sharkskin loafers. Garrett told us the man had been shadowing us since we'd left the post office; he'd appeared from an alley a few minutes after the Captain had paid the sergeant. Garrett said the only reason he'd become aware of him was he saw the man quickly turn away when he thought he was being observed. Obviously his cloak and dagger abilities hadn't progressed past the second grade; he'd been busted by an eighteen year old. Garrett noticed the man had maintained the same distance from us for over an hour. When we stopped, he stopped. And when we entered a premise he watched us from across the street, pretending to be interested in something else until we finished and came out. At one point, Garrett suggested we sneak up behind him and flip off his hat, but John grabbed his arm and smilingly shook his head no. Later, when we'd stopped for some tea, we watched the man cautiously find a table next to a market across the street and order a drink. While he was waiting he made a call from his cell phone. As the conversation progressed his mood turned sour, and for a brief moment he swore and gestured wildly. During this fit his coat fell open; there was a revolver in a holster under his left arm. John bristled and whispered something to Olaf, who nodded in agreement. It was clear to all of us that the man hadn't gotten what he wanted in the conversation. With childish impulsiveness he slammed the phone shut, shoved it into his breast pocket, swore loudly again, and kicked a wooden box of oranges in front of the market. Suddenly aware of his actions, he glanced furtively up and down the street to see if anyone had seen him, and then quickly hunched down in his chair. Scowling bitterly he gulped his drink and ordered another.

"The funniest thing about that dweeb is he's not even aware that we're aware of him. What a pink panther wannabe." Garrett laughed cynically. We all shook our heads and laughed loudly in agreement.

After finishing our herb teas, we continued taking in the colorful sights and sounds of the awakening nighttime city. In the distance the statue of 'Maria Pita' was just becoming visible. The last hour people in the streets had quadrupled and we found ourselves having to leisurely elbow our way through the celebratory throngs. Various musical groups were filling the cooling nighttime air with a noisy clamor. Suddenly, through the din, we began hearing Rorek and Lizzy yelling for us up the street. Betsy was the one that finally spotted them while standing on a chair. Our reunion was wildly uninhibited; laughing, hugs, kisses, and all of us dancing sailors' jigs in the middle of the street. We were causing a bit of a hubbub, but really didn't care about the smirks we were getting from some of the more hoity-toity snoots sticking their noses up in the air as they walked past us. It was so awesome to see them both again. You just don't realize how important someone is, or how much you love them, until they're not around for a while. Rorek had shed at least twenty pounds. He looked healthy and fit and his facial color had returned to normal. After we'd found a table Olaf brought them up to date about what'd happened since we'd last seen them a week ago. During the conversation we'd been keeping an eye on the peevish man standing at a mobile bar across the square. Out of the blue John grunted scornfully and stood up; in a second he'd vanished into the crowd. A few minutes later John had confronted him; within seconds he was talking heatedly right up in his face. Garrett was sitting on the edge of his chair watching John like a hawk. If John had given Garrett even the slightest look, he would have scrambled over there in an instant to give assistance. Finally, after a few moments of bickering, John grabbed his jacket collar and began escorting him in our direction. No one in the crowd cared. Much to his dismay he was forced to acquiesce to John's much greater strength and, when they'd reached our table, he'd become quite red-faced. Garrett, seeing John motion with his head, pushed a chair out with his foot, and, with both hands on his shoulders, forced him to sit down. Then he began swearing at John and threatening to get his relatives to take care of us. Lizzy asked the man if he would like something to drink. His rankled demeanor changed. For a moment he sat staring blankly. Then, as his predicament began taking root in his mind, he began to whimper and mumble in Spanish. Both his hands went up to his temples in frustration, and he started nervously fingering the hair around his sideburns. When John demanded that he open his jacket the heel of his left foot began flopping erratically against the chair leg. When he refused John forcibly reached down into his coat and pulled the 32 caliber revolver out of the holster and slipped it under a napkin.

"What's your name? The Captain asked. The peevish man shook his head, "No habla," he mumbled. Angered, the captain moved his chair closer and leaned into him. "What do you want, and why are you following us?" He asked a little more forcefully. "And don't you dare tell me you don't understand English; we heard you talking on the phone in English." The peevish man's eyes had begun to redden and he'd started glancing around fearfully. "Is someone watching us?" the Captain whispered. After hearing the question he broke down.

"I'm only doing what they told me to do." The man sniveled in broken English. "They're paying me a fortune, five hundred Euros; I think they're watching me right now."

"We *will* protect you while you're here with us, *but*, I want to know why you're following us," The Captain demanded.

"They want what they think you've found." He said, finally relenting, his shoulders slumping forward. "They've been watching you in Carino sir; two days ago they tried to intercept you on your diving site. Three ships were sent to box you in but all three failed. They're still all floating dead in the water, it's the strangest thing I've ever known, all three engines quitting at the same time. When they knew you were going to dock here they hired me to follow you and get as much information as I could. They assumed that you would drink and brag with each other. Then I could sit close to you and record what I'd heard." Sheepishly he pulled out a small hard disc recorder and handed it to Garrett. "You don't drink! And I can tell that you are good people. Please forgive me! I needed the money; I am not an evil man. I swear it! PLEASE, I swear it faithfully."

"Who are *they*? What do they know about us? Can you point them out to us?" John growled the questions in his ear.

"I've never seen them. Please; they call whenever they need my help and send a courier afterwards with the cash. They caused the taxi strike this afternoon; they knew you'd have to walk and I could easily get close to you. Please; I've seen their boat. It's in the harbor now; it followed you in this morning from up north."

"What does it look like?" Lizzy demanded.

"Blue aluminum hull, forty-five feet, white stripes, black sails, it's called the *Wormwood*."

"Once again . . . what do they want from us?" The Captain asked firmly, grabbing his shoulder.

"Please, forgive me sir; they desperately want the sword they think you've found." The Captain sat up straight with a shocked expression. "Please," the man cowered, "they say it has priceless treasure in it and a map inscribed on the blade. It's all I know, I swear, it's all I know sir. Please, can I go now, I feel sick."

"Who are they? Answer me right NOW!" John demanded, grabbing his upper arm. The man slumped down broken in spirit. With head in hands he softly mumbled: "It's the Mortiken sir; the evil ones want the sword, they think you have it."

Twenty-two

Sinking the *Wormwood* / the map

Quickly I paid for the meals. The number on the debit card was on an encrypted account father had established, and couldn't be traced in any of the conventional ways. Thankfully we didn't have to worry about anyone tracking our progress, or knowing our whereabouts, by how we used this particular card. Our transactions were safe. I suggested that we give the man some money for the information. Olaf agreed. When I handed him the money, the man grabbed my arm and pulled himself up to my ear and whispered: "Be careful, I think they're everywhere now. Merciful young master, please be careful. You've been called to something very great. I can feel it!" With that, he stood up, wiped off the front of his pants, adjusted his coat and hat, and vanished into the shadows around the side of the café. I wondered how the Mortiken could have possibly known about the Tempest. Even we didn't know if we had it yet. Were there really precious gems in the sword and a map inscribed on the blade? For a few moments we sat puzzled, but Rorek, coming back to his senses, suggested that we get back to the *Heimdall* at once. We all agreed.

"Oh sheesh, I forgot to give back his recorder," Garrett blurted as we were preparing. "I have it right here. I'll be right back boss." Garrett turned on heel and took off running full speed in pursuit of the man. "Senor, un momento, SENOR, SENOR . . . wait . . ."

"Garrett . . . GARRETT!" The Captain bellowed loudly. But Garrett was gone in an instant around the corner of the building.

"John, please go after him now!" The Captain cried out.

"He forgot his pistol, too, Captain," John yelled back over his shoulder, "I've got it here in my pocket; I'll get Garrett back sir, please don't worry." John was gone in a flash, following the same path the man and Garrett had taken moments earlier.

Ten minutes later Garrett and John stumbled back around the corner of the café with baffled looks on their faces; it was immediately clear that something terrible had happened. "Olaf," John gulped with an ashen face, "the man is dead. We found him about a block away next to a bench. Someone caved in his head with a club. We've got to leave this place, NOW!"

Looking around tensely Olaf pulled on his windbreaker and drank the last of his tea. "John, you and Garrett keep an eye behind us; let's get out of here now!" Grabbing Helga and Betsy's hands all three took off running. "Can you run brother?" Olaf shouted as he moved past Rorek. "No problem!" He assured him. As we moved out of the square, and onto one of the streets, we heard someone yell that the taxis were running again. Garrett hailed one and, much to the driver's annoyance, all eight of us stuffed inside. Twenty minutes later we'd reached the docks. After piling out, and paying the irritable driver, we took off running in the direction of the raft. Along our route, sitting on one of the harbor benches was the old man Lizzy had talked with earlier in the week. Lizzy stopped and extended her hand. "Senor Augusta, how very nice it is to see you again. Gabriel honey, would you come over please." He told us he'd been waiting six hours. How he'd known he could find us along this particular path was somewhat mystifying. He was curious to know if we'd decided to purchase the map. From former discussions we'd already decided that having it would be beneficial to the mission so Captain nodded his approval, after which I counted out one thousand Euros and put it into the man's hand.

"Muchas gracias," He nodded with a huge smile.

"You are most welcome, sir," I nodded and shook his hand. Next Lizzy hugged the man and offered him our collective thanks.

"Via con dios senora," he bowed politely to Lizzy. "I am most honored to have made your acquaintance; all the best to you and God bless you all." Waving he turned and shuffled off into the darkness.

Once aboard the raft John started scanning around the harbor through the binoculars. About halfway back he cried out and pointed, "I found the *Wormwood, Olaf!"* When we were all back aboard, and after we'd stowed the raft, Olaf, Rorek, and John climbed up into the wheel house and shut the door. Thirty minutes later the door flew open and John bolted down the stairs. Stopping a moment, he tossed the spies pistol out into the harbor and then ran below. When he returned, he was suited up with an air tank, an MKIII face mask, fins, a spear gun, a small hex cutting torch that he'd attached to his chest on the golden triangle, and a small light.

"Before John goes to work I want you all to know what we've decided." Rorek motioned us all together. "We're going to disable the *Wormwood.* He'll use the Hex torch to cut off the prop, the shaft, and the rudder. He'll also be cutting three holes in the hull at specific places, one being the approximate position of the bilge, one where the shaft exits the hull, and one just underneath the bow. The vessel will sink, over several hours, and be useless for anything but salvage." As Rorek explained further, the ladies began to express misgivings.

"What if someone's aboard?" Betsy asked nervously.

"What if someone sees the light? Helga added.

"What if someone hears him? Goodness Olaf, a man was brutally killed tonight. Shouldn't we just leave and forget about it? Oh goodness me, I feel uneasy about this," Lizzy complained.

"I can help, John, if you need me," Garrett offered.

"Wait a minute, just slow down here," the Captain interrupted, "we've already weighed the risks and they're worth taking. Garrett, John's going alone; remember, he was a Navy Seal, and he's been in much worse situations than this one. We've scrutinized the vessel with the big telescope and can't see anyone aboard. It's safe, so don't worry. The light and sounds are negligible; the vessel is far removed from any of the others in the harbor, see!" The Captain pointed. I could see that he was correct; there was at least two hundred yards between the *Wormwood* and every other vessel anchored in the harbor. "Let's pray now, and let John do his work. We're getting out of here as soon as he's back."

After an impassioned prayer from Lizzy, Helga hugged and kissed John and told him to be careful. Silently he slipped into the dark waters and sunk from sight. I mentioned to the Captain that we'd been aboard at least an hour now and the police cruiser hadn't showed up once to check our vessel. "I had a premonition that they were crooked, Gabriel, especially after I shook the sergeant's hand." Captain grimaced disdainfully and shook his head. "Keep an eye out anyway, ok son?" Sadly they never once showed up. Captain Olaf shut off the running lights and started the diesel. Garrett and I pulled up the forward anchor and locked down the capstan. Rorek uncovered the spotlight and got it ready to guide us through the harbor entrance. The Captain loaded a shotgun and put it down next to the wheelhouse door, where anyone could get to it in a matter of seconds.

The city was alive and noisy now. Everyone was drinking and dancing and making merry. We knew that during these revelries it was a good time to make our escape. Waiting for John was interminable; seconds seemed to us like minutes, and minutes seemed like hours. We were all huddled together now near the starboard railings, checking our watches, watching the harbor walk for anything suspicious, and looking for any sign on the water that may indicate John's return. Eighty minutes passed before he at last radioed to tell us that the mission had been successful, the *Wormwood* had been permanently disabled. Ten minutes later we saw his head surface a few yards off the port stern. As soon as he was on the diving platform Olaf maneuvered us out of the harbor entrance and into the ocean west towards Malpica. It was four hundred kilometers to the 'Ria de Vigo' and we were going to make good use of the time.

March 22nd

At 6:30 I was jolted awake by Helga and Lizzy's perfervid conversation. Apparently our determined women had awakened early and very keyed up to begin. They'd discovered an elaborately carved box inside one of the sealed crates. The key we'd discovered on the top of the Bares fit the lock. But opening it, according to them, was proving difficult due to the corrosion inside the ancient mechanism.

"Goodness," Captain Olaf exclaimed, taking a few steps back to size up the third box, "could this be the sword?"

"Oh Olaf, wouldn't that be something?" Lizzy gushed.

"Yah, maybe it is the sword. But the only way we'll know is if we figure out how to open the damn thing." Rorek grunted.

John arrived with a sleepy eyed Garrett by his side. Immediately John knelt down to examine the container. "Dudes, I was havin' some righteous dreams." Garrett grumbled. "This had better be good."

"The seals are different than the box with the tablets." John concluded. "What do you think Gabriel?" After scrutinizing them a moment I could see these *were* somewhat different; they looked like hardened resin seals. After a brief lesson from John, Rorek took on the tedious responsibility of loosening and shrinking the seals with a small torch. Since this was going to take some time Captain asked me to come up to the wheelhouse and help him. Betsy retreated into the kitchen and began preparations for breakfast while Lizzy, John, Helga and Rorek stayed outside the engine room to continue their efforts.

An hour later the breakfast bell rang; all dropped what they were doing and congregated in the galley to eat. Captain Olaf asked me to bring his breakfast up to the wheelhouse; he told me that if I cared to, I could help out with the work down below. After we'd eaten our labors continued on for three more hours. The ladies retreated to catch up on chores, and I got out the digital camera and began a step by step picture log of what was happening. The hardened resin seals had finally been loosened around the entire perimeter. Now, the task of removing the lid would begin. John and Rorek ascertained it was tightly fitted with wooden oval biscuits to the bottom box every two feet, and, also doweled every eight inches to a depth of half an inch in the lid and slightly deeper in the sides. On the top and bottom edges there were two grooves that appeared to have been put there so one could insert squared metal hooks and pull the lid straight up. Since we had no tools to accomplish this Rorek would have to construct them. After two hours of laboring Rorek had two square hardened steel hooks bent at ninety degree angles with two threaded steel rods to accommodate the length of the box. There were also eight nuts and washers to secure the hooks firmly in place so that the lid could be winched straight up. After the procedure was explained we fitted the hooks to the box and adjusting the rods to a ninety degree angle from the lid. Then, a small hydraulic winch was set up directly over the center of the box and the braided steel line was stretched taut. Rorek began slowly turning the crank. As he did I held the line steady and Garrett and John were on both ends holding firmly to the bottom part of the box as it began separating. After a small amount of upwards movement was achieved we heard a distinct release of pressure. Within seconds the room was overtaken by an acrid stench, similar to what we'd experienced with the tablets. After a few moments the dowels disengaged from the bottom box and the lid popped off. For a moment no one moved. Either this was a monumental discovery or just another old box filled with old artifacts.

"The others should be here for this." Garrett declared softly.

All of us agreed. Minutes later everyone had quietly gathered around the box. Slowly, as Garrett wheeled the winch away, and John steadied the lid, the contents of the box became suddenly visible under the work lights. The room fell into a hush and no word was spoken. For the rest of my life, I will never forget my first view and how it took my breath from me. Fitted expertly into a bed of tightly woven red clothe lay the legendary **Tempest Sword** waiting, as it had for centuries, to be awakened from a long soundless slumber. While scanning the inside of the box I noticed a small leather scroll wedged down next to the handle.

Twenty-three

What the scroll revealed

The scroll was an animal skin that had become very stiff with age. All of us knew that unrolling it like this would destroy whatever was on it. Lizzy suggested we use a spray bottle and moisten it, let it rehydrate, and then, on 20% power, warm it up slowly in the microwave with a bowel of water to help increase the malleability. Using this procedure, we were able to roll it open within thirty minutes. The message was written in an old Orknean dialect that I was able to translate.

A conspiracy of voices, like oil,
Sooth itching ears

Arcane lies and blinding darkness feed the inferno
Fading dreams of peaceful humankind
Slowly are abandoned
To the desires of flesh
Cruel winds,
Pestilent and insidious,
Embrace fragile vessels whispering
Fallacious destructive gospels . . . still, the seeker
Of Truth finds the narrow path unadorned, unpaved,
Winding and narrow, true wisdom embraces the only Man
Ever called the Way the Truth and the Life
And cries out save me.
The Tempest procured of Gamelin in vision will reveal
its fortune when the chosen one holds it high and cries
out for Christ's mercy . . .
King Agar

Agar was the powerful Viking ruler who'd been given the vision for the Rognvald's original journey. I remembered what'd been written in anticipation of that journey: *'Together and wretched we sail the raging unknown to find destinies embrace and complete the vision in honor to our great King.'* When I realized the magnitude of what'd been written here I began to weep.

Twenty-four

Along the Spanish coast

Two divisions of rivers exist along the northwestern and western shores of Spain. The **Rias Atlas** forms the most southern boundary of the Bay of Biscay. **La Ria De La Coruna**, **La Ria de Corme y Lage**, and **La Ria de Camarinas** act as the main northwestern estuaries. These rivers do not extend as deep into the Spanish mainland as their southern counterpart's, the **Rias Baja's**, and are less commercialized. Because of the information the old gentleman had shared with Lizzy, and our newly purchased map, we now had an opportunity to explore one of these southern Spanish estuaries that, in good faith, we'd prayerfully seized upon. Since we'd escaped from La Coruna we'd been staying close to the shoreline and consulting the charts every thirty minutes to avoid hidden reefs and shallow rocks. The diesel was purring like a kitten and we were making fifteen knots in calm seas. As soon as we'd rounded the **Cabo Finisterre Headland** Olaf announced over the ship's PA that this point of geography was the transition between the Northern and Southern Rias. Because of our time constraints we'd be sailing nonstop to the **Ria de Vigo** and were relegated to enjoying, and photographing, the view from the deck. Helga had been aloft for hours, keeping an eye out for any pursuers from La Coruna. There'd been no reports from her about anything threatening or out of the ordinary. Garrett was in the computer room watching on the VEW for anything that looked suspicious. On a whim he'd instructed the satellite to look down on the La Coruna harbor and was now utterly engrossed in what was happening around the *Wormwood.* Gleefully he shared with us that the only part of her still visible was the center mast. The harbor and the jetty were congested with police, harbor authorities, and the press. We could only hope that they were investigating the murder of the peevish spy, and would soon be remanding the perpetrator of that dastardly crime. The *Wormwood* incident, however, was another story entirely. Given all we knew about it we hoped that they would never find the ghost warriors who'd accomplished that wonderful deed.

I'd been given the privilege to photograph and notate everything that we'd recovered from the *Shallows of Three Rocks.* We'd all decided that nothing would be mentioned (on the cell phones or two way radios) about what we'd discovered, where we were going, or what our intentions were from this point forward. All communications about sensitive information, via anything electronic, would be encrypted and shared only with vital and trustworthy colleagues. Beginning now we were going to become like shadows, anonymous to everyone except our immediate family, Jonah, Roxanne, and my father. There was still some disquiet in us about someone possibly knowing about what we were doing. The journey was certainly becoming more perilous, but we were learning how to flow with whatever the day (or night) might bring. We had enemies now that would stop at nothing to get what they wanted. Given this I was very thankful Captain was given the insight to replace the frequency chips in our radios, and that we'd encrypted some of our most sensitive computer accounts. It was absolutely necessary that we become as imperceptible as possible, on every level.

Since Jonah and Roxanne departed, I'd accepted the duties of continuing her work. Roxanne had difficult shoes to fill; she was an extremely intelligent, organized, and fastidious woman. Given this, and out of respect and admiration, I'd dedicated myself to her tasks, and prayed that my efforts would be good enough to meet her excellent standards. It was determined that the sword would not be removed from the case at this time. This decision was made after prayer, and it was made unanimously. There was something about the Tempest that captivated us; a kind of magnificence surrounded the sword that filled us with awe. Why we were the ones privileged to discover it was truly a profound mystery. It seemed God's hand was strongly upon us in this matter. The case and lid for the Tempest were reconnected with steel bands and tightened. We'd stowed it in the safest place on the schooner; the small hydraulic room that stayed locked at all times. I'd sent encrypted e-mails, to Roxanne and Jonah, with a complete list of artifacts and pictures of everything we'd found. Since I'd never personally done business with the universities of Southern California, or Porto, I had shared my reluctance with Roxanne about disclosing our discoveries with anyone but her and Jonah. I suggested that they pursue what they wanted to do from their end and, if I could help in anyway, I was always available. All the artifacts were stowed now in sealed plastic containers and on each lid was a description of the contents. E-mail responses came back an hour later. Both raved about the photos and artifacts, but were deeply saddened because they'd not been able to be there for the unveiling of the Tempest. Both thanked me for not notifying the universities. They also confirmed the absolute necessity of keeping the 'old symbol' and the artifacts a secret from everyone. All of us agreed. It was getting more and more difficult knowing who we could trust and who our enemies were. The necessity for shrewdness and wisdom in all things was absolutely imperative. Continual prayer (Jonah had ministered) was the key to this, and thankfully the crew was involved daily in this spiritual discipline. Jonah had also mentioned talking with Regan Pendleton since he'd gotten home; he was feeling much less apprehensive about him. He'd felt strongly led to do some research on Regan's story to verify what he'd shared with us about his church's mission and himself. Everything he'd shared with us was true.

Jonah and Roxanne were profoundly engrossed with the recount of our exploits in La Coruna; they'd both agreed that now more than ever there was danger everywhere. They'd be praying about the authenticity of the new map, our safety, and, also for our eventual success in the Pontevedra Province. Jonah was preparing to take a church group up to **'Ghost Mountain'** in the Anza Borrego desert. They were planning on camping out for five days and six nights to write a pamphlet about the seasons we all go through when we feel isolated emotionally and spiritually from God and from one another. Jonah was concerned about us being in possession of the sword; he unquestionably saw this as an answer to prayer, but also saw the potential for evil to be thrust upon us if this knowledge got into the wrong hands. He once again exhorted us to be prayerful in all of our daily decisions. Roxanne was on Flores now. She was also filled with joy about the discovery and expressed her enthusiasm about our safe arrival April 1st. She considered sailing across the Atlantic with us an extraordinary opportunity, and was very much looking forward to learning how to become an able deckhand; she was also planning on bringing an ample supply of Dramamine. This evening the sunset was glorious. And the chance to sit quietly on deck and eat dinner together was superb. Another day had come to its conclusion, and we were all thankful to be alive and in each other's company.

March 23rd

After breakfast we unrolled the map to scrutinize what the old gentleman had created. It had been crafted with a wealth of acumen and minutiae, and it clearly revealed a complex set of streams that needed to be traversed in order to reach the goal. Ironically, an X marked the spot where the Norsemen were thought to be hidden. Early afternoon we anchored just off the port city of Vigo. I'd learned that in 1585, and in 1589 the English navigator, Sir Francis Drake, had attacked Vigo. Also in 1702, a combined compliment of British and Dutch treasure ships, from the new world, had been defeated and sunk in the harbor. As the stories were told, apparently some of the treasure had never been recovered and was still lying at the bottom. When John heard this he beamed with excitement and suggested that if we had some free time he knew exactly what he and Helga would be doing. Yes, it's true. Since John had saved Helga's life in the Mortiken mêlée; something had genuinely been brewing between them. Perhaps we'll get into more details in another chapter, or perhaps another book.

Around three we received clearance from the harbor master to anchor. We informed him that our intention was to venture inland for four or five days to explore and photograph the topography. They assured us that our schooner would be patrolled every twelve hours, along with all the other vessels. The only charge this time was our anchorage fee, and with this news the Captain smiled deeply. We had purchased three recreational permits. The cost was two hundred Euros. One was for fishing, one for camping, and one for hunting, and all good for thirty days. The rangers told us camping along the shorelines was acceptable as long as our fires were contained in some kind of rock or metal ring. They also demanded that all of our accumulated garbage must be taken back out with us. We assured them of our compliance. Because the bilge pump had become troublesome again Rorek opted to stay behind. This time he'd have to rebuild it completely. Thankfully all the parts he needed to complete the job had been purchased while we were in Edinburgh. Given his decision Lizzy contemplated whether she should stay aboard also. Of course Rorek balked. She'd done enough while nursing him, so he politely convinced her to join the others. When Rorek found out about the frozen dinners Betsy had put together he was overjoyed. He openly admitted he wasn't much of a cook and, with no way of going ashore; he was relegated to eating all his meals aboard the vessel. We agreed we'd be in touch at least once daily, and, if he encountered any problems, the harbor police were only minutes away.

Twenty-five

Into the Pontevedra Province

March 23rd

It has often been referred to as the Spanish Switzerland. Being a maritime province of Northwestern Spain, (formed in 1833 of districts taken from Galicia) the **Pontevedra Province** is bounded on the north by Corunna, on the east by Lugo and Orense, on the south by Portugal, and on the west by the Atlantic Ocean. Its shorelines exhibit unique character with small treacherous inlets and craggy mountainous islands just offshore. And though no mountaintop exceeded fifty-five hundred feet in the entire province; the sheer grandeur of its rugged beauty left us breathless when we first viewed it. According to our new map, this upcoming journey east would take us past the city of Vigo, and have us meandering through many diverse tributaries, into and out of the Mino River, around the southernmost parts of the province, and crisscrossing back and forth between the borders of Spain and Portugal. One of Europe's smallest countries, Portugal covers an area of 92,389 sq kilometers, and, along with Ireland, lies on Europe's' westernmost edge. Despite the fact that Portugal is one of the tiniest countries in Europe, it remains one of the most geographically diverse.

We'd determined that seven people in one 18'x 6' raft, along with all the supplies we needed, was too dangerous. To remedy this we'd be towing an eight foot diving raft to carry the bulk of our equipment and enough food for five days. Our gear included two compasses, two fishing poles with a box of tackle, one rifle, two shotguns, two hand weapons, five backpacks, one digital camera, one laptop with two extra batteries, extra petrol, seven long knives, medical supplies, sun screen, binoculars, one telescope, seven sleeping bags, seven small tents, utensils for cooking and eating, ledgers, extra clothes, and the map. We were headed into a region that was bounded on the north by the *Ulla River* and on the south by the *Minho River.* The old gentleman had informed Lizzy that sightings of the Northmen had, less than twenty years ago, emerged from the townships of *Valenca do Minho* and *Moncao* just south of the river on the northern Portuguese border. 'With the exception of the *Minho,*' he'd gone on, 'there are hundreds of short rivers, senora, especially in the rainy season. They roar out of the surrounding mountains and down into the *Ria de Vigo*, and eventually out to sea.' He'd assured her that we'd be traversing quite a few of those smaller rivers in our quest, (if we decided to venture out) and *Heimdall* would not be able to sail into those areas. Small vessels, like ours, could only go as far as the township of *Salvatierra.* 'Follow the flow of the water,' he'd repeated several times to her, 'always bear right against the flow on the journey up, always bear left with the flow on the journey back, so very simple. If you get lost senora, please follow the flow of the water, it will bring you back to the river. Do not fear, God will go with you, and He will bring you back.'

At 6:15 our journey inland began. "Take care and Godspeed," Rorek shouted and waved from the rails. "I'll call you later, brother," Olaf waved back. This morning there was a formidable fog that was limiting our visibility to no more than twenty feet. As we trolled past *Vigo,* the sounds of commerce had already awakened. A diverse clamor of blue-collar pulses, from iron foundries, the low consistent humming of petroleum refineries and processing plants, the muffled shouting of distant voices, the cawing of seagulls overhead, and the soft sputtering of the raft motor; all together were creating a surreal soundscape in the early morning environment. We were heading northeast towards the city of *Redondela.* After that we'd be navigating southeast through tributaries and rivulets towards the city of *Arbo* on the Minho River, near the Portuguese border. Somewhere, in that convoluted tangle of waterways, was the lost Norse settlement.

Garrett was perched on the bow of the raft. He'd brought along a bag of smooth stones and was preoccupied with skipping them out across the glassy surface.

"Be careful not to hit anyone honey, it's hard to see anything out there this morning." Lizzy said.

"Ok Liz," Garrett murmured, "This fog's awesome. I wonder where the dolphins went; think we'll see um again?"

"Not this trip son," Captain Olaf interjected, "salt water dolphins don't much care for fresh water."

"Oh yah boss yur right. Too bad, it woulda' helped break the monotony if they'd come along," Garrett brooded.

Thankfully the fog began clearing around ten. Now, through steadily thinning mists, sunlight was beginning to dance on the water in intermittent shafts. Around noon the fog dissipated completely which allowed the Captain to increase our speed to five knots. We'd taken a tack thirty yards from the shoreline where small whirlpools were forming in the shallower water because of the incoming tide. Almost six hours sedentary in the raft was taking a toll and all of us had succumbed to a quiet state of moody introspection. Suddenly the honking of a small air horn startled us.

"What the heck is that?" Garrett turned angrily and threw a rock in the direction of the sound. An old official looking vessel was chugging towards us off our port stern. Someone aboard was motioning for us to come about and stop. The name of the vessel had been burned off the bow and there were no identifying colors, or ensigns of origin.

"What do you think Olaf?" John looked troubled. "They have side arms and a small canon on the bow. Something feels wrong."

"I have no idea who these people are. But John, we're guests in this country and we can't appear lawless or uncompromising. Let's come about and see what they want. Tell the others to be on guard." John nodded reluctantly. His suspicions had put all of us on edge.

Captain decreased our speed and brought us alongside the other vessel. There were only two aboard. The older one was disgracefully obese, bald, and had tattoos all over his arms and neck. He was dressed in an official looking uniform with a fish and game patch on the right shoulder, a badge on his left pocket, and various medals and ribbons pinned to his right pocket. His clothes were tattered and cruddy and the younger man, in every way, looked the same as the older man, only without the tattoos.

The younger smirked and threw a filthy rope at Lizzy. "Take da rope, and tie it off on da oar lock, *NOW* missy cabron!" Lizzy cringed, but sullenly obliged the disrespectful request.

"Buenos dias," the older man hissed stepping out of the small wheelhouse as the sides of the two vessels quietly touched. "My name is Captain Miguel Jorge Demean Armando, and I am the most humble servant at your service." The man's ensuing smile revealed a mouth with half the teeth missing. The remaining, being blackened, diseased, or crooked, looked like old grave markers. Smears of tobacco bits were lodged in his gums and reminded me of the interior of an open rain soaked grave. Before anyone could respond he spit a mouthful of foul brown tobacco juice onto the side of the raft, right next to Lizzy's hand. Then his lip curled up evilly on the left side.

"Please forgive me, I missed!" He said mockingly.

"What's yur problem shit brain???" Garrett stood up furiously with clenched fists. "Don't spit at her, you moron!"

"Shut-up Cabron!" he shot back with his hand on his pistol. "I don't talk to little punks. Who's in charge here?"

"Try spittin' at me fat ass!" Garrett shot back with a ferocious expression; the young warrior in him was beginning to bristle.

The younger of the two, having slipped into the wheelhouse momentarily, had reemerged with an old sawed off shotgun; he began posturing defiantly. With stealth John changed places with Helga; one hand was discreetly on the handle of his titanium knife. Following John's example I also changed places with Betsy. When we sat back down she tightly gripped my hand and moved closer. The ruffian began smirking. Then he cocked the antique weapon.

"What's wrong carbons, are the little ladies afraid?" he asked mockingly as he pointed the weapon at us.

"Please, let's settle down now," Captain Olaf interjected coolly, motioning for all to remain calm, "I'm in charge senor'. What is it you want from us?" Looking down condescendingly, the fat man scowled. And as he hobbled closer he loudly broke gas.

"Oh sheesh pigs butt," Garrett shook his head disdainfully.

"What are your intentions in my province senor'," The fat man sneered. "Have you come to pillage innocent people?"

"No! Of course not! We're on a hunting, fishing, and camping trip. We'll be here for a few days. We have all the necessary permits. Would you like to see them?" Captain Olaf offered politely as he reached into his coat pocket. Listening attentively to the conversation, the younger one had quickly moved up behind the other. Unwittingly he had created a blind spot between himself and Garrett. John motioned towards Garrett to make him aware of this opportunity to overpower him. With his eyes he told him to wait for the precise moment. Garrett nodded quietly.

"Get your hand out of your pocket *NOW* filthy Cabron!" The fat man screamed. After pulling back the hammer of his pistol he shot into the air and then pointed it straight at Olaf's head. "You think I'm a fool cabron? Do you want to die right now? Stand up and put your hands in the air, all of you filthy pigs, *STAND UP NOW*!"

It was moments like these when God clearly anointed us for battle. The situation had gone too far; our lives were being threatened. And because of this, John, with one slight motion of his hand, set (the now bristling) Garrett into motion. With the nimbleness of a cat he pounced onto the deck and overwhelmed the younger man with a fierce blow to the chest and a jarring uppercut to his jaw. A second later he forced the staggering man down and put his knee right at the base of his neck.

"How's it feel you piece 'a crap?" Garrett snarled.

Awkwardly the older man spun around. John pulled out his knife and threw it handle first at his bloated hand; the pistol fell clinking onto the wooden deck. In an instant he bounded aboard and had squashed the (disgustingly flatulent) miscreant against the cabin wall in a painful arm lock. The man began screaming in pain.

"Gabriel . . ." Garrett motioned at the weapons.

Immediately I jumped aboard, too, and kicked the pistol and the shotgun into the water. When I glanced over at Betsy; she blew me a kiss and shook her head in admiration.

"Gabriel, steer the vessel towards that inlet!" The Captain bellowed, pointing towards the shore. "Get us out of sight! We're getting to the bottom of this right now! John, Garrett, tie them both through the forward scuppers face down! Get the vessel over there *NOW* son!" Lizzy quickly untied the rope holding the raft. Within seconds I'd engaged the creaking transmission and had slowly turned the sluggish vessel towards the inlet. A few seconds later Captain Olaf brought the raft alongside for the trip in. Fifteen minutes later we were anchored and hidden inside enormous overhanging mats of, what appeared to be, yellow South African Hottentot figs. The despicable duo was sitting on chairs with their hands and feet bound securely. I had never seen Captain as livid as he was. He began interrogating them in a manner I'd never seen before; he had no mercy whatsoever in his machinegun like inquiries. After examining the vessel we discovered the hold was filled with swag. It was obvious these two didn't work for the government, and they certainly weren't fish and game wardens. It appeared now that they were just common pirates. John found a rumpled operating permit and asked Captain Olaf if he could report the vessel to the authorities. Olaf suggested he wait until he'd established more facts in his interrogation. Seeing an opportunity Garrett moved over to the younger man and began lambasting him.

"You wanna piece a me? You wanna try me punk? I'll kick your stinkin' sorry butt! What kinda trip you on? Your mama must cry every day for you, you loser. You think what your doing is cool fool? Look at me you freakin' coward! I'll tie one hand behind my back and put on a blindfold and I'll still kick your sorry ass!" Garrett was furious and his taunting was relentless. After slapping his head sharply Garrett stomped angrily over to the older man and smacked him on the back of the head too. Then, when he began grumbling in protest, Garrett got right up in his face like a pit bull and growled: "Don't ever spit at a lady again, you understand me fat ass? You stink like a nasty sewer! Must be your rotten brains comin' outa your butt."

"Honey that's enough," Lizzy put her hand on Garrett's shoulder calmly. "All they're going to do now is beg."

As she had foretold both began begging for mercy. After kicking the deck angrily Garrett obeyed Lizzy and backed off. As he shuffled past John he got a smack on the chest and a nod for making the correct choice. Immediately Garrett softened. On the bow he sat down with his feet dangling over the edge and began playing his invisible drums. Soon peace had descended upon him once again.

After an hour of intense interrogation Olaf was convinced these men were murderers and thieves. Being in fear for their lives they'd confessed everything and afterwards continued sniveling like babies. After he'd finished Olaf instructed John to radio the authorities and give them a description of the men, the vessel, and also an explanation of what'd happened and how we'd been treated. The authorities were thrilled that they'd been caught and apologized for the inconvenience we'd been caused. They informed us these men were fugitives from *Braga Portugal*, and had eluded capture for almost two years. After they'd murdered the original owners of the vessel, there'd been dozens of complaints filed in Vigo concerning their mischief and robberies. We were instructed to disable the vessel, keep them securely tied up, and then continue on with our journey. A cruiser was going to be dispatched at once to impound the vessel and incarcerate them for a very long time. Many thanks were offered, and the police chief also informed us about the fifty thousand euro reward for their capture. When we heard the enormous sum we stared at each other speechless. Given that we'd already been blessed with all the finances we needed, Betsy suggested we donate it to some Christian church in the province, and we all agreed. After telling this to the chief he seemed baffled. "Are you very sure senor'? This is a small fortune here; many don't make it in a lifetime." After sharing our spiritual beliefs he finally understood and wished us Godspeed. He promised us the money would be delivered to a suitable church within twenty-four hours.

Two more hours of rafting brought us to a beautiful sandy inlet. Here there were steep rocky crags and weather rounded overhangs surrounded by Australian Eucalyptus, sweet chestnut, and Scots pine trees. It was a perfect place to stop for the evening. Nearby a waterfall flowed into a sandy bottomed pond, just twenty yards from where we'd be setting up. After we'd unloaded, and seven tents were up in a circle around the fire pit, we all took a refreshing swim together in the unseasonably warm late March air. Later, after a surprisingly excellent campsite dinner, Helga produced a small ledger she'd found in the wheelhouse. Scrawled inside was a list of what the rogues had stolen, who they'd pawned it to, and also descriptions of six other vessels they'd been in cahoots with. Helga pointed out one of the vessels descriptions and its name. It was the *Wormwood.*

Twenty-six

Our journey inland continues

6 am March 24th

Another fog was clinging to the land this morning like a moist ubiquitous blanket. We were convinced now that if this persisted our chances for finding the settlement would be seriously hindered. All of us were seated around a crackling fire sipping coffee and pondering what the day may bring. Our journey (thus far) had taken us forty miles inside the Pontevedra. We were learning that navigating a river like this required a certain kind of expertise, but, trying to find our way through diverse waterways and streams in a fog was a different challenge entirely. I was convinced that any caring sagacious group of individuals would have considered it prudent to turn back and wait for better weather. As it was, we weren't just any expedition. And, after praying, we all felt assured that things would work out if we pressed forward in faith. The waterfall, our rafts, even the shoreline was shrouded. Trees and moss covered overhangs hovered mysteriously around us. Similar to bears awakening and stretching from a long winter's hibernation they poked up around us, in ghostly irregular shapes, as if they'd been buried in snowdrifts. The huge Australian eucalyptus here resembled ethereal titans, ancient warriors silently watching us, and the fog accumulating on their leaves showered down in occasional bursts of heavy droplets. The waterfall and lapping waves were the only sounds, besides our breathing and the crackling fire, that were accompanying our prayerful introspections. Suddenly the silence was noisily broken. It was Rorek checking in. I realized, as the brothers talked, just how excellent these radios sounded. With twenty-five watt transmitting and receiving our ability to communicate effectively in this rugged topography was impressive. Rorek told us he'd been contacted the evening before by the affable Commander Portmanteau, the very same officer we'd consulted with concerning our unfortunate incident. According to the evening news there was big celebration in the port city of Vigo because of the capture of these thugs. The crew (once again) was being hailed as heroes. Fortunately no particulars had been shared; our names and the name of the schooner was still a mystery. Rorek also shared a dream he'd been given the night previous. It was a luminous idea that was eagerly embraced by all. His plan was to locate us with the 'Virtual Earth Watch' using my laptop as a link to the main computer and the weather station. It would allow us to navigate visually around the streams, rivulets, and obstacles that stood between us and our destination. Considering that we only had a few more days on our permits, we'd be using this idea for the rest of the journey. Hopefully the approach would prove productive in our efforts to successfully navigate a complicated terrain.

At seven the rafts were loaded and the journey inland continued. For thirty minutes our progress seemed fruitless. The fog was so thick we could barely see ten feet in front of the raft. Thankfully, after an hour of creeping, it began thinning enough to identify landmarks on the map. By 8:30 Helga and I were able to finally establish a positive link with our weather station and the satellite. The image was precise and clear. We could telescope down and see nothing but the rafts, and then zoom back out and see as much, or as little, as we wanted to see. We were surrounded by a dizzying amount of inlets, streams, and small lakes. Lizzy pointed out that they had an eerie likeness to the myriad blood vessels and capillaries in the human body, and I saw this as an inspired analogy. There were tiny islands everywhere now, and the maze of waterways was getting more tightly woven. No wonder the Norsemen had chosen this geography to hide in. Holding true to what the gentleman had instructed Lizzy to do; we bore right, against the current, and followed in precisely the same direction as the line on the map instructed. Because of the continual stream of information coming from the VEW, Olaf was able to effectively make adjustments to our course. During a late morning meal of tuna fish sandwiches, fruit, and tea, we calculated having covered fifty-seven miles inland. Rorek radioed Olaf while we were eating. Apparently he'd located rock formations near an area that betrayed the natural topography as having been altered; it was roughly eleven miles from our present position. He confirmed the location on the northern tip of the *Parque Nacional da Penenda-Geres.* It was an area between Spain and Portugal, on a tributary filled with small bays and lakes, about a mile from the Minho River. According to the geographical grid the anomaly was two miles in diameter. And though the area was overgrown by thick vegetation, Rorek could still vaguely make out the outlines of manmade structures built in quadrilateral patterns in a sizeable oval valley. Was it possible that what he'd seen was the lost settlement?

The farther inland we got the more unique our surroundings became. There were water snakes and small alligators slithering around us now. There were also red muskrats with long tails, glossy fur and enormously webbed rear feet, frolicking underwater next to the shoreline. We saw beaver building dams on small streams and (twice) we saw herds of wild boar foraging noisily at the water's edge. Farther inland we came upon a herd of deer grazing in flowered meadows of sediment rich soil, wreathed in mist. We also saw two gray Iberian Lynx's watching us from one of the trees; an animal we'd been told was an endangered species. For miles along the shoreline there were many rain filled indentations in the permeable bedrock; and all were surrounded by lush greenery, bulrushes, cattails, and exotic purple yellow pond lilies. Thick Spanish moss hung over the water's edge on cypress trees skewed from years of torrential rainfall and raging streams. These were filled with speckled warblers, black terns, sparrows, red winged nightjars, and pied flycatchers. Life abounded here richly, and the air was peaceful and sweet to breath. Early afternoon we came upon a flock of egrets circling around a thinning stand of enormous cypress trees; their monotone 'cuc cucs' echoed dissonantly amongst the trees and craggy outcroppings of rock. Captain Olaf stopped the raft and we all watched as they dove down into the dark waters and resurfaced with fish in their beaks. Others sat perched on thatched platforms of twigs and small branches. The cypress here served as perches for the Egret's nests. As it was, many of the trees appeared dead or dying, all having suffered the consequences of the droppings, which contained unusually destructive amounts of uric acid. Alas, life and death coexisting together. In the same moments we breathed in the oxygen that maintained our life, we exhaled the carbon dioxide that was deleterious to our existence, each breath, each second steadily advancing, a few moments closer to the time of our departure. What a mystery being alive and dying at the same moment.

"Hey . . . you're mumbling," Garrett poked me after taking his headphones off. "Are you waxing philosophic again?" Sheepishly shaking my head yes, I looked around reluctantly at the rest of the crew; they all knew my brain took strange detours.

"Captain . . . what time is it?" John asked. He looked disgruntled and had reeled in his fishing line.

"It's just about three John . . . why?"

"Oh . . .

"Captain . . ." Helga interrupted, "we appear to be very near the area Rorek told us about this morning."

"I didn't realize we were that close," Captain replied.

"We are, sir. According to the beacon, we're almost on top of it. It isn't more than an eighth mile from here."

"Perhaps we should set up camp for the evening and check it out." John suggested, grinning at Helga with hopeful eyes.

"I'm game. Is it good with everyone else?" The Captain asked. Everyone emphatically agreed.

After closely scrutinizing the shoreline, we discovered a fine location to set up camp for the evening. This part of the stream was a lot narrower than the river and streams we'd navigated earlier in the day; the widest part being no more than twenty-five feet, and at the most three or four feet deep. We'd come upon an eight foot wide channel. It extended about one hundred feet into the cliff wall and then opened up abruptly into a small secluded bay. The water here was crystal clear, about twenty feet deep, and was teeming with fish. John was ecstatic. He'd tried for hours today without a bite. But here was the captive audience he'd been dreaming of. Gleefully he and Helga began boasting as they excitedly tied their lures, they promised that they'd be catching dinner for all of us this evening. It was peaceful here. And there were no sounds except the occasional lapping of small waves on the shoreline. Curiously none of us had seen a trace of anything, or anyone, resembling Norsemen, or an ancient society, and this perplexed us. While discerning our surroundings we realized that this place was different than anything we'd seen on the journey thus far; the only trees I recognized here were the massive Scots pine. An area Garrett had walked past earlier had now captured my attention. It appeared to have once been a waterfall, but it was dry now and obstructed by rocks, smooth boulders, and scrubby vines. After sizing up the stair-like terracing I was taken by a sudden urge to climb up and explore the escarpment above. It felt as if invisible hands were drawing me to this, but how was I going to articulate such a whimsical idea in a way that the Captain would understand. It'd been thirty minutes since we'd stopped and all I could do was stand around mesmerized in my own thoughts. Garrett had made his way around to the other side of the bay and was preoccupied skipping stones and inspecting pieces of driftwood. John and Helga were fishing and succumbing to ardent fits of laughter when the curious perch began attacking their feathered spinners. Lizzy, Captain Olaf, and Betsy were setting up tents and putting together a makeshift kitchen for dinner and tomorrows breakfast. For some reason I'd been hesitant in asking permission to make the climb; my fears and insecurities warred against me often. At last, after mustering courage, I took an opportunity while he was taking a short break from his work.

"Captain, excuse me a moment sir. This may sound strange, but I have an overwhelming urge to climb that old waterfall there. I'm really curious to see what's on top of the escarpment. Is that something I could get your permission to do?" Captain chuckled. Then he bent down and snatched up a small stone and threw it over towards Garrett, who in turn, quickly threw one back. "It's funny you should ask son," He began, "we've been thinking the same thoughts, you and me. I saw that old waterfall the moment we beached the raft, and I wanted to do the very same thing. I'm really glad you offered. Of course, absolutely, go for it, but . . . I want you and Garrett to go together. And I want you to both carry a small sidearm; bring some water, a radio and a couple of flashlights. In fact put everything in these backpacks, take along some snacks too, it'll keep your strength; GARRETT, front and center!"

Garrett bolted over. "What's up Cap?"

"Son, you and Gabriel go ahead and climb that old waterfall over there, let's find out what's on top."

"Cool! I'm down with it big time boss. Let's go bubba."

"Thanks Captain Olaf, we'll be back before dark. By the way, how much time do we have before then?" I asked.

"Let's see . . . its three-thirty, probably seven, seven-thirty at the latest. Get up there, look around, and come right back down, I don't want you up there overnight, understand?"

"Aye sir . . . ready Garrett? See you later Captain, bye guys!" I yelled, waving at the rest of the crew.

"Gabriel, hold on," Betsy ran up, took my hands, and looked me straight in the eyes. "You be very careful Dr. Proudmore. Somebody cares about you oodles and oodles; don't be gone too long!" I smiled and shook my head no. Then she kissed my cheek and ran back to where they were constructing the makeshift kitchen. As we began our ascent it became apparent that this waterfall hadn't tumbled straight down off the cliff face; it'd meandered like a snake down through the granite and gouged out a small stepped canyon. Abrasive particles, suspended in cascading torrential runoff, had slowly sculpted this staircase with the precision of a craftsman and the vision of an artist.

After forty minutes of arduous climbing we at last reached the crest. Around us the plateau was demarcated with arboreal sculptures of red oak and Scots pine trees, bent, and twisted together inexorably from decades of desiccating winds. The ground was interspersed with buttercups and whortleberries; plants having pink flowers with blackish blue edible berries similar to the American huckleberry. The whole area was scattered over with an odd assortment of rocks covered in a fuzzy indigo moss. It was evident that this escarpment was really a multifarious high mountain plateau, an eclectic hodge-podge of indigenous and non-indigenous flora, which must have been brought by settlers from another part of the world. The view here was breathtaking. The Atlantic was visible on the distant horizon, as was the crew working and fishing below. Captain had calculated that in the sixty-eight miles we'd traveled inland, we'd climbed close to four thousand feet. On top of this twelve hundred foot plateau, we had to be on one of the highest points in the Pontevedra.

"Check it out," Garrett shouted from the northeast side of the plateau, "you ain't gonna believe it." He was laughing hilariously and threw a rock at me. When I reached him he was leaning over the edge holding onto a strong evergreen branch. Below us was hundreds of wooden structures overgrown with wild vegetation. I couldn't believe my eyes. The valley was surrounded on all sides by vertical granite cliffs, and spread out on centuries old alluvial fans were acres of evenly spaced trees. A swiftly moving river was entering from the south through a thick stand of forest which ran through the whole diameter of the settlement into a small lake on the Northwestern side. In the center of the settlement a large paddle wheel was turning in the current. Through the binoculars we could not discern any movement that might indicate a functioning society still living in this place. We radioed Captain Olaf and informed him. He congratulated our find, but also reminded us that it had been God's will that we'd trekked to the top of this plateau. We knew now that it existed and, like the Shallows of Three Rocks, we'd been the ones privileged to find it. The Captain instructed us to head back to camp at once. Dusk was coming and the nighttime sky was rapidly lowering a blanket around us. He also added that he hoped we'd developed a good appetite because there was fresh perch on the menu tonight. As we began the preliminaries for our descent, Garrett remembered suddenly he'd left the binoculars next to the evergreen tree on the other side of the plateau. "I'll be back in a flash dude!" He shouted as he bolted to the other side. A moment later I heard him whisper hoarsely for me to beat feet over. He was bubbling with excitement when I'd reached his side. "Check it out dude." He motioned below. I was shocked. On the northwestern edge of the lake a campfire was burning.

Twenty-seven

The hidden settlement

When Garrett and I returned the air was thick with the delicious aromas of breaded perch frying in butter, pan baked corn bread, and coffee. A crackling redolent fire was leaping high in the center of our circle of tents and all the crew were busy with preparations for our feast. It was magnificently undisturbed here and our hearts and minds were content. Precipitous granite walls surrounded us like giant movie screens and were reflecting back the flames in undulating reddish orange shapes. Across the small bay our shadows danced sinuously like ghostly giants with the flames. Above us the darkening sky was revealing more stars than I ever remember seeing. **Canis Major**, the big dog constellation, was directly over the campsite.

The ears, body, legs, and tail were readily discernible. The brilliant nose, (brightly defined by the blue white star Sirius) hung starkly in juxtapose with the black vastness of space. The beauty here was very moving. Dinner was superb, and afterwards we all reclined, full and contented, near the campfire in relaxed conversation. Being in this place, beneath clear starry skies, with my best friends was, in my estimation, a foretaste of heaven. I knew I was right where I belonged, with the people I was supposed to be with, and doing exactly what God wanted me to do. During our end of the day conversation we all agreed that we'd be leaving the campsite set up for another two or three nights to accomplish our work. Rorek said he'd e-mailed both Jonah and Roxanne to inform them about what we'd discovered. He also told them the pick-up date April 1st for Roxanne may well have to be pushed ahead to give us the time needed now to fully explore this discovery. He was awaiting their reply. Tomorrow, Captain, John, and I would be using the raft to gain entrance into the settlement. We would bring side-arms, a shotgun, the digital camera, extra clothes, underwear, first aid, two way radios, and enough food and boiled water for two long days of exploration. Garrett and Helga would perch up on the plateau; from this vantage they could help us maintain geographical bearings once we'd entered the settlement. Whether they'd be camped out overnight or not would be determined as circumstance unfolded. Lizzy and Betsy decided to stay in camp.

6 am March 25th

The bay this morning was a motionless mirror reflecting everything around it. And in the stillness every sound we made was being exaggerated radically because of the steep granite walls. Of course this encouraged Garrett's creative impulsiveness and, with great fervor, he broke out with every imaginable noise that human vocal cords were capable of making. Inspired by his lack of inhibition, the rest of us joined him. Those next few moments were life-changing. I am truly convinced that our creative bellowing had to have caused the angels to plug their ears. Within moments it'd become a maddening swirling guttural clamor that rose to such an obnoxious crescendo that we began seeing the fish darting for cover in the bay. Despite this we all ended up laughing so hard that some of us developed stomach cramps and began rolling around on the ground like children. Me, well, I laughed so hard I almost puked.

The air this morning was cool and sweet and the skies were dramatically different than the two previous mornings. The weather today I felt was perfect for our endeavors. Feeling optimistic, and excited to begin, we wolfed down a breakfast of leftover fish and canned fruit, joined hands, prayed, and afterwards completed our final preparations before departure. I was bringing along the laptop inside the waterproof housing. After some adjustments, I was able to establish a strong link with the weather station and the chain of VEW satellites. In Olaf's conversation with Rorek, he'd suggested that each party take along radios, and the solar powered chargers, so the entire crew could stay in constant contact. As it was our map was no longer useful. We were entirely dependent now on God, our personal intelligence, the VEW, and each other to accomplish what'd been laid before us to do. As we were motoring away I recalled how I'd struggled emotionally in the beginning days of this journey. But time had proven to me, beyond a shadow, that God's mighty hand was guiding this group of people; there were just too many occurrences that revealed divine fingerprints. If Lizzy had never bumped into the old gentleman we would have never known about the legends about the Northmen in the Pontevedra Province, and we'd never been given the opportunity to buy the map. Without the map we would never have located the lost settlement. If we hadn't encountered the peevish spy we would never have known about the circumstances surrounding the *Wormwood*, or that the Mortiken were in La Coruna manipulating business and watching us. If we'd never been confronted by the tattooed fatman we would never have known about their affiliation with the *Wormwood* and their criminal past. Everyday seemed to present us with a different set of circumstances, which placed us in a specific location, at exactly the time we needed to be there, to either meet someone or confront some situation that would propel us in a direction that repeated the same processes. So it was now, with our lives.

Forty five minutes after leaving camp Olaf, John, and I were staring at an enormous wall of vines woven together in a wildly disheveled mess. We'd turned off the larger river, into a semi hidden branch, and motored in about half a mile. Here the stream was colder than it was near camp, presumably because of snow melt from peaks farther south. The current was flowing swiftly under the enormous wall of fibrous vines in front of us. To our right and left there were stands of Oak, Scots pine, and Alder trees, but the banks were so tangled with dense growth that it was impossible to beach the raft to investigate. Something was fundamentally different here, the plants and trees did not appear indigenous to the area at all, and it'd been the same way up on top of the plateau. We were in the midst of a recondite landscape that defied geographical logic, and, as I mulled this my neck began to tingle. I realized a second time, and this time with no doubt, that the flora had purposely been brought in from somewhere else; it was the only explanation.

To keep the raft from ramming into the gate, Captain had put the motor in reverse at eight hundred rpm. This was keeping us at a temporary, albeit uncertain, standstill in the strong current and required his constant attention to maintain. Although it was apparent we were confronted with a large gate of sorts, the mechanism to open it was difficult to determine. The VEW was revealing a thick wall of plants, with our raft on one side, and the settlement on the other. But how were we going to get through? After grumbling Captain keyed on his radio.

"Garrett, do you copy?"

"Copy Cap . . . what's up?"

"Can you see the raft from where you are son?"

"Hold on! What did you say Helga? Oh cool! Captain, Helga's digging out the binoculars right now. Can you wait a minute?"

"Copy that son. Rorek, do you copy?" The Captains voice was beginning to reflect signs of exasperation.

"Loud and clear Olaf, what's wrong?"

"What do you see on the main computer brother?"

"The same as Gabriel's; it's the same signal Olaf."

"Oh crap, you're right, sorry 'bout that, thanks."

"Captain its Helga. Ok, Garrett's scanning the area with the binoculars, but he's shaking his head no to your question sir. We're not seeing you at all. That heavy stand of trees is blocking the view on your side of the river. Sorry Captain, we'll stay focused on that area and radio when we see something, Helga out!"

Olaf was discouraged, and his expression was showing me something I was thankful he wasn't putting into words. One of the things I loved about him was that you always knew where he was mentally and emotionally; he had the most expressive face I'd ever seen and he did *not* hide his emotions. Angry now, and frustrated, Captain somehow dropped his radio. As he bent over to pick it up his elbow hit the control toggle and the motor slipped into neutral. Before he could resolve it the raft had smashed into the tangled wall of vines and had thrown us all off our seats. Olaf cursed loudly. Then the strangest thing happened, which impressed upon me that God can use anything, in any circumstance, for His purposes. A second after we'd hit; the wall of vines shifted forward. Then it creaked open about two feet and stopped.

"OLAF," John shouted and pointed, "put it in forward sir, push against the wall right here." Captain's eyes were suddenly keen; he shook his head, as if he intuitively understood John's intentions. Seconds later the wall slowly began opening.

"Captain," Garrett shouted on the radio, "a whole section of trees is moving down where you're at, like a big door is opening."

"I'm seeing the same thing here." Rorek confirmed. "Whatever you're doing, it's working, congratulations brother."

Captain was radiant with satisfaction now. I could see the water was rapidly becoming shallower as the raft slowly moved forward; it was no more than three feet deep when John hurtled himself out of the raft. In the water he began to push the enormous tangled mass in an effort to maintain our impetus. In an effort to avoid the possibility of the raft being punctured, John put a seat cushion between the rafts bow and the wall, and then turned and yelled.

"Gabriel, I need some help!"

Breathing deeply I jumped into the water and began helping John push the mass of vines towards the shore. The water was frigid and my legs were tightening. John was complaining, as well, and had begun slapping at his quadriceps to encourage circulation. Captain had steady pressure on the gate to help facilitate our efforts. Unexpectedly, a frightening sound ripped through the air above us to the right. At once I was overwhelmed with agitation and dread. It was utterly fearsome sounding, as if the whole world was coming apart around us, and we were engulfed in it.

"IT'S FALLING," John screamed. "Move the raft *NOW, GO*!" Instantly the Captain veered port; the motor screaming in clouds of bluish gray smoke. "Gabriel, try to . . ." John's voice was buried in a deafening avalanche of ripping wood and collapsing branches. His face was filled with angst as he vigorously motioned for me to move to the other side of the stream. Then he dove as far away from the crumbling mass as he could. I followed him and swam with every ounce that I was able to muster. A moment later we both resurfaced and began running through the water towards the opposite shore. Thankfully the massive wall was falling away from us. We were out of harm's way and, as soon as we'd reached the shoreline, we both turned back, shivering, winded, and dripping wet. With a massive ripping crunch it crumbled in a heap. Afterwards an eerie stillness prevailed, like nothing had ever happened. Leaves, like snow, began floating down around us. Captain had taken the raft a ways into the encampment. He'd beached it up on the sand, shut off the motor, jumped out, and was running towards us when the radio on the raft began squawking loudly. Stopping short he ran back to retrieve it. The others had witnessed what'd happened and were frantic because they couldn't see us. It was clear to me that the mass of dust and leaves, floating down around us, was blocking any clear view of our area above on the plateau, or on the VEW. In the direction of the plateau, I could just barely make out the two small shapes of Garrett and Helga waving wildly in our direction. When I turned back, Captain Olaf had the radio in hand and was jogging towards us. He was reassuring everyone that we were safe, and that no one had gotten hurt. We were shivering uncontrollably now so we both began doing jumping jacks to warm up. When Olaf reached us he instructed us to run back to the raft and get out of our wet clothes. He said he'd start at once looking for dry wood so he could build a fire for us. Heeding his instructions we took off at a full gallop towards the raft; thankfully we'd had the foresight to bring along extra clothes.

An hour after the incident we were resting around a roaring campfire in dry clothes, sipping hot tea, and no worse for wear. Olaf had set up a make-shift site. There was a line strung between two trees for our clothes to dry on. A Coleman stove was warming up beans and water, a plastic tarp was staked out as a lean-to to rest under, and a stack of firewood had been gathered. The raft was half deflated and Captain was hovering over the bow fixing the small puncture. Thirty minutes later he looked over at us with a smile; the repair had been successful. Although it was only late morning, it felt as if we'd been through a long and trying day. No one had sustained any injuries, and we thanked God for keeping us safe through the ordeal. Following a short nap we began to ascertain our surroundings. We noticed a rocky knoll one hundred yards from the shoreline and determined that from this higher vantage point we'd be able to contemplate the valley much more effectively. Around us were vertical granite cliffs, which somehow reminded us of pictures we'd seen of Half Dome in Yosemite. We could see four areas were two dissimilar peaks came together in tortured canyons; here tributaries from above had once washed down forcefully into the valley. There were huge alluvial fans, at the base of the cliffs, made up of extremely rich soil and spread out over hundreds of acres. A wide variety of non-indigenous trees were growing in these areas which must have been imported and planted by the Rognvald descendants. Drainage canals had been dug where the water cascaded down from the escarpments; they were lined with two foot thick rock slabs. These directed runoff from storms towards the river in the center of the valley. Despite the roughness of appearance we could clearly recognize the engineering acumen it had taken to build all of these marvelous constructions.

As with all homogenous granite rock, we could see the ample evidence of the disintegration process everywhere. Millions of tons of rock had been exfoliated from the sheer granite walls and now lay in massive heaps on the valley floor from countless decades of heat and freezing. In some areas we could see where avalanches had destroyed many of the man-made structures at the base of the cliffs. Considering such a violent demise made me shudder. We'd ascertained the valley (from where we'd come in on the northwestern end) to be a mile and a half long and perhaps a mile in width. Laid out all over the valley there was hundreds of circular crannogs in different stages of decay. The name 'crannog' comes from the Irish word 'crann' which interpreted literally means tree. As I contemplated these constructions, I construed the circular shape as a physically strong structure for a building, with no part of the building bearing more load than another. They appeared to have been laid out in quadrilateral configurations, diamond patterns slowly moving up in elevation towards an enormous wooden structure on the top of the highest rocky plateau in the northeastern section of the valley, just east of the lake. Interspersed below this were bigger circular granite crannogs along with ornately carved rectangular wooden structures. To me this seemed to indicate a social hierarchy had existed in this colony. The higher the edifice was in altitude, and the larger and more ornate the construction appeared, the higher the social status was. There was one area where thousands of tons of rock had been exfoliated from the cliff walls. Here we saw what once had been a rock quarry set up to shape stones into usable building blocks. The evidence of this was apparent all over the higher areas in the northeastern valley, in the form of circular granite block crannogs, and also the rock linings in all the drainage channels. The Rognvald symbol was everywhere we looked. This confirmed that the valley had once been inhabited by Norsemen from the ancient Orknean tribe.

There was a broad variety of trees here, too, and each was confined to an area inclusive to its own particular genus. We had already seen Alder and Aspen where we'd come in, and Birch, Ash, and Oak were proliferating under the plateau where Garrett and Helga were presently stationed. Near the lake Hazelwood and Bird Cherry trees were widespread and still very healthy. It was irrefutable to me that the Norsemen had used all of these different genera in their constructions and furniture making. Where the gate had collapsed, in the southwestern part of the valley, there were also a wide variety of fruit trees, including strawberries, and whortleberries. Underneath most of them enormous mounds of rotting fruit had piled up four or five feet. Sadly the majority of the valley was overgrown with weeds and vines from long decades of neglect. Something terrible had happened here, something inexplicable. Further up the plateau we began investigating, and measuring, the crannogs that were still structurally intact; they were between twenty-five and thirty-five feet in diameter. Inside some of them we found usable furniture, pottery, and eating utensils. Each crannog appeared to have its own tool shop, outhouse, and poultry yard, which included a small wooden structure for animals, possibly pigs or cows. We found rusted iron hammers, iron axes, billhooks, and six foot long saws, in some of the buildings, which, from the configuration of the teeth, appeared to cut only in one direction. As we neared the lake, and the sun had just slipped behind the high granite walls, Captain Olaf made a sound suggestion.

"Perhaps we should return to the raft and get dinner going, it looks like we'll be spending the night here."

John and I agreed. Another day would be mandatory now to explore the Northern end of the valley. Near the shoreline we'd seen several water retrieval devices that were clearly not associated with Viking culture. It appeared that a form of engineering, from another culture, had been integrated successfully into this Norse society. As we prepared to return to the campsite, John discerned movement on the distant northwestern edge of the lake which compelled him to scan the area with the binoculars. "I see someone moving around over there," he told us, "and judging by the way the persons hobbling about it must be someone older." Moments later we began hearing the faint barking of a dog. Seconds after that Garrett radioed us.

"Hey Cap, dig it. We can see you from up here; you're on the southeastern edge of the lake. But you're not gonna believe it, Helga and me watched someone come out of that big structure to the east of you and walk over to western side of the lake, and I swear we heard a dog barking, did you hear it too?"

"We did son. What else can you see?" The Captain inquired.

"Hold on! We brought along John's night vision binoculars. I hope he doesn't get mad. Is that cool John? I thought we could use them, so did Helga." John shook his head yes and smiled.

"No problem son. Let us know as soon as you can see anything."

"Copy that Cap, we're on it." Garrett said.

"Rorek, can you see anything on the VEW?" Olaf asked.

"I'm in the engine room. Hold on, let me get back up."

"I guess you guys aren't coming home tonight, are you?" Lizzy asked. "Oh well . . . Betsy sends her love, and hopes everyone is fine. Is Gabriel ok? Betsy wants to know."

With a radiant grin Captain handed me the radio. "I'm fine Betsy. Everything's ok except for the fact that you're not here. I miss you too. It's awesome here. I'm taking a lot of pictures. Can't wait to share them with you, um, I mean with everyone. Captain fixed the raft earlier, and we've got a little camp set up on the south end. We're staying here for the night, everybody's fine, no injuries, so don't worry. There's a lot more we need to investigate tomorrow. You and Lizzy be safe, ok? We all love you, talk to you soon, Gabriel out."

As I handed over the radio Rorek came back on. "Olaf, I'm barely seeing what looks like a fire burning."

"We're seeing the same up here," Garrett concurred. "Someone started a fire right where we saw it last night."

"Ok . . . thanks son. By the way, are you and Helga planning on camping up there tonight?" The Captain asked.

"I think so, yes, it's too dark to get down now." Helga answered. "We have enough food and water, and there's enough wood up here. We brought along sleeping bags just in case. Garrett brought a pistol, and we have two radios, but we forgot the chargers. If we head back down tomorrow early afternoon, we'll be fine I'm sure."

"Alright lass, be safe, both of you, and don't take any chances. We'll check in first thing in the morning. Everyone have a good night. I love and miss all of you, Olaf out."

The fire near the lake was roaring now. In its light we could clearly make out a solitary person slowly moving about. Hopefully tomorrow we were going to find out who this was.

Twenty-eight

Floki Vildarsen

March 26th

After we'd dressed and toiletries were done, a breakfast of beans and coffee was hurriedly prepared in the light of two Coleman lanterns. For most (I'm sure) this collation might have sounded mediocre, but to us, it was satisfying this morning and we were very grateful. Diffuse pastel hues had just begun illuminating the sky as we adjusted our backpacks to begin. Captain radioed the rest of the crew snickering. "Rise and shine ya lubbers, no time for lazy butts lollygagging." After conveying our agenda for the day we exited the campsite with the chill morning air biting at our faces. At the river's edge, we stopped to contemplate the enormous tangled mass of vines and branches on the other side. For a while we stared in amazement, realizing that we could have all perished in this mishap. Once again we knew our loving God had been faithful and we gratefully offered up another prayer of thanks. Work today would include photographing the architectural styles of the four different crannogs, investigating the anomalous water retrieval devices, and hopefully we'd be discovering who was responsible for the fires on the northwestern corner of the lake. With these goals in mind we headed north along the river.

Around us we were seeing artistic details, we hadn't seen the previous day, on certain of the structures, and, a greater variety of non-indigenous flora scattered over the valley floor. It was evident that this place had not been occupied for some time, but I saw no indication of disease or death. There were no skeletons, and no areas that bore any resemblance to graveyards; by all appearances everyone had vanished. The farther we walked the more baffling it became. After an hour we came to the outer edge of the lake. My first thoughts were that it was strongly mesotrophic and about a mile in diameter. Considering the glut of flora encompassing the shoreline, I presumed the water had a moderate amount of dissolved nutrients built up over centuries which, in my opinion, would make it a middle-aged lake. Around the northern quadrants there were three places where the shoreline extended inland and partially circumvented several assemblies of various sized rock crannogs. Ditches appeared to have been dug purposely to channel water from the lake into these designated areas for personal use. They all were expertly lined on the bottom and sides with granite slabs fitted together like a puzzle. It was amazing work. The light bluish green water of the lake was clear, but it had a distinct sulfurous odor. It was fed by the river and also from rain runoff from the surrounding mountains. On the plateau, two days prior, Garrett and I could make out no apparent outlet for the lake. But seeing here that the lake was extremely healthy I knew there had to be one somewhere. After two more hours of close examination it was John who found the answer to this mystery. There was a large sinkhole on the northeastern end in an area surrounded on three sides by diverse rock formations. He radioed us to come and have a look. I recognized that the water, where he was, was the same color as it had been over the continental shelf; a blackish blue. Because of the proximity of the cliffs to this end of the lake, I deduced that the water communicated with deep caverns, or subterranean passages under the mountainous foundations, and exited at some place further down in elevation, perhaps one of the streams we'd passed on the way in. This would now explain logically the continual flow of water through the lake. It was evident now to me that some form of eutrophication had enriched (the more sedentary parts of) this lake with nourishment for many centuries. Except for two hundred yards around the sinkhole, most of the shorelines were copious in flora. We observed water-lilies, thirty to forty feet out, and the large flat floating leaves were teeming with colorful flowers. A steady supply of nutrients was generating lush growth all around the rooted plants along the shoreline and amongst the phytoplankton in the shallower waters. We'd taken note of the fact (once again) that no animals or birds resided here, and we hadn't seen fish in the lake or river. Something was wrong and I began seriously wondered if the barking we'd heard wasn't just echoes of falling rock. We could see where three edifices had once been standing just off the shoreline. They'd been built on timber pilings that had been tied together with what appeared to have once been strong leather straps, long since rotted. This area could have been docks for the fisherman and (possibly also) the longboats when they'd returned from journeys into the lower areas of the *Ria de Vigo*.

Here was another fact that I was troubled with; there were no boats or vessels, nothing tangible, not even the rotting remains of something.

This district had a pretense of upper class, much more so than the neighborhoods further south. The crannogs were larger and ornately carved here, and, in an area east of us (higher in elevation) solid wood structures were predominate. I remembered them being very similar in appearance to the ones that I'd seen during my vacations (in past years) in the Hebrides and Orkney islands. A gravelly road led from this lower-class area up to the enormous wooden structure on top of the plateau in the northeastern quadrant. At the lakes edge, next to the road, was one of the water retrieval devices we'd puzzled about the previous day. A thick oaken deck, twenty feet in diameter, had been constructed three feet above the ground. In the middle they'd cut a four foot circle that appeared as an open black throat. It descended straight down into the earth and was lined with two inch thick wooden panels as deep as we could see in the present light. At first I assumed it was an *Artesian well.* But the more I studied the construction the more I realized that this was not accurate. An elongated framework of wood, and a spiraling copper tube, eight inches in diameter, descended into the hole; this was attached to four blackened wooden bearings stabilized on a post connected to the surface of the deck. A large wheel, with two hand sized handles, apparently turned this mechanism. We all realized that the same sulfurous odors, that were around the periphery of the lake, had intensified here. I wondered if this had anything to do with the absence of animal life and fish in the valley. After mulling the apparatus for a few minutes Captain Olaf suddenly exclaimed: "It's an *Archimedean screw.* I remember studying this in college; this is a water raising device. This is how they brought usable water out of this well into these troughs here. But where would Viking's get ideas like this, this was invented by the Romans. Here, let's try something. John, you and Gabriel grab a hold of the handles and start turning, let's see if this device really does bring up water."

As we began turning the wheel, a deep throaty growl startled us, and then the rustling in the overgrowth intensified; something was moving towards us at a rapid pace. "SPREAD OUT!" The Captain ordered. Immediately John dropped down behind one of the corners of the wooden platform and readied his pistol. Just as Captain was reaching for his revolver a blurred tan shape burst through the bushes and launched itself directly at me. Before I could react I was knocked down flat on my back. My life began flashing in front of me as a mouth full of fangs approached my face. I was horrified. But instead of being mauled, a sloppy wet tongue started licking my forehead and nose. Within seconds warm slobber had begun dripping down my ear lobes and onto my chin. As suddenly as he'd downed me the mugger jumped off me and started bounding playfully around us and barking. It was a young Irish wolfhound. Turning he bolted to the edge of the bushes and grabbed a piece of wood and then ran back and dropped it at my feet. In readiness he stared into my eyes, motionless, poised for a game of fetch. Somewhat hesitantly, as Captain and John laughingly holstered their weapons, I reached down to pick up the piece of wood. Before I had a chance to throw it a banging metal sound came from the direction of the castle. At once the dog turned heel and bolted towards the plateau barking loudly. With the binoculars focused on him, John followed the wolfhound up to the large wooden edifice. "There's someone right outside the front door. A man; he's scratching the dog's head and motioning for us to come up, captain, he seems to be . . . oh gosh, he just fell over, something's wrong." Moments later mournful howling echoed hauntingly throughout the valley.

Without a word Captain started running up the gravel road as John and I followed.

He was ancient, with thin shoulder length hair, and a very thick reddish beard. His attire included coarse tan pants, worn leather ankle boots, and a tattered light blue shirt that hung down to his middle thigh. His eyes were cloudy, impenetrable, sunken, and the face and hands had deep lines from the storms of a very hard life. Impassively he fixed his eyes on us as we propped up his head and loosened his shirt. He seemed questioning, but peaceful, about our presence and nodded his head in thanks as we made him comfortable. The wolfhound was sitting near the old man's head and was watchful of our every move. John offered him a cup of water, which he greedily downed in an instant, and motioned for more. After he'd gulped the second glass his eyes cleared and his demeanor changed. After a few deep breathes he adjusted himself and began to speak. Captain Olaf and John looked at each other in frustration; they couldn't understand a word he was saying. Thankfully the dialect was recognizable to me; a blending of ancient Scottish from the periphery, and the old hebridean dialects my great-great grandfather used to speak. Though the language was archaic I understood the meanings of almost every word.

His name was Floki Vildarsen, and he was the last of this valley clan. Many generations had lived here and prospered, enjoying the peace and security they'd built over many years of labor. But he was the last, the chosen one, the man given the final mission to complete, before the end of this place. While I listened to Floki talk, and interpreted what he was saying, an abrupt tremor shook the valley for several seconds and then stopped. The old man's expression turned peaceful during the event and, as tears began forming in his eyes, he looked up towards heaven and started praying.

Suddenly our radio squawked into life. "I just heard there's been another earthquake up towards Ireland." Rorek was clearly distraught. "I don't know the exact coordinates yet but it was huge. It shook us pretty good. There's a lot of commotion here in the harbor, what's your status Olaf?"

"We're fine here Rorek. Is everyone else ok?" the Captain inquired. Everyone confirmed they were safe, a little shaken, but waiting for orders. "Ok, I'll be back with you all shortly, something incredible is happening here at the moment and we've got to finish. Garrett, you and Helga get back down to camp with Betsy and Liz."

"Copy that boss. We'll pack up and leave now, Garrett out."

The Captain motioned at me to continue. "Sir, he knew we were coming. He said he's been waiting for us. He said he was given a dream many years ago about a small group of outsiders who would eventually find this valley. He said, at least ten times, that this valley will be destroyed and that he has important information for us personally." The Captain seemed enthralled and motioned for me to continue. Floki pointed at the wolfhound and said he was the last animal in the settlement. He'd been born a year and a half prior. His name was Rolf. All the other dogs had since died and had been buried. Floki loved his companion dearly. With some effort he sat up and began shaking his head to reinforce what he was saying. Sighing he lay back and asked for more water. It was peculiar. He had (what seemed) an insatiable thirst; having drunk more in twenty minutes than I often did in a whole day. I assumed he must have collapsed earlier from dehydration. But considering the amount of water in this valley it seemed quite improbable. Something I couldn't put my finger on was nagging me.

"Mr. Vildarsen, why are you so thirsty?" I finally asked in the broken dialect.

"Good water all gone two days water killed everyone years ago except me and dog. I warned all clan leaders about poison killing wells, but no one believe me, so all people die in fortnight, quickly, no pain, they pass on to higher place than Valhalla."

His answer was perplexing. If everyone had died because of the water, why hadn't we? We'd drunk every day from the river, but not directly from the water in this valley. We'd brought along water from our primary campsite, and the only thing we'd done differently was we'd boiled and purified it. So why was Floki still alive? What had he consumed to survive for so long?

"Where are all the clan now sir?" I asked. With a flick of his hand, Floki motioned towards the enormous wooden castle behind him and muttered: **"All families waiting in wells of ash for the Christ!"** After interpreting this for Captain and John, we pondered for several minutes what this could mean. In the meantime Floki reached down inside his shirt and had pulled out two trinkets on a metal chain. One was a representation of a sword and the other was a cross. The cross was easy, but on closer examination we all realized that the sword was a tiny, but accurate copy of the *Tempest*.

"Captain, he keeps repeating that we have to get the *Tempest* home to the first tribe; he wants us to promise to get the *Tempest* home."

"Have you said anything about the sword to him Gabriel?"

"Not a word sir, not even a hint. What do you make of it? How in the world would he know we have it?" With a puzzled look the Captain shrugged his shoulders.

"Sir," I began . . .

Floki stopped me with an upraised hand. Then, while a low cough rumbled inside his chest, he began sharing: "No need for many words. I know that the Christ has sent you to me; you are here because the Holy One willed it, two days past now since good water ended for me and dog. Now is my time to linger patiently with sleeping families for the Christ to return. Valley will be destroyed. Our time here is over. I know that you have many questions but many will remain unanswered. This is the Christ's will; you must leave. My departure is almost upon me. Take Rolf. He is yours. This is the Christ's will. He will be your friend. He will recognize the first tribe when you find them. Christ will guide you to first tribe in foreign land. Fortune inside handle will honor those lost and strengthen Rognvald name should Christ tarry in His coming. Many will pursue sword. Many will try to defile sword. Many will try to steal sword. Do not let them! Be courageous in your journey young warriors. This is the Christ's will. Only one man can present sword to first tribe. That man is . . ."

Floki began wheezing and motioned at me for water. I realized, as he took the cup from me, that his skin had become cold. After drinking it down, he sighed deeply and slumped backwards. Tears were flowing down my cheeks now and Rolf was whimpering. Slowly he crawled forward and laid his head on the old man's chest. Floki pulled the dog closer and whispered something in his ear. When he'd finished the dog licked his face and lay down next to him. With a deep sigh, Floki looked up at me. His eyes began to cloud over. Impulsively taking hold of my wrist he pulled me close and, after laying his hand on my heart, he whispered: "You are now the chosen one Gabriel. My mantle is yours. Remember, son, **Christ before all else!"** Another earthquake rattled the valley suddenly. Moments later Floki Vildarsen's spirit took flight from all earthly limitations.

Twenty-nine

Rolf the wolfhound

I will never forget that moment Floki's spirit left him. The wolfhound started crying despondently and his mournful howling reverberated throughout the valley. During this expression of grief a third trembler shook the valley and jolted us back to the veracity of our circumstances. It was a cheerless reminder that we were in harm's way and needed to depart the valley as soon as possible. When we'd buried Floki the dog's howling ended and he came over to where I was. After licking my hand he laid his head against my leg and woofed softly.

"Wow! He bonded with you," John remarked. "I believe the old man told the dog he was yours Gabriel."

"Seems we've got a new crew member; the girls are gonna love this big shaggy guy." The Captain laughed throatily.

For some reason I kept seeing Rolf slobbering on me, and me constantly cleaning up after him. Then I imagined Captain yelling at me because he'd stepped in Rolf's crap, and him taking up my whole bed so I'd have to sleep on the floor, and dog hairs on everything. I saw him chasing seagulls and falling off the schooner, and me having to dive in to save him, and his enormous appetite frustrating Betsy. When I looked down at him again, he nuzzled the top of my hand and licked it. At that moment something changed in me and all my unsettled feelings vanished. Quietly I knelt down, grabbed both his cheeks, and whispered in his ear: "You're mine now dude, so let's try to make the best of it, ok?" Something in Rolf changed, too, and he began jumping up and down like a kangaroo and barking gleefully. After chasing his tail a moment he bolted down to the river's edge and picked up another stick. For a moment he stared towards Floki's grave and then he dropped the stick and sniffed at the water. Barking madly he turned and ran back to my side and sat down.

"Let's leave," the Captain motioned at us.

When we'd paid our final respects we began our trek back along the river's edge towards the raft. After walking in silence awhile we began discussing the steps necessary to get out of the Pontevedra as soon as possible; it was obvious the area was becoming unstable and could pose a grave threat to everyone's safety. We realized, too, that no matter how quickly we might travel, we still had almost sixty miles of streams and rivers to navigate, and we had to do it in a raft with seven people, a dog, and a utility raft in tow. The possibility of encountering another thick fog concerned us. But many things could go wrong that we had no control over. Given this we reconciled ourselves to press forward as rapidly, and as efficiently, as possible, and put our safe passage into God's hands.

"Something's been bugging me." John blurted suddenly.

"What's that?" The Captain asked.

"How did the old man know Gabriel's name?"

The question jolted me. Floki *had* called me by name, but never once had I shared that information in the conversation.

"I have absolutely no idea," The Captain finally muttered.

"I have no idea either Captain. But you know sir; Floki did say something else that was puzzling, too." I added.

"What's that?" The Captain inquired.

"He said, quote: *'I know you will have many questions, but many will remain unanswered, this is the Christ's will.'* Is it possible that this could be one of those questions?"

"Well . . . we'll certainly never have an answer for it, that's for certain. So I'd have to say yes, son." The Captain replied.

After we'd reached the secondary campsite, it took only thirty minutes to load the raft. Captain radioed ahead and told the others our intentions and that we'd inherited a new friend. Rorek balked, at once, and strongly suggested that we leave the dog at one of the humane shelters in Vigo. Everyone declined his suggestion. As soon as we'd arrived at the primary camp, and Rolf had jumped off the raft, his personality blossomed; he became a mischievous lovable clown, running and hiding, playing fetch with John, knocking Garrett down and wrestling with him, licking Betsy's hands, running in circles around me barking, and nipping playfully at Lizzy and Helga's feet. Everyone loved him.

March 27th

Small aftershocks had continued throughout the night. And just about the time you'd begin to drift off another jolt would sit you up straight; I knew that lack of rest would be dearly missed today. Regret was expressed as we motored away; we'd all been touched in numerous ways in this incredible place. This mysterious detour into the Pontevedra had been amazingly productive. We had over eight hundred photographs of our adventure. A detailed journal had been started, including visual records of all the architectural differences in the crannogs, what furniture and tools we found, the Archimedean screws in the wells, the lake and all its flora, the rock quarry, the drainage canals, and every different genus of tree in the valley. Sadly, because of circumstance, we were never given a chance to explore the wooden castle. Someday, perhaps, that may happen for us.

Rolf howled mightily as we entered the rivers swift current. Leaving behind the only environment he'd ever known must have been disconcerting. He was heading into the unknown, now, along with the rest of us. After a few minutes he finally quieted and crawled forward, around us and through our legs, up to the bow of the raft. There, as Garrett softly scratched his head, he curled up on the bottom and fell fast asleep. The journey downstream went without incident. Later in the afternoon we safely reached the harbor in Vigo under clear blue skies. Seeing the schooner again was a delight and Rorek embraced each of us as we boarded. When Rolf jumped aboard he at once sat down and stared at Rorek. Not knowing what to think Rorek stared back with quiet suspicion. For a few moments neither made a sound. But then, when our noble-minded canine politician trotted over and got up on his rear legs, with both paws on his shoulders, and licked his face, our engineer's laughter reverberated over the whole vessel. Rorek's prior suggestion (about leaving him at a humane shelter in Vigo) had now become a matter permanently resolved in favor of Rolf the Irish wolfhound. Very efficiently, and intelligently, he'd found a place in all of our hearts and was now a permanent part of the crew.

Thirty

South to Portugal

March 28th

After dressing, and running a comb through my tousled hair, I scurried up on deck; I needed to talk to someone about these wee morning hours. It was four-thirty. The brothers were in the wheelhouse plotting our course and listening to the Navtex for weather updates. John was on the big wheel. When Rolf saw me he bounded over with a happy yelp. And after licking my hand he bolted back to where Garrett was skipping stones from a bagful he'd collected at the primary campsite. We were headed southwest now towards Bayona; our goal was to reach Porto Portugal today, on the Douro River, one hundred and seventy kilometers from our present location. Helga reminded us that two delayed e-mails from Jonah and Roxanne had finally come through the evening before. They'd made inquiries about the hidden settlement in the Pontevedra, and had also shared the results from some analysis they had done. The water samples Jonah had taken from the shallows had finally come back. The lab at the university had established that nothing peculiar existed in the water, on the surface, or in the cavern, where we'd retrieved the artifacts. There'd only been a slight elevation of sulfur in the cavern and a nominal difference in saline levels. It appeared that everything we'd discovered had been miraculously preserved just for us. The leather scroll, we'd retrieved on top of volcano rock, had been obscured and extensive chemical treatments hadn't revealed anything useful. The lab technicians believed certain parts of the writings were done at the last minute and the scroll had been rolled up wet. Because of this, areas of the scroll had been destroyed. Helga reminded me that I still had the hard disc recorder we'd taken from the peevish spy stashed in my berth and that we needed to ascertain whether or not there was anything pertinent on it that may affect our journey negatively. Since I wasn't required at present I decided to use the next few hours to e-mail mother and father, and also surf the internet. While writing I realized that almost a month had passed since I'd departed Aberdeen. For one thing I felt like a different person. I was stronger physically and had muscles appearing in my upper body and legs that I never knew existed before. Three weeks previous, Garrett, John and I had begun a regimen of weights and calisthenics. It was a brisk thirty minute daily workout that was really helping me with strength, flexibility, and confidence. John was also teaching us fighting skills he'd learned in the Navy Seals and he was looking forward to teaching us more about scuba-diving in the months ahead.

The brothers had decided to purchase ten thousand rounds of ammunition for our weapons, and, British Berkefeld water filters to use on our protracted journey across the Atlantic. Everyone was also in need of new clothing and shoes, toiletries, batteries, and a host of other things. This stop in Porto would be crucial for personal supplies and the vessels requirements. The University of Porto had authorized loaning us some powerful laser technology to use in our quest. Apparently the universities of Porto, and Southern California had authorized a financial grant for the *Heimdall's* covert mission. They also had offered us the use of newly developed equipment to field test and write reports on. They were bowled over with the reports we'd sent them of our discoveries of 'Volcano rock' and the 'Shallows of Three Rocks' and were eager to analyze the digital photos of the hidden settlement, and throughout the Pontevedra Province. A new website was being built by an aggregate of universities now expressing interest in our journey. When completed it would be offering the public an abbreviated glimpse into some of the new information along with downloadable high resolution photos. Everything (except personal information and names, pictures of the *Tempest,* or any other classified artifacts) would be made available to the public free of charge. At this point even Regan Pendleton wasn't aware of our discovery of the *Tempest*, and neither were the Universities. We all knew that if this ever became common knowledge we would become a target for the media, the Mortiken, and every other scumbag that wanted glory for someone else's hard work.

Because of the crew's dedicated commitment, in pursuing the Rognvald's ancient route to America's west coast, a new college course was being developed for the winter season in Southern California, and also at the University of Alaska. They had kindly (and in my estimation sagaciously) offered Roxanne the professorship. It was an honor she did not hesitate to accept. Much was changing in the world and I was very thankful that we were in God's plan concerning our endeavors. I was really looking forward to a burgeoning relationship with Betsy, and I also knew that John felt the same way about Helga.

"Everyone up at the wheelhouse now," the Captain announced on the vessels PA. As I raced out the door I glanced over at the clock; it was nine-thirty. "We've received distressing news from Roxanne," the Captain began, as he climbed down the stairs. "It looks like the Mortiken have launched a full scale invasion against the Azorean Archipelagoes now. They've attempted raids on *Viana do Castelo* and *Porto* sometime earlier this week. Someone suggested they might be trying to manipulate certain shipping ports in the EC, and, of course we all know that Porto has that huge harbor that can accommodate anything. The military was on bi-yearly maneuvers all along the Spanish and Portuguese coastlines. Because of this they were able to stymie what they were trying to do. Three Mortiken vessels evaded capture however; they used a thick fog to their advantage and were last tracked heading west towards the islands of *Santa Maria* and *Sao Miguel* in the eastern Azores. These vessels are a great deal larger than the smacks we encountered on the barges; they're diesel driven and carry no sails. These two islands are under Mortiken control, now, and a lot of people have died trying to defend them." The Captain paused a moment and sipped his coffee. Then he continued. "Shortly after John destroyed the *Wormwood,* Roxanne received an encrypted message from a colleague vacationing there. Riots had erupted between harbor officials, and a group of businessmen that had recently defected to the European community from the Middle East. Apparently someone was very disgruntled with what'd been accomplished."

"Was there anything mentioned about the fatman's vessel?"

"Yes Liz there was. Evidently after they'd heard about the capture of their southern operatives, and the impoundment of the stolen vessel, they were enraged. It's unclear why, perhaps the ledger Helga found had some information they didn't want getting out. By the way, on that thought Helga, go through that book again, carefully please, and see if there's anything we missed the first time. Perhaps there's something in it useful to us."

"Aye sir, we'll do it right after we're done here." Helga replied.

Olaf nodded his thanks and continued. "The day after we left La Coruna, three vessels anchored off-shore. Those same men, Roxanne's colleague said, boarded a small speedboat and went out to rendezvous with them. Little is known about what transpired aboard those ships, but I'm thinking it must have been a prearranged tactical meeting. She observed launches taking people from the two smaller vessels over to the larger vessel, and all of them were carrying weapons. Four hours later the businessmen boarded a helicopter that flew out to meet them, and then the three vessels headed west. I mentioned already what happened after that." The Captain paused a few moments with his head down, and then continued. "Really, this is crumby news for us. Our plans have changed once again. We've all got some serious praying and thinking to do. It looks like we're heading right back into harm's way. Let's have a meeting tomorrow; I want to hear everyone's thoughts and ideas about what's going on. Also we've got to restock everything; this is the lowest we've been in a very long time."

The bell on Helga's computer rang over the ships PA; another e-mail had just come through. "Give me a moment Captain, this might be important." When Helga returned her face was flushed. "Captain, it's from Roxy. Should I read it?"

"Aye lass, by all means," He responded tersely.

Brothers and sisters, I love you all so very much.

As an addendum to my last letter, the Mortiken are moving quickly. I understand there's over one hundred in this new assault. The islands of Terciera and Sao Jorge have also been taken over, along with Sao Miguel and Santa Maria. Everyone involved in island government have been murdered. This is horrifying, and unconscionable. The island of Pico has Navy docked in the harbor there, and also a regiment of marines are on deployment for their bi-yearly maneuvers. Hopefully they will be able to do something. Graciosa and Faial Island are still clear of invaders, but they're preparing for the worst. Many people have opted to fly to the mainland from all of the islands. The military have ordered Resell, Lira and I to leave Flores. We're leaving behind everything we found in the caves. We've hidden it all in a cave just southwest of the Albarnaz lighthouse on the Ponta do Albarnaz; it's marked with a cross so we can find it again. There are seven boxes of artifacts we've kept. Most of the photographic records are on disc now, and I'll be carrying those personally. I've also mailed several backup copies to both universities and Jonah. The three of us are at the airport now as I'm writing this on my laptop. We leave in twenty minutes; they're straight through flights so we'll be in Porto by ten am today.

Here's my itinerary . . .

Resell and Lira will have a truck waiting for them. It belongs to another graduate student they know. Before they head back to Vila Real, they'll be dropping me off in the Rebeira district. It's on the northern side of the Douro

River right on the boardwalk, about thirty yards before the Dom Luis Bridge. There's a little restaurant called the 'Casa Filha da Mae Preta' there. I'll stay inside until you arrive. I'll leave a white handkerchief tied on the railing overlooking the river. Please be safe, things are getting desperate here now. The whole city of Porto is on military alert, they're checking everyone coming and going. Captain Olaf, it might be wise to anchor off the coast and take the raft in after dark. It would bring less attention to what we're doing. The raft is big enough to carry all the equipment and four people safely. I love you all dearly, oh yes; the new technology is on the loading dock, right by the restaurant, in three large unmarked boxes. I had the University deliver it that way to facilitate our time, and not generate any curiosity in our being there. As far as I can tell no one has a clue about us, except Regan Pendleton, and he knows very little. Jonah's beginning to trust him a lot more now though, I pray that continues.

P.S. I just saw on Earthnet news that the Vigo prison was raided last night and two men were murdered . . . no names or faces yet. See y'all soon, love Roxanne. Roxanne@earthnet.net

The Captain had that daunting expression again when Helga finished reading. Immediately we all huddled together and began laying out plans for replenishing our supplies, filling our fuel and water tanks, and getting Roxanne without being noticed. We all agreed that, after we'd anchored south of the township of *Matosinhos*, John, Garrett and I would be taking the raft up the Douro to fetch

Roxy and the new technology. The Captain figured it was about eight kilometers to the restaurant. Lord willing, if all went as planned, we should be in and out in three hours.

Lizzy went on-line to learn more about the raid on the prison. Strangely the news about it was being blocked. Were the two men murdered in the Vigo prison the tattooed fatman and his accomplice? Was this the way they cleaned up their messes? I wondered who those EC businessmen were, and what their actual agenda was. It seemed the Mortiken had substantial money and power accumulating behind them, now, from varied sources, and their evil agenda was being embraced by many more than just their own kind. An ancient wickedness was beginning to proliferate.

Thirty-one

Rescuing Roxanne

A grouping of islands, three miles south of the hamlet, and two miles from the mouth of the Douro River, was our present destination. Captain was planning on anchoring there to launch our rescue mission into Porto. After praying we lowered the raft into the water and the three of us boarded. We'd decided to dress dark, camouflage our faces, bring John's night vision binoculars, carry a light sidearm each, small lithium flashlights, and radios with ear pieces. Garrett started the motor. But just as we were about to shove off Helga's cell phone rang. She told us it was Roxanne and motioned to wait. The conversation took longer than expected so we turned the motor off to conserve gas. Ten minutes later Helga motioned for us to come back aboard and then called the rest of the crew topside. When everyone was present she updated us.

"She's at the restaurant, she's safe, and there's hardly anyone there tonight because of the new city-wide restrictions. The laser technology is next to the concrete stairs. As of now no one is suspicious about her, or the boxes. She tied a white handkerchief to the railing as a marker. There are many new developments around Porto tonight, she said, and they're spreading quickly into all the outlying areas. The military are everywhere, monitoring everyone moving about the city. They're patrolling the waterfront every hour, and the river every thirty minutes with helicopters. She said a new system of permits is required to move about and do business with. They have to be on your person at all times or else you can be jailed. She said all the refueling depots along the Douro have been shut down indefinitely. When she realized the extent of what was happening Roxanne admitted that she was at a loss about what to do. She decided to pray for direction and then felt compelled to call Resell and Lira. Here's where it gets hopeful sir . . . they both understood and suggested if we could make it to *Leiria* their uncle had a fueling depot just five kilometers northwest of the city. His business supply's all the local fishermen and the smaller ocean going vessels like ours. He also owns a general market where we should be able to purchase all our food and everything else we need. They also mentioned that uncle has a very large assortment of ammunition and weapons hidden up in the hills; their other uncle is a gunrunner for the paramilitary in Portugal, and Spain, and if we can tell him at least six hours ahead of our arrival, the order will be waiting for us. Fortunately there's nothing else in that area, no other businesses or homes for miles, so, it's very possible we could get in and out and no one would even know we'd been there. There's a catch though Captain. We have to get there before six tomorrow morning, because tomorrow morning at eight they won't be able to do business with anyone unless they've obtained a permit from Porto. The second catch is that he wants paper Euros up front, no checks, no credit, and no debit cards."

The Captain held up his hand and turned towards me. "Son, how much cash do you have left from that last transaction with the map maker?"

"I still have four thousand Euros sir."

"Excellent, wonderful, praise God hallelujah and pass the chili, we'll have enough to refuel, purchase ammo, and replenish all we need then." Captain's demeanor brightened and a salubrious optimism began to prevail in his expression again. "Rorek, let's you and I put together lists. As soon as the boys leave I'll come below and help out." Turning on heel Rorek scuffled below decks. "Betsy, get everyone's personal lists together. Helga, contact Roxanne again and have her get in touch with Resell and Lira. Ask them to contact their uncle and confirm that we'll be there on time. Get a phone number so we can order the ammunition personally. Also get a fax number so we can send along our shopping list. This is unfolding nicely people. Alright men, it's time for business. Go get Roxy and the equipment." The Captain shook his head optimistically and gave us a thumb up as we climbed back down into the raft.

Garrett started the motor. A few seconds later we roared off towards the Douro River. I began having strange misgivings about what we might be headed into this evening. Lights along the shoreline began flickering on shortly after we'd passed through the mouth of the river. I could see an increase of activity in the villages along the river, but no one seemed to notice us. A strange uneasiness came over me as we passed the fishing boats headed upriver. It felt as if some heavy oppression was on everyone. I wondered if the Mortiken attempt to take over the city might have had a deleterious effect on the emotions of these citizens. John was laying down in the bow peering through the night vision binoculars. Garrett began maneuvering the raft closer to the shoreline to take advantage of a forming mist.

"Men . . . where are you now?"

The Captains sudden question startled us. John turned and motioned for me to answer so he could continue searching the shoreline. "Sir its Gabriel," I whispered back in the mouthpiece. "According to the map we're just now passing the Ponta de Arrabida; Massarelos is on our port. I estimate we have another two miles before we approach the *Dom Luis Bridge*. River traffic is gone sir, hardly any traffic on the riverfront roads either. Garrett's got us about ten yards off the northern side of the river in shallower water."

"Copy that Gabriel. Do the others have their earpieces in, can they both hear me?" I glanced over at John and Garrett and they both nodded that they could.

"Roger that sir, loud and clear."

"Ok, here's an up-date, listen carefully now. I contacted uncle, a wonderfully accommodating man, too; we'll rendezvous with him on the *Lis River* tomorrow morning at six and depart by seven. That's exactly ten hours from now. Rorek ordered ammunition. Uncle said no problem; it'll be waiting for us in unmarked crates. We got everything on our list. Betsy also sent our food, supplies, and personal items list via fax. When he received it he assured me he had everything in stock. He'll have all of our supplies and frozen foods packaged and ready to go when we get there. Refueling will be the biggest time consumer; it'll take about forty-five minutes. He informed me there's plenty of diesel and propane, but he's only got twenty gallons of gasoline for the raft. His main delivery is still three days away, it'll have to do for now. We have a lot of water to cover in a short amount of time. Get your job done safely men and get back home ASAP . . . Olaf out!"

"Captain, before you sign off . . ." A thought had suddenly come to me about Roxanne.

"Go ahead Gabriel."

"Perhaps you could phone Roxanne and suggest that she pay her bill, exit the restaurant, and wait for us down next to the river. We can get the crates and her aboard in a minimum amount of time that way."

"We should be at the bridge in about fifteen minute's sir." John whispered in addition.

"Hold on men." The Captain answered. There was silence for several minutes. "Alright, we've got a go on the idea, it's very logical son, thanks. Helga's calling Roxanne. I'll get back with you when she's done." Several minutes more went by before the Captain responded. "Roxanne loved the idea, she's paying her bill as we speak, and she'll be down next to the water in five minutes. Let me know when you make contact with her . . . Olaf out."

Later John motioned suddenly for silence. With hand signals he made us aware of a fully gunned military cruiser scanning the water and boardwalks methodically with a powerful spotlight. Garrett killed the motor. Silently we drifted towards the retaining wall. As soon as we were next to it we took a hold of the docking rings, to avoid drifting, and we all hunched down. Thankfully there was a thick mist now hovering two feet above the water that we vanished into. After several minutes Garrett whispered: "Two hundred yards, starboard bow; Roxanne's next to the water on those concrete stairs, she's right beneath that stupid white handkerchief. It'll stick out like a sore thumb if the spotlight hits it. I hope the military cruiser doesn't get suspicious about the stupid thing and try to bust her." John and I murmured in agreement. Seconds later Roxanne bolted up the stairs, removed the handkerchief, and then ran back down the stairs and vanished. John whispered that he could just barely see her, through the binoculars, crouching behind one of the pilings next to water's edge. A few seconds later Helga contacted us.

"I overheard your conversation and called Roxy. She'd been watching the cruiser for a while and was getting concerned. Garrett, you were right about the handkerchief. It was a good idea in theory, but not in tonight's circumstances. She was considering going back up to the restaurant to avoid being detained and interrogated. I guess the safest place tonight is inside a building. She's very relieved you can see her. She'll stay hidden and wait."

"Copy that. Oh gosh! Helga, the cruiser stopped. They've killed their engine. The spotlight is moving around right above us; oh gosh, we've got to stay out of sight. We'll keep you posted, Gabriel out."

The possibility of being detained filled us all with a terrible trepidation. With a limited window of opportunity we needed to maintain our schedule. It was going to be difficult, though, and given these circumstances none of us were going to get any sleep tonight. It was very quiet on the river now. The only sounds were a monotonous bubbling current against the concrete walls and the occasional radio conversations aboard the military cruiser. The vessel was only twenty yards from us now. My heart was beating like a war drum, but there was absolutely nothing we could do except shake our heads helplessly and wait. The intense spotlight was arching back and forth just above our heads, at times coming only inches away from illuminating our position. I hoped that their only interest would be the thoroughfare above us tonight. In the tense stillness it was Garrett's prayer over the radio that filled me once again with faith and hope.

"Father God in heaven, in the name of Jesus Christ, the author and sustainer of our lives, we all agree right now Lord, all the

members of the crew agree, that you will create a distraction to take this military cruiser away from us so we can accomplish this job you've given us to do. Thank you Lord Christ, ahead of time, in your blessed name amen."

Seconds later the cumbersome stillness was shattered by the sudden loud blaring of the cruisers radio. Central command was reporting that a Mortiken platoon had been spotted at the Campanha train station and also Porto's main airport. The motor exploded into life and, with a sudden intense churning of the water, the vessel spun around and roared upriver. A few seconds later a deadly helicopter gunship flew by us ten feet above the water's surface. As soon as they were out of site we knew it was time to make our move. Garrett sprang into action and, with the motor screaming; we raced towards the dock where Roxanne was waving franticly with both arms. Within seconds we were next to the concrete stairs.

"I'm really glad to see you guys. Thank God you're here and safe. The wait was beginning to drive me nuts."

I helped Roxanne aboard and got a huge hug for my efforts. Bubbling with excitement, and apprehension, she quickly huddled down on the forward seat and wrapped her coat tightly around her neck and ears. While Garrett held us stable, John bounded off the raft and handed the crates, and Roxanne's luggage, down to me. Within a few breathless moments we were all aboard again and racing back.

"Captain Olaf," I shouted in the radio mouthpiece, "we're on our way. Roxanne is safe, and we have everything aboard."

"Copy that, Gabriel, excellent work men. Get back here as soon as you can, Olaf out."

Moments after I'd keyed off the radio we began hearing an ominous chatter of gunfire and low explosive thuds in the distance. Somewhere in Porto another battle with the Mortiken had begun.

Thirty-two

Racing against time

The motor was screaming wide open and in a matter of minutes we'd all been soaked to the skin. Garrett's skill in piloting the raft (high speed) was evident here and, like his solitary penchant for skipping stones; he had us bouncing back to the *Heimdall,* holding on for dear life. As soon as we'd arrived those on the schooner sprang into action. Unloading our cargo, and hoisting the raft out of the water, took only minutes. Captain had already weighed anchor and the diesel was warm and ready to go. Now we'd be racing against time to reach our next destination. It was wonderful seeing Roxanne again and we all exchanged hugs and jabbered like children. It seemed as if a month had passed since we'd watched her sad face in the rear window of the taxi pulling away on the docks of La Coruna. After showers, and a fresh change of clothes, we all met in the galley for hot chocolate and Betsy's freshly prepared torpedo sandwiches. Rolf wandered in and introduced himself. Roxanne and he bonded immediately. While we ate she e-mailed Jonah (from my laptop) and gave him our coordinates and itinerary for the next twenty-four hours. Fortunately he'd brought along his laptop, on his Ghost Mountain excursion, to stay in touch with us; his response came within fifteen minutes. He sent his love to all, and was very relieved that she was safe. Concerned about our race against time for supplies, he assured us that he and the church group would begin praying for our safety and success. Jonah informed us that he was beginning to read on-line reports about a violent insurrection erupting in *Panama City, Colon'*, in the country of Columbia, and also in the cities of *Cartagena* and *Barranquilla*. Because the details were sketchy he gave us several URL's so we could keep abreast of these hotspots also. If these areas became too embroiled in skirmishes our original route to South California would be seriously compromised.

It was mandatory that we refuel and resupply; because if we didn't there was no way that we could continue on. In all their years of sailing this stop was the most critical the two brothers could ever remember. We still had one hundred and eighty kilometers to go and if one thing happened to interfere we weren't going to reach our appointment on time. After dinner John went up on deck to man the spotlight to help Rorek navigate through the darkness. Rolf sauntered idly up with him and flumped down a few feet away. After a while he got up and chased his tail for a few moments and then stood up with his paws on the rear rails and began howling out into the brisk ocean air. John, as it happened, was deeply moved by Rolf's impromptu performance and saw a perfect opportunity to let off some steam himself. Let it be known to the reader that their performance will forever haunt my dreams. The horrifying sonic disturbance created between John and Rolf, (in those interminable moments) broke all world records for weird, and left us all seriously stupefied. Out of love and respect none of us mentioned anything to either.

March 29th

At five the skies were just beginning to show a faint wash of light. No one had slept at all, except Rolf, who was still snuggled up in his 'blankie' and snoring soundly under the raft. Helga and John were up in the crow's nest watching for the *Lis River.* Garrett was on the bow spotlight busily scanning for any obstacles. As it was we were making surprising time, as if some secret current was transporting us faster than the schooner was capable of moving on its own. At five fifteen John alerted us that the river entrance was in sight. Olaf began to steer closer towards the shore to safely access the turbulent mouth of the river.

"Captain, can you see them, off the port bow?" John shouted down and pointed from the crow's nest.

When I saw what he was talking about my heart began rejoicing. As the rest of the crew ran up on deck Rolf awakened with a jolt. And after shaking himself briskly he made his way over to the railings and sat down and began cleaning his paws and face. The dolphins were jumping and laughing excitedly. They were very happy to see us as we were them. I knew God's hand had to be in these encounters because of the timing. I was convinced, now more than ever, that they were here to help us accomplish something that we were incapable of doing ourselves. After we'd entered the river's mouth the dolphins rolled up on their sides and waved with their flukes. Then they veered away towards a small island near the mouth; it appeared that they were going to wait for our return. John and Helga were huddled together now with the Captain and Rorek. After a short talk Helga gave her cell phone to Captain. I presumed he was contacting Resell and Lira's Uncle to tell him our present coordinates so he could prepare for our arrival. As he talked Captain was nodding and smiling, and shortly thereafter he handed the phone back to Helga and he picked up the radio.

"Crew, I've just contacted uncle. We're only a few miles away from him now. All our supplies are packaged and waiting and he's got employees on the dock ready to help us refuel and facilitate our time. These people are awesome. He's going to package up the frozen food now so it will be ready to load when we arrive. I figure twenty more minutes. Gabriel and Garrett, get the gangplank ready, Olaf out."

Minutes later Helga burst back on deck and thrust a piece of paper into the Captain's hand. When he'd read it his demeanor darkened. Clearly distraught he handed his radio to Helga and she keyed on. "Crew, just received another up-date from Jonah, here let me read it.

> *Captain Olaf and crew,*
>
> *Our first route across the Atlantic, through the Panama Canal, has been compromised. The violence has escalated dramatically there in the last twelve hours. Not only is Panama City and Colon being attacked; now Portobello and Porvenir are also under assault. The violence up in Columbia has been squashed though and the military are now in control there, they've also called in the American marines. It appears now that the Mortiken are behind this new wave of violence. They've been spotted throughout all of these cities, I just mentioned, and it looks like they're trying to take over the Canal. The Middle Eastern allies,*

they're in allegiance with, have destroyed several key positions along the Chagres River; this river supplies the water necessary to operate the locks of the Panama Canal. They've also tried to blow up the dam holding back the Gatun Lake, but this attempt was unsuccessful. If they stop the flow of the Chagres River, the locks on the Canal won't be able to function; all traffic through the Canal will stop. Now, I'd like to rendezvous with the Heimdall on the Madeira Islands before you head to Flores to discuss our new route to America. As of now I can free up seven days, but this number could possibly increase. I think there might be a cancellation of one of my expeditions. These islands belong to the European Union so you'll need Euros to do business, or a good encrypted card. I think I remember Gabriel saying his Father had given him one. A rest might be very beneficial for all of you now. Please prayerfully discuss this and let me know as soon as possible after you've taken aboard all your supplies.

Your brother in Christ, and fellow warrior-Jonah"

As we chewed over these new developments, a sudden shout from Garrett alerted us to a young man running along the shore waving franticly. He was pointing upstream at a grouping of various sized buildings. Captain slowed the vessel and maneuvered us in towards the wooden pier. When we'd tied off the mooring lines and lowered the plank, uncle ran onboard and warmly greeted us. His wife and two others followed afterwards with coffee and warm cinnamon buns smothered in butter. These we devoured greedily and then put our minds towards the business at hand. Two of uncle's employees began the tedious refueling process, while three others began moving sixty boxes and crates aboard. Under uncles watchful eye the process went smoothly. When they'd finished, Captain motioned me over to where he was standing. As I was he put up three and a half fingers. Then uncle handed the Captain a piece of paper which he put into his breast pocket without reading. Bowing respectfully I handed thirty-five hundred Euros to the short, balding man we knew only as uncle. Smiling he motioned for his wife and employees to gather around. When they had, they joined hands and bowed, and then saluted the Captain in military fashion and retreated back into the trees towards the market. Olaf was ecstatic and raised both fists in victory as he scurried back up the gangplank. Rolf bounded after him barking excitedly. Back aboard he lay down next to Olaf's feet in the wheelhouse and began licking his paws. After giving the order to cast off the fore and aft lines, Captain motioned for Rorek and me to crank in the plank.

We'd done it!

Our race against time had been successful and very productive. Before we departed we all joined hands and thanked God for the victory. We were refueled, restocked, and had acquired all the ammunition we'd ordered. We were completely prepared now for the next leg of our journey. Minutes after we left the river, and had entered into the Atlantic, our dolphins appeared alongside us. Racing ahead, they began jumping, chattering, and squeaking. Then suddenly, and for no apparent reason, they stopped dead in the water just off the bow and stared. Bewildered, Captain Olaf stopped the schooner. I could see from his expression that he was perplexed about something. Climbing down from the wheelhouse he walked over to the rails and stared blankly at the water for a few moments while twisting his moustache.

"*OH* . . . I remember now!" He blurted. Then he reached into his shirt pocket and pulled out a piece of paper.

"What is it Captain?" I asked, coming up next to him.

"This note uncle gave me, he asked me to read it before we got too far underway." He began smiling. A few moments later he handed it to me with a wink. "Read this, and then tell all the others that we're going to take a break for a few days, starting this morning." With that he laughed heartily, slapped his thigh, and began punching the air as he climbed back up into the wheelhouse. Rolf sat up alertly as he entered and barked several times as Olaf vigorously scratched his head. Here's what uncle had written.

> *Salutations . . . Resell and Lira have spoken so very highly of you. They love Roxanne and their affiliation with her work and also your wonderful journey. Thank you so much for your business today, it was truly appreciated. My brother Rodolfo appreciates your business also, he sends his regards and apologizes that he was not there to meet you. Because of this he would be pleased and honored to offer you the following: He has a dear friend in Peniche who has agreed to let all of you stay at his beachfront inn for three days and nights at Rodolfo's expense. Your arrival has already been established and all is paid. You check in at 10am this morning and don't have to leave until 10am April 1st. His name is Ernesto Padilla, and the inn is of the same name. Please enjoy my friends, and may God bless and protect you on your journey ahead. Regards, uncle*

The crew was ecstatic and then suddenly very tired. At nine-thirty Captain Olaf anchored inside a small harbor on a jaggy peninsula next to the picturesque rural community of *Peniche*. Wearily we all checked into the **'Ernesto Padilla Inn'** at ten and, as we were politely escorted to our individual rooms, we murmured to one another that we'd meet for dinner at eight.

Thirty-three

Ernesto Padilla's Inn

When the door of my room closed I fell into a kind of faint and collapsed onto the large bed. Mercifully, I descended into a deep sleep. Drawn from my vivid dreams I was jolted awake around seven by a loud knocking on the door.

"Rise and shine dill-dork! I can't believe how loud you snore; I thought it was an earthquake, I think you need to see a doctor. Either that or you need therapy immediately."

It was Garrett, again being himself, and humorous. He went on to tell me that we were going to be treated to a most sumptuous feast and I needed to get ready. Groggily I answered with a halfhearted, ok, and stumbled into the shower. Within an hour I was downstairs, dressed and looking decent, in the rustic dining room facing the Atlantic. Most of the crew was already congregated around an elaborate indoor waterfall sipping herb tea and coffee. Dressed in red shorts, a white t-shirt emblazoned with a cross, and blue tennis shoes, Garrett sauntered over. "Your sweetie's in the kitchen with Roxy and the executive chef. They've got something awesome fur dinner, dude. They started at four, while you were still snoring up a storm. Dude, you were so loud I thought a freight train de-railed. I felt the earth move under my feet man." I looked at Garrett with a sheepish expression and shrugged my shoulders. "We're the only people in town tonight," he continued, "that meatball over there, the one dressed like a lounge singer, said the place is ours. We can get whatever we want until Monday morning at ten for no charge . . . totally cool!"

Garrett had pointed at a refined man in his early sixties. He sported a waxed moustache and was dressed in an old fashioned baby blue tuxedo, a garish bolo tie, brown and white penny loafers with two old copper pennies and pink socks; he looked exactly like Garrett had described him. When he'd noticed Garrett pointing, he scurried over to where we were standing and extended his hand to me; I could hardly restrain snickering when Garrett began poking me in the ribs.

"Good evening young master," he began politely, "it is my sincere pleasure to make your acquaintance. Welcome to the world famous Ernesto Padilla's Inn, a place where travelers confront Portuguese hospitality at its finest, and develop bravura memories that last a lifetime. May I offer you something cold or hot young sir, or possibly some tantalizing spirits?"

"Thank you sir, you are most genial." I responded back. "But I never consume liquor, ever. If it wouldn't be too much trouble, sir, I would delight exceedingly in having a cup of hot apple cinnamon herb tea with a dash of cinnamon powder on top, and a small wedge of lime on the side. Oh . . . and if you don't mind, a bag of oyster crackers would complement the tea delightfully."

Garrett snickered as I spoke. But when I bowed to Ernesto, he snorted and made his way back across the room. For some peculiar reason I'd begun responded to Ernesto's affectations with embellished manners and feigned politeness of my own, but I don't think he picked up on it. If he had; he was far too much a gentleman to react negatively to my whimsical behavior. He bowed politely to me and then, with a slight scowl, scurried away. He barked an order to an older waitress behind the bar, who, in a matter of minutes, brought me my order and handed me the evening's menu.

"Dig on that menu." Garrett yelled from across the room. "When you're done come on over and take a look at this lobster tank, these red crackers are monsters man."

I waved and then acknowledged to him that I'd be over in a few minutes. The atmosphere was soft, warm and inviting, and the aromas drifting throughout were mouth-watering. In the background uninspired elevator renditions of early classics were playing inconspicuously. After exploring the spacious room I decided to peruse the menu and moved over under a light by the main entrance. In wonderment my eyes opened as I read.

First course: *Lobster Bisque soup, or phyllo crusted Roquefort and Goat cheese crostata salad with candied walnuts, cherries, and white balsamic vinaigrette.*

Second course: 1. *Lobster Thermador-broiled spiny lobster tail topped with creamy white wine mustard sauce.* 2. *Petite Filet Mignon with caramelized shiitake mushrooms.* 3. *Lobster Puerto Nuevo-spiny lobster tail* *fried in butter and white wine, and served with rice, beans, and seasoned tortilla chips.*

Third course: *Apple crisp a La Mode, or;*

A. *Golden Raisin Banana Bread pudding with almond cream*
B. *Pumpkin Cheese Cake with cranberry sauce or*
C. *Double Fudge Brownie sundae*

Dinner was an extravaganza. And while the menu had so eloquently tantalized us with the names of what we'd be consuming, the actual process of ingesting the food was unequaled in its rewards. Tonight we gorged ourselves with delight, and afterwards leaned back in satiated repose. Betsy and Roxanne giggled as they ate, and shyly accepted the flood of kudos they received for their extraordinary skills; I could tell they were very pleased with what they'd created. After the table was cleared Ernesto and his charming crew doted on us all evening. A short time after dinner we moved to the center of the lodge and sat down in a circle around a warm crackling fire. We conversed lightly for the next hour. At eleven pm Captain Olaf stood up and opened the floor for discussion about Jonah's newest request to rendezvous in the Madeira Islands. It took only minutes for us to agree that his idea was crucial in reestablishing our trans-Atlantic route.

Thirty-four

The Madeira Islands

April 1st

We'd all benefited greatly from the down time and each of us was reenergized and eager to continue on. Farewells with Ernesto lasted (what seemed) an hour. And after finally breaking free of the congeniality and niceties, *and* his offer for a pair each of the inns personalized penny loafers, (which we respectfully declined) we all waved goodbye, and hurried back aboard to prepare for departure. Captain Olaf had e-mailed Jonah before he'd retired the evening before. He'd informed him of our intentions to rendezvous with him in Funchal Bay. Jonah had responded quickly and with unbridled joy. Our plan was to meet him at twelve o'clock the morning of April

3rd. He suggested that we anchor in the bay just west of the Lido Complex. He'd make reservations for us at the Pestana Palms Hotel in advance; hopefully this would work. Considering the up-coming journey was well over a thousand kilometers Captain decided to sail two days non-stop as we had through the Bay of Biscay. The dolphins had remained near the entire time we'd been ashore. And now, since we'd re-boarded, they'd become playfully agitated and quite anxious to get underway. I sensed once again that they knew something we didn't. But what could that be? Captain maneuvered us carefully through the rocks and reefs and when we'd safely reached deeper water, the order to *raise sails* reverberated over the vessel's PA. Soon we were flying southwest towards the Madeira Islands. It was amazing to me just how alive you felt sailing this swiftly. This morning the weather was exceptional. Sixty-five degrees, clear blue skies, and a sea dappled with small waves and very occasional whitecaps, a Beaufort number four as I recalled from the Captain's lesson. North of us the sky was darkening up with thunderheads. Was this what the dolphins had been agitated about? Rorek told us the BBC's shipping reports were forecasting a major storm moving east into the Bay of Biscay and towards the western shores of France. For now this set our minds at ease. When we were five miles offshore, and just before sailing through a large area of iridescent plankton, the dolphins vanished. But as soon as we'd cleared the plankton they rejoined us off our starboard stern; it looked like they were staying with us for the duration.

It was Rolf's first time under sails and the poor guy was having trouble establishing his *sea legs*. For a while he just couldn't find his center of gravity and he wobbled about with a bewildered expression. Howling in frustration Rolf finally gave up, deposited a mess on the deck, shook vigorously, and stumbled below decks. Immediately I got out the deck hose and washed the enormous mishap into the ocean, all under the vigilant frown of Captain Olaf. When I'd finished he offered a half-hearted smirky smile and one thumb up. Making my way up towards the bow, and bracing against the biting wind, I began deeply inhaling the invigorating salt air and thinking back.

The e-mails between Jonah and I had increased. We were communicating every two or three days now, and a very special relationship was being forged between us. Jonah would reminisce, with extemporaneous regularity; about someone whom he'd shared many adventures with from his distant past. As I slowly gleaned more and more details from our many exchanges, I began to understand a great deal more about this bewildering relationship that [at times] troubled him deeply. This person seemed to occupy a place of prominence and respect in Jonah's heart; I speculated that this individual might be a close friend or possibly even a family member. I also knew that Jonah and this person had worked together for a number of years artistically. With some degree of imaginative acumen they had successfully composed very compelling music that had been influential in many people's lives. The feelings Jonah would share about this person were infused with an idiosyncratic blend of love, respect, disdain, grief and anger, and he'd often refer to him as '*a years past polemic antagonist.*' Even though Jonah would never disclose enough details to satisfy my curiosity, I decided early on not to ask too many questions concerning whoever this might be. It appeared there were many unresolved feelings with this strange Delphic personality, and I had no intention of ever offending my special friend with exasperating questions, so I just listened. I would sometimes hear him describe the person as a '*pontifical and disputatious character, a self-absorbed egoist, with a foul opinion of everyone, and anything he couldn't control.*' Often, in the same breath, Jonah's despondent recollections would suddenly and quite dramatically change, then his descriptions of this person would then become Pollyannaish. *'I never met a more gifted songwriter,'* he would reminisce sanguinely. *'I remember those two magical years when this person was as good a musical artist as anyone on the planet, but something dreadful happened in his heart, something very dark, and terrible, Gabriel.'* It was in one of our well-structured late night conversations that I believe my eyes were clearly opened to something I'd never known. *He was a member of Jonah's family, I was sure of it now!* Almost ghostlike, the certainty of the matter began to overwhelm me in an all-encompassing confluence of foul gray shades. Because of the strength of these troubling thoughts I began notating them in my journal. A storm of tears began to foment inside me as I realized the abysmal mindset that had trapped Jonah's antagonist for so many years. He had been controlled by a consuming *'perception of rejection'* by others. I shuddered, realizing how many of Gods wonderful blessings he had deprived himself of with his unfortunately deceptive choices. Jonah had taught me that the Holy Spirit's work in other believer's lives was always intended to be a wondrous way God would bless his children through others. This was a beautifully simple plan, with the intention of teaching us how to share with each other, and accept each other, in Christ. We were supposed to make others more important than ourselves. Giving was always more important than getting. We were supposed to humble ourselves to one another; the very way that Jesus humbled Himself for us in his profound sacrifice. Blessing one another mercifully in Christ, with the gifts He had given us was the way He had designed it. Alas, a nefarious mindset had emerged in the antagonists early impressionable years that had consumed him completely.

If they don't accept me, I won't accept them! I'll be better at rejecting others than they are at rejecting me. I will never let myself be touched by anything, except those things that are, (in my estimation) situations and/or people that I can manipulate or control.

I saw that this was not so much pride, at first, as it was a fear of his own personal weakness' and inabilities becoming known to all of those around him. These facts had never been concealed from anyone though, especially those closest to him. People had always seen him for who he was, and, had simply accepted him, or rejected him, based on his very own merit or how he treated them. It was really uncomplicated in my mind: you act like a jerk, people pull away, you treat others with respect and love, and people move in. It was clear now that a spirit of control had dominated him in all of his thoughts because of what he had unfortunately assumed others were thinking about him. Slowly he'd built a fortress around his heart to protect himself from perceived rejections, which were really just his own exaggerated fears. Daily, he played out this defensively composed "Magnum Opus" with the impassioned abandon of an emotionally wounded virtuoso. Jonah showed me that for years his antagonist had been wretchedly deceived, the mental strongholds he assumed protected him, had slowly and completely deceived him. Prides lascivious, but mellifluously convincing voice had turned an artist's heart into a cold dungeon, hard as flint, with little light, no real joy, or acceptance or appreciation of what others had accomplished. The condition had slowly become a morbid blend of his festering old emotional wounds, tearlessly stagnant in old reams of flagrantly rotten lies he'd agreed with for decades. I realized early on that this man was one of Jonah's greatest regrets, and he was also a man that had brought him great joy. I truly wished on many occasions that I could have been in possession of a magic wand; I would have simply waved it, and changed this tempestuous situation for the better for my new friend. But alas . . . magic wands are alive only in make believe, and the seasons of real life had to be played out to their conclusions, no matter how I wished otherwise.

The lunch bell pulled me my thoughts. After glancing at my watch I realized three hours had passed. For some reason it seemed that much less time had gone by. While we were seating ourselves Helga came in with a new e-mail from Jonah. "I gave a copy of this to the Captain and Rorek," she began, "and after they read it they told me to come down and read it to ya'll. Here's what he wrote:

> *I've been back for two days. It was a great experience, thankfully the book is finished. I've been on the internet talking to my contacts in Europe, and a professor Roxanne and I know from Rabat Morocco. He has contacts up in Tangier and Oran in Algeria that have begun an underground virtual network to track the Mortiken progress; we have access to their website. They're reporting that the recent affiliation they've established with those Middle Eastern businessmen has gained momentum. They're tracking a vast amount of money being funneled into different areas for the purchase of used military equipment and weapons. Apparently it's coming down through the Mediterranean. Financial accounts are being set up in Rome, Athens Greece, Hamburg Germany, Alexandria Egypt, Damascus Syria, and Jiddah Saudi Arabia. In a few days another will be open in Panama City, along with a full-fledged military installation somewhere in the Chagres National Park outside of Portobello. Someone is dumping billions into this, and there's speculation that*

it might be coming down from Russia. The Panama Canal has been effectively shut down. Golfo de Uraba and the Golfo Del Darien are regrettably under Mortiken control. The country has erupted in violent conflict over control of the Panama Canal. The magnetic disturbances are raging across Iceland, Norway, Sweden, and Finland and also across Russia now. It moved in unexpectedly last night, and glaciers are already beginning to melt in various areas from the heat. You might be able to get some images from the VEW; all other communication is down for the duration of the storms. I certainly praise God that we haven't been exposed to this anomaly yet. Somehow, the Mortiken are aware that the Tempest has been located. I understand they have a supreme leader now, his name is Amalek Baaldur. He's an enormous man, like a giant, and he wants the sword found, but scattered internet reports state that they have no idea where it is. I received an encrypted e-mail from Regan Pendleton yesterday stating that the Rognvald clan in Concello de Carino could be leaving the escarpment in June. Regan's church in Vermont, with the help of a host of other churches along the eastern seaboard, has financed the purchase of a very large used freighter. They are in the process now of outfitting it to accommodate the removal of hidden clans around the world, and move them up to the Northwestern territories of America. The rest is vague. Apparently there's a large gathering of ancient Rognvald tribes somewhere between September-November of this year. I believe Regan mentioned the island of Kodiak. He said he would be in touch later when he had more information. I have no idea what this means, but it sounds like a large conflict might be brewing between the Baaldurians and the Rognvalds. I'll see you on the 3rd in Madeira. My flight leaves tomorrow morning at 4:00am and takes me to Miami for a thirty minute layover. Then I board a Trans-Atlantic flight to Lisbon. After Lisbon I head to Funchal. All flights into the Azores have now ceased. Sao Miguel, Santa Maria, Terciera and Sao Jorge are in chaos. The American Marines are involved, and appear to be gaining ground; their weaponry is much more sophisticated. Santa Cruz and Flores are still thankfully clear of aggression for the time being. This will help us get back in to pick up the artifacts without being seen. I'll contact you again tomorrow. By the way, I think it might be wise to communicate only on the encrypted account from here on out, things are getting critical, and the "Old Symbol" needs to get home to the first tribe safely. I love you all dearly. Jonah

It was evident now that many areas around the world were capitulating to Mortiken and the Middle Eastern influence. More than ever the need to stay anonymous and low-profile was crucial to our safety. My respect for Jonah was growing daily. He truly was a man that God had given an important vision to, and thankfully he was pursuing it zealously. While enjoying a wonderful midday meal, I was suddenly taken with the idea of accomplishing some specifics on the voyage over to Madeira. Considering that Roxanne's curiosity, about the Tempest, was getting the best of her I offered my suggestion to the Captain on the radio while everyone listened.

"Captain, this is Gabriel. Are you too busy to talk sir?"

"No, what's on your mind son?"

"Sir, I've been thinking, considering the unfolding situation worldwide, the information Jonah has just relayed to us, all the work we need to accomplish, and Roxanne's curiosity, perhaps we should make use of our time on the way to Madeira to study the sword. Also sir, it might be a good time to uncrate the new laser technology and figure out what we have and how we're going to use it."

"Is everyone sitting at the table Gabriel?"

"Yes sir, we're all here."

"Ok, here's what I think. If studying the sword is something we should do now, I'm all for it. Actually, I'm really curious about the map and what's possibly inside the handle. It's your decision Roxanne. John, why don't you and Helga figure out what the new equipment really is? We'll be in the wheelhouse. Remember, we're sailing around the clock this trip. Thanks Gabriel."

"Captain, we'll begin now." John blurted, pushing back from his chair and motioning towards Helga. Roxanne's eyes were blazing with excitement and she almost fell backwards off of her chair in an effort to grab the radio.

"Olaf, I'm starting now with Garrett and Gabriel."

"Sounds good, keep me informed."

The three of us ran towards the hydraulic room and Garrett unlocked the door. Carefully we removed the case and put it up on the metal work table next to the main diesel. Then, all of us rolled up our sleeves to begin work.

Thirty-five

Chameleon Surface Adapting Technology & a fabled fortune

April 2nd

John radioed and asked if it we might break and meet with him ASAP. A few minutes later he rushed top-side, overwhelmed with enthusiasm, with a boisterous Rolf in hot pursuit. For the first time ever I was witnessing something in the man that I'd never seen, an endearing departure from his ordinarily imperturbable character. Garrett and I were waiting when he arrived. We were standing with the Captain and Rorek, and all of us listened breathlessly as he shared the stunning statistics about what the university had actually loaned us.

It wasn't offensive laser weapons at all, not like the space guns you'd see in the movies, these were shields designed not only to enshroud the entire vessel but also each one of us. This would be accomplished with discreet modular devices attached anywhere on our person, or worn around the waist on a belt. Utilizing a **'Chameleon Surface Adapting Technology',** it employed laser dispersion to spread the effect instantly throughout the initiators pre-designated space. These devices would very effectively allow the wearers to appear precisely like the surrounding areas, no matter what angle they were viewed from. This was certainly not your stereotypical cloaking device, regularly seen in science-fiction movies. Although we would still be physically vulnerable, and anyone around us could hear any noise we might make, we would apparently be rendered invisible, even in the closest proximity. The personal modular units were powered by a coin shaped battery installed inside the device, but the battery was only necessary on the start-up. After the chameleon effect was achieved then naturally occurring light waves would maintain the field indefinitely. As long as the chip was empowered, it would continually evaluate the terrain or environment as it changed, or as we moved. The schooner, or us individually, could appear like anything we were around, the ocean or the backdrop of a mountainous island, a rain storm, or even snow if we encountered it, generating zero distortion from any angle in the detached viewing field. John showed us that to effectively camouflage the schooner we would have to install a series of strategically placed chips about the size of a one inch thick credit card in twenty-four different locations around the exterior of the vessel. These statistical calculations had been accomplished by scientists at the university, based on measurements and specifications they'd received from Roxanne about the *Heimdall.* The chips would be attached with a specially designed two part adhesive that would adhere to anything. Each mast would take two chips; one at the base and one at the pinnacle. The perimeter of the vessel had to be outfitted every twenty feet at the base of the deck railings, which would require ten chips to complete the circumference. Any structures larger than a twelve foot quadrangle would need one placed at each corner. The wheelhouse would require four chips, and the main cabin house would also require four, bringing us to a total of twenty-four. The base unit, or brains of the technology, was somewhat bulky, approx 36" in length, 24" in height, and 12" in width, and came with a water proof, crush resistant stainless steel structure. This unit maintained electronic equilibrium during times of swift sailing, or storms, and also generated the Continuity of Realism (or COR) when the Chameleon technology was in use. Much like the CPU of a computer, it was filled with modular boards that could be replaced quickly if we ever encountered problems. The unit was also equipped with safeguards against all environmental equations known thus far, this in relationship to the devastating heat of the drought, the electro-magnetic disturbances worldwide, or any form of electrical discharge. If unknown parameters were ever encountered the chip would make a note of the new anomaly, print it out digitally, and could then be up-dated over the internet from another networked source, or the new information could be typed in manually from any compatible computer terminal. This central unit would have to be in the center of the vessel, which on the *Heimdall* was at the base of the center mast. This would effectively enshroud the entire vessel.

"Captain Olaf, let me give you a demonstration, sir; this will blow you away." John said excitedly. Carefully he attached an oval object, about the size of a large belt buckle, to his shirt pocket and walked to the stern of the vessel. "Here we go guys." John smiled as he turned on the device. Instantly John vanished.

"John, where are you?" A stunned Captain Olaf leaned out the doorway of the wheelhouse.

"I'm standing right in front of you sir at the bottom of the stairs."

Captain Olaf impulsively jumped back a few steps and peered intently towards the bottom of the wheelhouse steps, shaking his head and chuckling. "Extend your hand sir." John asked. I watched the Captain extend his hand out the door, and immediately saw it being vigorously shaken by John's.

"This is incredible," the Captain gasped, "I can't see you at all John, there's nothing, where are you now?"

"Here I am sir." John laughed and turned off the unit. The Captain spun around to John's smiling face standing right behind him. We were all stunned, this was unbelievable. The Captain and Rorek whispered for a few moments and then Rorek turned and asked: "What will it take to get this installed John?"

"Sir . . . after mathematical calculations—which will help us establish exact placement of the chips so we can achieve optimal coverage without any holes—about six to eight hours and three men." John replied.

Rorek looked over at Olaf and shrugged. "Let's get it done today men. John, you, Rorek, and Garrett get busy, do whatever you have to, I think I have a plan to spring on Jonah with this gizmo."

"Gabriel, you can go below and continue with Roxanne."

"No problem sir," I responded. "She was a bit frustrated when Garrett and I left earlier."

"Have you found out anything?" The Captain asked.

"Nothing worth talking about; the inscriptions on the hilt of the blade don't make any sense. The information on the one side seems to be continued on the other side. Roxanne scanned the etchings and fed it into her software program about ancient and modern maps. That was around eight yesterday evening sir; it hasn't given us anything yet."

"Alright son, we'll talk more at dinnertime. Hopefully by then we'll have something that we can all sink our teeth into."

Roxanne was feeling dejected. Nothing spectacular had been discovered, except the dimensions, and the fact that it was physically heavy. Yesterday, after removing the sword from the case, I discovered it to be unbalanced towards the handle. And although it was easy to move around above my head, it was very difficult to hold in front of me. The sword was exactly fifty-three inches in length, but only thirty-eight inches of the length was the blade itself. Twelve inches of the blade, on both sides, was magnificently etched with (what appeared to be) a map. The elaborate wooden handle, and the three weighted pommels, comprised seventeen inches of the overall length; I'd never seen a handle this large. Earlier this morning, when we'd put the sword on a delicate fulcrum to test the balance, we found it to be an incredible six lbs handle heavy, which confirmed my initial assessment about the sword being unbalanced. There was something nagging me that I just couldn't put my finger on, something we'd read earlier in the journey, something significant.

"Roxanne lets pray," I blurted in frustration. "Something is bugging me about this." After we'd finished I still couldn't resolve what was nagging me. In need of a break we both went above to check on the progress of the new installations, and to breathe some fresh air. The horizon was just as ominous as it had been yesterday. One small wooden ship was visible, now, off our port stern; it was headed into the intermittent flashes of lightening in the distance that were now moving closer. As we watched a brilliant flash of lightening exploded on the surface about two miles out. It was loud and spectacular and the dolphins disappeared. Suddenly I knew what'd been nagging me; it was something I'd read on the leather scroll.

"I remember now!" Roxanne knew at once what I was talking about. "Excellent, let's go!" she cried back. Once below we pulled up one of the computer files we'd made of King Agar's writing's we'd discovered in the Tempest case. Here's what it said: *'The Tempest procured of Gamelin in vision will reveal its fortune when the chosen one holds it high and cries out for Christ's mercy.'* Roxanne looked perplexed. "What do you think it means?" My heart began beating like a drum; something Floki had said to me came flooding back.

"Roxanne, just before Floki died he whispered something to me. *'You are now the* ***chosen one*** *Gabriel,'* he said, *'my mantle is yours. Remember son, Christ before all else!'* Look what the line King Agar wrote says. *'When the* ***chosen one*** *holds it high and cries out for mercy'.* Could it be me Roxanne? Could I be the chosen one they're talking about?" Roxanne stared at me with eyes as large as dinner plates. After jumping up, stumbling backwards, knocking her chair down and almost falling, she deftly regained her balance, and then bolted over to the table. After clutching the Tempest in both hands she turned and handed it to me. "Do what it says Gabriel!" She said breathlessly. But I couldn't, something felt wrong. "No Roxy. Not until the whole crew is in agreement. It's our way. From the very first day it's been our way, and I don't think it's wise to change it." Roxanne shook her head in quiet agreement. "You're so right Gab, absolutely, I'm sorry; I got caught up in the moment. Let's tell everyone at dinner."

Having traveled an outstanding distance on consistent winds, Captain Olaf decided to break sails and anchor for the evening on unique shallow reefs well-known in the area. We were now on a longitudinal parallel with Casablanca in Morocco, and about one hundred and fifty kilometers from Funchal Bay in the Madeira's. Our rendezvous with Jonah was set for twelve noon tomorrow, but the desire to stop awhile and collect ourselves was weighing on everyone. Why the Captain had chosen this peculiar area in the middle of the ocean was a mystery that I will never forget. During dinner Helga mentioned that Jonah had confirmed his arrival. He'd also said that he'd freed up eighteen days and would be staying with us until we'd left Flores. Roxanne was pleased with this news. The others informed us that the *Chameleon Surface Adapting Technology*, (CSAT) was installed and ready for testing first thing in the morning. Roxanne kept poking me in the ribs to share our new discovery, but I was too embarrassed. Finally flustered, and irritated with my shyness, she decided to share what I'd discovered. For some moments all sat speechless. Finally breaking the silence, Helga suggested we pray for God's will and, if we all felt unified, let Gabriel accomplish what'd been written so many centuries ago, and just recently confirmed by Floki Vildarsen. After doing so, we all moved into the engine room. Each person prayed in unity about what we all felt led to do, and, after doing so, I broke ranks with the others and grasped the sword in both hands and held it point down. The crew was standing in a semi-circle, still holding hands, when I was suddenly overwhelmed and began praying aloud: "Father God, I admit to knowing very little about you and your son, but Lord, I am humbly drawn to you now with shaking hands, a pounding heart, and in eager anticipation. In obedience to your will for my life, Father, I pray for your son Jesus Christ to forgive me my sins, for they are many Lord. Please indwell me now with your eternal life, and put my name in your blessed Book of Life, Lord make me a new creature in the Risen Christ. I admit my absolute need for you now, thank you Holy Spirit. In faith now,

Lord, I lift up this symbol that you've let us discover, this miraculous symbol, and I ask Holy One for your wisdom and MERCIES!"

As soon as I'd thrust the Tempest up a deafening thunder roared, accompanied with a bolt of lightning, which illuminated the interior of the *room in* a sudden white flash. With my heart pounding and tears running down my cheeks, I slowly brought the sword down and placed it on the table. As I did I felt the center pommel move, as if the lid of a jar had come loose.

"Captain, this center pommel just loosened. What should I do?"

"What does your heart tell you Gabriel?"

"Alright then sir . . . here I go."

From each side of the table Garrett and John held the sword up slightly as I turned the pommel. Slowly, brilliantly engineered threads brought the cap out until it separated and fell off into my hand. "It's all yours now dude." Garrett murmured, as they handed the sword to me. Inside was a leather plug that I removed with long needle nose pliers. After taking a deep breath I turned the sword handle down. Noisily dozens of uncut blood red rubies spilled out onto the table.

Thirty-six

In the eye of the Storm/ rendezvousing with Jonah

Something remarkable happened to me after offering up that prayer; a mystifying presence, beggaring description, had suddenly indwelt me in a place that I never knew existed. I'd stepped through a portal and was now in possession of something ineffable, something magnificently loving, and gloriously forever. Words feel meager as I try to describe (to the reader) what happened. My heart was swelling with love, now, and around me everything seemed magical; all I felt like doing was praising God for his mercies and faithfulness. An intellectual fog had been lifted from my mental processes, and, in the void that remained, a deep peace had been deposited inside of me. It felt as if I were a magnificent eagle, flying in crystal pure air, under the wings of wisdom and love from ages past, present and future. I was certainly not where I'd started in my early years. Seemingly all the disenchantment and emptiness I'd experienced (pursuing religion) had been vanquished in one inscrutable moment. The unquenchable thirst that had plagued me for years had suddenly been satisfied and I knew that the Truth had found me and that I had accepted Him. Now, without a doubt, I was part of His blessed and eternal family.

There were sixty-six rubies, varying slightly in size, and between 3-4 carats each. Lizzy had worked with a precious gems broker in her late twenty's; she recalled that rubies of this (extremely rare) kind and quality fetched a substantially higher price (in the right market) than even the best diamonds would. After examining them carefully she considered that these could easily command a price of two hundred thousand dollars per carat, and estimated the find, even uncut, at near fifty million dollars. I surmised, in large scale modern conflict, that fifty million dollars was not a large sum of money. There was, however, something indeterminate about what this fortune of rubies really represented and what it was destined for, or even how it would be used. Somewhere inside me, now, I had faith that God would reveal these facts to us in His time.

The weather was becoming increasingly unstable since we'd departed Peniche. What we'd watched in the distance was now approaching us. The northern horizon was surging with a blackened reverberating fury. The Captain had chosen an area of shoals, strangely shallow for this area of the Atlantic, to anchor on. This semi-hidden formation was configured like a small wheel inside a larger rim he'd told us. The larger rim was eight to ten feet deep, one hundred yards wide, and approximately one and a half miles in diameter. Inside that rim was two hundred yards of water, maybe one hundred and fifty feet deep. After that the ocean floor abruptly jutted back up towards the circular shaped center reef, similar to a submerged island. On this innermost seamount, in twelve feet of water, *Heimdall* was firmly anchored. In less than an hour the rain began with a soft intermittent pattering, and then slowly increased as intense displays of lightening split the sky with fiercely luminous fingers. In a matter of thirty minutes the rains became torrential, and our once clear visibility became almost completely obscured. A powerful weather system was approaching, and it was placing our lives, and the schooner, in a position of vulnerability that we'd never faced before. Earlier, Captain Olaf had instructed us to drop the fore and aft anchors, lash the raft tightly, remove the satellite dish, and securely lock all the sails down. Everything loose on deck had been brought below and secured, all gas valves were shut off, the food cabinets and refrigerators were locked tightly, and all portholes were pressure sealed against the probability of high seas. After everything had been done to protect ourselves, Rorek asked us to congregate in the galley to prepare for the storms savage onslaught.

Imagining what kind of damage a storm like this might wreak was beginning to short-circuit my fraying emotions. I was mentally and emotionally edgy; more so than I'd ever been in my life. The Navtex reports were relaying numbing statistics. An enormous front was making its way down from the Arctic Ocean. It had come into existence somewhere between Norway and Greenland four days ago. A high pressure trough had kept the storm in check, for the first three days, and had isolated it between the two countries. Then, the jet stream had shifted, approximately ten pm on April 1st, and had pushed the storm's path due south. Instead of bouncing east and west between the two countries (like a ping-pong ball between two paddles) the storm was now headed directly towards us. The front was twenty-five hundred kilometers in width and was generating ninety mph winds. Having already wreaked havoc on Iceland, Ireland, Scotland, and England, the storm was ravaging the western shores of France and the northern shores of Spain in the Bay of Biscay now with forty foot waves. Apparently we'd be getting the westernmost edge of this storm, which, thankfully, had been downgraded twenty percent. According to our weather station, the consistent wind speed at our anchorage was fifty mph, and gusts were seventy-five to ninety mph; no one would be allowed on deck without hurricane gear and safety tethers attached.

Lightening was etching the sky in erratic white hot traceries, and it was hitting the ocean's surface with the ferocity of a striking snake. The thunder that followed was irregularly explosive and, at times, required us all to cover our ears. I sensed the monstrous heart of the storm upon us now. Around me most of the crew was grimacing and tightly huddled in small groups. Lizzy was wiping a flood of tears from her eyes and had begun cringing at each thunderous explosion. Roxanne was as wide-eyed as I'd ever seen her, and she was tightly clutching the safety rail on the cabin wall. Helga and John were tightly embraced at one of the tables next to the wall; Helga was crying. Captain Olaf and Rorek were sitting in the center of the room holding onto the center deck supports. Garrett was the only one standing. In boldness he was shouting at the storm with an impassioned bravado. Wildly playing his invisible drums, with the irregular rhythms of exploding thunder, he began dancing and spinning in tight concentric circles as if a savage spirit had gripped his heart. Somehow his eccentric behavior was imparting faith in me to rise up and stand strong. I suddenly realized that God would never allow us to be destroyed here; we had a job to accomplish. A moment later low rumbling explosions began shaking the vessel. A once Captain and Rorek jumped up and began doing a sailor's jig and laughing in gut-wrenching guffaws. It seemed Garrett's war dance was affecting everyone. As I pulled Betsy nearer she put her arms around my neck and then, with tears welling up in her eyes, she kissed me. "Please know that I love you," she murmured. There was no time to consider Betsy's loving expression because Captain Olaf had begun shouting in a voice infused with exuberance.

"Everyone, top-side; I want to show you something. Praise God hallelujah and pass the chili! Our God is a mighty God, and He loves us. See what He's done for us!" I caught a blur in my right peripheral. Rorek was stumbling out the galley door laughing with binoculars in hand. Deeply infused, now, with their optimism, the crew struggled up the stairs in cautious pursuit. The wind whipped around us mercilessly. It was ripping at our skin and raingear as if hundreds of invisible fists were pummeling us at the same moment. On deck everyone attached nylon safety tethers to the rails. Betsy clung to me white-knuckled. Hunched over and squinting out in the direction Captain Olaf was pointing, I gasped at the incredible sight unfolding around us, and pointed it out to Betsy. Now, I fully understood the reason for the Captain and Rorek's abounding joyfulness; we were anchored safely in the eye of the storm.

"Look where He put us to protect us . . ." The Captain once again shouted over the mighty din of the storm. "HALLELUJAH! PRAISE YOU MOST HIGH! PRAISE YOUR HOLY NAME!"

From the north enormous walls of water cascaded down in thundering mountains of white foam. But here, where we were anchored; the water was relatively tranquil. Anchored firmly on the center of these reefs, in the middle of the ocean; we were being protected from the onslaught of the storms enormous seas. It was incredible. Mammoth waves were crashing on the outer rim (as they would on the shores of any beach) but because of the configuration of these reefs they were powerless to regenerate their momentum after being absorbed by the deep water of the inner circle. All we were subject to were the ramping mounds of whitewater. I knew now that if we'd been anchored outside the outer rim, in the deeper water, I would never have been able to write this narrative; we'd all be dead; this storm was a killer.

Massive black walls roared past the outer rim of the circular reef with frothy white crests and huge sheets of over spray flying off the upper edges. I felt as if we were inside the hidden settlement again, on the valley floor looking up at the enormous cliffs surrounding us, only this time it was mountainous cliffs of water roaring past us with the force of a hundred freight trains. Father God had put us in a place where we could see, hear, feel, and taste what was happening around us, but the full strength of the storm would never touch us. For several hours we stayed topside, mesmerized by this display of oceanic fury. Around the beginning of the third hour the crew began singing and praising God loudly, and then, as if a hand had passed over the water, the ferocity of the storm subsided over a period of forty-five minutes. At the beginning of the fourth hour the clouds began dissipating and I began rejoicing in a way I'd never known before. Betsy and I hugged like school children. God had thoroughly preserved us as He had with Daniel in the lion's den, Noah in the flood, and Shadrach, Meshach and Abednigo in the fiery furnace. Our Lord had taken us through a great tempest unharmed.

It was Garrett who'd first noticed that Rolf was nowhere to be found. After the weather had subsided we all dispersed and moved about the vessel calling for him. There was no response. Sadly, after relinquishing ourselves to the wolfhound's sad fate, we decided to retire to our berths and try and get some rest before leaving in the morning. When I'd reached my berth a miserable torrent of tears had begun flowing down my cheeks. While undressing I took off my wristwatch and then accidentally dropped it. A sudden erratic motion caused it to slide under my bunk and, as I got down on my knees to retrieve it, I heard the soft whimpering of Rolf. Slowly, a frazzled shaggy face emerged from the shadows. Seeing it was me he crawled out, sneezed several times, and began shaking himself vigorously. For a few moments we both stared at each other without a sound. Impulsively I grabbed him in both arms and hugged him; at once his energetic barking reverberated around the vessel. I realized, then and there, that Rolf would forever be attached to my heart, and that I had a friend for life.

April 3rd 6 am

Following a few hours of fitful sleep we met in the galley. The early morning forecasts were confirming that, despite the storm having ended, a huge swell would be persisting for several days. The north shores of the Madeira Islands were being inundated with thirty foot waves. Thankfully our next anchorage was on the southern shores of the main island in considerably calmer waters. It was colder this morning than anytime yet this year. We needed our heaviest jackets, gloves and hats to perform efficiently in the bitingly cold wind. Large waves were still pummeling the northern parts of the reef, but nothing like a few hours previous. Captain Olaf, closely watching the rhythm of the sea, had calculated ten to fifteen minute intervals between the greater and lesser swells. It was during this lull that we weighed both anchors, hoisted sails, and made good our escape.

Several hours later

I was comfortably ensconced now in the Captain and Rorek's superb library. I was curious to learn more about where we were presently heading. The *Madeira Islands* were discovered accidentally by the Portuguese in the fifteenth century. Originally they were known (by the Roman Empire) as the Purple Islands. This grouping is located three hundred and sixty miles west of Morocco, and five hundred and forty miles southwest of Lisbon, in the Atlantic Ocean. All are volcanic in nature, mountainous, and overflowing with beautiful flowers, hence the early Roman designation, the Purple Islands. The rugged coast of Madeira Island is a series of steep gorges, all emptying into the sea. Madeira and Porto Santo are the only inhabited islands. There are four different groupings of archipelagoes in the central eastern Atlantic; mere specks on most maps, and, mostly unknown except to those who have enjoyed the legendary Canary Islands in Portuguese pirate folklore and the movies. The northern of the four, the Azorean Archipelagoes, are located directly west of Portugal. The most southern are the Canary Islands. These are located west of Morocco and the Cape-Verde Archipelagoes, and west of Senegal and Mauritania on the western African coast.

Helga and John had been up in the crow's nest since seven, hunched against the bitter cold winds, and keeping a lookout for the Captain. Suddenly John's gleeful announcement over the radios, *"LAND HO",* reverberated to the cheers of the crew. It was exactly eleven am. Distracted from my research I raced up on deck with Rolf in hot pursuit. Eagerly we situated ourselves on the bow to take in the show. Directly in front of us was the northern shore of Porto Santo, the northernmost of the Madeira Islands. The city, we'd be docking at, was nestled on an amphitheatre like formation that began on the beach and rose twelve hundred meters on gentle slopes.

12:30

Jonah contacts Roxanne. Jonah is now waiting for us at the 'Lido Complex' in Funchal Bay. Reservations for ten had been made at the Pestana Palms Hotel for the evening.

1:00

Captain Olaf maneuvers towards the pier adjacent to the Lido and gives orders to tie off the fore and aft lines. Fifteen minutes later the gangplank is lowered.

1:20

The entire crew is reunited on the docks. Jonah warmly embraces his wife, and that is followed up with many long loving kisses. After that he hugs each of us. Something is wrong with him. I can sense melancholy flowing out of him. As soon as Rolf had been introduced, and a slobbery bond was formed, Jonah began speaking.

"Praise God you're all safe and sound. The flight over was long and wearisome. From Lisbon here I thought we weren't going to make it; my faith was tested. That storm was the fiercest I can ever remember flying in. I'm so thankful we're back together again, I love you all so very much!" Jonah reached for Roxanne. Embracing her tightly he began weeping bitterly. In moments all of us had joined him and Rolf began howling despondently. Surely we must have been a pathetic sight to any casual observer, but none of us cared; a powerful healing was happening between us. Never before had I seen Rorek, Garrett, or the Captain cry, but something refreshing rolled over me as they did, and the love I had for these people grew more than ever. Right there on the docks all ten of us (with Rolf in the middle) joined hands in a circle and gave thanks to our Lord Jesus Christ for delivering us through a terrible tempest safely and bringing us all back together. We were all surely learning more, in the last month, about our little mustard seed faith. We knew now that fear and pride were the greatest destroyers of any faith walk. Given this we purposed to pray about everything together pertaining to our journey, and always walk in God's love with one another. From now on when a problem arose between any of the crew, we would sit down immediately and prayerfully discuss it openly so God's Holy Spirit could give us wisdom and help us work it out. We weren't going to let petty problems fester because we were too proud to admit personal weaknesses. We knew that, in so doing, this would always keep the air clear between us from anything that might interfere with God's plan for us individually or collectively in the times ahead.

Shortly after checking in we met in the restaurant for lunch and another conversation with Jonah. He informed us that, because of a last minute cancellation from one of his clients, he was able to free up the best part of a month before he'd have to return to Pine Valley. This was most excellent news, especially for Roxanne who shed tears of joy. Jonah's next job was at the beginning of May; he'd be leading another expedition into southern Utah around Lake Powell. After lunch we decided that remaining two weeks in the Madeira's (resting, exploring, eating, writing, hiking, fishing, camping, and exercising) was essential for our mental, emotional, and physical health. Much to John and Helga's delight they'd discovered an exciting opportunity (online) to indulge in some sport fishing in a little parish (the oldest on the island) called Canical. They had already reserved two little cabanas in the village for their stay and were leaving the following morning on the raft. Jonah and Roxanne were going to rent scooters to explore the island for a few days. After that they were going to charter a speedboat to explore and photograph the unpopulated outer islands as soon as the storm swell had subsided. During the conversation John invited Garrett, Betsy, and me to join them for diving and spear-fishing on the reefs. After agreeing to meet them towards the end of the week they promised to contact us (on the radios we'd all be carrying) to make arrangements. Before we could leave we'd agreed to help Captain and Rorek run tests on the newly installed CSAT and up-date our software for the **V**irtual **E**arth **W**atch. This would take us two days. After that we'd be taking Rolf, and full backpacks, and hiking over to *Porto do Moniz* on the northern side of the island. After several days of camping and exploring we'd rent scooters and head over to rendezvous with John and Helga in *Canical*. The brother's had also decided to re-visit *Ponta de Sao Lourenco*. After Rorek's wife had passed, fifteen years previous, they'd both escaped here for three months of grieving and healing. Lizzy would stay at the *Pestana Palms* with Olaf and Rorek. After that she was going to tackle the daunting job of cleaning the schooner from top to bottom. We all prayed for her strength and focus. All of us promised to rendezvous with the *Heimdall* towards the end of the second week to prepare for our journey to *Isla Flores*. So it was, now, in the first week of April, our second month out, that God gave us a very special time to rest and recreate.

Thirty-seven

A dangerous encounter/ beyond the Isle of Flowers

April 20th

The first time I'd heard about the new Mortiken menace was several weeks earlier, after Jonah had returned from Ghost Mountain. He was resting at his home in Pine Valley when the news had arrived in an encrypted e-mail from **the professor**; a brilliantly gifted man he and Roxanne had worked with several years previous in Rabat Morocco. This information had been sent to the professor from his contacts in Tangier, Oran in Algeria, and a village on the Strait of Messina in Sicily. Now, since we'd left the Madeira's, there'd been a flood of information coming to Jonah (via encrypted e-mail again) about what'd really happened in January, what was happening at present, and what we should expect in the very near future.

The supreme Mortiken leader had revealed himself for the first time in January outside the city of Messina. He was companioned with the only female collaborator ever seen publicly with the Mortiken. It was now being reported that the brutality they'd exhibited had stunned the villagers in the surrounding coastal areas in the week long skirmish. Fortunately they'd failed in their attempt to establish control over the chemical trade there, but this fact had never been corroborated in the media. Details of the battle had been covered up by a military governmental affiliation in the Mediterranean who, together, had begun pursuing an underground program of disinformation and covert retaliation. It'd been strategically leaked, to the EC media, from unknown sources, that the two leaders were in the process (now) of gathering resources to produce chemical weapons. Because of this threat new laws had been put into effect which required that anyone viewing suspicious activity must contact their local authorities, who in turn would contact the affiliation on a special web address given to all European city governments. Time would tell whether or not this newly implemented program would be effective in curbing this grievous evil.

Shortly after the battle the two leaders had vanished.

His name was **Amalek Baaldur**. And he was a tremendous anomaly among men who stood over eleven feet in height, and weighed approximately nine hundred pounds. Some high profile websites were theorizing that he might be a descendant from the ancient race of Nephilim first mentioned in a cryptic passage from the Holy Bible in Genesis 6:4. *His female companion* was known only by the designation **Krystal Blackeyes**. Nothing was known about her except what the media narrative was saying, and what the military had discovered in photographs during the weeklong battle in Messina. She was apparently small in stature; five foot five, but there were many reports that she was in possession of an unsurpassed wickedness that bore upon everything, and everyone, she was around. It was being said her voice was unbelievably stentorian and that Mortiken soldiers cowered in fear when she spoke. She was frightening, cunning, and deceitful, and eye witness reports were claiming that her eyes turned completely black when she was confronted or spoken to by anyone except Amalek. The woman and the giant were never seen apart.

I recalled, through my youth, listening to fantastic stories about giants that inhabited the North Channel area in the Shetland Islands. These seasoned storytellers, most of them retired fishermen, had shared riveting tales about Viking outcasts wandering aimlessly for generations waiting for a leader to come forth and unify their vengeful efforts. There were numerous accounts of fishing vessels vanishing, and hundreds of people (who'd ventured into the maze of islands) disappearing and never being heard from again. Dozens of stories from reputable pilots abounded. After navigating slightly off course, and flying over the more remote islands, some reported seeing huge bonfires. Sometimes confused about what they thought they saw, they would circle back for visual confirmation, watching in astonishment as groups of sordid beings, huge in stature, danced in strange rituals around these roaring fires. It was also reported that their bellowing was so thunderous that it could be heard in the airplanes as they flew over. Passed down from generation to generation, these tales had persisted for hundreds of years and had remained unrivaled in any of the other northern folklore. These, ironically, were the very tales my family had always kept secretive and had never talked about openly.

In the eighth and ninth centuries history revealed the Shetlands having been invaded by powerful Vikings, who ruled until 1472. The recognized religious split between the two main tribes had occurred shortly before that year, possibly 1469. Some of the nation embraced Christianity, and some, the Baaldurian doctrine of blood witchcraft, violence, and human sacrifice. After the Baaldurians were defeated, in their uprising against the Rognvald's, they'd disappeared into the islands making up the north Orknean and Shetland Archipelagoes. The Vikings remaining visible were added to the domains of the 'Kings of Scotland', having established, for all time, a sound and honorable legacy in their choices. Recently it'd been confirmed (from European military commanders and satellite surveillance) that a giant was aboard one of the vessels rampaging now in the Azores.

The southern shores of the ***Isle of Flowers*** became visible to us through the early morning mists on the twentieth. Europe ended here, on the western shores of Flores. There was only one thing left for us to do; retrieving the artifacts Roxanne and her assistant's had hidden in the cave. Tomorrow we'd be sailing from this part of the world for the USA; a long journey around Cape Horn, through the Drake Passage, and then north to Southern California.

Our time in the Madeira's had proven excellent. We were rested and focused and all of us felt well prepared for the next phase of our journey. The vessel was immaculate. The Captain was overjoyed and the rest of us were truly blown away. What Lizzy accomplished had been an amazing feat of diligence and focus. She was being hailed now as a champion and had received a new nickname from us; Ms. Amazing. The CSAT was operating flawlessly. And just prior to John and Helga reuniting with us the Captain had engaged the technology to satisfy some monkey business that'd been festering in him since finding out what it was capable of. It was the very first time I'd seen this side of the Captain's personality. As they came around the far point John stopped the raft and took out the binoculars. I could see that both of them were becoming more and more confused as they slowly trolled about calling out for us. At one point Helga began crying and I heard her blubbering that we'd left without them. This went on for twenty minutes; far too long in my estimation. But the Captain persisted still. And it was only after John accidentally bumped into the shrouded schooner, and both of them almost fell overboard, that he finally felt released from the joke that he'd originally planned for Jonah a few weeks earlier. As they winched the raft back aboard Olaf was the only one on the crew laughing. I could clearly see, from John's *'ok buddy, you wanna play that way'* expression, that he was considering serious payback in the near future. I truly thanked God that I would not be the recipient of his schemes.

There were eleven of us (including the wolfhound) living aboard the schooner now. Rolf was an excellent canine, and also a very good camper and hiker. Very intelligent, and always cognizant of his role, he offered all of us delightful diversions with his boisterous personality, frolicking antics, and dependable friendship. Given the circumstances I'd even trained him to do his business regularly in an old oil pan. When this had been successfully accomplished, Captain hugged me in front of the crew as they laughed and applauded.

Sometime later

"Captain, do you copy?" Helga cried out distraughtly.

"Go ahead lass."

"We have the north shore of Flores on the VEW. We can see the northern lighthouse, and the Ponta do Albarnaz where Roxy stashed the artifacts. Sir . . . we've got company."

"I did *not* want to hear that . . . damn!" Angrily the Captain hit the large wheel with both hands. His buoyant good natured disposition had changed instantly and gruffly he ordered all sails down. Rapidly the mood aboard changed. It appeared now that our premonitions, about encountering the Mortiken again, had become a reality. Within twenty minutes we were motionless in the water and had gathered near the computer screen to assess what we were confronted with. One of the three vessels was anchored on the northern side of the island several hundred yards outside the surf line. Three Mortiken were ashore, and we counted ten more visible now on deck. There were five boxes lying on the sand, and more were being carried out from the cave. Roxanne cried out dismally after she'd assessed the situation.

"Oh no, oh no, Jonah . . . please say it isn't true! They've found the cave, they're stealing the artifacts."

"What!" Jonah bent towards the screen to see clearer.

"Oh my Lord Roxy, this can't be happening . . . not after all those weeks of work. What are we going to do now honey?"

"Captain Olaf!" John's tone distressed me. He was stationed in the crow's nest with the large telescope. "There's another vessel moving in from the east sir, they're on a tack towards the northern shore. Also sir, can't tell how many from here, but there's a lot of large men on the deck of this one."

"Engage the CSAT now, anyone!" The Captain ordered. "Lord willing, they haven't seen us. Rorek . . ."

"Gabriel, Garrett, topside *NOW*, I need help!" Rorek barked. "John, stay up above and monitor that vessel!"

"Aye . . ." John responded.

Within seconds the CSAT had rendered us invisible. Rorek engaged the electric motor, which allowed us to move soundlessly towards the island. I saw this as an exceptional strategy because we were producing no discernible wake that would give away our position. Soon we heard shots in the distance from the approaching vessel.

"Can you tell what the gunfire's about? What are they shooting at John?" Captain Olaf asked.

"They just executed several people and threw them overboard. There's also a large contained fire on the bow of the vessel, and some began dancing around it."

"Jonah, you and Roxanne try and contact anyone on-line or by phone. Try calling the airport at Santa Cruz, see if anyone is still on the island. I want some information. Why are these vessels here? How do they know about the artifacts? Why are they stealing them? What in the world is going on? Continue monitoring the VEW Helga and keep us up-dated. Install earpieces in your radios crew; Lizzy please help with this. I recall them being in the bottom drawer of the ammo locker in my berth. Remain silent from here on out, everyone! Gabriel, explain to Rolf what's happening, and keep him still. Garrett, you and Betsy bring up weapons for everyone. My pistol too, Garrett, and make sure the chamber and the belt is full."

"Gotcha Cap, we're on it big time. Beat feet sissy!"

Captain Olaf had brought the schooner to a dead stop around twelve. We were floating motionlessly just west of a tiny island one hundred yards from Isla Flores; *Ilheu de Maria Vaz*. Everyone was in the galley eating lunch, and discussing the situation. Asleep under one of the larger chairs; Rolf awakened suddenly and jumped up. The chair flew straight up in the air and landed with a noisy crash. Grunting, and with eyes wide and piercing, Garrett pushed his chair back and began whispering in John's ear. A few moments later they both slapped high hands and John turned towards the rest of us.

"Garrett just reminded me about the special package Rodolpho added to the order we picked up in Leiria, Olaf. He gave us eight magnetic mines with radio detonation controllers. This wasn't part of our original order; he gave them to us for free. Anyway, sir, there's a way we can deal a death blow to these bums. It'll be a bit risky, but, with God's help we can do this; we have everything we need aboard to make it happen." John stood quietly for a few moments. Then, with a huge grin, he shook his head and said: "Let's sink the filthy scumbags. We did it with the *Wormwood,* and we can do it with these bums."

Thirty-eight

A final dangerous encounter before we depart European waters

John and Garrett's plan was indeed inspired. It was a simple, unassailable way to rid us, and the world, of several more pieces of this malignant and growing threat. Since none of us could formulate a better alternative to their strategy, we all agreed to proceed. After intense group prayer plans were carefully laid out for a pre-dawn mission (on the twenty-first) while they were recovering from their drunken merrymaking the night before. Using the mathematical grid option on the VEW satellite for exact dimensions, our engineer decided to attach the weapons ten feet forward of the props, dead center on the hull, and then, with a radio controlled firing mechanism, detonate the vessels from a safe distance. On the VEW we could see two ships anchored within fifty yards of one another. Over twenty Mortiken were milling about on the beaches now. Several had opened the cases and were rummaging through the contents. There appeared to be a growing frustration between them. It appeared to me that they couldn't find something they were looking for; several of them had begun fighting and others were randomly firing weapons into the air.

All our phone calls had been fruitless. No one knew anything. There was no one on Isla Flores now; all had been evacuated several weeks earlier. There was one last possibility. Roxanne suggested that Jonah e-mail Regan Pendleton. Regan's response came within thirty minutes. His answers were plausible and very informative. I could clearly see that Jonah was finally beginning to trust Regan and his involvement in our endeavors. Regan was convinced the Mortiken invasion of the Azores was an attempt to find the Tempest Sword, and establish an outpost for controlling North Atlantic trade routes. Regan's church network had intercepted encoded messages in early April. As he told it, Amalek Baaldur was promising great wealth and power to the one who could capture or destroy the ***'Ghost Vessel'*** that was creating so many problems for them. Regan reminded us that *we* were that vessel, and that our successes of late had become a thorn in the side of both the Mortiken and their Middle Eastern connection. He went on to say that renovations had been completed on the enormous freighter the churches had purchased, and that it would be moving down to Concello de Carino, late June, to remove the entire Rognvald clan and relocate them. Clans from the North Cape in Norway, the island of Jan Mayen in the Norwegian Sea, the Faroe Islands, and the Northern Orkney Islands would already be aboard. Then they'd be voyaging down to the South Sandwich Islands in the Scotia Sea, and Elephant Island in the Southern Shetlands to pick up the few remaining clans scattered throughout the South Atlantic Ocean. Their final destination would be Kodiak Island for the reunification of the Rognvald clans with the First Tribe. This was apparently scheduled for September of this year. Despite the danger we may confront in the morning, we slept like babies, safely enshrouded in the CSAT, two kilometers from the other vessels. At four in the morning Captain Olaf started the electric motor and silently maneuvered us into position. After testing the temperature of the water (and finding it frigid) John decided wetsuits would be necessary.

5am

Captain anchored a quarter kilometer from the two targets. A soft radiance had begun highlighting the eastern horizon, and hovering above our heads was a glimmering of moonlight oozing through a thick mist. This mist was obscuring parts of the island, but down on the waters smooth black surface it was crystal clear. In the distance we could hear the crashing of waves over rocks, and hoped that this white noise would help cover any sound we might make. The running lights of the enemy vessels had become visible now; the conditions were perfect to launch our clandestine mission.

5:15 am

Even though Rolf was bubbling with enthusiasm he clearly comprehended the absolute necessity for silence. He was a very intelligent dog that would quickly acclimate to any circumstance, and had proven himself worthy in every situation we'd already experienced. As a precaution we kept all of the lights aboard turned off. After group prayer, John, Jonah, and Rorek slipped into the black water and sunk out of sight. They were carrying directional beacons with them. In this way we could safely help them navigate with the computer. When in close proximity to the other vessels they would engage the red diving lights to attach the mines and set the detonation frequencies.

5:35 am

Jonah checked in for the first time. "Radio check copy?"

"We copy loud and clear." Captain Olaf whispered back.

"Conditions are dismal. Undercurrent is erratic. Very black, can't see our hands in front of our faces. Good grief what's that?" Jonah's transmission ended suddenly and the radios went silent. For several minutes we waited breathlessly for an up-date. At last John's laughing voice broke the suspense. "Dolphins are back. I can hardly believe this, it's incredible. Thought they were sharks, freaked us out. I think they're guiding us towards the vessels. Are we still on course?"

"Right on course, a hundred fifty yards from preliminary target now, straight ahead." Helga responded.

While John was talking, the incredible role dolphins had already played in our journey came flooding back to me. How could they just appear exactly when we needed them? It was amazing. Unquestionably a part of God's mercy on our journey was manifested in these creatures appearing exactly when we needed them.

"Any movement aboard the other vessels yet, can we engage our lights?" Rorek asked after John had finished.

"No movement. Go ahead with the RDL's (red diving lights). That thick mist has dropped on the surface now." Captain Olaf replied.

"Copy that, the mist will help hide our bubbles. RDL's are engaged. Hull of preliminary target is dead ahead; have reached bottom of vessel. John is attaching mine to designated area. Frequency has been set, moving to secondary target now. Dolphins still with us, holding onto top fins, they're pulling us over to target. Water is starting to get lighter."

"Copy that, Rorek," Olaf responded.

The eastern horizon was developing a golden glow. The men had thirty minutes before they had to be back aboard; at that point the sun would crest the horizon with a flood of light and they'd be much more vulnerable.

5:55 am

"Under secondary target," Jonah radioed, "John successful. Attached mine and frequency has been set. Mission accomplished, heading back; see you in a few."

6:10 am

Diver's bubbles were clearly visible now off the port. Quietly the Captain ordered Garrett and me to pull up the anchor. Dolphins were silently milling about the stern of the vessel when all three men hoisted themselves onto the diving platform and began removing their gear. On the first vessel we watched as a lone Mortiken stumbled up on deck and lit a cigarette.

Then a horrible chain of events happened.

We were two hundred yards west of them when an earthquake suddenly began shaking the area around Flores. Instantly the dolphins scattered. While we were being bounced about we heard Garrett scream that the red light was blinking on the CSAT's main box on deck. Apparently the technology had failed and we were now visible to the enemy. Less than a minute later the lone Mortiken on deck became aware of our presence and began screaming and hitting the rails; the ***'Ghost Vessel'*** had appeared in front of him and he was terrified. Within minutes the decks of both vessels were swarming with men gesticulating wildly in our direction. All at once they stopped and stood frozen in shock until one of the leaders screamed an order. Without delay men on the first vessel began uncovering the large weapon on the bow. Shortly thereafter shells began exploding in the water around us. The second vessel started their engines and began turning around so they could bring their bow weapon to bear on us. Having already started the *Heimdall's* diesel, Captain Olaf was focused on maneuvering away. Suddenly an aftershock shook the area once again. This time John lost his footing and fell against the port rails; the radio controlled firing mechanism, he was holding, fell into the ocean and sank from view. We were shocked. Now we had no way of detonating the magnetic mines. The second vessel had come about and was now pursuing us head on. The noise was overwhelming. Shells were exploding in the water around us every thirty seconds; thankfully none were finding their mark. After a cursory order from Olaf, Helga got out her rifle and began targeting the Mortiken gunners. One by one they fell in lifeless heaps. Still, as the fallen were pushed aside and others took their places, the thunderous onslaught of the bow cannon continued. The second vessel was charging towards our starboard and it was frighteningly apparent that their bow gun was trained directly on us. From the wheelhouse door, Rorek shouted towards Helga about the new danger. At once she brought her keen eye to bear and one Mortiken after another began dropping. They were infuriated, their efforts were being successfully thwarted by one woman, and they knew it. Helga's marksmanship was devastating their attempts to destroy the *Heimdall,* and this fact was giving us all hope and joyfulness.

A lone dolphin had surfaced near the diving platform; Lizzy noticed something in its mouth. Not knowing what it was she made John aware. Nodding back, he cautiously made his way over towards the stern. Laughing joyfully, he low-crawled onto the diving platform and began petting the dolphins head and then kissed its nose. After removing the object from its mouth he radioed Captain Olaf with the news. He was ecstatic. Miraculously, the dolphin had retrieved the RCFM from the sea floor and had brought it back up still perfectly intact. The whole crew erupted in cheers and whistles and began praising God; it was undeniable now the He was guiding these creatures to our benefit. The Mortiken had begun firing back with hand weapons and old rifles. Bullets were whizzing around us, but not one shot was finding flesh. Some had gotten so frustrated with Helga that they'd begun throwing rocks at us. Eagerly Garrett responded to them in similar manner. Only much to their dismay, his rocks consistently found their marks and theirs consistently fell short.

"OLAF," John screamed from the stern, "we need two hundred yards before I detonate . . . pedal to the metal sir!" Captain shook his head and the diesel roared. Within minutes we were three hundred yards from the other vessels. Without warning the Captain slowed us down, jumped out the wheelhouse door, and ran towards the stern. John looked over at the Captain for his order to detonate. The whole crew moved in around him and quietly waited. Rolf was barking excitedly now; he had both paws on the rear rails watching. After a few moments Captain Olaf turned towards John.

"Take um out John!" He hissed.

John uncovered the switch and flicked it up.

A low thunderous WHOMP shook the surface violently around the vessels. Both of them heaved up amidships on thick humps and then sucked back down in a cauldron of whitewater. With a deafening roar and the grind of ripping metal, they exploded simultaneously in balls of fire and began sinking. Within minutes both vessels had disappeared in boiling cauldrons of steam, smoke, and frantic screams. For the next fifteen minutes, we stood hunched over the railings, staring out at an empty ocean surface, where just moments before a ruthless enemy was bent on killing us. Flotsam slowly began bobbing up to the surface, but there wasn't one survivor. Captain Olaf finally came back to his senses and quickly rousted everyone to their posts; it was time to leave. Using the Captain's telescope, Roxanne and Jonah methodically searched the cave where the artifacts had been stashed; sadly not a trace of anything remained anywhere. Everything had either been taken aboard the Mortiken vessels, or, destroyed by the earthquake. It seemed now that we had in our possession only what God wanted us to have and nothing more. And after an hour of grieving, and consolation from her husband, Roxanne found herself convinced of this fact also. Thankfully, there was still a photographic journal of all the work we'd accomplished together, and in this Roxanne found reassurance.

So it was now, on the 21st of April, after almost two months and many incredible adventures together, that Captain Olaf, Rorek, John, Garrett, Jonah, Roxanne, Helga, Betsy, Lizzy, Rolf and I departed the waters of the European continent to begin our three month voyage to Southern California.

About the Author

Born in Chicago Illinois, and now residing in La Mesa California, Richard Lloyd Cederberg is a man with spiritual vision and creative determination. For much of his life he has chosen to express life's mysteries, joys, and struggles thru music, poetry, short stories, and now, his first novel about one young man's adventurous passage into manhood in a changing world. Richard began writing in his early teens. His motivation was the Bible, the brilliance of Jules Verne, Robert Lewis Stevenson, Edgar Rice Burroughs, and numerous intrepid authors. Having created purpose driven characters, exemplifying humankind's exigent struggle in the world system, the 'Monumental Journey' series purposes to illustrate the importance of all people finding Truth, their gifts and callings, and then pursuing them against all odds.

Made in the USA
Coppell, TX
26 March 2021

52444389R00194